Georg Lunge

The Alkali-Makers Handbook

Georg Lunge

The Alkali-Makers Handbook

ISBN/EAN: 9783337382551

Printed in Europe, USA, Canada, Australia, Japan

Cover: Foto ©Andreas Hilbeck / pixelio.de

More available books at **www.hansebooks.com**

THE

ALKALI-MAKERS' HANDBOOK.

TABLES AND ANALYTICAL METHODS FOR MANUFACTURERS
OF SULPHURIC ACID, NITRIC ACID, SODA, POTASH,
AND AMMONIA.

BY

GEORGE LUNGE, Ph.D.,

Professor of Technical Chemistry, Zurich;

AND

FERDINAND HURTER, Ph.D.,

Consulting Chemist to the United Alkali Co., Limited.

SECOND EDITION,
ENLARGED AND THOROUGHLY REVISED.

LONDON: WHITTAKER & CO., 2, WHITE HART STREET,
PATERNOSTER SQUARE.

GEORGE BELL & SONS: YORK STREET,
COVENT GARDEN.

1891.

PREFACE TO THE FIRST EDITION.

MOST practical chemists and manufacturers have long felt the want of uniformity in analytical methods, tables of specific gravities, etc., employed by buyers and sellers for the valuation of chemicals, and by manufacturers for controlling and superintending their various processes. Want of uniformity in this respect is constantly leading to disagreements, and prevents exact comparison of results.

In order to terminate the confusion, Mr. Stroof, manager of the Griesheim Alkali Works, suggested to the German Society of Alkali Makers that they should have a standard manual published. This suggestion was adopted, a committee of seven, of owners and managers of high reputation, was appointed, and the first of the undersigned was induced to collect and sift the material for such a manual.

The first condition imposed upon him was to state only one method for each analytical operation for the preparation of standard solutions and for sampling the materials. Only one method was to be chosen, in order that no discrepancies might arise, which would certainly happen if two or more methods had been introduced.

In selecting the one standard method, the first and most important consideration was, that the method should permit a certain indispensable degree of accuracy. No pains were spared to arrive at a satisfactory result in this respect. Where there was a choice between several equally accurate methods, the one occupying least time and requiring least apparatus, or one already widely known and employed, was preferred.

The author prepared a draft, which, together with various suggestions from others, was fully discussed at the several meetings of the committee. These meetings were held at intervals of six and twelve months respectively, in order to give the author and his assistants time to carry out experimental researches, to clear up any doubtful points. Most of these experiments have been described in a report published partially in the *Journal of the Society of Chemical Industry*, 1882, pp. 12, 55, and 91. Public criticism was then invited, and several important contributions were thus obtained. Ultimately, after the complete manuscript had been circulated among the members of the committee, it was agreed to on all points.

The methods described in this little work are thus acknowledged by the united voice of the German Alkali and Ammonia manufacturers as the most suitable, and are not the arbitrary choice of the author. Many of the processes, the description of which frequently only occupies a few lines, are the result of many a month of arduous labour, and of subsequent anxious discussion by all concerned.

The want of standard tables of specific gravities of various solutions, was felt quite as much as the want of standard analytical methods. For some substances such tables had never been constructed, and for very few substances indeed were the data provided to reduce the specific gravity of the solution to a normal temperature. The author and his colleagues have striven to remedy this defect by a careful examination of the existing tables, and by supplying new ones where required.

In addition a number of general tables, useful to alkali manufacturers, have been provided. Every care has been taken to ensure the accuracy of these tables, many of them, particularly those referring to atomic weights, percentage composition, and analytical factors, having been entirely recalculated.

The German edition, the small compass of which but little betrays the labour expended upon it, was issued with the expectation that it would be accepted as a standard work by all German Alkali manufacturers, by their customers, and by commercial analysts. This expectation has already been realized in a great measure. It has already become customary to make these analytical methods and specific gravity tables binding in all transactions between buyers and sellers, until the progress of science necessitates the substitution of more accurate methods and tables in future editions.

From many sides the desire has been expressed that this little work should be made accessible to the English public. For this purpose the co-operation of the second of the undersigned was obtained. To him is due the extensive labour of recalculating all the tables for English weights and measures. In making these calculations every one of the tables was, as far as possible, reconstructed from the original data by graphic interpolation. Errors of computation were avoided as much as possible by the use of Thomas' Arithmometer and Fuller's Calculator; and the hope is expressed that the tables, based on the English weights and measures, will be found equally reliable as those based on the metric system. The chapters on Deacon's process and on chimney-testing are also due to him, and in general he has adapted the work to suit the wants of English manufacturers. But in no essential particular does this edition deviate from the German, a few additions excepted.

PREFACE TO THE SECOND EDITION.

In this edition numerous small errors of the first edition, almost unavoidable in such a case, have been corrected, and many minor improvements have been made. Moreover, for reasons explained by one of us in the *Journal of the Society of Chemical Industry* (1890, p. 1013), a considerable number of new methods for analysis have been introduced.

The new tables for specific gravities of sulphuric, hydrochloric, and nitric acid, and of liquor ammoniæ, constructed with extreme care by one of us, with his assistants, have been substituted for the tables of Kolb and Carius contained in the first edition.

All suggestions for alterations which have reached us since the publication of the first edition have been carefully considered, and have been adopted wherever it was possible and consistent with our endeavour to maintain unchanged the general scope and character of the book.

As the size of the page has been somewhat increased, the designation "handbook" has been substituted for "pocketbook" in the title.

G. LUNGE.
F. HURTER.

ZURICH AND WIDNES,
August, 1891.

NOTE.

ALL *temperatures* are indicated in degrees centigrade, unless the contrary is expressed.

The *atomic weights* are stated in table No. 1 in round numbers, and these are made use of in all calculations contained in this book. This has been done because the so-called correct atomic weights are not accepted equally by all chemists, and are subject to alteration by new researches, whilst there is practically no disagreement concerning the rounded-off atomic weights of the more important elements, and these are, at any rate, sufficiently near the truth for all technical purposes. An exception has been made for platinum, for which the figure adopted by all German potash manufacturers and analytical chemists has been retained.

We have, however, also added a table giving the values of atomic weights assumed by Ostwald to be the nearest approximations to the truth.

CONTENTS.

GENERAL TABLES.

TABLE I.—ATOMIC WEIGHTS, EQUIVALENT WEIGHTS (IN ROUND NUMBERS), AND VALENCY OF ELEMENTS.

	Symbol and Valency.	Atomic Weight.*	Equivalent Weight.
Aluminium	Al^{IV}	27·5	13·75
Antimony	$Sb^{III\ V}$	122	122
Arsenic	$As^{III\ V}$	75	75
Barium	Ba^{II}	137	68·5
Beryllium	Be^{II}	9·4	4·7
Bismuth	$Bi^{III\ V}$	208	208
Boron	Bo^{III}	11	11
Bromine	$Br^{I\ VII}$	80	80
Cadmium	Cd^{II}	112	56
Caesium	Cs^{I}	133	133
Calcium	Ca^{II}	40	20
Carbon	$C^{IV\ II}$	12	6
Cerium	Ce^{IV}	137	68·5
Chlorine	$Cl^{I\ VII}$	35·5	35·5
Chromium	$Cr^{II\ IV\ VI}$	52 5	26·25
Cobalt	$Co^{II\ VI}$	59	29·5
Copper	Cu^{II}	63·5	31·75
Didymium	Di^{IV}	144	72
Erbium	Er^{III}	170·6	85·3
Fluorine	F^{I}	19	19
Gold	Au^{III}	197	197
Hydrogen	H^{I}	1	1
Indium	In^{III}	113	56·5
Iodine	$I^{I\ VII}$	127	127
Iridium	$Ir^{IV\ VI}$	193	96·5
Iron	$Fe^{II\ IV\ VI}$	56	28
Lanthanum	La^{IV}	139	69·5
Lead	$Pb^{II\ IV}$	207	103 5
Lithium	Li^{I}	7	7
Magnesium	Mg^{II}	24	12
Manganium	$Mn^{II\ VII}$	55	27·5
Mercury	Hg^{II}	200	100
Molybdenum	Mo^{VI}	96	48
Nickel	Ni^{II}	59	29 5
Niobium	Nb^{V}	94	47
Nitrogen	$N^{III\ V}$	14	14
Osmium	$Os^{IV\ VI}$	199	99·5
Oxygen	O^{II}	16	8
Palladium	$Pd^{II\ IV\ VI}$	106	53
Phosphorus	$P^{III\ V}$	31	31
Platinum	$Pt^{II\ IV\ VI}$	197·18†	98 59
Potassium	K^{I}	39	39
Rhodium	$Rh^{II\ IV\ VI}$	104	52
Rubidium	Rb^{I}	85	85
Ruthenium	$Ru^{IV\ VIII}$	104	52
Selenium	$Se^{II\ IV\ VI}$	79	39·5
Silicium	Si^{IV}	28	14
Silver	Ag^{I}	108	108
Sodium	Na^{I}	23	23
Strontium	Sr^{II}	87·5	43·75
Sulphur	$S^{II\ IV\ VI}$	32	16

* These atomic weights are used throughout this book.
† Adopted by Potash Convention for calculating Analyses of Potassium salts.

TABLE I.—ATOMIC WEIGHTS, Etc. (*continued*).

	Symbol and Valency.	Atomic Weight.*	Equivalent Weight.
Tantalium...........................	Ta^V	182	182
Tellurium	Te$^{II\ IV\ VI}$	125	62·5
Thallium	Tl$^{I\ III}$	204	204
Thorium	Th^{IV}	231·5	231·5
Tin	Sn^{IV}	118	59
Titanium	Ti^{IV}	48	24
Uranium	Ur^{VI}	240	240
Vanadium	V^V	51	25·5
Wolframium........................	W^{VI}	184	92
Yttrium..............................	Y^{III}	88	44
Zinc	Zn^{II}	65	32·5
Zirconium	Zr^{IV}	90	45·0

* These atomic weights are used throughout this book.

TABLE I(a).—ACCURATE ATOMIC WEIGHTS (Ostwald).

Elements.	O=16	H=1	Elements.	O=16	H=1
Aluminium	27·1	27·01	Molybdenum	95·9	95·6
Antimony...............	120·3	119·92	Nickel	59·0	58·82
Arsenic	75·0	74·78	Niobium	97·2	96·9
Barium	137·0	136·6	Nitrogen	14·041	14·00
Beryllium...............	9·10	9·07	Osmium	192·0	191·40
Bismuth	208·0	207·3	Oxygen	16·0	15·95
Boron	11·01	10·97	Palladium	106·0	105·7
Bromine	79·963	79·71	Phosphorus...........	31·03	30·93
Cadmium	112·1	111·75	Platinum...............	194·8	194·2
Caesium	132·9	132·50	Potassium	39·14	39·02
Calcium	40·0	39·87	Rhodium...............	103·0	102·7
Carbon	12·00	11·96	Rubidium	85·4	85·14
Cerium	140·2	139·75	Ruthenium	103·8	103·48
Chlorine	35·45	35·34	Samarium	150·0	149·5
Chromium	52·3	52·13	Scandium	44·1	43·96
Cobalt	59·0	58·81	Selenium...............	79·1	78·85
Copper	63·3	63·10	Silicium	28·40	29·31
Didymium { Pr......	143·6	143·14	Silver	107·938	107·60
{ Nd......	140·8	140·37	Sodium	23·06	22·99
Erbium..................	166·0	165·5	Strontium	87·5	87·2
Fluorine	19·00	18·94	Sulphur	32·06	31·96
Gallium	69·9	69·68	Tantalum	129·0	128·60
Germanium	72·3	72·08	Tellurium	125·0	124·60
Gold	197·2	196·60	Thallium	204·1	203·5
Hydrogen...............	1·0032	1·00	Thorium	232·4	231·7
Indium	113·7	113·33	Thulium	171·0	170·4
Iodine	126·86	126·466	Tin	118·1	117·72
Iridium	193·2	192·6	Titanium	48·1	47·95
Iron	56·0	55·83	Uranium	239·4	238·65
Lanthanum	138·5	138·0	Vanadium	51·2	51·04
Lead	206·91	206·3	Wolframium	184·0	183·40
Lithium	7·03	7·01	Ytterbium	173·2	172·65
Magnesium	24·38	24·30	Yttrium	88·7	88·4
Manganium	55·0	54·83	Zinc	65·5	65·3
Mercury	200·4	199·8	Zirconium	90·7	90·42

TABLE 2.—SYMBOLS, MOLECULAR AND EQUIVALENT
COMPOUNDS, IMPORTANT

No.	COMPOUNDS.	Molecular Formula.*	Molcr. weight.
1	Aluminium oxide	Al_2O_3	103
2	hydrate	$Al_2'(HO)_6$	157
3	chloride	Al_2Cl_6	263
4	sulphate	$Al_2(SO_4)_3$	343
5	sulphate, cryst.	$Al_2(SO_4)_3+18aq$	667
6	Ammonia	NH_3	17
7	alum	$Al(NH_4)(SO_4)_2+12aq$	453·5
8	Ammonium carbonate	$\{$ $H(NH_4)CO_3+(NH_4)CO_2NH_2\}$	157
9	chloride	NH_4Cl	53·5
10	magnesium arsenate	$Mg(NH_4)AsO_4+\frac{1}{2}aq$.	190
11	magnesium phosphate, cryst.	$Mg(NH_4)PO_4+6aq$	245
12	nitrate	NH_4NO_3	80
13	phosphate	$(NH_4)_2HPO_4$	132
14	sodium phosphate	$(NH_4)NaHPO_4+4aq$.	209
15	platinum chloride	$(NH_4)_2PtCl_6$	446·18
16	sulphate	$(NH_4)_2SO_4$	132
17	sulphocyanate	NH_4CNS	76
18	Arsenic oxide	As_2O_5	230
19	Arsenious oxide	As_2O_3	198
20	trisulphide	As_2S_3	246
21	Barium monoxide	BaO	153
22	hydrate	$Ba(HO)_2$	171
23	hydrate, cryst.	$Ba(HO)_2+8aq$	315
24	carbonate	$BaCO_3$	197
25	chloride	$BaCl_2+2aq$	244
26	sulphate	$BaSO_4$	233
27	Calcium monoxide	CaO	56
28	hydrate	$Ca(HO)_2$	74
29	carbonate	$CaCO_3$	100
30	chloride	$CaCl_2$	111
31	chloride, cryst.	$CaCl_2+6aq$	219
32	chlorate	$Ca(ClO_3)_2$	207
33	hypochlorite	$Ca(OCl)_2$	143
34	phosphate, monobasic	$CaH_4(PO_4)_2$	234
35	phosphate, dibasic	$CaHPO_4$	136
36	phosphate, tribasic	$Ca_3(PO_4)_2$	310
37	sulphate, anhydrous	$CaSO_4$	136

* Modern notation and atomic weights.

WEIGHTS, AND PERCENTAGE COMPOSITION OF CHEMICAL TO THE ALKALI INDUSTRY.

No.	Equivalent Formula.†	Equivlt. weight.	Percentage Composition.
1	Al_2O_3	51·5	Al 53·40, O 46·60
2	$Al_2O_3\,3HO$	78·5	Al_2O_3 65·61, H_2O 34·39
3	Al_2Cl_3	134	Al 20·52, Cl 79·48
4	$Al_2O_3 3SO_3$	171·5	Al_2O_3 30·03, SO_3 69·97
5	$Al_2O_3 3SO_3 + 18HO$	333·5	Al_2O_3 15·44, SO_3 35·98, H_2O 48·58
6	NH_3	17	N 82·35, H 17·67
7	$Al_2O_3 3SO_3 + NH_4OS\,O_3 + 24HO$	458·5	Al_2O_3 11·35, NH_3 3·75, SO_3 35·29, H_2O [49·61
8	$3NH_3 4CO_2 + 2HO$	157	NH_3 32·49, CO_2 56·05, H_2O 11·46
9	NH_4Cl	53·5	NH_3 31·77, H Cl 68·23
10	$2MgONH_4O\,AsO_5 + HO$	190	MgO 21·05, As_2O_5 60·53, NH_3 8·95, H_2O 9·47
11	$2MgONH_4OPO_5 + 12 HO$	245	MgO 16·30, NH_3 6·93, P_2O_5 29·09, H_2O 47·68
12	NH_4ONO_5	80	NH_3 21·25, N_2O_5 67·50, H_2O 11·25
13	$2NH_4OHOPO_5$	132	NH_3 25·68, P_2O_5 53·93, H_2O 20·39
14	$NH_4ONaOHOPO_5 + 8HO$	209	NH_3 8·13, Na_2O 14·83, P_2O_5 33·97, H_2O 43·06
15	$NH_4ClPtCl_2$	223·09	NH_3 7·62, Pt 44·19, Cl 47·74, H_2·45
16	NH_4OSO_3	66	NH_3 25·76, SO_3 60·61, H_2O 13·63
17	$NH_4C_2NS_2$	76	NH_4 22·37, H 1·31, CN 34·21, S 42·11
18	AsO_5	115	As 65·22, O 34·78
19	AsO_3	99	As 75·76, O 24·24
20	AsS_3	123	As 60·98, S 39·02
21	BaO	76·5	Ba 89·54, O 10·46
22	$BaOHO$	85·5	BaO 89·47, H_2O 10·53
23	$BaO9HO$	157·5	BaO 48·60, H_2O 51·40
24	$BaOCO_2$	98·5	BaO 77·60, CO_2 22·40
25	$BaCl + 2HO$	122	Ba Cl 85·24. H_2O 14·76
26	$BaOSO_3$	116·5	BaO 65·67, SO_3 34·33
27	CaO	28	Ca 71·43, O 28·57
28	$CaOHO$	37	CaO 75·67, H_2O 24·33
29	$CaOCO_2$	50	CaO 56·00, CO_2 44·00
30	$CaCl$	55·5	Ca 36·05, Cl 63·95
31	$CaCl + 6HO$	109·5	$CaCl_2$ 50·69, H_2O 49·31
32	$CaOClO_5$	103·5	CaO 27·05, Cl_2O_5 72·95
33	$CaOClO$	71·5	CaO 39·16, Cl 49·65, O 11·19
34	$CaO2HOPO_5$	117	CaO 23·93, P_2O_5 60·68, H_2O 15·38
35	$2CaOHOPO_5$	136	CaO 41·18, P_2O_5 52·20, H_2O 6·62
36	$3CaOPO_5$	155	CaO 54·19, P_2O_5 45·81
37	$CaOSO_3$	68	CaO 41·18, SO_3 58·82

† Old notation and atomic weights.

SYMBOLS, MOLECULAR AND EQUIVALENT WEIGHTS, AND PER-

No.	COMPOUNDS.	Molecular formula.	Molcr. weight.
38	Calcium sulphate, cryst. (gypsum)...	$CaSO_4 + 2aq$	172
39	sulphite...........................	$CaSO_3$.....................	120
40	thiosulphate.....................	CaS_2O_3	152
41	sulphide..........................	CaS........................	72
42	pentasulphide	CaS_5......................	200
43	Carbonic acid, dioxide	CO_2	44
44	oxide..................	CO	28
45	Carburetted hydrogen : methane......	CH_4......................	16
46	ethylene......	C_2H_4	28
47	Copper chloride	$CuCl_2$	134·5
48	oxide...................	CuO......................	79·5
49	sulphide	CuS.......................	95·5
50	Copper (cuprous) sulphide	Cu_2S	159
51	sulphate	$CuSO_4 5aq$	249·5
52	Hydrochloric acid	HCl.......................	36·5
53	Hypochlorous anhydride	Cl_2O.....................	87
54	acid	$HClO$	52·5
55	Iron, oxide, ferric...................	Fe_2O_3	160
56	ferric hydrate...................	$Fe_2(OH)_6$	214
57	ferrous chloride..............	$FeCl_2$....................	127
58	cryst.	$FeCl_2 4aq$.................	199
59	ferric chloride..............	Fe_2Cl_6	325
60	Iron, ferrous sulphide.............	FeS.......................	88
61	bisulphide (pyrites)	FeS_2	120
62	protosulphate	$FeSO_4 7aq$	278
63	Lead monoxide (litharge)..............	PbO	223
64	carbonate	$PbCO_3$	267
65	chloride	$PbCl_2$....................	278
66	sulphate	$PbSO_4$....................	303
67	sulphide	PbS.......................	239
68	dioxide...................	PbO_2	239
69	Magnesium oxide.......................	MgO	40
70	hydrate	$Mg(HO)_2$	58
71	chloride	$MgCl_2$....................	95
72	cryst.	$MgCl_2 + 6aq$	203
73	carbonate	$MgCO_3$	84
74	sulphate	$MgSO_4 + 7aq$	246
75	pyrophosphate	$Mg_2P_2O_7$................	222
76	Manganous oxide.......................	MnO	71
77	Manganous manganic oxide	Mn_3O_4...................	229

CENTAGE COMPOSITION OF CHEMICAL COMPOUNDS—*Continued.*

No.	Equivalent Formula.	Equivlt. weight.	Percentage Composition.
38	$CaOSO_3 + 2HO$	86	CaO 32·56, SO_3 46·51, H_2O 20·93
39	$CaOSO_2$	60	CaO 46·67, SO_2 53·33
40	$CaOS_2O_2$	76	CaO 36·84, SO_2 42·11, S 21·05
41	CaS	36	Ca 55·56, S 44·44
42	CaS_5	100	Ca 20·00, S 80·00
43	CO_2	22	C 27·27, O 72·73
44	CO	14	C 42·85, O 57·15
45	C_2H_4	16	C 75·00, H 25·00
46	C_4H_4	28	C 85·72, H 14·28
47	CuCl	67·25	Cu 47·21, Cl 52·79
48	CuO	39·75	Cu 79·87, O 20·13
49	CuS	47·75	Cu 66·49, S 33·51
50	Cu_2S	79·5	Cu 79·87, S 20·13
51	$CuOSO_5 5HO$	124·75	CuO 31·86, SO_3 32·06, H_2O 36·03
52	HCl	36·5	Cl 97·26, H 2·74
53	ClO	43·5	Cl 81·61, O 18·39
54	ClOHO	52·5	Cl 67·62, O 30·48, H 1·90
55	Fe_2O_3	80	Fe 70·0, O 30·0
56	$Fe_2O_3 3HO$	107	Fe_2O_3 74·77, H_2O 25·23
57	FeCl	63·5	Fe 44·09, Cl 55·91
58	$FeCl 4HO$	99·5	$FeCl_2$ 63·82, H_2O 36·18
59	Fe_2Cl_3	162·5	Fe 34·46, Cl 65·54
60	FeS	44	Fe 63·64, S 36·36
61	FeS_2	60	Fe 46·67, S 53·33
62	$FeOSO_3 7HO$	139	Fe 20·14, O 5·76, SO_3 28·78, H_2O 45·32
63	PbO	111·5	Pb 92·83, O 7·17
64	$PbOCO_2$	133·5	PbO 83·52, CO_2 16·48
65	PbCl	139	Pb 74·46, Cl 25·54
66	$PbOSO_3$	151·5	PbO 73·60, SO_3 26·40
67	PbS	118·5	Pb 86·61, S 13·39
68	PbO_2	119·5	Pb 86·61, O 13·39
69	MgO	20	Mg 60·00, O 40·00
70	MgOHO	29	MgO 68·96, H_2O 31·04
71	MgCl	47·5	Mg 25·26, Cl 74·74
72	$MgCl + 6HO$	101·5	$MgCl_2$ 46·80, H_2O 53·2
73	$MgOCO_2$	42	MgO 47·62, CO_2 52·38
74	$MgOSO_3 + 7HO$	123	MgO 16·26, SO_3 32·52, H_2O 51·22
75	$2MgOP O_5$	111	MgO 36·04, P_2O_5 63·96
76	MnO	35·5	Mn 77·47, O 22·58
77	Mn_3O_4	114·5	Mn 72·05, O 27·95

SYMBOLS, MOLECULAR AND EQUIVALENT WEIGHTS, AND PER-

No.	COMPOUNDS.	Molecular formula.	Molcr. weight.
78	Manganic oxide	Mn_2O_3	158
79	Manganese dioxide	MnO_2	87
80	Manganous chloride	$MnCl_2$	126
81	sulphate	$MnSO_4$	151
82	Nitrosulphonicacid, nitrososulphuric acid, chamber crystals }	$SO_2(OH)(ONO)$..........	127
83	Nitrous oxide	N_2O..................	44
84	Nitric oxide	NO	30
85	Nitrous anhydride	N_2O_3	76
86	Nitric peroxide, tetroxide	$NO_2[N_2O_4]$	46
87	Nitric acid..................	HNO_3	63
88	Phosphoric anhydride	P_2O_5	142
89	acid, ortho	H_3PO_4..................	98
90	acid, pyro	$H_4P_2O_7$	178
91	acid, meta	HPO_3	80
92	Platinum chloride	$PtCl_4$	339·18
93	Potassium oxide	K_2O..................	94
94	hydrate	KOH	56
95	bichromate	$K_2Cr_2O_7$	295
96	carbonate	K_2CO_3	138
97	bicarbonate	$KHCO_3$	100
98	chlorate..................	$KClO_3$..................	122·5
99	chloride..................	KCl	74·5
100	ferricyanide, red prussiate	$K_6Fe_2(NC)_{12}$	658
101	ferrocyanide, yellow prus- [siate	$K_4Fe(NC)_63aq$	422
102	iodide	KJ	166
103	nitrate	KNO_3..................	101
104	permanganate	$KMnO_4$	158
105	phosphate	K_2HPO_4	174
106	platinum chloride	K_2PtCl_6	488·18
107	silicate	K_2SiO_3	154
108	sulphate..................	K_2SO_4..................	174
109	bisulphate..................	$KHSO_4$	136
110	sulphide..................	K_2S..................	110
111	sulphite..................	K_2SO_32aq	194
112	bisulphite	$KHSO_3$	120
113	sulphocyanate	$KCNS$..................	97
114	Potash, alum	$KAl(SO_4)_212aq$	474·5
115	Selenious anhydride	SeO_2	111
116	Silicic acid, anhydride	SiO_2...	60
117	Silver chloride..................	$AgCl$	143·5

CENTAGE COMPOSITION OF CHEMICAL COMPOUNDS—*Continued.*

No.	Equivalent Formula.	Equivlt. weight.	Percentage Composition.
78	Mn_2O_3	79	Mn 69·62, O 30·38
79	MnO_2	43·5	Mn 63·22, O 36·78
80	$MnCl$	63	Mn 43·65, Cl 56·35
81	$MnOSO_3$	75·5	MnO 47·02, SO_3 52·98
82	$2SO_3HONO_3$	127	SO_3 62·99, N_2O_3 29·92, H_2O 7·09
83	NO	22	N 63·64, O 36·36
84	NO_2	30	N 46·67, O 53·33
85	NO_3	38	N 36·84, O 63·16
86	NO_4	46	N 30·44, O 69·56
87	NO_5HO	63	N_2O_5 85·71, H_2O 14·29
88	PO_5	71	P 43·66, O 56·34
89	PO_53HO	98	P_2O_5 72·45, H_2O 27·55
90	PO_52HO	89	P_2O_5 79·77, H_2O 20·23
91	PO_5HO	80	P_2O_5 88·75, H_2O 11·25
92	$PtCl_2$	169·59	Pt 58·13, Cl 41·7
93	KO	47	K 82·98, O 17·02
94	$KOHO$	56	K_2O 83·93, H_2O 16·07
95	$KO2CrO_3$	147·5	K_2O 31·86, CrO_3 63·14
96	$KOCO_2$	69	K_2O 68·12, CO_2 31·88
97	$KOHOCO_2$	100	K_2O 47·00, CO_2 44·00, H_2O 9·00
98	$KOClO_5$	122·5	K_2O 38·37, Cl 28·98, O 32·65
99	KCl	74·5	K 52·35, Cl 47·65
100	$3KCyFe_2Cy_3$	329	K 35·56, Fe 17·02, CN 47·42
101	$2KCyFeCy3HO$	211	K 37·03, Fe 13·25, CN 36·93, H_2O 12·79
102	KJ	166	K 23·49, J 76·51
103	$KONO_5$	101	K_2O 46·54, N_2O_3 53·46
104	$KOMn_2O_7$	158	K_2O 29·75, Mn_2O_7 70·25
105	$2KOHOPO_5$	174	K_2O 54·02, P_2O_5 40·81, H_2O 5·17
106	$KClPtCl_2$	244·09	Pt 40·39, Cl 43·63, K 15·98 (KCl 30·52)
107	$KOSiO_2$	77	K_2O 61·04, SiO_2 38·96
108	$KOSO_3$	87	K_2O 54·02, SO_3 45·98
109	$KOHO2SO_3$	136	K_2O 34·56, SO_3 58·83, H_2O 6·62
110	KS	55	K 70·91, S 29·09
111	$KOSO_22HO$	97	K_2O 48·45, SO_2 33·00, H_2O 18·55
112	$KOHO2SO_2$	120	K_2O 39·17, SO_2 53·33, H_2O 7·50
113	KC_2NS_2	97	K 40·21, C 12·37, N 14·43, S 32·99
114	$\begin{Bmatrix} KOSO_3 + Al_2O_33SO_3 \\ + 24HO \end{Bmatrix}$	474·5	K_2O 9·91, Al_2O_3 10·84, SO_3 33·73, H_2O 45·52
115	S_2O_2	55·5	Se 71·17, O 28·83
116	SiO_2	30·0	Si 46·67, O 53·33
117	$AgCl$	143·5	Ag 75·26, Cl 24·74

SYMBOLS, MOLECULAR AND EQUIVALENT WEIGHTS, AND PER-

No.	COMPOUNDS.	Molecular formula.	Molcr. weight.
118	Silver nitrate	$AgNO_3$	170
119	sulphide............................	Ag_2S	248
120	Sodium oxide	Na_2O	62
121	hydrate	$NaHO$	40
122	chloride	$NaCl$	58·5
123	aluminate	$Na_6Al_2O_6$	289
124	borate	$Na_2B_4O_7 10aq$..........	382
125	carbonate, anhydrous........	Na_2CO_3	106
126	carbonate, monohydrated ...	Na_2CO_3aq	124
127	carbonate, decahydrated crst.	$Na_2CO_3 10aq$	286
128	bicarbonate	$NaHCO_3$.................	84
129	chlorate	$NaClO_3$	106·5
130	hypochlorite	$NaOCl$	74·5
131	nitrate.............................	$NaNO_3$	85
132	phosphate	$Na_2HPO_4 12aq$	358
133	silicate.............................	Na_2SiO_3	122
134	sulphate	Na_2SO_4	142
135	cryst.	$Na_2SO_4 10aq$	322
136	bisulphate	$NaHSO_4$	120
137	sulphite	$Na_2SO_3 6aq$	234
138	bisulphite	$NaHSO_3$	104
139	thiosulphate, hyposulphite...	$Na_2S_2O_3 5aq$	248
140	sulphide	Na_2S	78
141	pentasulphide	Na_2S_5	206
142	hydrogen sulphide	$NaSH$..............	56
143	Sulphurous anhydride	SO_2	64
144	Sulphuric anhydride	SO_3	80
145	Sulphuric acid, monohydrate	H_2SO_4	98
146	pyro	$H_2S_2O_7$	178
147	Thiosulphuric acid, hyposulphurous acid	$H_2S_2O_3$	114
148	Trithionic acid	$H_2S_3O_6$	194
149	Tetrathionic acid....................	$H_2S_4O_6$	226
150	Pentathionic acid	$H_2S_5O_6$	258
151	Sulphuretted hydrogen	H_2S.................	34
152	Stannous chloride	$SnCl_2 2aq$	225
153	Water................................	H_2O	18
154	Zinc oxide.............................	ZnO	81
155	chloride	$ZnCl_2$.................	136
156	sulphate	$ZnSO_4$.................	161
157	cryst.	$ZnSO_4 7aq$	287
158	sulphide	ZnS.................	97

CENTAGE COMPOSITION OF CHEMICAL COMPOUNDS—*Continued.*

No.	Equivalent Formula.	Eqnivlt. weight.	Percentage Composition.
118	$AgONO_5$	170	Ag 63·53, NO_3 36·47
119	AgS	124	Ag 87·09, S 12·91
120	NaO	31	Na 74·19, O 25·81
121	NaOHO	40	Na_2O 77·50, H_2O 22·50
122	NaCl	58·5	Na 39·32, Cl 60·68
123	$3NaOAl_2O_3$	144·5	Na_2O 64·36, Al_2O_3 35·64
124	$NaO2BO_3+10HO$	191·0	Na_2O 16·23, B_2O_3 36·65, H_2O 47·12
125	$NaOCO_2$	53	Na_2O 58·49, CO_2 41·51
126	$NaOCO_2+HO$	62	Na_2O 50·00, CO_2 35·48, H_2O 14·52
127	$NaOCO_2+10HO$	143	Na_2O 21·68, CO_2 15·39, H_2O 62·93
128	$NaOHO2CO_2$............	84	Na_2O 36·90, CO_2 52·38, H_2O 10·71
129	$NaOClO_5$	106·5	Na_2O 29·10, Cl_2O_5 70·90
130	NaOClO.................	74·5	Na_2O 41·61, Cl_2O 58·39
131	$NaONO_5$................	85	Na_2O 36·47, N_2O_5 63·53
132	$2NaOHOPO_5+24HO$	358	Na_2O 17·32, P_2O_5 19·84, H_2O 62·84
133	$NaOSiO_2$................	61	Na_2O 50·82, SiO_2 49·18
134	$NaOSO_3$................	71	Na_2O 43·66, SO_3 56·34
135	$NaOSO_3+10HO$	161	Na_2O 19·25, SO_3 24·84, H_2O 55·91
136	$NaOHO2SO_3$............	120	Na_2O 25·83, SO_3 66·67, H_2O 7·50
137	$NaOSO_2+6HO$.........	117	Na_2O 26·50, SO_2 27·35, H_2O 46·15
138	$NaOHO2SO_2$............	104	Na_2O 29·81, SO_2 61·54, H_2O 8·65
139	$NaOS_2O_2+5HO$	124	Na_2O 25·00, S 12·90, SO_2 25·80, H_2O 36·30
140	NaS........................	39	Na 58·97, S 41·03, corresponding to
141	NaS_5	103	Na_2S 37·86, S_4 62·14 [79·49 Na_2O
142	NaSHS	56	Na_2S 69·65, H_2S 30·35
143	SO_2	32	S 50·00, O 50·00
144	SO_3........................	40	S 40·00, O 60·00
145	$HOSO_3$	49	SO_3 81·63, H_2O 18·37
146	$HO2SO_3$.................	89	H_2SO_4 55·06, SO_3 44·94
147	HOS_2O_2	57	SO_2 56·14, S 28·07, H_2O 15·79
148	HOS_3O_5	97	SO_3 41·24, SO_2 32·99, S 16·49, H_2O 9·23
149	HOS_4O_5.................	113	SO_3 35·39, SO_2 28·32, S 28·32, H_2O 7·97
150	HOS_5O_5	129	SO_3 31·01, SO_2 24·81, S 37·20, H_2O 6·03
151	HS	17	S 94·12, H 5·88
152	$SnCl+2HO$	112·5	Sn 52·44, Cl 31·56, H_2O 16·00
153	HO	9	H 11·11, O 88·89
154	ZnO.......................	40·5	Zn 80·25, O 19·75
155	ZnCl	68	Zn 47·79, Cl 52·21
156	$ZnOSO_3$..................	80·5	ZnO 50·31, SO_3 49·69
157	$ZnOSO_3+7HO$	143·5	ZnO 28·22, SO_3 27·87, H_2O 43·91
158	ZnS........................	48·5	Zn 67·01, S 32·99

TABLE 3.—FACTORS FOR CALCULATING

Substance Weighed.	Substance to be determined.
Ammonium.	
Ammonium Chloride, NH_4Cl	Ammonia, NH_3 ....
Ammonium platinum chloride, $(NH_4)_2PtCl_6$ .... {	Ammonium oxide $(NH_4)_2O$ ....
	Ammonia, NH_3 ....
	Nitrogen, N ....
Arsenic.	{
Arsenic trisulphide, As_2S_3 .... }	Arsenic, As ....
	Arsenic trioxide, As_2O_3 ....
	Arsenic Anhydride, As_2O_5 ....
Ammonium magnesium arsenate, $Mg(NH_4)AsO_4 + \frac{1}{2}aq$ .... {	Arsenic, As ....
	Arsenic trioxide, As_2O_3 ....
	Arsenic anhydride, As_2O_5 ....
Barium.	
Barium sulphate, $BaSO_4$ .... }	{ BaO ....
Barium carbonate, $BaCO_3$ .... } Barium oxide,	{ BaO ....
Barium silico fluoride, $BaSiF_6$ .... }	{ BaO ....
Calcium.	
Calcium sulphate, $CaSO_4$ .... } Calcium oxide,	{ CaO ....
Calcium carbonate, $CaCO_3$	{ CaO ....
Carbon.	
Carbonic anhydride, CO	Carbon, C ....
Calcium carbonate, $CaCO_3$ .... } Carbonic anhydride,	{ CO_2 ....
Barium carbonate, $BaCO_3$	{ CO_2 ....
Chlorine.	{ Chlorine, Cl ....
Silver chloride, AgCl .... {	Hydrochloric acid, HCl ....
	Chloric anhydride, Cl_2O_5 ....
	Sodium chloride, NaCl ....
Copper.	
Copper oxide, CuO..........................	Copper, Cu ....
Cuprous sulphide, Cu_2S .... {	Copper, Cu ....
	Cupric oxide, CuO ....
Iron.	
Ferric oxide, Fe_2O_3 .... {	Iron, Fe ....
	Ferrous oxide, FeO ....
Lead.	
Lead monoxide, PbO......................	Lead, Pb ....
Lead sulphate, $PbSO_4$ .... {	Lead, Pb ....
	Lead oxide, PbO ....
Lead sulphide, PbS...................... {	Lead, Pb ....
	Lead oxide, PbO ....
Lead, Pb	Lead oxide, PbO

GRAVIMETRIC ANALYSES.

1	2	3	4	5	6	7	8	9
0·31776	0·63552	0·95328	1·27104	1·58880	1·90656	2·22132	2·54208	2·85934
0·11654	0·23308	0·34962	0·46616	0·58270	0·69924	0·81578	0·93232	1·04886
0·07620	0·15240	0·22860	0·30480	0·38100	0·45720	0·53340	0·60960	0·68580
0·06276	0·12552	0·18828	0·25104	0·31380	0·37656	0·43932	0·50208	0·56484
0·60975	1·21950	1·82925	2·43900	2·04875	3·65850	3·26825	4·87800	5·48775
0·80488	1·60976	2·41464	3·21552	4·02440	4·82928	5·63416	6·43904	7·24392
0·93496	1·86992	2·80488	3·73984	4·67480	5·60976	6·54472	7·47968	8·41464
0·39473	0·78946	1·18419	1·57892	1·97365	2·36838	2·76311	3·15784	3·55257
0·52105	1·04210	1·56315	2·08420	2·60525	3·12630	3·64735	4·16840	4·68945
0·60526	1·21052	1·81578	2·42104	3·02630	3·63156	4·23682	4·84208	5·44734
0·65665	1·31330	1·96995	2·62660	3·28325	3·93990	4·59655	5·25320	5·90985
0·77655	1·55310	2·32965	3·10620	3·88275	4·65930	5·43585	6·21240	6·98895
0·54839	1·09678	1·64517	2·19356	2·74195	3·29034	3·83873	4·38712	4·93551
0·41176	0·82352	1·23528	1·64704	2·05880	2·47056	2·88232	3·29408	3·70584
0·56000	1·12000	1·68000	2·24000	2·80000	3·36000	3·92000	4·48000	5·04000
0·27273	0·54546	0·81819	1·09092	1·36365	1·63638	1·90911	2·18184	2·45457
0·44000	0·88000	1·32000	1·76000	2·20000	2·64000	3·08000	3·52000	3·96000
0·22335	0·44670	0·67005	0·89340	1·11675	1·34010	1·56345	1·78680	2·01015
0·24739	0·49478	0·74217	0·93956	1·23695	1·48434	1·73173	1·97912	2·22651
0·25435	0·50870	0·76305	1·01740	1·27175	1·52610	1·78045	2·03480	2·28915
0·52613	1·05226	1·57839	2·10452	2·63065	3·15678	3·68291	4·20904	4·73517
0·40767	0·81534	1·22301	1·63068	2·03835	2·44602	2·85369	3·26136	3·66903
0·79874	1·59748	2·39622	3·19496	3·99370	4·79244	5·59118	6·38992	7·18866
0·79874	1·59748	2·39622	3·19496	3·99370	4·79244	5·59118	6·38992	7·18866
1·00000	2·00000	3·00000	4·00000	5·00000	6·00000	7·00000	8·00000	9·00000
0·70000	1·40000	2·10000	2·80000	3·50000	4·20000	4·90000	5·60000	6·30000
0·90000	1·80000	2·70000	3·60000	4·50000	5·40000	6·30000	7·20000	8·10000
0·92825	1·85650	2·78475	3·71300	4·64125	5·56950	6·49775	7·42600	8·35425
0·68317	1·36634	2·04951	2·73268	3·41585	4·09902	4·78219	5·46536	6·14853
0·73597	1·47194	2·20791	2·94388	3·67985	4·41582	5·15179	5·88776	6·62373
0·86611	1·73222	2·59833	3·46444	4·33055	5·19666	6·06277	6·92888	7·79499
0·93305	1·86610	2·79915	3·73220	4·66525	5·59830	6·53135	7·46440	8·39745
1·07730	2·15460	3·23190	4·30920	5·38650	6·46380	7·54110	8·61840	9·69570

FACTORS FOR CALCULATING

Substance Weighed.	Substance to be determined.
Hydrogen.	
Water, H_2O..............................	Hydrogen, H..............................
Magnesium.	
Magnesium sulphate, $MgSO_4$............	Magnesia, MgO..........................
Magnesium pyrophosphate, $Mg_2P_2O_7$	Magnesia, MgO..........................
Manganese.	
Mangano-manganic oxide, Mn_3O_4	Manganese, Mn..........................
Manganese sulphide, MnS.............. $\big\{$	Manganese, Mn..........................
	Manganous oxide, MnO ....
Nitrogen.	
Ammonium platinum chloride,	
$(NH_4)_2PtCl_6$	Nitrogen, N ....
Platinum, Pt	Nitrogen, N ....
Phosphorus.	$\big\{$ Phosphoric anhydride, P_2O_5 ....
Magnesium pyrophosphate, $Mg_2P_2O_7$	$\big\{$ Phosphorus, P ....
Potassium.	
Potassium sulphate, K_2SO_4..............	Potassium oxide, K_2O..................
Potassium chloride, KCl	Potassium oxide, K_2O..................
Potassium platinum chloride, K_2PtCl_6	$\big\{$ Potassium oxide, K_2O ....
	$\big\{$ Potassium chloride, KCl ....
Sodium.	
Sodium sulphate, Na_2SO_4	Sodium oxide, Na_2O ....
Sodium carbonate, Na_2CO_3..............	Sodium oxide, Na_2O ....
Sodium chloride, NaCl....................	Sodium oxide, Na_2O ....
Sulphur.	Sulphur, S..............................
Barium sulphate, $BaSO_4$ .... $\big\{$	Sulphuric anhydride, SO_3 ....
	Sulphurous anhydride, SO_2 ....
	Sodium sulphate, Na_2SO_4 ....
Zinc.	
Zinc oxide, ZnO...........................	Zinc, Zn ....
Zinc sulphide, ZnS .... $\big\{$	Zinc, Zn ....
	Zinc oxide, ZnO ....

GRAVIMETRIC ANALYSES—*continued.*

1	2	3	4	5	6	7	8	9
0·11111	0·22222	0·33333	0·44444	0·55555	0·66666	0·77777	0·88888	1·00000
0·33333	0·66666	1·00000	1·33333	1·66666	2·00000	2·33333	2·66666	3·00000
0·36036	0·72072	1·08108	1·44144	1·80180	2·16216	2·52252	2·88288	3·24324
0·72052	1·44104	2·16156	2·88208	3·60260	4·32312	5·04364	5·76416	6·48468
0·63218	1·26436	1·89654	2·52872	3·16090	3·79308	4·42526	5·05744	5·68962
0·81609	1·63218	2·44827	3·26436	4·08045	4·89654	5·71263	6·52872	7·34481
0·06276	0·12552	0·18828	0·25104	0·31380	0·37656	0·43932	0·50208	0·56484
0·14200	0·28400	0·42600	0·56800	0·71000	0·85200	0·99400	1·13600	1·27800
0·63964	1·27928	1·91892	2·55856	3·19820	3·83784	4·47748	5·11712	5·75676
0·27928	0·55856	0·83784	1·11712	1·39640	1·67568	1·95496	2·23424	2·51352
0·54023	1·08046	1·62069	2·16092	2·70115	3·24138	3·78161	4·32184	4·86207
0·63087	1·26174	1·89261	2·52348	3·15435	3·78522	4·41609	5·04696	5·67783
0·19255	0·38510	0·57765	0·77020	0·96275	1·15530	1·34785	1·54040	1·73295
0·30521	0·61042	0·91563	1·22084	1·52605	1·83126	2·13647	2·44168	2·74689
0·43662	0·87324	1·30986	1·74648	2·18310	2·61972	3·05634	3·49296	3·92958
0·58491	1·16982	1·75473	2·33964	2·92455	3·50946	4·09437	4·67928	5·26419
0·52991	1·05982	1·58973	2·11964	2·64955	3·17946	3·70937	4·23928	4·76919
0·13734	0·27468	0·41202	0·54936	0·68670	0·82404	0·96138	1·09872	1·23606
0·34335	0·68670	1·03005	1·37340	1·71675	2·06010	2·40345	2·74680	3·09015
0·27467	0·54934	0·82401	1·09868	1·37335	1·64802	1·92269	2·19736	2·47203
0·60944	1·21888	1·82832	2·43776	3·04720	3·65664	4·26608	4·87552	5·48496
0·80295	1·60590	2·40885	3·21180	4·01475	4·81770	5·62065	6·42360	7·22655
0·67078	1·34156	2·01234	2·68312	3·35390	4·02468	4·69546	5·36624	6·03702
0·83539	1·67078	2·50617	3·34156	4·17695	5·01234	5·84773	6·68312	7·51851

TABLE 4.—SOLUBILITY OF DIFFERENT SALTS.

REMARK.—The solubility is given in parts of the anhydrous salt dissolved by 100 parts of water.

100 Water Dissolve.	Cold.	Boiling.
Alum, ammonia	9	422
potash	9·5	357
Aluminium sulphate	33	89
Ammonium oxalate	4·5	40·8
nitrate	199	...
sulphate	66	100
Barium chloride	35	60
hydrate	5	10
nitrate	8	35
Boric acid	2	21
Bromine	3	...
Calcium carbonate	0·0036	...
chloride	400	...
hydrate	0·128	0·079
nitrate	400	...
sulphate	0·23	0·21
Copper acetate	7	19·8
nitrate	127	...
sulphate	21	75
Iron protosulphate	20	178
Lead acetate	46	71
chloride	3	5
nitrate	48	139
sulphate	·008	...
Magnesium oxide	·002	·002
carbonate	·02	...
chloride	200	400
Manganous chloride	62	123
Oxalic acid	11·5	100
Potassium hydrate	200	...
chromate (neutral)	48	...
bichromate	10	102
oxalate (acid)	2·5	10
sulphite	100	...
thiosulphate	deliquescent	...
bitartrate	0·4	10·5
tartrate (neutral)	133	296
cyanide	122	...
ferrocyanide	28	91
ferricyanide	40	82
iodide	141	221
Sodium acetate	85	150
borate	4	55
hydrate	61	...
thiosulphate	50	more than 200

SOLUBILITY OF DIFFERENT SALTS—*continued*.

100 Water Dissolve.	Cold.	Boiling.
Sodium phosphate.............................	12	...
sulphite	25	100
Strontium hydrate	1·6	84·8
nitrate	20	113
chloride	53	102
Tartaric acid	76	200
Tin (stannous) chloride	270	...
Zinc chloride	300	...
sulphate............................	50	95

TABLE 5.—SOLUBILITY OF CERTAIN SALTS AT DIFFERENT TEMPERATURES.

Ammonium Carbonate.

100 parts water dissolve (Berzelius) at

18° 25 parts
17 30
32 37
41 40
49 50

Ammonium Chloride.

100 parts water dissolve at

15° 35·68 parts NH_4Cl (Gerlach)
19 36·8 (Schiff)
100 100

Calcium Chloride.

1 part anhydrous $CaCl_2$ dissolves (Kremers) at

10·2° in 1·58 parts water
20 1·35
40 0·83
60 0·72

1 part $CaCl_2$, 6aq., dissolves at

10° in 0·5 parts water
16 0·25
100 every proportion

Magnesium Sulphate (Epsom Salts).

100 parts water dissolve (Gay-Lussac and Tobler) at

0° 24·7 $MgSO_4$ as cryst. salt
10 30·5
20 35·0
25 37·1
30 39·8
40 47·0
50 49·7
55 52·8
60 55·9
70 60·4
80 65·1
90 70·3
105·5 132·50 (Griffiths)

Potassium Carbonate.

(1) *Anhydrous* (Osann).

1 part dissolves at

3° in 1·05 parts water
6 0·962
12·6 0·900
26 0·747
70 0·490
15 0·922 (Gerlach).

c

SOLUBILITY OF CERTAIN SALTS AT DIFFERENT
TEMPERATURES—*continued.*

(2) Crystallized (Poggiale).

100 parts water dissolves at

0° $83.12K_2CO_3 = 131.15K_2CO_3, 2aq.$

10	88.72	142.50
20	94.06	153.70
30	100.00	166.85
40	106.20	180.07
50	112.90	196.60
60	119.24	212.35
70	127.10	232.84
80	134.25	252.57
90	143.18	278.72
100	153.66	311.85
135	205.11	526.10

Potassium Bicarbonate.

100 parts water dissolve (Poggiale) at

0°	19.61 parts $KHCO_3$
10	23.23
20	26.91
30	30.57
40	34.15
50	37.92
60	41.85
70	45.24

Potassium Chlorate.

100 parts water dissolve at

0°	3.33	parts $KClO_3$ (Gay-Lus-
13.32	5.60	sac)
15.37	6.03	
21.43	8.44	
35.02	12.05	
49.08	18.96	
74.89	35.40	
104.78	60.24	
17	6.68	(V. Meyer)
18	6.82	
98	55.50	

Potassium Chloride.

100 parts water dissolve at

0°	29.21	KCl (Gay-Lussac)
11.8	34.6	(Kopp)
13.8	34.9	
15.6	35	
19	34.58	(Gay-Lussac)
52	43.59	
79	50.93	
109.6	59.26	

Potassium Nitrate.

100 parts water dissolve at

0°	13.32	parts KNO_3 (Gay-Lus-
5.01	16.72	sac)
11.67	22.23	
17.91	29.31	
24.94	38.40	
35.13	54.82	
45.10	74.66	
54.72	97.05	
65.45	125.42	
79.72	169.27	
97.66	236.45	
114.5	284.61	

Potassium Sulphate.

100 parts water dissolve at

12.5°	10	K_2SO_4 (Brandes and Firn-
15	10.38	haber)
31.25	14	
37.5	17	
50	25	
56.25	22	
68.75	21.95	
87.5	25	
100	26	
101.7	21.21	

Sodium Carbonate.

100 parts water dissolve at

[(Loewel)

0°	6.97	$Na_2CO_3 21.33Na_2CO_3 10aq.$
10	12.06	40.94
15	16.20	63.20
20	21.71	92.82
25	28.50	149.13
30	37.24	273.64
32	59	(Mulder)
34—79	46.2	
80	45.9	
85	45.7	
90	45.6	
95	45.4	
100	45.1	

Boiling point of the saturated
solution 106°

SOLUBILITY OF CERTAIN SALTS AT DIFFERENT
TEMPERATURES—*continued*.

Sodium Bicarbonate.

100 parts water dissolve at

0° 6·90 $NaHCO_3$ (Dibbits)
10 8·15
20 9·60
30 11·10
40 12·70
50 14·45
60 16·40

Sodium Chloride.

100 parts water dissolve at

—15°	32·78 NaCl (Poggiale)
—10	33·49
— 5	34·22
0	35·52
+5	35·68
9	35·74
14	35·87
25	36·13
40	36·64
50	36·98
60	37·25
70	37·88
80	38·22
90	38·87
100	39·61
109·7	40·35

Sodium Chlorate.

100 parts water dissolve at

0° 81·9 $NaClO_3$ (Kremers)
20 99
40 128·5
60 147·1
80 175·6
100 232·6
120 333·3

Sodium Nitrate.

100 parts water dissolve at

— 6'	68·80 NaNO₃ (Poggiale)
+0	79·75
10	84·30
16	87·63

20· 89·55
30 95·87
40 102·81
50 111·13
60 119·94
70 129·63
80 140·72
90 158·63
100 168·20
120 225·30

The saturated solution boils at 122°

Sodium Sulphate.

100 parts water dissolve (Gay-Lussac) at

0°	5·02Na₂SO₄	12·17Na₂SO₄,10aq
11·67	10·12	26·88
13·30	11·74	31·33
17·91	16·73	48·28
25·05	28·11	99·48
28·76	37·35	161·53
30·75	43·05	215·77
31·84	47·37	270·22
32·73	50·65	322·12
33·88	50·04	312·11
40·15	48·78	291·44
45·04	47·81	276·91
50·40	46·82	262·35
59·79	45·42	...
70·61	44·35	...
84·42	42·96	...
108·17	42·65	...

Sodium Thiosulphate (hyposulphite).

100 parts water dissolve (Mulder) at

0°	47·6 Na₂S₂O₃ as cryst. salt
16	65
20	69
25	75
30	82
35	89
40	98
45	109
47	114
60	192

(Kremers)

TABLE 6.—SOLUBILITY OF SOME GASES IN WATER.

At a pressure of 760mm.=29·92in. (Bunsen).

1 Vol. Water dissolves at °C.	Nitrogen.	Hydrogen.	Oxygen.	Carbon Dioxide.	Carbon Monoxide.	Nitrous Oxide.	Nitric Oxide. (In Alcohol.)	Hydrogen Sulphide.	Sulphur Dioxide.	Ammonia.	Atmosph. Air.
0°	0·02035	0·0193	0·04114	1·7967	0·03287	1·3052	0·31606	4·3706	68·861	1049·6	0·02471
1	0·01981	0·0193	0·04007	1·7207	0·03207	1·2005	0·31282	4·2874	67·003	1020·8	0·02406
2	0·01932	0·0193	0·03907	1·6481	0·03131	1·2172	0·30928	4·2053	65·169	993·3	0·02345
3	0·01884	0·0193	0·03810	1·5787	0·03057	1·1752	0·30604	4·1243	63·360	967·0	0·02287
4	0·01838	0·0193	0·03717	1·5126	0·02987	1·1846	0·30290	4·0442	61·576	941·9	0·02237
5	0·01794	0·0193	0·03628	1·4497	0·02920	1·0451	0·29965	3·9652	59·816	917·9	0·02179
6	0·01752	0·0193	0·03554	1·3901	0·02857	1·0575	0·29630	3·8872	58·080	895·0	0·02128
7	0·01713	0·0193	0·03465	1·3339	0·02796	1·0210	0·29405	3·8103	56·369	873·1	0·02080
8	0·01675	0·0193	0·03389	1·2809	0·02739	0·9858	0·29130	3·7345	54·683	852·1	0·02034
9	0·01640	0·0193	0·03317	1·2311	0·02686	0·9520	0·28965	3·6596	53·021	832·0	0·01992
10	0·01607	0·0193	0·03250	1·1847	0·02635	0·9196	0·28909	3·5558	51·383	812·8	0·01953
11	0·01577	0·0193	0·03189	1·1416	0·02588	0·8885	0·28363	3·5132	49·770	794·3	0·01916
12	0·01549	0·0193	0·03133	1·1018	0·02544	0·8588	0·28127	3·3415	48·182	775·6	0·01882
13	0·01523	0·0193	0·03082	1·0653	0·02504	0·8304	0·27901	4·3708	46·618	759·6	0·01851
14	0·01500	0·0193	0·03034	1·0321	0·02466	0·8034	0·27685	3·3012	45·079	743·1	0·01822
15	0·01478	0·0193	0·02989	1·0020	0·02432	0·7778	0·27478	3·2326	43·504	727·2	0·01795
16	0·01458	0·0193	0·02949	0·9753	0·02402	0·7535	0·27281	3·1651	42·073	711·8	0·01771
17	0·01441	0·0193	0·02914	0·9519	0·02374	0·7306	0·27094	3·0986	40·608	696·9	0·01750
18	0·01426	0·0193	0·02884	0·9318	0·02350	0·7090	0·26917	3·0331	39·165	682·3	0·01732
19	0·01423	0·0193	0·02858	0·9150	0·02329	0·6888	0·26750	2·9687	37·749	668·0	0·01717
20	0·01403	0·0193	0·02838	0·9014	0·02312	0·6700	0·26592	2·9053	36·216	654·0	0·01701

TABLE 7.—SOLUBILITY OF AMMONIA IN WATER BY WEIGHT.

(Solubility by Volume in Table 6.) 1g. Water Dissolves at 760 mm.
pressure (Roscoe and Dittmar).

At	g NH_3	At	g NH_3	At	g NH_3	At	g NH_3
0°	· 0·875	16°	0·582	30°	0·408	44°	0·275
2	0·833	18	0·554	32	0·382	46	0·259
4	0·792	20	0·526	34	0·362	48	0·244
6	0·751	22	0·499	36	0·343	50	0·229
8	0·718	24	0·474	38	0·324	52	0·214
10	0·679	26	0·449	40	0·307	54	0·200
12	0·645	28	0·426	42	0·290	56	0·185
14	0·612						

TABLE 8.—SOLUBILITY OF CHLORINE IN WATER.

(Schönfeld.)

1 Vol. Water absorbs Vols. Chlorine, calculated at 10° and 760 mm. pressure.

At	Vol. Chlor.	At	Vol. Chlor.	At	Vol. Chlor.	At	Vol. Chlor.
10°	2·5852	18°	2·2405	26°	1·9099	34°	1·5984
11	2·5413	19	2·1984	27	1·8695	35	1·5555
12	2·4977	20	2·1565	28	1·8295	36	1·5166
13	2·4543	21	2·1148	29	1·7895	37	1·4785
14	2·4111	22	2·0734	30	1·7490	38	1·4406
15	2·3681	23	2·0322	31	1·7104	39	1·4029
16	2·3253	24	1·9912	32	1·6712	40	1·3655
17	2·2828	25	1·9504	33	1·6322		

TABLE 9.—SOLUBILITY OF HYDROGEN CHLORIDE IN WATER.

1. BY WEIGHT (Roscoe and Dittmar). 1g. Water absorbs at 760mm.
pressure.

At	g HCl	At	g HCl	At	g HCl	At	g HCl
0°	0·825	16°	0·742	32°	0·665	48°	0·608
4	0·804	20	0·721	36	0·649	52	0·589
8	0·788	24	0·700	40	0·633	56	0·575
12	0·762	28	0·682	44	0·618	60	0·561

SOLUBILITY OF HYDROGEN CHLORIDE IN WATER—*continued.*

2. By Volume (Deicke).—1ccm. Water absorbs at a pressure of 760mm.

At	ccm. HCl	Spec. Grav. of the Acid Formed.	Percentage of HCl in same.
0°	525·2	1·2257	45·148
4	497·7	1·2265	44·361
8	480·8	1·2185	43·828
12	471·8	1·2148	43·277
14	462·4	1·2074	42·829
18	451·2	1·2064	42·311
18·25	450·7	1·2056	42·283
28	435·0	1·2014	41·536

TABLE 10.—SPECIFIC GRAVITIES OF DIFFERENT SOLIDS.

Alderwood	0·5–0·6	Brickwork	1·5–1·7
Alumina, anhydrous	4·15	Bricks, ordinary	1·4–2·2
Alum, ammonia	1·626	Brass	8·4–8·7
potash	1·724	Calamine	4·1–4·5
Alumina sulphate, cryst.	1·596	Chalk	1·8–2·7
Aluminium	2·76	Calcium chloride, cryst.	1·612
Alumstone	2·8	chloride, anhydrous	2·240
Ammonium nitrate	1·707	silicate	2·9
sulphate	1·77	carbonate	2·7
chloride	1·528	phosphate	3·18
Anhydrous gypsum	2·96	sulphate, anhydrous	2·927
Anthracite	1·4–1·7	Calcspar	2·72
Antimony	6·7	Cannel coal	1·16–1·27
Arsenious acid	3·884	Cement	2·7–3·05
Arsenic acid	4·250	China clay, kaolin	2·21
Asphalt	1·1–1·2	Charcoal, organic	1·57
Ashwood	0·7–0·8	wood	0·3–0·5
Barium chloride, cryst.	2·664	Coke, porous	0·4
carbonate	4·56	Coal, porous	1·16–1·63
sulphate (spar)	4·73	Copper, metallic, cast	8·726
hydrate, cryst.	1·66	hammered	8·94
Bauxite		pyrites	4·1–4·8
Basalt	2·8–3·2	oxide	6·48
Beechwood, dry	0·7–0·8	sulphide	2·27
Birchwood, dry	0·7–0·8	Cuprous sulphide	5·97
Bismuth	9·85	Clay	1·8–2·6
Borate of magnesia (boracite)	2·9	Cryolite	2·96
		Elmwood	0·67
Borax, crystallised	1·692	Fat, animal	0·92
Boric acid, crystallised	1·479	Felspar	2·5–2·6
fused	1·880	Fibres, vegetable	1·51
Brown coal, lignite	1·2–1·4	Firwood, dry	0·6

SPECIFIC GRAVITIES OF DIFFERENT SOLIDS—*continued.*

Firebricks	1·85	Pinewood, red	0·5
Flint	2·7	Platinum	21·1
Glass, green	2·642	Pockwood	1·263
plate	2·450	Poplar	0·38
crystal, Bohem.	2·9–3·0	Porcelain	2·1–2·5
flint, Engl.	3·4–3·44	Porphyry	2·8
Glauber's salt, cryst.	1·52	Potash	2·3
anhydrous	2·68	Potassium carbonate	2·264
Granite	2·5–2·9	chlorate	2·35
Gypsum, plaster-of-paris	2·322	chloride	1·945
cast, dry	·97	chromate	2·603
Heavy spar	4·3–4·48	nitrate	2·058
Iodine	4·948	sulphate	2·66
Iron, wrought	7·4–7·9	bisulphate	2·277
grey, cast	6·6–7·3	hydrate	2·044
white, cast	7·1–7·9	Quartz	2·7
peroxide	5·22	Resin	1·07
hydrated oxide	3·94	Rock salt	2·1–2·2
magnetic oxide	5·4	Sal-ammoniac	1·528
carbonate	3·87	Sand, dry	1·4–1·6
sulphate, cryst.	1·904	damp	1·9–2·0
pyrites, white	4·65–4·88	Sandstone	1·9–2·5
pyrites	5·18	Silver	10·6
Larchwood	0·44–0·5	Silver chloride	5·501
Lignite	1·2–1·4	Slate	2·7
Lime, burnt, quick	3·08	Sodium carbonate, anh.	2·509
Limewood	0·5	carbonate cryst.	1·454
Litharge	9·36	chloride	2·078
Lead, cast	11·3	nitrate	2·226
red	8·62	sulphate	2·63
chromate	6·00	sulphide	2·471
acetate, cryst.	2·895	thiosulphate	1·736
carbonate	6·47	hydrate	2·130
nitrate	4·40	Steel	7·80
sulphide	7·505	Steel, cast	7·92
sulphate	6·169	hardened	7·66
chloride	5·802	Sulphur, native	2·069
Magnesia, calcined	3·2	sticks, fresh	1·98
carbonate	2·94	sticks, old	2·05
Magnesite	2·9–3·1	soft, amorphous	1·96
Magnesium sulph., cryst.	1·751	Sulphuric anhydride	1·97
chloride, cryst.	1·558	Tin, cast	7·21–7·4
Manganese peroxide	2·94	hammered	7·475
native	4·7–5·0	Willowwood	0·5–0·58
Marble	2·5–2·8	Witherite	4·30
Nickel	8·9	Zinc, cast	6·8
Oakwood, dry	0·85–0·95	rolled	7·2
Phosphorus, yellow	1·826	blende	3·9–4·2
red	2·106	oxide	5·73
Pinewood, white	0·55	sulphate	2·036

TABLE II.—WEIGHT OF SUBSTANCES AS STORED.

SUBSTANCE.	1 Cub. Metre Weighs	1 Cub. Foot Weighs	Tons per Cub. Foot.
	Kilo.	lb. a.d.p.	
Bricks	2100	131	·0584
Cement	1200	75	·0335
Clay, damp	1650	103	·0459
dry	1570	98	·0437
Limestone and other Building Stones	2000	125	·0558
Mortar (lime and sand).....................................	1800	112	·0500
Quicklime...	1000	62·5	·0279
Sand, dry	1330	83	·0370
damp	1770	110	·0491
Wood, Beech Logs	400	24·5	·0107
Fir Logs	330	20·5	·0091
Oak Logs..	420	26	·0116
RAW MATERIALS, ETC., FOR ALKALI WORKS.			
Pyrites, broken pieces	2500	156	·0696
smalls	2340	146·5	·0654
burnt..	1520	95·0	·0424
Nitre	1310	81·5	·0364
Nitrecake (acid Sulphate of Soda).....................	1335	83	·0375
Salt...	689	43	·0192
Saltcake..	1180	73·5	·0328
Limestone (small pieces)	1400	87·5	·0391
Black Ash (lumps)...	962	60	·0268
Alkali Waste (wet)..	1268	79	·0352
Soda Salts ($Na_2CO_3 + H_2O$) (drained)................	810	50·5	·0225
Soda Ash (unground)..	1195	74·5	·0332
Soda Crystals	1010	63	·0281
Bicarbonate (ground).......................................	986	61·5	·0274
Quicklime (small lumps)	1058	66	·0295
Sieved Lime (for Bleaching Powder)..................	497–598	31–37	·0151
Bleaching Powder	721–834	45–52	·0216
Manganese, Native..	2210	138	·0616
Limestone Dust	1550	96·5	·0431
Coke (for filling towers)...................................	417–534	26–33	·0131
Flints „ „	1600	100	·0446
Cinders (ashes)...	738	46	·0205

TABLE 12.—SPECIFIC GRAVITY OF DIFFERENT LIQUIDS.

	Specific Gravity.	At Temp.		Specific Gravity.	At Temp.
Alcohol	0·7989	12·5	Nitrogen peroxide		
Acetic acid	1·061	17	(liquid)	1·45	...
Bisulphide of carbon	1·272	...	Olive oil	0·917	15
Benzene	0·85	15·5	Petroleum	0·78-0·81	15
Coal tar	1·15	15	Rapeseed oil	0·9136	15
Ether	0·723	12·5	Sulphurous anhy-		
Glycerine	1·260	15	dride (liquid)	1·45	−20
Linseed Oil	0·9347	15	Sea water	1·02-1·04	15
Mercury	13·596	0	Spirits of turp'ntine	0·865	15

TABLE 13.—SPECIFIC GRAVITY AND PERCENTAGE OF SATURATED SOLUTIONS.

The percentage refers to anhydrous salt.

	Temperature.	Percentage of Salt.	Specific Gravity.	Degrees Twaddell.
Ammonium chloride	15	26·80	1·0776	15·5
sulphate	19	50·00	1·2890	57·8
Barium chloride	15	25·97	1·2827	56·5
Calcium chloride	15	40·66	1·4110	82·2
Magnesium sulphate	15	25·25	1·2880	57·6
Potassium chloride	15	24·90	1·1723	34·4
carbonate	15	52·02	1·5708	114
nitrate	15	21·07	1·1441	28·8
sulphate	15	9·92	1·0831	16·6
Sodium chloride	15	26·395	1·2043	40·8
carbonate	15	14·85	1·1535	30·7
nitrate	19·5	46·25	1·3804	76
sulphate	15·0	11·95	1·1117	22·3

TABLE 14.—SPECIFIC GRAVITY OF GASES AND VAPOURS.

North Latitude, 52° 30′, 130 feet above sea level.

Gas.		Molecular weight.	Specific gravity. Air=1.	Grams per litre at 760mm. & 0° C.	Grains per cub. foot. 29·92″ & 32° F.	Lbs. per * cub. foot 29·92″ & 32° F.
Ammonia	NH_3	17	0·58890	0·76199	332·96	·01757
Atmospheric air	...	...	1·00000	1·293909	565·16	·08074
Bromine	Br_2	160	5·52271	7·14588	3122·1	·4460
Chlorine	Cl_2	71	2·44921	3·16906	1384·73	·1978
Carbonic oxide	CO	28	0·96709	1·25133	546·78	·07811
Carbonic anhydride	CO_2	44	1·51968	1·96633	859·21	·12274
Ethylene	C_2H_4	28	0·96744	1·25178	546·98	·07814
Hydrogen	H_2	2	0·06928	0·08958	39·1439	·0055919
Hydrogen chloride	HCl	36·5	1·25922	1·62932	711·94	·1017
Iodine	I_2	254	8·756	11·328	4949·90	·7071
Methane	CH_4	16	0·55297	0·71549	312·64	·04466
Mercury	Hg	200		8·9582	3914·39	·5592
Nitrogen	N_2	28	0·97010	1·25523	548·47	·07835
Nitrous oxide	N_2O	44	1·52269	1·97028	860·90	·1229
Nitric oxide	NO	30	1·03767	1·34261	586·66	·08381
Nitrous anhydride	N_2O_3	76	2·630	3·40412	1487·46	·2125
Nitric peroxide	NO_2	46	1·592	2·06089	900·81	·1286
„ „	N_2O_4	92	3·184	4·12078	1800·63	·2572
Oxygen	O_2	32	1·10521	1·43003	624·85	·08926
Sulphuretted hydrogen	H_2S	34	1·17697	1·52290	665·44	·09506
Sulphurous anhydride	SO_2	64	2·21295	2·86386	1251·19	·1787
Sulphur	S_2	64	2·2155	2·86663	1252·59	·1789
Water	H_2O	18	0·62182	0·80458	351·57	·05022

* For calculations with large quantities of gas, it is sufficiently accurate to assume that 10,000 cubic feet weigh as many cwt. as the molecular weight of the gas divided by 4 indicates. For example, 10,000 cubic feet of sulphuretted hydrogen weigh $\frac{34}{4}=8·5$ cwt. (Exactly, it would be 8·433 cwt.)

TABLE 15.—LINEAR EXPANSION OF DIFFERENT SUBSTANCES.

By variation of temperature from 0° to 100° C. (32°-212° F.)

Brass	0·001868	1 : 535
Charcoal from oak	0·001200	1 : 833
fir	0·00100	1 : 1000
Copper	0·001718	1 : 582
Glass, flint..	0·000817	1 : 1219
white	0·000861	1 : 1161
green	0·000766	1 : 1305
Gold	0·001466	1 : 682
Iron, wrought	0·001235	1 : 812
cast	0·001110	1 : 901
Lead	0·002848	1 : 351
Marble of Carrara	0·000849	1 : 1178
St. Beat	0·000418	1 : 2392
Platinum	0·000884	1 : 1132
Silver	0·001908	1 : 524
Solder, hard	0·002058	1 : 486
Steel, hardened	0·001240	1 : 807
not hardened...........................	0·001079	1 : 927
Tin	0·001988	1 : 516
Water	0·015588	1 : 71·4
Zinc	0·002942	1 : 340

TABLE 16. — COMPARISON OF DIFFERENT THERMOMETRIC SCALES.

$$t°C = \tfrac{4}{5}t°R = \tfrac{9}{5}t + 32°F; \quad t°R = \tfrac{5}{4}t°C = \tfrac{9}{4}t + 32°F; \quad t°F = \tfrac{5}{9}(t-32)°C = \tfrac{4}{9}(t-32)°R.$$

By Celsius's (Centigrade) degrees as units.

Cels.	Réaum.	Fahr.	Cels.	Réaum.	Fahr.	Cels.	Réaum.	Fahr.	Cels.	Réaum.	Fahr.	Cels.	Réaum.	Fahr.	Cels.	Réaum.	Fahr.
-40	-32	-40	-16	-12.8	+3.2	+8	+6.4	+46.4	+32	+25.6	+89.6	+55	+44	+131	+78	+62.4	+172.4
39	31.2	38.2	15	12	5	9	7.2	48.2	33	26.4	91.4	56	44.8	132.8	79	63.2	174.2
38	30.4	36.4	14	11.2	6.8	10	8	50	34	27.2	93.2	57	45.6	134.6	80	64	176
37	29.6	34.6	13	10.4	8.6	11	8.8	51.8	35	28	95	58	46.4	136.4	81	64.8	177.8
36	28.8	32.8	12	9.6	10.4	12	9.6	53.6	36	28.8	96.8	59	47.2	138.2	82	65.6	179.6
35	28	31	11	8.8	12.2	13	10.4	55.4	37	29.6	98.6	60	48	140	83	66.4	181.4
34	27.2	29.2	10	8	14	14	11.2	57.2	38	30.4	100.4	61	48.8	141.8	84	67.2	183.2
33	26.4	27.4	9	7.2	15.8	15	12	59	39	31.2	102.2	62	49.6	143.6	85	68	185
32	25.6	25.6	8	6.4	17.6	16	12.8	60.8	40	32	104	63	50.4	145.4	86	68.8	186.8
31	24.8	23.8	7	5.6	19.4	17	13.6	62.6	41	32.8	105.8	64	51.2	147.2	87	69.6	188.6
30	24	22	6	4.8	21.2	18	14.4	64.4	42	33.6	107.6	65	52	149	88	70.4	190.4
29	23.2	20.2	5	4	23	19	15.2	66.2	43	34.4	109.4	66	52.8	150.8	89	71.2	192.2
28	22.4	18.4	4	3.2	24.8	20	16	68	44	35.2	111.2	67	53.6	152.6	90	72	194
27	21.6	16.6	3	2.4	26.6	21	16.8	69.8	45	36	113	68	54.4	154.4	91	72.8	195.8
26	20.8	14.8	2	1.6	28.4	22	17.6	71.6	46	36.8	114.8	69	55.2	156.2	92	73.6	197.6
25	20	13	1	0.8	30.2	23	18.4	73.4	47	37.6	116.6	70	56	158	93	74.4	199.4
24	19.2	11.2	0	0	32	24	19.2	75.2	48	38.4	118.4	71	56.8	159.8	94	75.2	201.2
23	18.4	9.4	+1	+0.8	33.8	25	20	77	49	39.2	120.2	72	57.6	161.6	95	76	203
22	17.6	7.6	2	1.6	35.6	26	20.8	78.8	50	40	122	73	58.4	163.4	96	76.8	204.8
21	16.8	5.8	3	2.4	37.4	27	21.6	80.6	51	40.8	123.8	74	59.2	165.2	97	77.6	206.6
20	16	4	4	3.2	39.2	28	22.4	82.4	52	41.6	125.6	75	60	167	98	78.4	208.4
19	15.2	2.2	5	4	41	29	23.2	84.2	53	42.4	127.4	76	60.8	168.8	99	79.2	210.2
18	14.4	0.4	6	4.8	42.8	30	24	86	54	43.2	129.2	77	61.6	170.6	100	80	212
17	13.6	+1.4	7	5.6	44.6	31	24.8	87.8									

TABLE 16B.—BY FAHRENHEIT DEGREES AS UNITS.

Fah.	Cel.	Réau.
−40	−40·0	−32·0
−39	39·4	31·6
−38	38·9	31·1
−37	38·3	30·7
−36	37·8	30·2
−35	37·2	29·8
−34	36·7	29·3
−33	36·1	28·9
−32	35·6	28·4
−31	35·0	28·0
−30	34·4	27·6
−29	33·9	27·1
−28	33·3	26·7
−27	32·8	26·2
−26	32·2	25·8
−25	31·7	25·3
−24	31·1	24·9
−23	30·6	24·4
−22	30·0	24·0
−21	29·4	23·6
−20	28·9	23·1
−19	28·3	22·7
−18	27·8	22·2
−17	27·2	21·8
−16	26·7	21·3
−15	26·1	20·9
−14	25·6	20·4
−13	25·0	20·0
−12	24·4	19·6
−11	23·9	19·1
−10	23·3	18·7
−9	22·8	18·2
−8	22·2	17·8
−7	21·7	17·3
−6	21·1	16·9
−5	20·6	16·4
−4	20·0	16·0
−3	−19·4	−15·6
−2	18·9	15·1
−1	18·3	14·7
0	17·8	14·2
+1	17·2	13·8
2	16·7	13·3
3	16·1	12·9
4	15·6	12·4
5	15·0	12·0
6	14·4	11·6
7	13·9	11·1
8	13·3	10·7
9	12·8	10·2
10	12·2	9·8
11	11·7	9·3
12	11·1	8·9
13	10·6	8·4
14	10·0	8·0
15	9·4	7·6
16	8·9	7·1
17	8·3	6·7
18	7·8	6·2
19	7·2	5·8
20	6·7	5·3
21	6·1	4·9
22	5·6	4·4
23	5·0	4·0
24	4·4	3·6
25	3·9	3·1
26	3·3	2·7
27	2·8	2·2
28	2·2	1·8
29	1·7	1·3
30	1·1	0·9
31	0·6	0·4
32	+0·0	+0·0
33	+0·6	+0·4
34	1·1	0·9
35	1·7	1·3
36	2·2	1·8
37	2·8	2·2
38	3·3	2·7
39	3·9	3·1
40	4·4	3·6
41	5·0	4·0
42	5·6	4·4
43	6·1	4·9
44	6·7	5·3
45	7·2	5·8
46	7·8	6·2
47	8·3	6·7
48	8·9	7·1
49	9·4	7·6
50	10·0	8·0
51	10·6	8·4
52	11·1	8·9
53	11·7	9·3
54	12·2	9·8
55	12·8	10·2
56	13·3	10·7
57	13·9	11·1
58	14·4	11·6
59	15·0	12·0
60	15·6	12·4
61	16·1	12·9
62	16·7	13·3
63	17·2	13·8
64	17·8	14·2
65	18·3	14·7
66	18·9	15·1
67	19·4	15·6
68	20·0	16·0
69	+20·6	+16·4
70	21·1	16·9
71	21·7	17·3
72	22·2	17·8
73	22·8	18·2
74	23·3	18·7
75	23·9	19·1
76	24·4	19·6
77	25·0	20·0
78	25·6	20·4
79	26·1	20·9
80	26·7	21·3
81	27·2	21·8
82	27·8	22·2
83	28·3	22·7
84	28·9	23·1
85	29·4	23·6
86	30·0	24·0
87	30·6	24·4
88	31·1	24·9
89	31·7	25·3
90	32·2	25·8
91	32·8	26·2
92	33·3	26·7
93	33·9	27·1
94	34·4	27·6
95	35·0	28·0
96	35·6	28·4
97	36·1	28·9
98	36·7	29·3
99	37·2	29·8
100	37·8	30·2
101	38·3	30·7
102	38·9	31·1
103	39·4	31·6
104	40·0	32·0
105	+40·6	+32·4
106	41·1	32·9
107	41·7	33·3
108	42·2	33·8
109	42·8	34·2
110	43·3	34·7
111	43·9	35·1
112	44·4	35·6
113	45·0	36·0
114	45·6	36·4
115	46·1	36·9
116	46·7	37·3
117	47·2	37·8
118	47·8	38·2
119	48·3	38·7
120	48·9	39·1
121	49·4	39·6
122	50·0	40·0
123	50·6	40·4
124	51·1	40·9
125	51·7	41·3
126	52·2	41·8
127	52·8	42·2
128	53·3	42·7
129	53·9	43·1
130	54·4	43·6
131	55·0	44·0
132	55·6	44·4
133	56·1	44·9
134	56·7	45·3
135	57·2	45·8
136	57·8	46·2
137	58·3	46·7
138	58·9	47·1
139	59·4	47·6
140	60·0	48·0
141	+60·6	+48·4
142	61·1	48·9
143	61·7	49·3
144	62·2	49·8
145	62·8	50·2
146	63·3	50·7
147	63·9	51·1
148	64·4	51·6
149	65·0	52·0
150	65·6	52·4
151	66·1	52·9
152	66·7	53·3
153	67·2	53·8
154	67·8	54·2
155	68·3	54·7
156	68·9	55·1
157	69·4	55·6
158	70·0	56·0
159	70·6	56·4
160	71·1	56·9
161	71·7	57·3
162	72·2	57·8
163	72·8	58·2
164	73·3	58·7
165	73·9	59·1
166	74·4	59·6
167	75·0	60·0
168	75·6	60·4
169	76·1	60·9
170	76·7	61·3
171	77·2	61·8
172	77·8	62·2
173	78·3	62·7
174	78·9	63·1
175	79·4	63·6
176	80·0	64·0
177	+80·6	+64·4
178	81·1	64·9
179	81·7	65·3
180	82·2	65·8
181	82·8	66·2
182	83·3	66·7
183	83·9	67·1
184	84·4	67·6
185	85·0	68·0
186	85·6	68·4
187	86·1	68·9
188	86·7	69·3
189	87·2	69·8
190	87·8	70·2
191	88·3	70·7
192	88·9	71·1
193	89·4	71·6
194	90·0	72·0
195	90·6	72·4
196	91·1	72·9
197	91·7	73·3
198	92·2	73·8
199	92·8	74·2
200	93·3	74·7
201	93·9	75·1
202	94·4	75·6
203	95·0	76·0
204	95·6	76·4
205	96·1	76·9
206	96·7	77·3
207	97·2	77·8
208	97·8	78·2
209	98·3	78·7
210	98·9	79·1
211	99·4	79·6
212	100·0	80·0

TABLE 17.—CONVERSION OF CELSIUS INTO FAHRENHEIT DEGREES ABOVE 100 AND VICE VERSA.

Divide the degrees above 100 into hundreds and a remainder. The figure corresponding to the hundreds is taken from the following tables and added to that corresponding to the remainder as taken from Table 17. If, on converting Fahrenheit into Celsius, the "remainder" amounts to 32°, or below this, the degrees Celsius corresponding to it are negative (below freezing point), and hence must be *deducted* from the figures of the following table. Also take notice, for example, that 300° F. is not = 166·7° C., but = 166·7 − 17·8, or = 111·1 + 37·7 = 148·9° C.

A.

Cels.	Fahr.	Cels.	Fahr.	Cels.	Fahr.	Cels.	Fahr.
100	180	600	1080	1100	1980	1600	2880
200	360	700	1260	1200	2160	1700	3060
300	540	800	1440	1300	2340	1800	3240
400	720	900	1620	1400	2520	1900	3420
500	900	1000	1800	1500	2700	2000	3600

B.

Fahr.	Cels.	Fahr.	Cels.	Fahr.	Cels.	Fahr.	Cels.
100	55·6	1000	556·6	1900	1055·6	2800	1555·6
200	111·1	1100	611·1	2000	1111·1	2900	1611·1
300	166·7	1200	666·7	2100	1166·7	3000	1666·7
400	222·2	1300	722·2	2200	1222·2	3100	1722·2
500	277·8	1400	777·8	2300	1277·8	3200	1777·8
600	333·3	1500	833·3	2400	1333·3	3300	1833·3
700	388·9	1600	888·9	2500	1388·9	3400	1888·9
800	444·4	1700	944·4	2600	1444·4	3500	1944·4
900	500	1800	1000	2700	1500		

TABLE 18.—FUSING POINTS.

	C.	F.
Aluminium	700°	1292°
Antimony	432	809
Asphalt	100	212
Bismuth	260	500
Boric Acid	186	367
Brass	900	1652
Bromine	−22	−7·6
Bronze	900	1652
Cadmium	316	600
Cobalt	1500	2732
Colophonium	135	275
Copper	1100	2012
Cupric chloride	498	928
Cuprous chloride	434	813
Fat, oxen	40	104
sheep	42	107·6
pig	27	80·6
Fluorspar	902	1655
Glass	1200	2192
Glass containing lead	1000	1832
Gold	1075	1967
Iron, cast, white	1075	1967
grey	1275	2327
wrought	1550	2822
Iodine	113	235·4
Lead	326	618
oxide	954	1749
chloride	498	928
Magnesium	500	932
Mercury	−39	−38·2
Mercuric chloride	293	560
Naphthalene	79	174·2
Nickel	1500	2732
Palm oil	29	84·2
Paraffin	45–60	113–140
Pitch (coal tar)	150–200	300–400
Phosphorus	44	111·2

FUSING POINTS—*continued.*

	C.	F.
Platinum	1775	3227
Potassium chlorate	359	678
iodide	634	1173
carbonate	834	1533
nitrate	329	624
Stearic acid	70	158
Steel	1375	2507
Silver, metallic	960	1760
chloride	451	843·8
nitrate	217	422
Strontium chloride	825	1517
Selenium	217	422
Sodium chloride	772	1421
sulphate	861	1581
nitrate	316	600
chlorate	302	575
carbonate	814	1497
Spermaceti	45–50	113–122
Thallium	290	554
Tin	230	446
Wax, bee's	62–70	143–158
Zinc	412	773

TABLE 19.—BOILING POINTS.

	C.	F.
Alcohol, absolute	78°	172·4°
Ammonia, anhydrous	−38·5	−37·3
nitrate, satur. solution	164	327
Barium chloride, satur. solution	104·4	220
Bisulphide of carbon	47·0	116·6
Benzene	80·4	177
Bromine	63·0	145·4
Calcium chloride, satur. solution	179·5	355·1
66 per cent. solution	156	312·8
33 per cent. solution	128	262·4

BOILING POINTS.—*Continued.*

	C.	F.
Calcium nitrate, satur. solution	152	305·6
Carbon dioxide	−78	−108
Ether	85	95
Hydrochloric acid, 20·2 per cent. HCl	110	230
Iodine ....above	200	392
Methylic alcohol	60	140
Mercury	357	674·6
Naphthalene	217	422·6
Nitric acid, most concentrated	86	186·8
specific gravity 1·42	121	249·8
Nitrous anhydride	−2	28·4
oxide	−88	−126
Nitrogen peroxide	28	82·4
Potassium chloride, satur. solution	110	230
chlorate, satur. solution	105	221
acetate, satur. solution	169·4	336·9
carbonate, satur. solution	135	275
nitrate, satur. solution	118	244·4
Sodium chloride satur. solution	108·4	227·1
acetate „ „	124·4	255·9
carbonate „ „	106	222·8
phosphate „ „	106·6	223·8
nitrate „ „	122	251·6
Sulphur	448	838
Sulphuric acid, H_2SO_4	326	618·8
anhydride α	15	59
β	50	122
Sulphurous anhydride	−10	14
Turpentine, spirits of	160	320

TABLE 20.—REDUCTION OF THE VOLUME OF

I. Table for reducing the volumes

0°	1°	2°	3°	4°	5°	6°	7°	8°	9°	10°	0°
1	0·996	0·993	0·989	0·986	0·982	0·978	0·975	0·972	0·968	0·965	1
2	1·993	1·985	1·978	1·971	1·964	1·957	1·950	1·943	1·936	1·929	2
3	2·989	2·978	2·967	2·957	2·946	2·936	2·925	2·915	2·904	2·894	3
4	3·985	3·971	3·956	3·942	3·928	3·914	3·900	3·886	3·872	3·859	4
5	4·982	4·964	4·946	4·928	4·910	4·893	4·876	4·858	4·841	4·824	5
6	5·978	5·956	5·935	5·913	5·892	5·871	5·850	5·830	5·809	5·788	6
7	6·974	6·949	6·924	6·899	6·874	6·850	6·825	6·801	6·777	6·753	7
8	7·970	7·942	7·913	7·885	7·856	7·828	7·800	7·773	7·745	7·718	8
9	8·967	8·934	8·902	8·870	8·838	8·807	8·775	8·744	8·713	8·682	9
10	9·963	9·927	9·891	9·856	9·820	9·785	9·750	9·716	9·681	9·647	10
11	10·96	10·92	10·88	10·84	10·80	10·76	10·73	10·69	10·65	10·61	11
12	11·96	11·91	11·87	11·83	11·78	11·74	11·70	11·66	11·62	11·57	12
13	12·95	12·91	12·86	12·81	12·76	12·72	12·68	12·63	12·59	12·54	13
14	13·95	13·90	13·85	13·80	13·75	13·70	13·65	13·60	13·55	13·50	14
15	14·95	14·89	14·84	14·78	14·73	14·68	14·63	14·57	14·52	14·47	15
16	15·94	15·88	15·83	15·77	15·71	15·66	15·60	15·55	15·49	15·43	16
17	16·94	16·87	16·82	16·75	16·69	16·64	16·58	16·52	16·46	16·40	17
18	17·93	17·87	17·81	17·74	17·67	17·61	17·55	17·49	17·43	17·36	18
19	18·93	18·86	18·79	18·72	18·65	18·59	18·53	18·46	18·39	18·33	19
20	19·93	19·85	14·78	19·71	19·64	19·57	19·50	19·43	19·36	19·29	20
21	20·93	20·84	20·77	20·69	20·62	20·55	20·48	20·40	20·33	20·26	21
22	21·92	21·84	21·76	21·68	21·60	21·53	21·45	21·37	21·30	21·22	22
23	22·92	22·83	22·75	22·66	22·58	22·51	22·43	22·35	22·26	22·18	23
24	23·92	23·82	23·74	23·65	23·56	23·48	23·40	23·32	23·23	23·15	24
25	24·91	24·81	24·73	24·64	24·55	24·46	24·38	24·29	24·20	24·11	25
26	25·91	25·81	25·72	25·62	25·53	25·44	25·35	25·26	25·17	25·08	26
27	26·90	26·80	26·71	26·61	26·52	26·42	26·33	26·23	26·13	26·04	27
28	27·90	27·79	27·69	27·59	27·50	27·40	27·30	27·20	27·10	27·01	28
29	28·90	28·78	28·68	28·58	28·48	28·38	28·28	28·17	28·07	27·97	29
30	29·89	29·78	29·67	29·57	29·46	29·36	29·25	29·15	29·04	28·94	30
31	30·89	30·77	30·66	30·55	30·44	30·34	30·23	30·12	30·01	29·91	31
32	31·88	31·76	31·65	31·54	31·42	31·32	31·20	31·09	30·98	30·87	32
33	32·88	32·76	32·64	32·52	32·40	32·30	32·18	32·06	31·94	31·84	33
34	33·88	33·75	33·63	33·51	33·38	33·27	33·15	33·03	32·91	32·80	34
35	34·87	34·74	34·62	34·50	34·37	34·25	34·13	34·01	33·88	33·77	35
36	35·87	35·74	35·61	35·48	35·35	35·23	35·10	34·98	34·85	34·73	36
37	36·87	36·73	36·60	36·47	36·33	36·21	36·08	35·95	35·82	35·70	37
38	37·86	37·72	37·59	37·45	37·32	37·19	37·05	36·92	36·79	36·66	38
39	38·86	38·71	38·58	38·44	38·30	38·16	38·03	37·89	37·75	37·62	39
40	39·85	39·71	39·56	39·42	39·28	39·14	39·00	38·86	38·72	38·59	40
41	40·85	40·70	40·55	40·41	40·26	40·12	39·98	39·83	39·69	39·55	41
42	41·85	41·69	41·54	41·39	41·24	41·10	40·95	40·80	40·66	40·52	42
43	42·84	42·68	42·53	42·38	42·22	42·08	41·93	41·78	41·62	41·48	43
44	43·84	43·68	43·52	43·37	43·20	43·05	42·90	42·75	42·59	42·45	44
45	44·84	44·67	44·51	44·35	44·19	44·03	43·88	43·72	43·56	43·41	45
46	45·83	45·66	45·50	45·34	45·17	45·01	44·85	44·69	44·53	44·38	46
47	46·83	46·65	46·48	46·32	46·15	45·99	45·83	45·66	45·50	45·34	47
48	47·83	47·65	47·48	47·31	47·13	46·97	46·80	46·63	46·47	46·31	48
49	48·82	48·64	48·47	48·29	48·12	47·95	47·78	47·60	47·44	47·27	49
50	49·82	49·64	49·46	49·28	49·10	48·93	48·75	48·58	48·41	48·24	50

GASES TO NORMAL TEMPERATURE AND PRESSURE.

of gases to a temperature of 0° C.

0°	1°	2°	3°	4°	5°	6°	7°	8°	9°	10°	0°
51	50·82	50·63	50·45	50·26	50·08	49·91	49·73	49·55	49·38	49·21	51
52	51·81	51·62	51·44	51·25	51·06	50·89	50·70	50·52	50·35	50·17	52
53	52·81	52·62	52·43	52·24	52·05	51·87	51·68	51·49	51·31	51·13	53
54	53·81	53·61	53·42	53·22	53·03	52·84	52·65	52·46	52·28	52·10	54
55	54·80	54·60	54·41	54·21	54·01	53·82	53·63	53·44	53·25	53·06	55
56	55·80	55·60	55·40	55·19	54·99	54·80	54·60	54·41	54·22	54·03	56
57	56·80	56·59	56·39	56·18	55·97	55·78	55·58	55·38	55·19	54·99	57
58	57·79	57·58	57·37	57·16	56·95	56·76	56·55	56·35	56·16	55·96	58
59	58·79	58·57	58·37	58·15	57·93	57·74	57·53	57·32	57·12	56·92	59
60	59·78	59·56	59·35	59·13	58·92	58·71	58·50	58·30	58·00	57·88	60
61	60·78	60·56	60·34	60·12	59·90	59·69	59·48	59·27	59·06	58·85	61
62	61·78	61·55	61·33	61·10	60·88	60·67	60·45	60·24	60·03	59·81	62
63	62·77	62·54	62·32	62·09	61·86	61·65	61·43	61·21	60·99	60·77	63
64	63·77	63·53	63·31	63·07	62·84	62·63	62·40	62·18	61·96	61·74	64
65	64·76	64·53	64·30	64·06	63·83	63·61	63·38	63·15	62·93	62·70	65
66	65·76	65·52	65·29	65·04	64·81	64·58	64·35	64·13	63·89	63·67	66
67	66·75	66·51	66·27	66·03	65·79	65·56	65·33	65·10	64·86	64·63	67
68	67·75	67·50	67·26	67·02	66·77	66·54	66·30	66·07	65·83	65·60	68
69	68·75	68·50	68·25	68·01	67·75	67·52	67·28	67·04	66·80	66·56	69
70	69·74	69·49	69·24	68·99	68·74	68·50	68·25	68·01	67·77	67·53	70
71	70·74	70·48	70·23	69·98	69·72	69·48	69·23	68·98	68·74	68·49	71
72	71·74	71·48	71·22	70·96	70·70	70·46	70·20	69·95	69·71	69·46	72
73	72·73	72·47	72·21	71·95	71·69	71·44	71·18	70·93	70·67	70·42	73
74	73·73	73·46	73·20	72·93	72·66	72·41	72·15	71·90	71·64	71·39	74
75	74·72	74·45	74·19	73·92	73·65	73·39	73·13	72·87	72·61	72·35	75
76	75·72	75·45	75·18	74·90	74·63	74·37	74·10	73·84	73·58	73·32	76
77	76·72	76·44	76·17	75·89	75·61	75·35	75·08	74·81	74·55	74·28	77
78	77·71	77·43	77·15	76·87	76·59	76·33	76·05	75·78	75·51	75·25	78
79	78·71	78·42	78·14	77·86	77·58	77·31	77·03	76·75	76·48	76·21	79
80	79·70	79·42	79·13	78·85	78·56	78·28	78·00	77·73	77·45	77·18	80
81	80·70	80·41	80·12	79·83	79·54	79·26	78·98	78·70	78·42	78·14	81
82	81·69	81·40	81·11	80·82	80·52	80·24	79·95	79·67	79·39	79·11	82
83	82·69	82·39	82·10	81·81	81·51	81·22	80·93	80·64	80·36	80·07	83
84	83·69	83·39	83·09	82·79	82·49	82·20	81·90	81·61	81·32	81·04	84
85	84·68	84·38	84·08	83·78	83·47	83·17	82·88	82·58	82·20	82·00	85
86	85·68	85·37	85·07	84·76	84·45	84·15	83·85	83·55	83·26	82·97	86
87	86·68	86·37	86·06	85·75	85·43	85·13	84·83	84·53	84·23	83·93	87
88	87·67	87·36	87·05	86·73	86·42	86·11	85·80	85·50	85·20	84·90	88
89	88·67	88·35	88·04	87·72	87·40	87·09	86·78	86·47	86·16	85·86	89
90	89·67	89·34	89·02	88·70	88·38	88·07	87·75	87·44	87·13	86·82	90
91	90·66	90·34	90·01	89·69	89·36	89·05	88·73	88·41	88·10	87·79	91
92	91·66	91·33	91·00	90·67	90·34	90·03	89·70	89·38	89·07	88·75	92
93	92·66	92·32	91·99	91·66	91·33	91·01	90·68	90·36	90·03	89·72	93
94	93·65	93·31	92·98	92·64	92·31	91·98	91·65	91·33	91·00	90·68	94
95	94·65	94·31	93·97	93·63	93·29	92·96	92·63	92·30	91·97	91·65	95
96	95·65	95·30	94·96	94·61	94·27	93·94	93·60	93·27	92·94	92·61	96
97	96·64	96·29	95·95	95·60	95·25	94·92	94·58	94·24	93·91	93·57	97
98	97·64	97·28	96·93	96·58	96·24	95·90	95·55	95·21	94·87	94·54	98
99	98·64	98·27	97·92	97·57	97·22	96·87	96·53	96·18	95·84	95·50	99
100	99·63	99·27	98·91	98·56	98·20	97·85	97·50	97·16	96·81	96·47	100

REDUCTION OF THE VOLUME OF GASES TO

Table for reducing the volumes of gases

0°	11°	12°	13°	14°	15°	16°	17°	18°	19°	20°	0°
1	0·961	0·958	0·955	0·951	0·948	0·945	0·941	0·938	0·935	0·932	1
2	1·923	1·916	1·909	1·903	1·896	1·889	1·883	1·876	1·869	1·864	2
3	2·884	2·874	2·864	2·854	2·844	2·834	2·824	2·815	2·805	2·795	3
4	3·845	3·832	3·818	3·805	3·792	3·779	3·766	3·753	3·740	3·727	4
5	4·807	4·790	4·773	4·757	4·740	4·724	4·707	4·691	4·675	4·659	5
6	5·768	5·747	5·728	5·708	5·688	5·668	5·648	5·629	5·609	5·591	6
7	6·720	6·705	6·682	6·659	6·636	6·613	6·590	6·567	6·544	6·523	7
8	7·690	7·663	7·637	7·610	7·584	7·558	7·531	7·506	7·479	7·454	8
9	8·652	8·621	8·591	8·562	8·532	8·502	8·472	8·444	8·414	8·386	9
10	9·613	9·579	9·546	9·513	9·480	9·447	9·414	9·382	9·349	9·318	10
11	10·57	10·53	10·50	10·46	10·43	10·39	10·35	10·32	10·28	10·25	11
12	11·53	11·49	11·45	11·42	11·38	11·33	11·30	11·26	11·21	11·18	12
13	12·49	12·45	12·41	12·36	12·32	12·28	12·24	12·20	12·15	12·11	13
14	13·45	13·41	13·36	13·31	13·27	13·22	13·17	13·13	13·08	13·04	14
15	14·42	14·37	14·32	14·27	14·22	14·17	14·12	14·07	14·02	13·97	15
16	15·38	15·32	15·27	15·22	15·17	15·11	15·06	15·01	14·96	14·91	16
17	16·34	16·28	16·23	16·17	16·12	16·06	16·00	15·95	15·89	15·84	17
18	17·30	17·24	17·18	17·12	17·06	17·00	16·94	16·89	16·82	16·76	18
19	18·26	18·20	18·14	18·07	18·01	17·95	17·89	17·83	17·76	17·70	19
20	19·23	19·16	19·09	19·03	18·96	18·89	18·83	18·76	18·69	18·64	20
21	20·19	20·12	20·04	19·98	19·91	19·84	19·77	19·70	19·62	19·57	21
22	21·15	21·08	21·00	20·93	20·86	20·78	20·71	20·64	20·56	20·50	22
23	22·11	22·03	21·95	21·88	21·80	21·73	21·65	21·58	21·50	21·43	23
24	23·07	22·99	22·91	22·83	22·75	22·67	22·59	22·51	22·43	22·37	24
25	24·03	23·95	23·86	23·78	23·70	23·61	23·54	23·45	23·37	23·30	25
26	25·00	24·91	24·81	24·73	24·65	24·56	24·48	24·39	24·30	24·23	26
27	25·96	25·87	25·77	25·69	25·60	25·50	25·42	25·33	25·23	25·16	27
28	26·92	26·82	26·72	26·64	26·54	26·45	26·36	26·27	26·17	26·09	28
29	27·88	27·78	27·68	27·59	27·49	27·39	27·30	27·20	27·10	27·02	29
30	28·84	28·74	28·64	28·54	28·44	28·34	28·24	28·15	28·05	27·95	30
31	29·80	29·70	29·59	29·49	29·39	29·28	29·18	29·09	28·99	28·87	31
32	30·76	30·66	30·55	30·44	30·34	30·23	30·12	30·03	29·92	29·81	32
33	31·72	31·61	31·50	31·39	31·28	31·17	31·06	30·97	30·86	30·74	33
34	32·68	32·57	32·46	32·34	32·23	32·12	32·01	31·90	31·79	31·68	34
35	33·65	33·53	33·41	33·30	33·18	33·06	32·95	32·84	32·73	32·61	35
36	34·61	34·49	34·37	34·25	34·13	34·01	33·89	33·78	33·66	33·54	36
37	35·57	35·45	35·32	35·20	35·08	34·95	34·83	34·72	34·59	34·47	37
38	36·53	36·40	36·28	36·15	36·02	35·90	35·77	35·66	35·53	35·40	38
39	37·49	37·36	37·23	37·10	36·97	36·84	36·71	36·59	36·46	36·34	39
40	38·45	38·32	38·18	38·05	37·92	37·79	37·66	37·53	37·40	37·27	40
41	39·41	39·28	39·14	39·00	38·87	38·73	38·60	38·47	38·34	38·20	41
42	40·37	40·24	40·09	39·95	39·82	39·68	39·54	39·41	39·27	39·13	42
43	41·33	41·19	41·05	40·90	40·76	40·62	40·48	40·35	40·21	40·07	43
44	42·30	42·15	42·00	41·86	41·71	41·57	41·43	41·28	41·14	41·00	44
45	43·26	43·11	42·95	42·81	42·66	42·51	42·37	42·22	42·08	41·93	45
46	44·29	44·07	43·91	43·76	43·61	43·46	43·31	43·16	43·01	42·86	46
47	45·18	45·03	44·86	44·71	44·56	44·40	44·25	44·10	43·94	43·79	47
48	46·14	45·98	45·82	45·66	45·50	45·35	45·19	45·04	44·88	44·72	48
49	47·10	46·94	46·77	46·61	46·45	46·29	46·13	45·97	45·81	45·65	49
50	48·07	47·90	47·73	47·57	47·40	47·24	47·07	46·91	46·75	46·59	50

NORMAL TEMPERATURE AND PRESSURE.

to a temperature of 0° C.—*continued*.

0°	11°	12°	13°	14°	15°	16°	17°	18°	19°	20°	0°
51	49·03	48·86	48·69	48·52	48·35	48·18	48·01	47·85	47·68	47·52	51
52	49·99	49·82	49·64	49·47	49·30	49·13	48·95	48·79	48·62	48·45	52
53	50·95	50·77	50·59	50·42	50·24	50·07	49·89	49·72	49·55	49·38	53
54	51·91	51·73	51·55	51·37	51·19	51·02	50·54	50·66	50·49	50·32	54
55	52·87	52·69	52·50	52·33	52·14	51·93	51·78	51·60	51·43	51·25	55
56	53·84	53·65	53·46	53·28	53·09	52·91	52·72	52·54	52·36	52·18	56
57	54·80	54·61	54·41	54·23	54·04	53·86	53·66	53·48	53·29	53·71	57
58	55·76	55·56	55·37	55·18	54·98	54·80	54·60	54·42	54·23	54·04	58
59	56·72	56·52	56·32	56·13	55·93	55·74	55·54	55·35	55·16	54·97	59
60	57·68	57·47	57·28	57·08	56·88	56·68	56·48	56·29	56·09	55·91	60
61	58·64	58·43	58·23	58·03	57·83	57·63	57·42	57·23	57·02	56·84	61
62	59·60	59·39	59·19	58·98	58·78	58·57	58·36	58·17	57·96	57·77	62
63	60·56	60·35	60·14	59·93	59·72	59·52	59·30	59·11	58·90	58·11	63
64	61·53	61·31	61·10	60·88	60·67	60·46	60·25	60·04	59·83	59·64	64
65	62·49	62·26	62·05	61·84	61·62	61·40	61·19	60·98	60·77	60·57	65
66	63·45	63·22	63·01	62·79	62·57	62·35	62·13	61·92	61·70	61·50	66
67	64·41	64·18	63·96	63·74	63·52	63·29	63·07	62·86	62·63	62·43	67
68	65·37	65·13	64·92	64·69	64·46	64·23	64·01	63·80	63·57	63·36	68
69	66·33	66·09	65·87	65·64	65·41	65·18	64·95	64·73	64·50	64·30	69
70	67·29	67·05	66·82	66·59	66·36	66·13	65·90	65·67	65·44	65·23	70
71	68·25	68·01	67·77	67·54	67·31	67·07	66·84	66·61	66·38	66·16	71
72	69·21	68·97	68·73	68·49	68·26	68·02	67·78	67·55	67·31	67·09	72
73	70·17	69·92	69·68	69·44	69·20	68·96	68·72	68·49	68·26	68·03	73
74	71·14	70·88	70·64	70·40	70·15	69·91	69·66	69·42	69·18	68·96	74
75	72·10	71·84	71·59	71·35	71·10	70·85	70·61	70·37	70·12	69·89	75
76	73·06	72·80	72·55	72·30	72·05	71·80	71·55	71·30	71·05	70·82	76
77	74·02	73·76	73·51	73·25	73·00	72·74	72·49	72·24	71·98	71·75	77
78	74·93	74·71	74·46	74·20	73·94	73·69	73·43	73·18	72·92	72·68	78
79	75·94	75·67	75·41	75·15	74·89	74·63	74·37	74·11	73·85	73·61	79
80	76·90	76·63	76·37	76·10	75·84	75·58	75·31	75·06	74·79	74·54	80
81	77·86	77·59	77·32	77·05	76·79	76·52	76·25	76·00	75·73	75·47	81
82	78·82	78·55	78·28	78·00	77·74	77·47	77·19	76·94	76·66	76·40	82
83	79·78	79·50	79·23	78·95	78·68	78·41	78·13	77·87	77·60	77·34	83
84	80·75	80·46	80·19	79·91	79·63	79·35	79·08	78·81	78·53	78·27	84
85	81·71	81·42	81·14	80·86	80·58	80·30	80·02	79·75	79·47	79·20	85
86	82·67	82·38	82·10	81·81	81·53	81·24	80·96	80·69	80·40	80·13	86
87	83·63	83·33	83·05	82·76	82·48	82·19	81·90	81·63	81·33	81·06	87
88	84·59	84·29	84·01	83·71	83·42	83·13	82·84	82·57	82·27	81·99	88
89	85·56	85·25	84·96	84·66	84·37	84·08	83·78	83·50	83·22	82·93	89
90	86·52	86·21	85·92	85·62	85·32	85·02	84·72	84·44	84·14	83·86	90
91	87·48	87·17	86·87	86·57	86·27	85·96	85·66	85·33	85·07	84·79	91
92	88·44	88·13	87·83	87·52	87·22	86·91	86·60	86·32	86·01	85·72	92
93	89·40	89·08	88·78	88·47	88·16	87·85	87·54	87·25	86·95	86·66	93
94	90·36	90·04	89·73	89·42	89·11	88·80	88·49	88·19	87·88	87·59	94
95	91·33	91·00	90·68	90·38	90·06	89·74	89·43	89·13	88·82	88·52	95
96	92·29	91·96	91·64	91·33	91·01	90·69	90·37	90·07	89·75	89·45	96
97	93·25	92·92	92·59	92·28	91·96	91·63	91·31	91·00	90·08	90·38	97
98	94·21	93·87	93·55	93·23	92·90	92·58	92·25	91·94	91·62	91·31	98
99	95·17	94·83	94·50	94·18	93·85	93·52	93·19	92·88	92·55	92·24	99
100	96·13	95·79	95·46	95·13	94·80	94·47	94·14	93·82	93·49	93·18	100

REDUCTION OF THE VOLUME OF GASES TO
Table for reducing the volumes of gases

0°	21°	22°	23°	24°	25°	26°	27°	28°	29°	0°
1	0·929	0·926	0·922	0·919	0·916	0·913	0·910	0·907	0·904	1
2	1·857	1·851	1·845	1·839	1·832	1·826	1·820	1·814	1·808	2
3	2·786	2·777	2·767	2·758	2·749	2·739	2·730	2·721	2·712	3
4	3·714	3·702	3·690	3·677	3·665	3·652	3·640	3·628	3·616	4
5	4·643	4·628	4·612	4·597	4·581	4·566	4·551	4·535	4·520	5
6	5·572	5·553	5·534	5·516	5·497	5·479	5·461	5·442	5·424	6
7	6·500	6·479	6·457	6·435	6·413	6·392	6·371	6·349	6·328	7
8	7·429	7·404	7·379	7·354	7·330	7·305	7·281	7·256	7·232	8
9	8·357	8·330	8·302	8·274	8·246	8·218	8·191	8·163	8·136	9
10	9·286	9·255	9·224	9·193	9·162	9·131	9·101	9·070	9·040	10
11	10·21	10·18	10·15	10·11	10·07	10·04	10·01	9·98	9·94	11
12	11·14	11·11	11·07	11·03	10·99	10·96	10·92	10·88	10·85	12
13	12·07	12·03	11·99	11·95	11·91	11·87	11·83	11·79	11·75	13
14	13·00	12·96	12·91	12·87	12·83	12·78	12·74	12·70	12·66	14
15	13·93	13·88	13·84	13·79	13·74	13·70	13·65	13·61	13·56	15
16	14·86	14·81	14·76	14·71	14·66	14·61	14·56	14·51	14·46	16
17	15·79	15·73	15·68	15·63	15·58	15·52	15·47	15·42	15·37	17
18	16·71	16·66	16·60	16·55	16·49	16·44	16·38	16·33	16·27	18
19	17·64	17·58	17·53	17·47	17·41	17·35	17·29	17·23	17·18	19
20	18·57	18·51	18·45	18·39	18·32	18·26	18·20	18·14	18·08	20
21	19·50	19·43	19·37	19·31	19·24	19·17	19·11	19·05	18·98	21
22	20·43	20·36	20·29	20·23	20·15	20·09	20·02	19·95	19·89	22
23	21·36	21·29	21·21	21·15	21·07	21·00	20·93	20·86	20·79	23
24	22·28	22·21	22·14	22·07	21·99	21·91	21·84	21·77	21·70	24
25	23·21	23·14	23·06	22·99	22·90	22·83	22·75	22·68	22·60	25
26	24·14	24·06	23·98	23·91	23·82	23·74	23·66	23·58	23·50	26
27	25·07	24·99	24·90	24·83	24·73	24·65	24·57	24·49	24·41	27
28	26·00	25·91	25·82	25·74	25·65	25·57	25·48	25·40	25·31	28
29	26·93	26·84	26·75	26·67	26·57	26·48	26·39	26·30	26·22	29
30	27·86	27·77	27·67	27·58	27·49	27·39	27·30	27·21	27·12	30
31	28·79	28·70	28·59	28·50	28·41	28·30	28·21	28·12	28·02	31
32	29·72	29·62	29·51	29·42	29·32	29·22	29·12	29·02	28·93	32
33	30·65	30·55	30·44	30·34	30·24	30·13	30·03	29·93	29·83	33
34	31·57	31·47	31·36	31·26	31·10	31·04	30·94	30·84	30·74	34
35	32·50	32·40	32·28	32·18	32·07	31·96	31·85	31·75	31·64	35
36	33·43	33·32	33·20	33·10	32·99	32·87	32·76	32·65	32·54	36
37	34·36	34·25	34·12	34·02	33·90	33·78	33·67	33·56	33·45	37
38	35·29	35·17	35·05	34·93	34·82	34·70	34·58	34·47	34·35	38
39	36·22	36·10	35·97	35·85	35·74	35·61	35·49	35·47	35·26	39
40	37·14	37·02	36·90	36·77	36·65	36·52	36·40	36·28	36·16	40
41	38·07	37·95	37·82	37·69	37·57	37·43	37·31	37·19	37·06	41
42	39·00	38·87	38·74	38·61	38·48	38·35	38·22	38·09	37·97	42
43	39·93	39·80	39·66	39·53	39·40	39·26	39·13	39·00	38·87	43
44	40·85	40·72	40·59	40·45	40·32	40·17	40·04	39·91	39·78	44
45	41·78	41·65	40·51	41·37	41·23	41·09	40·95	40·82	40·68	45
46	42·71	42·57	42·43	42·29	42·15	42·00	41·86	41·72	41·58	46
47	43·64	43·50	43·35	43·21	43·06	42·91	42·77	42·63	42·49	47
48	44·57	44·42	44·27	44·12	43·98	43·83	43·68	43·54	43·39	48
49	45·50	45·35	45·19	45·04	44·80	44·74	44·59	44·44	44·30	49
50	46·43	46·28	46·12	45·97	45·81	45·66	45·51	45·35	45·20	50

NORMAL TEMPERATURE AND PRESSURE.

to a temperature of 0° C.—*continued.*

0°	21°	22°	23°	24°	25°	26°	27°	28°	29°	0°
51	47·36	47·20	47·04	46·89	46·73	46·57	46·42	46·26	46·10	51
52	48·29	48·13	47·96	47·81	47·64	47·49	47·33	47·16	47·01	52
53	49·22	49·06	48·89	48·73	48·56	48·40	48·24	48·07	47·91	53
54	50·14	49·98	49·81	49·65	49·48	49·31	49·15	48·98	48·82	54
55	51·07	50·91	50·73	50·57	50·39	50·23	50·06	49·89	49·72	55
56	52·00	51·83	51·65	51·49	51·31	51·14	50·97	50·79	50·62	56
57	52·93	52·76	52·58	52·41	52·22	52·05	51·88	51·70	51·53	57
58	53·86	53·68	53·50	53·32	53·14	52·97	52·79	52·61	52·43	58
59	54·79	54·61	54·42	54·24	54·06	53·88	53·70	53·51	53·34	59
60	55·72	55·53	55·34	55·16	54·97	54·79	54·61	54·42	54·24	60
61	56·65	56·46	56·26	56·08	55·89	55·70	55·52	55·33	55·14	61
62	57·58	57·38	57·19	57·00	56·80	56·62	56·43	56·23	56·05	62
63	58·51	58·31	58·11	57·92	57·72	57·53	57·34	57·14	56·95	63
64	59·42	59·23	59·03	58·84	58·64	58·44	58·25	58·05	57·86	64
65	60·36	60·16	59·95	59·76	59·55	59·36	59·16	58·96	58·76	65
66	61·29	61·08	60·87	60·68	60·47	60·27	60·07	59·86	59·66	66
67	62·22	62·01	61·79	61·60	61·38	61·18	60·98	60·77	60·57	67
68	63·15	62·93	62·72	62·51	62·30	62·10	61·89	61·68	61·47	68
69	64·08	63·86	63·64	63·43	63·22	63·01	62·80	62·58	62·38	69
70	65·00	64·79	64·57	64·35	64·13	63·93	63·71	63·49	63·28	70
71	65·93	65·71	65·49	65·27	65·05	64·83	64·62	64·40	64·18	71
72	66·86	66·64	66·42	66·19	65·96	65·75	65·53	65·30	65·09	72
73	67·79	67·57	67·34	67·11	66·88	66·66	66·44	66·21	65·99	73
74	68·61	68·49	68·26	68·03	67·80	67·57	67·35	67·12	66·90	74
75	69·64	69·42	69·18	68·95	68·71	68·49	68·26	68·03	67·80	75
76	70·57	70·34	70·10	69·87	69·63	69·40	69·17	68·93	68·70	76
77	71·50	71·27	71·03	70·79	70·54	70·31	70·08	69·84	69·61	77
78	72·43	72·19	71·95	71·70	71·46	71·22	70·99	70·75	70·51	78
79	73·36	73·12	72·87	72·62	72·38	72·14	71·90	71·65	71·42	79
80	74·29	74·04	73·79	73·54	73·30	73·05	72·81	72·56	72·32	80
81	75·22	74·97	74·71	74·46	74·22	73·96	73·72	73·47	73·22	81
82	76·15	75·89	75·63	75·38	75·13	74·88	74·63	74·37	74·13	82
83	77·08	76·82	76·56	76·30	76·05	75·79	75·54	75·28	75·03	83
84	78·00	77·74	77·48	77·22	76·96	76·70	76·45	76·19	75·94	84
85	78·93	78·67	78·40	78·14	77·88	77·62	77·36	77·10	76·84	85
86	79·86	79·59	79·32	79·06	78·80	78·53	78·27	78·00	77·74	86
87	80·79	80·52	80·25	79·98	79·71	79·44	79·18	78·91	78·65	87
88	81·72	81·44	81·17	80·90	80·63	80·36	80·09	79·82	79·55	88
89	82·65	82·37	82·09	81·82	81·55	81·27	81·00	80·72	80·46	89
90	83·57	83·30	83·02	82·74	82·46	82·18	81·91	81·63	81·36	90
91	84·50	84·22	83·94	83·66	83·38	83·09	82·82	82·54	82·26	91
92	85·43	85·15	84·86	84·58	84·29	84·01	83·73	83·44	83·17	92
93	86·36	86·08	85·79	85·50	85·21	84·92	84·64	84·35	84·07	93
94	87·28	87·00	86·71	86·42	86·13	85·83	85·55	85·26	84·98	94
95	88·21	87·93	87·63	87·34	87·04	86·75	86·46	86·17	85·88	95
96	89·14	88·85	88·55	88·26	87·96	87·66	87·37	87·07	86·78	96
97	90·07	89·78	89·48	89·18	88·87	88·57	88·28	87·98	87·69	97
98	91·00	90·70	90·40	90·09	89·79	89·48	89·19	88·89	88·59	98
99	91·93	91·63	91·32	91·01	90·71	90·40	90·10	89·79	89·50	99
100	92·86	92·55	92·24	91·93	91·62	91·31	91·01	90·70	90·40	100

TABLE 21.—REDUCTION OF VOLUMES OF

Deduct from the pressure read off at the barometer 1 mm. for temperatures

760	710	712	714	716	718	720	722	724	726	728	760
1	0·934	0·937	0·940	0·942	0·945	0·947	0·950	0·953	0·955	0·958	1
2	1·808	1·874	1·879	1·884	1·890	1·895	1·900	1·905	1·911	1·916	2
3	2·803	2·810	2·818	2·826	2·834	2·842	2·850	2·858	2·866	2·874	3
4	3·738	3·747	3·758	3·768	3·779	3·789	3·800	3·810	3·821	3·832	4
5	4·672	4·685	4·697	4·711	4·724	4·736	4·750	4·763	4·777	4·790	5
6	5·607	5·621	5·637	5·653	5·669	5·684	5·700	5·716	5·732	5·747	6
7	6·540	6·558	6·577	6·595	6·614	6·631	6·650	6·668	6·687	6·705	7
8	7·474	7·494	7·516	7·537	7·558	7·578	7·600	7·621	7·642	7·663	8
9	8·409	8·431	8·456	8·479	8·503	8·526	8·550	8·573	8·598	8·621	9
10	9·34	9·37	9·40	9·42	9·45	9·47	9·50	9·53	9·55	9·58	10
11	10·28	10·31	10·34	10·36	10·39	10·42	10·45	10·48	10·51	10·54	11
12	11·21	11·24	11·27	11·30	11·34	11·37	11·40	11·43	11·46	11·50	12
13	12·14	12·18	12·21	12·24	12·28	12·31	12·35	12·38	12·41	12·45	13
14	13·08	13·12	13·16	13·19	13·23	13·26	13·30	13·34	13·37	13·41	14
15	14·02	14·06	14·10	14·13	14·17	14·21	14·25	14·29	14·33	14·37	15
16	14·95	14·99	15·03	15·07	15·11	15·15	15·20	15·24	15·28	15·33	16
17	15·88	15·93	15·98	16·02	16·06	16·10	16·15	16·19	16·23	16·28	17
18	16·82	16·87	16·92	16·96	17·01	17·05	17·10	17·15	17·19	17·24	18
19	17·76	17·81	17·86	17·90	17·95	18·00	18·05	18·10	18·15	18·21	19
20	18·68	18·74	18·79	18·84	18·90	18·95	19·00	19·05	19·11	19·16	20
21	19·62	19·68	19·73	19·78	19·84	19·90	19·95	20·00	20·06	20·12	21
22	20·55	20·61	20·67	20·72	20·78	20·84	20·90	20·96	21·01	21·07	22
23	21·40	21·55	21·61	21·66	21·73	21·79	21·85	21·91	21·97	22·03	23
24	22·43	22·49	22·55	22·61	22·68	22·74	22·80	22·86	22·92	22·99	24
25	23·35	23·42	23·49	23·55	23·62	23·69	23·75	23·81	23·88	23·95	25
26	24·29	24·36	24·43	24·50	24·57	24·64	24·70	24·77	24·83	24·90	26
27	25·23	25·30	25·37	25·44	25·51	25·58	25·65	25·72	25·79	25·86	27
28	26·16	26·23	26·30	26·37	26·45	26·53	26·60	26·67	26·74	26·82	28
29	27·10	27·17	27·24	27·31	27·40	27·48	27·55	27·62	27·70	27·78	29
30	28·03	28·10	28·18	28·26	28·34	28·42	28·50	28·58	28·66	28·74	30
31	28·97	29·04	29·12	29·20	29·29	29·37	29·45	29·53	29·62	29·70	31
32	29·90	29·98	30·06	30·14	30·23	30·32	30·40	30·48	30·57	30·66	32
33	30·83	30·91	31·00	31·08	31·17	31·26	31·35	31·43	31·52	31·61	33
34	31·77	31·85	31·94	32·03	32·12	32·21	32·30	32·39	32·48	32·57	34
35	32·71	32·79	32·88	32·97	33·07	33·16	33·25	33·34	33·44	33·53	35
36	33·64	33·73	33·82	33·91	34·01	34·10	34·20	34·29	34·39	34·49	36
37	34·57	34·66	34·76	34·86	34·96	35·05	35·15	35·25	35·35	35·45	37
38	35·50	35·60	35·70	35·80	35·90	36·00	36·10	36·20	36·30	36·40	38
39	36·44	36·54	36·64	36·74	36·85	36·95	37·05	37·15	37·26	37·37	39
40	37·38	37·48	37·58	37·68	37·79	37·89	38·00	38·10	38·21	38·32	40
41	38·31	38·41	38·52	38·62	38·74	38·84	38·95	39·05	39·17	39·28	41
42	39·23	39·35	39·46	39·57	39·69	39·79	39·90	40·01	40·12	40·23	42
43	40·18	40·29	40·40	40·51	40·62	40·73	40·85	40·96	41·08	41·19	43
44	41·11	41·22	41·34	41·44	41·56	41·68	41·80	41·91	42·03	42·16	44
45	42·05	42·16	42·28	42·39	42·52	42·63	42·75	42·87	42·99	43·11	45
46	42·98	43·10	43·22	43·34	43·46	43·58	43·70	43·82	43·94	44·06	46
47	43·91	44·03	44·15	44·27	44·40	44·52	44·65	44·77	44·90	45·03	47
48	44·84	44·96	45·09	45·22	45·35	45·47	45·60	45·72	45·85	45·98	48
49	45·78	45·91	46·04	46·17	46·30	46·42	46·55	46·67	46·80	46·94	49
50	46·72	46·85	46·97	47·11	47·24	47·36	47·50	47·63	47·77	47·90	50

GASES TO A PRESSURE OF 760 MM.

bet. 0° and 12° C., and 2 mm. bet. 13° and 19° C., 3 mm. bet. 20° and 25° C.

760	710	712	714	716	718	720	722	724	726	728	760
51	47·05	47·79	47·92	48·05	48·18	48·31	48·45	48·59	48·73	48·86	51
52	48·58	48·72	48·85	48·99	49·13	49·26	49·40	49·54	49·08	49·82	52
53	49·52	49·66	49·79	49·93	50·07	50·21	50·35	50·48	50·64	50·78	53
54	50·45	50·59	50·73	50·87	51·01	51·15	51·30	51·44	51·59	51·73	54
55	51·38	51·53	51·67	51·82	51·96	52·10	52·25	52·39	52·54	52·69	55
56	52·32	52·47	52·61	52·76	52·91	53·05	53·20	53·35	53·50	53·05	56
57	53·25	53·41	53·55	53·70	53·85	54·00	54·15	54·30	54·45	54·60	57
58	54·19	54·34	54·49	54·64	54·79	54·94	55·10	55·25	55·41	55·56	58
59	55·13	55·28	55·43	55·59	55·74	55·89	56·05	56·21	56·37	56·52	59
60	56·07	56·22	56·37	56·53	56·69	56·84	57·00	57·16	57·32	57·47	60
61	57·00	57·15	57·31	57·47	57·63	57·79	57·95	58·11	58·27	58·43	61
62	57·93	58·09	58·25	58·41	58·58	58·74	58·90	59·06	59·23	59·39	62
63	58·87	59·03	59·19	59·35	59·52	59·68	59·85	60·01	60·18	60·35	63
64	59·80	59·96	60·13	60·30	60·47	60·63	60·80	60·97	61·14	61·30	64
65	60·74	60·90	61·07	61·24	61·41	61·58	61·75	61·92	62·09	62·26	65
66	61·67	61·84	62·01	62·18	62·35	62·52	62·70	62·87	63·05	63·22	66
67	62·60	62·77	62·95	63·12	63·30	63·47	63·65	63·82	64·00	64·18	67
68	63·54	63·71	63·89	64·06	64·24	64·42	64·60	64·78	64·96	65·13	68
69	64·47	64·65	64·83	65·01	65·19	65·37	65·55	65·73	65·91	66·09	69
70	65·40	65·58	65·77	65·95	66·14	66·32	66·50	66·68	66·87	67·05	70
71	66·34	66·52	66·71	66·89	67·08	67·26	67·45	67·63	67·82	68·01	71
72	67·27	67·46	67·65	67·83	68·02	68·21	68·40	68·59	68·78	68·97	72
73	68·20	68·39	68·58	68·77	68·97	69·16	69·35	69·54	69·73	69·92	73
74	69·14	69·33	69·53	69·72	69·92	70·11	70·30	70·49	70·69	70·88	74
75	70·07	70·27	70·47	70·66	70·86	71·05	71·25	71·44	71·64	71·84	75
76	71·01	71·21	71·41	71·60	71·80	72·00	72·20	72·40	72·60	72·80	76
77	71·94	72·14	72·34	72·54	72·75	72·95	73·15	73·35	73·55	73·75	77
78	72·87	73·07	73·28	73·48	73·69	73·89	74·10	74·30	74·51	74·71	78
79	73·80	74·01	74·22	74·42	74·63	74·84	75·05	75·25	75·46	75·67	79
80	74·74	74·94	75·16	75·37	75·58	75·78	76·00	76·21	76·42	76·63	80
81	75·67	75·88	76·10	76·31	76·53	76·74	76·95	77·16	77·37	77·58	81
82	76·60	76·82	77·04	77·25	77·47	77·68	77·90	78·11	78·33	78·54	82
83	77·54	77·76	77·98	78·19	78·41	78·63	78·85	79·07	79·28	79·50	83
84	78·47	78·69	78·91	79·13	79·35	79·57	79·80	80·02	80·24	80·46	84
85	79·41	79·63	79·86	80·08	80·31	80·53	80·75	80·97	81·10	81·41	85
86	80·34	80·57	80·80	81·02	81·25	81·47	81·70	81·92	82·15	82·37	86
87	81·28	81·50	81·74	81·96	82·19	82·42	82·65	82·87	83·10	83·33	87
88	82·21	82·44	82·68	82·90	83·13	83·36	83·60	83·83	84·06	84·29	88
89	83·15	83·38	83·62	83·85	84·08	84·31	84·55	84·78	85·02	85·25	89
90	84·09	84·31	84·56	84·79	85·03	85·26	85·50	85·73	85·98	86·21	90
91	85·02	85·25	85·50	85·73	85·98	86·21	86·45	86·69	86·93	87·17	91
92	85·95	86·19	86·44	86·68	86·92	87·16	87·40	87·64	87·89	88·13	92
93	86·89	87·12	87·38	87·62	87·87	88·11	88·35	88·59	88·84	89·08	93
94	87·82	88·06	88·32	88·56	88·81	89·05	89·30	89·54	89·80	90·04	94
95	88·76	89·01	89·26	89·50	89·75	90·00	90·25	90·50	90·75	91·00	95
96	89·69	89·94	90·20	90·45	90·70	90·95	91·20	91·45	91·70	91·95	96
97	90·62	90·87	91·13	91·38	91·64	91·89	92·15	92·40	92·66	92·91	97
98	91·56	91·82	92·07	92·33	92·59	92·84	93·10	93·35	93·62	93·87	98
99	92·49	92·75	93·01	93·26	93·53	93·79	94·05	94·31	94·57	94·83	99
100	93·42	93·68	93·95	94·21	94·47	94·74	95·00	95·26	95·53	95·79	100

REDUCTION OF VOLUMES OF GASES

Deduct from the pressure read off at the barometer 1 mm. for temperatures

760	730	732	734	736	738	740	742	744	746	748	760
1	0·961	0·963	0·966	0·968	0·971	0·974	0·976	0·979	0·982	0·984	1
2	1·921	1·926	1·932	1·937	1·942	1·947	1·953	1·958	1·963	1·968	2
3	2·882	2·889	2·898	2·905	2·913	2·921	2·929	2·937	2·945	2·953	3
4	3·842	3·852	3·864	3·874	3·884	3·895	3·905	3·916	3·926	3·937	4
5	4·803	4·816	4·830	4·842	4·855	4·868	4·882	4·895	4·908	4·921	5
6	5·763	5·779	5·796	5·810	5·826	5·842	5·858	5·874	5·890	5·905	6
7	6·724	6·742	6·762	6·779	6·797	6·816	6·834	6·853	6·871	6·889	7
8	7·684	7·705	7·728	7·747	7·768	7·790	7·810	7·832	7·853	7·874	8
9	8·645	8·668	8·693	8·716	8·739	8·763	8·787	8·811	8·834	8·858	9
10	9·61	9·63	9·66	9·68	9·71	9·74	9·76	9·79	9·82	9·84	10
11	10·57	10·59	10·62	10·65	10·68	10·71	10·74	10·77	10·80	10·82	11
12	11·53	11·56	11·59	11·62	11·65	11·68	11·71	11·75	11·78	11·81	12
13	12·49	12·52	12·55	12·59	12·62	12·66	12·69	12·73	12·76	12·79	13
14	13·45	13·48	13·52	13·56	13·59	13·63	13·66	13·70	13·74	13·78	14
15	14·41	14·44	14·48	14·52	14·56	14·60	14·64	14·69	14·73	14·77	15
16	15·37	15·41	15·45	15·49	15·53	15·58	15·62	15·67	15·71	15·75	16
17	16·33	16·37	16·41	16·46	16·50	16·55	16·60	16·65	16·69	16·73	17
18	17·29	17·33	17·38	17·43	17·47	17·52	17·57	17·62	17·67	17·72	18
19	18·25	18·29	18·35	18·40	18·45	18·50	18·55	18·60	18·65	18·70	19
20	19·21	19·26	19·32	19·37	19·42	19·47	19·53	19·58	19·63	19·68	20
21	20·17	20·22	20·28	20·34	20·39	20·44	20·50	20·56	20·61	20·66	21
22	21·13	21·19	21·25	21·31	21·36	21·42	21·48	21·54	21·59	21·65	22
23	22·09	22·15	22·21	22·27	22·33	22·39	22·45	22·51	22·57	22·64	23
24	23·05	23·11	23·18	23·24	23·30	23·36	23·43	23·50	23·56	23·63	24
25	24·01	24·07	24·14	24·21	24·27	24·34	24·41	24·48	24·54	24·61	25
26	24·97	25·04	25·11	25·18	25·24	25·31	25·38	25·45	25·52	25·59	26
27	25·93	26·00	26·07	26·14	26·21	26·28	26·36	26·43	26·50	26·58	27
28	26·89	26·96	27·04	27·12	27·18	27·26	27·33	27·41	27·48	27·56	28
29	27·85	27·92	28·00	28·08	28·15	28·23	28·31	28·39	28·47	28·55	29
30	28·82	28·89	28·97	29·05	29·13	29·21	29·29	29·37	29·45	29·53	30
31	29·78	29·86	29·94	30·02	30·10	30·18	30·26	30·35	30·43	30·51	31
32	30·74	30·82	30·91	30·99	31·07	31·15	31·24	31·33	31·41	31·50	32
33	31·70	31·78	31·87	31·96	32·04	32·13	32·21	32·30	32·39	32·48	33
34	32·66	32·75	32·84	32·93	33·01	33·10	33·19	33·28	33·37	33·46	34
35	33·62	33·71	33·80	33·89	33·98	34·07	34·17	34·27	34·36	34·45	35
36	34·58	34·67	34·77	34·86	34·95	35·05	35·15	35·25	35·34	35·43	36
37	35·54	35·63	35·73	35·83	35·92	36·02	36·12	36·22	36·32	36·42	37
38	36·50	36·60	36·70	36·80	36·90	37·00	37·10	37·20	37·30	37·40	38
39	37·47	37·57	37·67	37·77	37·87	37·97	38·07	38·18	38·28	38·39	39
40	38·42	38·52	38·64	38·74	38·84	38·95	39·05	39·16	39·26	39·37	40
41	39·38	39·48	39·60	39·71	39·81	39·92	40·02	40·14	40·24	40·36	41
42	40·34	40·44	40·56	40·68	40·78	40·89	41·00	41·12	41·22	41·34	42
43	41·30	41·41	41·53	41·64	41·75	41·86	41·97	42·10	42·20	42·32	43
44	42·27	42·38	42·50	42·62	42·73	42·84	42·95	43·07	43·18	43·30	44
45	43·22	43·34	43·46	43·58	43·69	43·81	43·93	44·06	44·17	44·29	45
46	44·18	44·30	44·42	44·54	44·66	44·78	44·90	45·03	45·15	45·27	46
47	45·15	45·26	45·39	45·52	45·64	45·76	45·88	46·01	46·13	46·26	47
48	46·10	46·23	46·36	46·49	46·61	46·73	46·85	46·99	47·12	47·24	48
49	47·06	47·19	47·32	47·44	47·57	47·70	47·83	47·97	48·10	48·23	49
50	48·03	48·16	48·30	48·42	48·55	48·68	48·82	48·95	49·08	49·21	50

TO A PRESSURE OF 760 MM.—*Continued.*

between 0° and 12° C., 2 mm. between 13° and 19° C., 3 mm. between 20° and 25° C.

760	730	732	734	736	738	740	742	744	746	748	760
51	48·99	49·12	49·26	49·39	49·52	49·65	49·79	49·93	50·06	50·19	51
52	49·96	50·08	50·22	50·36	50·49	50·63	50·77	50·91	51·04	51·18	52
53	50·91	51·05	51·19	51·33	51·46	51·60	51·75	51·89	52·02	52·16	53
54	51·87	52·01	52·16	52·30	52·44	52·58	52·72	52·87	53·01	53·15	54
55	52·83	52·98	53·13	53·27	53·41	53·55	53·70	53·85	53·99	54·14	55
56	53·79	53·94	54·09	54·23	54·37	54·52	54·68	54·83	54·97	55·11	56
57	54·75	54·90	55·05	55·20	55·35	55·50	55·65	55·80	55·95	56·10	57
58	55·71	55·86	56·02	56·17	56·32	56·47	56·63	56·78	56·93	57·08	58
59	56·67	56·83	56·99	57·14	57·29	57·44	57·60	57·76	57·92	58·07	59
60	57·63	57·79	57·95	58·10	58·26	58·42	58·58	58·74	58·90	59·05	60
61	58·59	58·75	58·91	59·07	59·23	59·39	59·56	59·72	59·88	60·04	61
62	59·55	59·72	59·88	60·04	60·20	60·36	60·53	60·70	60·86	61·02	62
63	60·51	60·68	60·85	61·01	61·17	61·34	61·51	61·68	61·84	62·00	63
64	61·47	61·64	61·81	61·98	62·15	62·32	62·49	62·66	62·82	62·99	64
65	62·43	62·60	62·77	62·94	63·11	63·28	63·46	63·64	63·81	63·98	65
66	63·39	63·57	63·74	63·91	64·08	64·26	64·44	64·62	64·79	64·96	66
67	64·35	64·53	64·71	64·88	65·05	65·23	65·41	65·59	65·77	65·94	67
68	65·31	65·50	65·68	65·85	66·02	66·20	66·38	66·56	66·74	66·92	68
69	66·27	66·45	66·64	66·82	67·00	67·18	67·37	67·55	67·73	67·91	69
70	67·24	67·42	67·61	67·79	67·97	68·16	68·34	68·53	68·71	68·89	70
71	68·20	68·39	68·58	68·76	68·94	69·13	69·32	69·51	69·69	69·88	71
72	69·16	69·35	69·54	69·73	69·92	70·11	70·30	70·49	70·68	70·86	72
73	70·12	70·31	70·51	70·69	70·88	71·08	71·27	71·47	71·66	71·85	73
74	71·08	71·28	71·48	71·66	71·85	72·05	72·25	72·45	72·64	72·83	74
75	72·04	72·24	72·44	72·63	72·82	73·02	73·22	73·42	73·62	73·82	75
76	73·00	73·20	73·40	73·60	73·80	74·00	74·20	74·40	74·60	74·80	76
77	73·96	74·17	74·37	74·57	74·77	74·97	75·18	75·39	75·59	75·79	77
78	74·93	75·12	75·33	75·53	75·74	75·95	76·16	76·37	76·57	76·77	78
79	75·88	76·09	76·30	76·50	76·71	76·92	77·13	77·34	77·55	77·75	79
80	76·84	77·05	77·27	77·47	77·68	77·90	78·10	78·32	78·53	78·74	80
81	77·80	78·02	78·23	78·44	78·65	78·87	79·08	79·30	79·51	79·72	81
82	78·76	78·98	79·20	79·41	79·62	79·84	80·06	80·28	80·50	80·71	82
83	79·72	79·94	80·16	80·38	80·60	80·82	81·04	81·26	81·48	81·69	83
84	80·68	80·90	81·12	81·34	81·56	81·79	82·01	82·24	82·46	82·68	84
85	81·64	81·87	82·10	82·31	82·53	82·76	82·99	83·22	83·44	83·66	85
86	82·60	82·83	83·06	83·28	83·50	83·73	83·97	84·20	84·42	84·64	86
87	83·56	83·79	84·02	84·25	84·48	84·71	84·94	85·17	85·40	85·62	87
88	84·52	84·76	85·00	85·22	85·45	85·68	85·92	86·15	86·38	86·61	88
89	85·48	85·72	85·98	86·19	86·42	86·66	86·89	87·13	87·36	87·59	89
90	86·45	86·68	86·93	87·16	87·39	87·63	87·87	88·11	88·34	88·58	90
91	87·41	87·65	87·89	88·12	88·36	88·61	88·85	89·09	89·33	89·56	91
92	88·37	88·61	88·86	89·09	89·33	89·58	89·82	90·07	90·31	90·55	92
93	89·33	89·57	89·82	90·06	90·30	90·55	90·80	91·05	91·29	91·53	93
94	90·29	90·54	90·79	91·03	91·27	91·53	91·78	92·03	92·27	92·51	94
95	91·25	91·50	91·75	92·00	92·25	92·50	92·75	93·00	93·25	93·50	95
96	92·21	92·46	92·72	92·97	93·22	93·47	93·73	93·93	94·23	94·48	96
97	93·17	93·43	93·68	93·93	94·19	94·45	94·71	94·96	95·22	95·47	97
98	94·13	94·39	94·65	94·90	95·16	95·42	95·68	95·94	96·20	96·45	98
99	95·09	95·35	95·61	95·87	96·13	96·39	96·66	96·92	97·18	97·43	99
100	96·05	96·32	96·58	96·84	97·11	97·37	97·63	97·89	98·16	98·42	100

REDUCTION OF VOLUMES OF GASES

Deduct from the pressure read off at the barometer 1 mm. for temperatures

760	750	752	754	756	758	762	764	766	768	770	760
1	0·987	0·989	0·992	0·995	0·997	1·003	1·005	1·008	1·011	1·013	1
2	1·974	1·979	1·984	1·989	1·995	2·005	2·011	2·016	2·021	2·026	2
3	2·960	2·968	2·976	2·984	2·992	3·007	3·016	3·024	3·032	3·039	3
4	3·947	3·958	3·968	3·979	3·990	4·010	4·021	4·032	4·042	4·052	4
5	4·934	4·947	4·960	4·974	4·987	5·013	5·026	5·040	5·053	5·066	5
6	5·921	5·937	5·952	5·968	5·984	6·016	6·032	6·047	6·063	6·079	6
7	6·908	6·926	6·944	6·963	6·982	7·018	7·037	7·055	7·074	7·092	7
8	7·894	7·916	7·936	7·958	7·979	8·021	8·042	8·063	8·084	8·106	8
9	8·881	8·905	8·929	8·952	8·977	9·023	9·048	9·071	9·095	9·119	9
10	9·87	9·89	9·92	9·95	9·97	10·03	10·05	10·08	10·11	10·13	10
11	10·85	10·88	10·91	10·94	10·97	11·03	11·06	11·09	11·12	11·14	11
12	11·84	11·87	11·90	11·94	11·97	12·04	12·07	12·10	12·13	12·16	12
13	12·83	12·86	12·89	12·93	12·96	13·04	13·07	13·10	13·14	13·17	13
14	13·82	13·85	13·88	13·92	13·96	14·04	14·07	14·11	14·15	14·17	14
15	14·81	14·84	14·87	14·92	14·96	15·04	15·08	15·12	15·16	15·19	15
16	15·79	15·83	15·87	15·91	15·95	16·05	16·09	16·13	16·17	16·21	16
17	16·78	16·82	16·86	16·91	16·95	17·05	17·09	17·14	17·18	17·22	17
18	17·77	17·81	17·85	17·90	17·95	18·05	18·10	18·15	18·19	18·23	18
19	18·75	18·80	18·85	18·90	18·95	19·05	19·10	19·15	19·20	19·25	19
20	19·74	19·79	19·84	19·89	19·95	20·05	20·11	20·16	20·21	20·26	20
21	20·72	20·77	20·83	20·89	20·94	21·05	21·11	21·17	21·22	21·27	21
22	21·71	21·76	21·82	21·88	21·94	22·06	22·12	22·18	22·23	22·28	22
23	22·70	22·75	22·81	22·88	22·94	23·06	23·12	23·18	23·24	23·30	23
24	23·69	23·74	23·80	23·87	23·93	24·06	24·13	24·19	24·25	24·31	24
25	24·67	24·73	24·80	24·87	24·93	25·06	25·13	25·20	25·26	25·32	25
26	25·66	25·72	25·79	25·86	25·93	26·06	26·14	26·21	26·27	26·34	26
27	26·65	26·71	26·78	26·86	26·93	27·07	27·15	27·22	27·28	27·35	27
28	27·63	27·70	27·77	27·85	27·92	28·07	28·15	28·23	28·29	28·36	28
29	28·62	28·69	28·76	28·84	28·92	29·07	29·16	29·24	29·30	29·37	29
30	29·60	29·68	29·76	29·84	29·92	30·07	30·16	30·24	30·32	30·39	30
31	30·59	30·67	30·75	30·84	30·92	31·08	31·17	31·25	31·33	31·41	31
32	31·58	31·66	31·74	31·83	31·92	32·08	32·17	32·26	32·34	32·42	32
33	32·56	32·65	32·73	32·82	32·91	33·08	33·18	33·27	33·35	33·43	33
34	33·55	33·64	33·73	33·82	33·91	34·09	34·18	34·28	34·36	34·45	34
35	34·54	34·63	34·72	34·82	34·91	35·09	35·19	35·28	35·37	35·46	35
36	35·52	35·62	35·71	35·81	35·91	36·09	36·19	36·29	36·38	36·47	36
37	36·51	36·61	36·71	36·81	36·90	37·09	37·20	37·30	37·39	37·49	37
38	37·50	37·60	37·70	37·80	37·90	38·10	38·20	38·30	38·40	38·50	38
39	38·49	38·59	38·69	38·80	38·90	39·10	39·21	39·31	39·41	39·51	39
40	39·47	39·58	39·68	39·79	39·90	40·10	40·21	40·32	40·42	40 52	40
41	40·46	40·56	40·67	40·79	40·89	41·11	41·22	41·33	41·43	41·54	41
42	41·44	41·55	41·66	41·78	41·89	42·11	42·22	42·34	42·44	42·55	42
43	42·43	42·54	42·66	42·78	42·89	43·11	43·23	43·35	43·45	43·56	43
44	43·42	43·53	43·65	43·77	43·89	44·12	44·23	44·35	44·46	44·58	44
45	44·40	44·52	44·64	44·76	44·88	45·12	45·24	45·36	45·47	45·59	45
46	45·39	45·51	45·63	45·76	45·88	46·12	46·24	46·36	46·48	46·60	46
47	46·38	46·50	46·63	46·76	46·88	47·12	47·25	47·38	47·49	47·61	47
48	47·36	47·49	47·62	47·75	47·87	48·13	48·25	48·39	48·51	48·63	48
49	48·35	48·48	48·61	48·74	48·87	49·13	49·26	49·40	49·52	49·64	49
50	49·34	49·47	49·60	49·74	49·87	50·13	50·26	50·40	50·53	50·66	50

TO A PRESSURE OF 760 MM.—*Continued.*

between 0° and 12° C., 2 mm. between 13° and 19° C., 3 mm. between 20° and 25° C.

760	750	752	754	756	758	762	764	766	768	770	760
51	50·33	50·46	50·60	50·74	50·87	51·14	51·27	51·41	51·54	51·67	51
52	51·32	51·45	51·59	51·73	51·87	52·14	52·28	52·42	52·55	52·68	52
53	52·30	52·44	52·58	52·73	52·87	53·14	53·28	53·42	53·56	53·70	53
54	53·29	53·43	53·57	53·72	53·86	54·14	54·28	54·43	54·57	54·72	54
55	54·28	54·42	54·56	54·71	54·86	55·15	55·29	55·44	55·58	55·73	55
56	55·26	55·41	55·56	55·71	55·86	56·15	56·29	56·45	56·59	56·74	56
57	56·25	56·40	56·55	56·70	56·85	57·15	57·30	57·45	57·60	57·76	57
58	57·24	57·39	57·54	57·69	57·85	58·15	58·30	58·46	58·61	58·77	58
59	58·22	58·38	58·53	58·69	58·85	59·16	59·31	59·47	59·62	59·78	59
60	59·21	59·37	59·52	59·68	59·84	60·16	60·32	60·47	60·63	60·79	60
61	60·20	60·36	60·52	60·68	60·84	61·16	61·32	61·48	61·64	61·81	61
62	61·19	61·35	61·51	61·67	61·84	62·16	62·33	62·49	62·65	62·82	62
63	62·17	62·34	62·50	62·67	62·83	63·17	63·33	63·50	63·67	63·84	63
64	63·16	63·33	63·49	63·66	63·83	64·17	64·34	64·51	64·68	64·85	64
65	64·15	64·32	64·49	64·66	64·83	65·17	65·34	65·51	65·69	65·86	65
66	65·13	65·31	65·48	65·65	65·82	66·17	66·35	66·52	66·70	66·88	66
67	66·12	66·30	66·47	66·64	66·82	67·18	67·35	67·53	67·71	67·89	67
68	67·10	67·29	67·46	67·64	67·82	68·18	68·36	68·54	68·72	68·90	68
69	68·09	68·28	68·45	68·63	68·82	69·18	69·36	69·54	69·73	69·91	69
70	69·08	69·26	69·44	69·63	69·82	70·18	70 37	70·55	70·74	70·92	70
71	70·07	70·25	70·43	70·62	70·81	71·19	71·37	71·56	71·75	71·94	71
72	71·05	71·24	71·43	71·62	71·81	72·19	72·38	72·57	72·76	72·95	72
73	72·04	72·23	72·42	72·61	72·81	73·19	73·38	73·57	73·77	73·97	73
74	73·03	73·22	73·41	73·61	73·80	74·19	74·39	74·58	74·78	74·98	74
75	74·01	74·21	74·40	74·60	74·80	75·20	75·39	75·59	75·79	75·99	75
76	75·00	75·20	75·40	75·60	75·80	76·20	76·40	76·60	76·80	77·01	76
77	75·99	76·19	76·39	76·59	76·79	77·20	77·40	77·60	77·81	78·02	77
78	76·97	77·18	77·38	77·58	77·79	78·20	78·41	78·61	78·82	79·03	78
79	77·96	78·17	78·37	78·58	78·79	79·21	79·41	79·62	79·83	80·04	79
80	78·94	79·16	79·36	79·58	79·79	80·21	80·42	80·63	80·84	81·06	80
81	79·93	80·15	80·35	80·57	80·79	81·21	81·42	81·64	81·85	82·07	81
82	80·92	81·14	81·35	81·56	81·78	82·21	82·43	82·65	82·87	83·09	82
83	81·91	82·13	82·34	82·56	82·78	83·22	83·44	83·66	83·88	84·10	83
84	82·90	83·12	83·34	83·56	83·78	84·22	84·44	84·66	84·89	85·11	84
85	83·88	84·11	84·33	84·55	84·78	85·22	85·45	85·67	85·90	86·13	85
86	84·87	85·10	85·32	85·55	85·78	86·22	86·46	86·67	86·91	87·14	86
87	85·85	86·08	86·31	86·54	86·77	87·23	87·56	87·68	87·92	88·15	87
88	86·84	87·07	87·30	87·54	87·77	88·23	88·47	88·69	88·93	89·17	88
89	87·82	88·06	88·29	88·53	88·77	89·23	89·47	89·70	89·94	90·18	89
90	88·81	89·05	89·29	89·52	89·77	90·23	90·48	90·71	90·95	91·19	90
91	89·80	90·04	90·28	90·52	90·76	91·24	91·48	91·72	91·96	92·21	91
92	90·79	91·03	91·27	91·51	91·76	92·24	92·49	92·73	92·97	93·22	92
93	91·77	92·02	92·26	92·51	92·76	93·24	93·49	93·74	93·98	94·23	93
94	92·76	93·01	93·26	93·50	93·75	94·24	94·49	94·74	94·99	95·24	94
95	93·74	94·00	94·25	94·50	94·75	95·25	95·50	95·75	96·00	96·26	95
96	94·73	94·98	95·24	95·49	95·75	96·25	96·51	96·76	97·01	97·27	96
97	95·72	95·97	96 23	96·49	96·75	97·25	97·51	97·77	98·02	98·29	97
98	96·70	96·96	97·22	97·48	97·74	98·25	98·52	98·77	99·03	99·30	98
99	97·69	97·95	98·21	98·48	98·74	99·26	99·52	99·78	100·04	100·31	99
100	98·68	98·95	99·21	99·47	99·74	100·26	100·53	100·79	101·05	101·32	100

TABLE 21ʙ.—FACTORS FOR REDUCING A GIVEN VOLUME OF GAS TO NORMAL TEMPERATURE AND PRESSURE.

0° Centigrade, and 760 millimetres, or 32° Fahrenheit, and 29·92 inches barometric pressure.

Centigrade.		0·0	1·1	2·2	3·3	4·4	5·6	6·7	7·8	8·9
Fahrenheit.		32°	34°	36°	38°	40°	42°	44°	46°	48°
In.	Milli-metre.									
27·5	698·5	·9191	·9154	·9116	·9079	·9043	·9007	·8972	·8936	·8899
27·6	701·0	·9224	·9188	·9149	·9112	·9076	·9039	·9005	·8969	·8932
27·7	703·6	·9258	·9221	·9183	·9145	·9109	·9072	·9037	·9001	·8964
27·8	706·1	·9291	·9254	·9215	·9179	·9142	·9105	·9070	·9034	·8996
27·9	708·6	·9325	·9288	·9249	·9212	·9174	·9138	·9102	·9067	·9029
28·0	711·2	·9358	·9321	·9282	·9244	·9208	·9170	·9135	·9099	·9061
28·1	713·7	·9391	·9354	·9315	·9278	·9241	·9203	·9167	·9131	·9093
28·2	716·3	·9425	·9387	·9348	·9310	·9273	·9236	·9200	·9164	·9125
28·3	718·8	·9458	·9421	·9382	·9344	·9306	·9269	·9233	·9197	·9158
28·4	721·3	·9491	·9454	·9415	·9377	·9339	·9301	·9265	·9229	·9190
28·5	723·9	·9525	·9487	·9448	·9410	·9372	·9334	·9298	·9262	·9223
28·6	726·4	·9558	·9520	·9481	·9443	·9405	·9367	·9331	·9294	·9255
28·7	728·9	·9592	·9554	·9514	·9476	·9438	·9400	·9364	·9327	·9287
28·8	731·5	·9625	·9587	·9547	·9509	·9471	·9432	·9396	·9359	·9320
28·9	734·0	·9659	·9620	·9580	·9542	·9504	·9465	·9429	·9392	·9352
29·0	736·6	·9692	·9654	·9613	·9575	·9536	·9498	·9462	·9424	·9385
29·1	739·1	·9725	·9687	·9647	·9608	·9569	·9531	·9494	·9457	·9417
29·2	741·6	·9758	·9720	·9680	·9610	·9602	·9563	·9527	·9489	·9449
29·3	744·2	·9792	·9753	·9713	·9674	·9635	·9596	·9559	·9522	·9481
29·4	746·7	·9826	·9787	·9746	·9707	·9668	·9629	·9592	·9554	·9514
29·5	749·3	·9859	·9820	·9779	·9740	·9701	·9662	·9624	·9587	·9546
29·6	751·8	·9893	·9853	·9812	·9773	·9733	·9694	·9657	·9619	·9578
29·7	754·3	·9926	·9887	·9845	·9806	·9766	·9727	·9690	·9652	·9611
29·8	756·9	·9959	·9920	·9879	·9839	·9800	·9760	·9722	·9684	·9643
29 9	759·4	·9993	·9954	·9912	·9872	·9832	·9793	·9755	·9717	·9676
30·0	762·0	1·0026	·9987	·9945	·9905	·9865	·9826	·9788	·9749	·9708
30·1	764·5	1·0060	1·0020	·9978	·9938	·9898	·9858	·9820	·9782	·9740
30·2	767·0	1·0093	1·0053	1·0011	·9971	·9931	·9891	·9853	·9814	·9773
30·3	769·6	1·0126	1·0086	1·0044	1·0004	·9964	·9924	·9885	·9846	·9805
30·4	772·1	1·0160	1·0120	1·0078	1·0037	·9997	·9957	·9918	·9879	·9837
30·5	774·7	1·0194	1·0153	1·0111	1·0070	1·0030	·9989	·9950	·9911	·9870
30·6	777·2	1·0227	1·0186	1·0144	1·0103	1·0063	1·0022	·9983	·9944	·9902
30·7	779·7	1·0260	1·0220	1·0177	1·0136	1·0096	1·0055	1·0016	·9976	·9935
30·8	782·3	1·0294	1·0253	1·0210	1·0169	1·0128	1·0087	1·0048	1·0009	·9967
30·9	784·8	1·0327	1·0286	1·0243	1·0202	1·0164	1·0120	1·0081	1·0041	1·0000
31·0	787·4	1·0360	1·0319	1·0276	1·0235	1·0194	1·0153	1·0114	1·0074	1·0032

FACTORS FOR REDUCING A GIVEN VOLUME OF GAS TO NORMAL TEMPERATURE AND PRESSURE.—*Continued.*

0° Centigrade, and 760 millimetres, or 32° Fahrenheit, and 29·92 inches barometric pressure.

Centigrade.	10·0	11·1	12·2	13·3	14·4	15·6	16·7	17·8
Fahrenheit.	50°	52°	54°	56°	58°	60°	62°	64°

In.	Milli-metre.							
27·5	698·5	·8867	·8832	·8797	·8763	·8728	·8695	·8661	·8628
27·6	701·0	·8900	·8864	·8829	·8795	·8760	·8726	·8693	·8660
27·7	703·6	·8932	·8897	·8861	·8827	·8792	·8758	·8724	·8691
27·8	706·1	·8964	·8928	·8893	·8859	·8823	·8790	·8756	·8722
27·9	708·6	·8996	·8960	·8925	·8890	·8855	·8821	·8787	·8754
28·0	711·2	·9029	·8992	·8957	·8922	·8887	·8853	·8819	·8785
28·1	713·7	·9060	·9025	·8989	·8954	·8919	·8884	·8850	·8816
28·2	716·3	·9093	·9057	·9021	·8986	·8951	·8916	·8882	·8848
28·3	718·8	·9125	·9089	·9053	·9018	·8983	·8948	·8913	·8879
28·4	721·3	·9157	·9121	·9085	·9050	·9014	·8979	·8945	·8911
28·5	723·9	·9189	·9153	·9117	·9082	·9046	·9011	·8976	·8942
28·6	726·4	·9222	·9185	·9149	·9114	·9077	·9043	·9008	·8973
28·7	728·9	·9254	·9218	·9181	·9145	·9109	·9074	·9039	·9005
28·8	731·5	·9286	·9250	·9213	·9177	·9141	·9196	·9071	·9036
28·9	734·0	·9318	·9282	·9245	·9209	9173	·9138	·9102	·9067
29·0	736·6	·9351	·9314	·9277	·9241	·9205	·9169	·9134	·9099
29·1	739·1	·9383	·9346	·9309	·9273	·9236	·9201	·9165	·9130
29·2	741·6	·9415	·9378	·9341	·9305	·9268	·9233	·9197	·9162
29·3	744·2	·9448	·9410	·9373	·9336	·9300	·9264	·9228	·9193
29·4	746·7	·9480	·9443	·9405	·9368	·9332	·9296	·9260	·9224
29·5	749·3	·9512	·9475	·9437	·9400	·9363	·9328	·9291	·9256
29·6	751·8	·9544	·9506	·9469	·9432	·9395	·9359	·9323	·9287
29·7	754·3	·9577	·9539	·9501	·9464	·9427	·9390	·9354	·9318
29·8	756·9	·9609	·9571	·9533	·9496	·9459	·9422	·9386	·9350
29·9	759·4	·9641	·9603	·9565	·9528	·9490	·9454	·9417	·9381
30·0	762·0	·9673	·9635	·9597	·9560	·9522	·9486	·9449	·9413
30·1	764·5	·9706	·9667	·9629	·9591	·9554	·9517	·9480	·9444
30·2	767·0	·9738	·9700	·9661	·9623	·9586	·9549	·9512	·9475
30·3	769·6	·9770	·9731	·9693	·9655	·9617	·9580	·9543	·9507
30·4	772·1	·9802	·9764	·9725	·9687	·9649	·9612	·9575	·9538
30·5	774·7	·9835	·9796	·9757	·9719	·9681	·9643	·9606	·9569
30·6	777·2	·9867	·9828	·9789	·9751	·9712	·9675	·9638	·9601
30·7	779·7	·9899	·9860	·9821	·9782	·9744	·9707	·9669	·9632
30·8	782·3	·9931	·9892	·9853	·9815	·9776	·9738	·9701	·9664
30·9	784·8	·9963	·9924	·9885	·9846	·9807	·9770	·9732	·9695
31·0	787·4	·9996	·9956	·9917	·9878	·9840	·9801	·9764	·9726

48

FACTORS FOR REDUCING A GIVEN VOLUME OF GAS TO NORMAL TEMPERATURE AND PRESSURE.—*Continued.*

0° Centigrade, and 760° millimetres, or 32° Fahrenheit, and 29·92 inches barometric pressure.

Centigrade.		18·9	20	21·1	22·2	23·3	24·4	25·6	26·7
Fahrenheit.		66°	68°	70°	72°	74°	76°	78°	80°
In.	Milli-metre.								
27·5	698·5	·8595	·8568	·8530	·8498	·8466	·8435	·8403	·8372
27·6	701·0	·8626	·8594	·8561	·8529	·8497	·8465	·8434	·8403
27·7	703·6	·8658	·8625	·8592	·8560	·8528	·8496	·8464	·8433
27·8	706·1	·8689	·8656	·8623	·8591	·8559	·8527	·8495	·8463
27·9	708·6	·8720	·8687	·8654	·8622	·8589	·8557	·8525	·8494
28·0	711·2	·8751	·8718	·8685	·8653	·8620	·8588	·8556	·8524
28·1	713·7	·8783	·8750	·8716	·8684	·8651	·8619	·8587	·8555
28·2	716·3	·8814	·8781	·8747	·8714	·8682	·8649	·8617	·8585
28·3	718·8	·8845	·8812	·8778	·8745	·8713	·8680	·8648	·8616
28·4	721·3	·8876	·8843	·8809	·8776	·8743	·8711	·8678	·8646
28·5	723·9	·8908	·8874	·8840	·8807	·8774	·8741	·8709	·8677
28·6	726·4	·8939	·8905	·8872	·8838	·8805	·8772	·8739	·8707
28·7	728·9	·8970	·8936	·8903	·8869	·8836	·8803	·8770	·8738
28·8	731·5	·9002	·8968	·8934	·8900	·8866	·8833	·8800	·8768
28·9	734·0	·9033	·8999	·8965	·8931	·8897	·8864	·8831	·8798
29·0	736·6	·9064	·9030	·8996	·8962	·8928	·8895	·8862	·8829
29·1	739·1	·9095	·9061	·9027	·8993	·8959	·8925	·8892	·8859
29·2	741·6	·9127	·9092	·9050	·9023	·8990	·8956	·8923	·8890
29·3	744·2	·9158	·9123	·9089	·9054	·9020	·8987	·8953	·8920
29·4	746·7	·9189	·9154	·9120	·9085	·9051	·9017	·8984	·8951
29·5	749·3	·9220	·9186	·9151	·9116	·9082	·9048	·9014	·8981
29·6	751·8	·9252	·9217	·9182	·9147	·9113	·9079	·9045	·9012
29·7	754·3	·9283	·9248	·9213	·9178	·9144	·9109	·9076	·9042
29·8	756·9	·9314	·9279	·9244	·9209	·9174	·9140	·9106	·9072
29·9	759·4	·9345	·9310	·9275	·9240	·9205	·9171	·9137	·9103
30·0	762·0	·9377	·9341	·9306	·9271	·9236	·9201	·9167	·9133
30·1	764·5	·9408	·9372	·9337	·9302	·9267	·9232	·9198	·9164
30·2	767·0	·9439	·9403	·9368	·9333	·9297	·9263	·9228	·9194
30·3	769·6	·9470	·9435	·9329	·9363	·9328	·9293	·9259	·9225
30·4	772·1	·9502	·9466	·9430	·9394	·9359	·9324	·9280	·9255
30·5	774·7	·9533	·9497	·9461	·9425	·9390	·9355	·9320	·9286
30·6	777·2	·9564	·9528	·9492	·9456	·9421	·9385	·9351	·9316
30·7	779·7	·9595	·9559	·9523	·9487	·9451	·9416	·9381	·9346
30·8	782·3	·9627	·9590	·9554	·9518	·9482	·9447	·9412	·9377
30·9	784·8	·9658	·9621	·9585	·9549	·9513	·9477	·9442	·9407
31·0	787·4	·9689	·9653	·9616	·9580	·9544	·9508	·9473	·9438

TABLE 22.—VOLUMES OF WATER
At different Temperatures (Kopp).

Temp. Cels.		Temp. Cels.		Temp. Cels.	
0	1	14	1·000556	40	1·007531
1	0·999947	15	1·000695	45	1·009541
2	0·999908	16	1·000846	50	1·011766
8	0·999885	17	1·001010	55	1·014100
4	0·999877	18	1·001184	60	1·016590
5	0·999883	19	1·001370	65	1·019302
6	0·999903	20	1·001567	70	1·022246
7	0·999938	21	1·001776	75	1·025440
8	0·999986	22	1·001995	80	1·028581
9	1·000048	28	1·002225	85	1·031894
10	1·000124	24	1·002465	90	1·035397
11	1·000213	25	1·002715	95	1·039094
12	1·000314	80	1·004064	100	1·042986
18	1·000429	85	1·005697		

TABLE 22B.—REDUCTION OF WATER PRESSURE
To Mercurial Pressure.

aq	Hg	aq	Hg	aq	Hg	aq	Hg	aq	Hg
1	0·07	28	1·70	45	3·32	67	4·94	89	6·57
2	0·15	24	1·77	46	8·39	68	5·02	90	6·64
8	0·22	25	1·84	47	8·47	69	5·09	91	6·72
4	0·80	26	1·92	48	8·54	70	5·17	92	6·79
5	0·37	27	1·98	49	8·62	71	5·24	98	6·86
6	0·44	28	2·07	50	3·69	72	5·31	94	6·94
7	0·52	29	2·14	51	3·76	73	5·39	95	7·01
8	0·59	80	2·21	52	3·84	74	5·46	96	7·08
9	0·66	31	2·29	53	3·91	75	5·54	97	7·16
10	0·74	82	2·36	54	3·99	76	5·61	98	7·23
11	0·81	88	2·44	55	4·06	77	5·68	99	7·31
12	0·89	84	2·51	56	4·13	78	5·76	100	7·88
13	0·96	85	2·58	57	4·21	79	5·83	200	14·76
14	1·03	86	2·66	58	4·28	80	5·90	800	22·14
15	1·12	87	2·73	59	4·35	81	5·98	400	29·52
16	1·18	88	2·80	60	4·43	82	6·05	500	36·90
17	1·26	89	2·58	61	4·50	83	6·13	600	44·28
18	1·33	40	2·95	62	4·58	84	6·20	700	51·66
19	1·40	41	3·03	63	4·65	85	6·27	800	59·04
20	1·88	42	3·10	64	4·72	86	6·35	900	66·42
21	1·55	43	3·17	65	4·80	87	6·42	1000	78·80
22	1·62	44	3·25	66	4·87	88	6·49		

E

TABLE 23.—TENSIONS OF AQUEOUS VAPOUR

between − 20 and + 118° C. in millimetres mercury (Magnus).

T	mm	T	mm	T	mm
−20°	0·916	+15°	12·677	+50°	92·0
19	0·999	16	13·519	51	96·6
18	1·089	17	14·409	52	101·5
17	1·186	18	15·351	53	106·6
16	1·290	19	16·345	54	111·9
15	1·408	20	17·396	55	117·4
14	1·525	21	18·505	56	123·1
13	1·655	22	19·675	57	129·1
12	1·796	23	20·909	58	135·3
11	1·947	24	22·211	59	141·8
10	2·109	25	23·582	60	148·6
9	2·284	26	25·026	61	155·6
8	2·471	27	26·547	62	162·9
7	2·671	28	28·148	63	170·5
6	2·886	29	29·832	64	178·4
5	3·110	30	31·602	65	186·6
4	3·361	31	33·5	66	195·1
3	3·624	32	35·4	67	204·0
2	3·900	33	37·5	68	213·2
1	4·205	34	39·6	69	222·7
0	4·525	35	41·9	70	232·6
+1	4·867	36	44·3	71	242·9
2	5·231	37	46·8	72	258·5
3	5·619	38	49·4	73	264·6
4	6·032	39	52·1	74	276·0
5	6·471	40	55·0	75	287·9
6	6·989	41	58·0	76	300·2
7	7·436	42	61·1	77	312·9
8	7·964	43	64·4	78	326·1
9	8·525	44	67·8	79	339·8
10	9·126	45	71·4	80	353·9
11	9·756	46	75·2	81	368·6
12	10·421	47	79·1	82	383·7
13	11·130	48	83·2	83	399·4
14	11·882	49	87·5	84	415·6

TENSION OF AQUEOUS VAPOUR—*Continued.*

T	mm	T	mm	T	mm
+85°	432·3	+97°	681·7	+109°	1041·3
86	449·6	98	707·0	110	1077·3
87	467·5	99	733·1	111	1114·3
88	486·0	100	760·0	112	1152·3
89	505·0	101	787·7	113	1191·4
90	524·8	102	816·3	114	1231·7
91	545·1	103	845·7	115	1273·0
92	566·1	104	876·0	116	1315·5
93	587·8	105	907·1	117	1359·1
94	610·2	106	939·2	118	1403·9
95	633·3	107	972·3		
96	657·1	108	1006·3		

TABLE 23B.—TENSION OF AQUEOUS VAPOUR FOR TEMPERATURES FROM 40° C.

Temperature.	Tension in mm.	In atmospheres.	Pressure per square centm. in kilos.
+ 40°	54·906	0·072	0·07465
45	71·391	0·094	0·09706
50	91·982	0·121	0·12505
55	117·478	0·154	0·15972
60	148·791	0·196	0·20323
65	186·945	0·246	0·25417
70	233·098	0·306	0·31692
75	288·517	0·380	0·39227
80	354·643	0·466	0·48217
85	433·041	0·570	0·58877
90	525·450	0·691	0·71440
95	633·778	0·834	0·86168
100	760·00	1·000	1·03330
105	906·41	1·193	1·23236
110	1075·87	1·415	1·46210
115	1269·41	1·673	1·72592
120	1491·28	1·962	2·02755
125	1743·88	2·294	2·37098
130	2030·28	2·671	2·76037
135	2353·73	3·097	3·20013

TENSION OF AQUEOUS VAPOUR FOR TEMPERATURES FROM 40° C.—*Continued*.

Temperature.	Tension in mm.	In atmospheres.	Pressure per square centm. in kilos.
+140	2717·63	3·575	3·69490
145	3125·55	4·112	4·24950
150	3581·23	4·712	4·86904
155	4088·56	5·380	5·55881
160	4651·62	6·120	6·32434
165	5274·54	6·940	7·17127
170	5961·66	7·844	8·10547
175	6717·48	8·838	9·13302
180	7546·39	9·929	10·2601
185	8453·23	11·122	11·4930
190	9442·70	12·424	12·8383
195	10519·73	13·841	14·3025
200	11688·96	15·380	15·8923
205	12955·66	17·047	17·6145
210	14324·80	18·848	19·4760
215	15801·33	20·791	21·4835
220	17890·00	22·881	23·6439
225	19097·04	25·127	25·9643
230	20026·40	27·534	28·4515

TABLE 24.—TENSION OF AQUEOUS VAPOUR IN INCHES OF MERCURY FROM 1° TO 100° FAH.

Temperature Fahrenheit.	Inches of Mercury.	Temperature Fahrenheit.	Inches of Mercury.
1	·046	11	·071
2	·048	12	·074
3	·050	13	·078
4	·052	14	·082
5	·054	15	·086
6	·057	16	·090
7	·060	17	·094
8	·062	18	·098
9	·065	19	·103
10	·068	20	·108

TENSION OF AQUEOUS VAPOUR IN INCHES OF MERCURY FROM 1° TO 100° FAH.—*Continued.*

Temperature Fahrenheit.	Inches of Mercury.	Temperature Fahrenheit.	Inches of Mercury.
21	·113	61	·537
22	·118	62	·556
23	·123	63	·576
24	·129	64	·596
25	·135	65	·617
26	·141	66	·639
27	·147	67	·661
28	·153	68	·685
29	·160	69	·708
30	·167	70	·733
31	·174	71	·759
32	·181	72	·785
33	·188	73	·812
34	·196	74	·840
35	·204	75	·868
36	·212	76	·897
37	·220	77	·927
38	·229	78	·958
39	·238	79	·990
40	·247	80	1·023
41	·257	81	1·057
42	·267	82	1·092
43	·277	83	1·128
44	·288	84	1·165
45	·299	85	1·203
46	·311	86	1·242
47	·323	87	1·282
48	·335	88	1·323
49	·348	89	1·366
50	·361	90	1·401
51	·374	91	1·455
52	·388	92	1·501
53	·403	93	1·548
54	·418	94	1·596
55	·433	95	1·646
56	·449	96	1·697
57	·465	97	1·751
58	·482	98	1·806
59	·500	99	1·862
60	·518	100	1·918

TABLE 24B.—TENSION OF AQUEOUS VAPOUR.

Temperature Fahrenheit.	Inches of Mercury.	Atmospheres.	Lbs. per square inch.
100	1·918	·064	·941
110	2·577	·086	1·267
120	3·427	·114	1·676
130	4·502	·150	2·205
140	5·858	·196	2·883
150	7·546	·252	3·705
160	9·628	·322	4·734
170	12·18	·407	5·984
180	15·27	·510	7·498
190	19·01	·635	9·336
200	23·46	·784	11·53
212	29·92	1·000	14·706
220	35·01	1·170	17·19
230	42·34	1·415	20·80
240	50·89	1·701	25·01
250	60·81	2·032	29·87
260	72·27	2·415	35·50
270	85·41	2·855	41·97
280	100·4	3·356	49·34
290	117·5	3·927	57·73
300	136·8	4·572	67·22
310	158·6	5·301	77·94
320	183·1	6·120	89·98
330	210·5	7·035	103·4
340	241·1	8·058	118·5
350	275·0	9·198	135·2
360	312·6	10·45	153·6
370	354·0	11·83	178·9
380	399·6	13·35	196·3
390	449·6	15·02	220·8
400	504·4	16·86	247·9
410	563·9	18·84	277·0
420	628·8	21·01	309·9
430	699·2	23·37	343·6
440	775·3	25·91	380·9

TABLE 25.—VARIATION OF BOILING POINT OF WATER

with different barometric pressures.

Boiling Point.		Barometric Pressure.	
Centigrade.	Fahrenheit.	Millimetres.	Inches.
98·5	209·80	720·15	28·352
98·6	209·48	722·75	28·455
98·7	209·66	725·35	28·557
98·8	209·84	727·96	28·660
98·9	210·02	730·58	28·763
99·0	210·20	733·21	28·866
99·1	210·38	735·85	28·970
99·2	210·56	738·50	29·075
99·3	210·74	741·16	29·179
99·4	210·92	743·88	29·283
99·5	211·10	746·50	29·390
99·6	211·28	749·18	29·495
99·7	211·46	751·87	29·601
99·8	211·64	754·57	29·707
99·9	211·82	757·28	29·814
100·0	212·00	760·00	29·921
100·1	212·18	762·73	30·029
100·2	212·36	765·46	30·137
100·3	212·54	768·20	30·244
100·4	212·72	771·95	30·392

TABLE 26.—SPECIFIC HEATS.

(Regnault.)

a.—SOLIDS AND LIQUIDS.

Water = 1·0000.

Antimony	·0508	Platinum	·0324
Bismuth	·0308	Phosphorus	·1187
Brass	·0939	Sulphur	·2026
Bricks	·189—·241	Silver	·0570
Carbon	·2411	Steel (Hard)	·1175
Copper	·0951	Steel (Soft)	·1165
Glass	·1937	Tin	·0562
Gold	·0824	Zinc	·0956
Iron (Cast)	·1298	Alcohol	·7000
Iron (Wrought)	·1138	Mercury	·0333
Lead	·0314	Sulphuric Acid	·3350

b.—GASES AND VAPOURS.

	Air=1·000 at Constant Pressure.	Water=1·0000.	
		Constant Volume.	Constant Pressure.
Atmospheric Air	1·00000	0·1687	0·2377
Alcohol Vapour	1·8986	0·3200	0·4513
Carbonic Acid	0·9104	0·1535	0·2164
Carbonic Oxide	1·0798	0·1758	0·2479
Ether Vapour	2·0235	0·3411	0·4810
Hydrogen	14·3281	2·4146	3·4046
Nitrogen	1·0265	0·1780	0·2440
Oxygen	0·9180	0·1548	0·2182
Water Vapour	1·9794	0·3337	0·4750

TABLE 27.—MATHEMATICAL TABLES.

Circumference and area of circles, squares, cubes, square and cube roots.

n	πn $\bigcirc$	$\pi \dfrac{n^2}{4}$ ●	n^2	n^3	$\sqrt{n}$	$\sqrt[3]{n}$
1·0	3·142	0·7854	1·000	1·000	1·0000	1·0000
1·1	3·456	0·9503	1·210	1·331	1·0488	1·0323
1·2	3·770	1·1310	1·440	1·728	1·0955	1·0627
1·3	4·084	1·3273	1·690	2·197	1·1402	1·0914
1·4	4·398	1·5394	1·960	2·744	1·1832	1·1187
1·5	4·712	1·7672	2·250	3·375	1·2247	1·1447
1·6	5·027	2·0106	2·560	4·096	1·2649	1·1696
1·7	5·341	2·2698	2·890	4·913	1·3038	1·1935
1·8	5·655	2·5417	3·240	5·832	1·3416	1·2164
1·9	5·969	2·8353	3·610	6·859	1·3784	1·2386
2·0	6·283	3·1416	4·000	8·000	1·4142	1·2599
2·1	6·597	3·4636	4·410	9·261	1·4491	1·2806
2·2	6·912	3·8013	4·840	10·648	1·4832	1·3006
2·3	7·226	4·1548	5·290	12·167	1·5166	1·3200
2·4	7·540	4·5239	5·760	13·824	1·5492	1·3389
2·5	7·854	4·9087	6·250	15·625	1·5811	1·3572
2·6	8·168	5·3093	6·760	17·576	1·6125	1·3751
2·7	8·482	5·7256	7·290	19·683	1·6432	1·3925
2·8	8·797	6·1575	7·840	21·952	1·6733	1·4095
2·9	9·111	6·6052	8·410	24·389	1·7029	1·4260
3·0	9·425	7·0686	9·00	27·000	1·7321	1·4422
3·1	9·739	7·5477	9·61	29·791	1·7607	1·4581
3·2	10·053	8·0425	10·24	32·768	1·7889	1·4736
3·3	10·367	8·5530	10·89	35·987	1·8166	1·4888
3·4	10·681	9·0792	11·56	39·304	1·8439	1·5037
3·5	10·996	9·6211	12·25	42·875	1·8708	1·5183
3·6	11·310	10·179	12·96	46·656	1·8974	1·5326
3·7	11·624	10·752	13·69	50·653	1·9235	1·5467
3·8	11·938	11·341	14·44	54·872	1·9494	1·5605
3·9	12·252	11·946	15·21	59·319	1·9748	1·5741
4·0	12·566	12·566	16·00	64·000	2·0000	1·5874
4·1	12·881	13·203	16·81	68·921	2·0249	1·6005
4·2	13·195	13·854	17·64	74·088	2·0494	1·6134
4·3	13·509	14·522	18·49	79·507	2·0736	1·6261
4·4	13·823	15·205	19·36	85·184	2·0976	1·6386
4·5	14·137	15·904	20·25	91·125	2·1213	1·6510
4·6	14·451	16·619	21·16	97·336	2·1448	1·6631
4·7	14·765	17·349	22·09	103·823	2·1680	1·6751

TABLE 27.—MATHEMATICAL TABLES.—*Continued.*

Circumference and area of circles, squares, cubes, square and cube roots.

n	πn ○	$\dfrac{n^2}{\pi\ 4}$ ●	n^2	n^3	$\sqrt{n}$	$\sqrt[3]{n}$
4·8	15·080	18·096	23·04	110·592	2·1009	1·6869
4·9	15·394	18·857	24·01	117·649	2·2136	1·6985
5·0	15·708	19·685	25·00	125·000	2·2361	1·7100
5·1	16·022	20·428	26·01	132·651	2·2583	1·7213
5·2	16·336	21·237	27·04	140·608	2·2804	1·7325
5·3	16·650	22·062	28·09	148·877	2·3022	1·7435
5·4	16·965	22·902	29·16	157·464	2·3238	1·7544
5·5	17·279	23·758	30·25	166·375	2·3452	1·7652
5·6	17·593	24·630	31·36	175·616	2·3664	1·7758
5·7	17·907	25·518	32·49	185·193	2·3875	1·7863
5·8	18·221	26·421	33·64	195·112	2·4083	1·7967
5·9	18·535	27·340	34·81	205·379	2·4290	1·8070
6·0	18·850	28·274	36·00	216·000	2·4495	1·8171
6·1	19·164	29·225	37·21	226·981	2·4698	1·8272
6·2	19·478	30·191	38·44	238·328	2·4900	1·8371
6·3	19·792	31·173	39·69	250·047	2·5100	1·8469
6·4	20·106	32·170	40·96	262·144	2·5298	1·8566
6·5	20·420	33·183	42·25	274·625	2·5495	1·8663
6·6	20·735	34·212	43·56	287·496	2·5691	1·8758
6·7	21·049	35·257	44·89	300·763	2·5884	1·8852
6·8	21·363	36·317	46·24	314·432	2·6077	1·8945
6·9	21·677	37·393	47·61	328·509	2·6268	1·9038
7·0	21·991	38·485	49·00	343·000	2·6458	1·9129
7·1	22·305	39·592	50·41	357·911	2·6646	1·9220
7·2	22·619	40·715	51·84	373·248	2·6833	1·9310
7·3	22·934	41·854	53·29	389·017	2·7019	1·9399
7·4	23·248	43·008	54·76	405·224	2·7203	1·9487
7·5	23·562	44·179	56·25	421·875	2·7386	1·9574
7·6	23·876	45·365	57·76	438·976	2·7568	1·9661
7·7	24·190	46·566	59·29	456·533	2·7749	1·9747
7·8	24·504	47·784	60·84	474·552	2·7929	1·9832
7·9	24·819	49·017	62·41	493·089	2·8107	1·9916
8·0	25·133	50·266	64·00	512·000	2·8284	2·0000
8·1	25·447	51·530	65·61	531·441	2·8461	2·0083
8·2	25·761	52·810	67·24	551·368	2·8636	2·0165
8·3	26·075	54·106	68·89	571·787	2·8810	2·0247
8·4	26·389	55·418	70·56	592·704	2·8983	2·0328

TABLE 27.—MATHEMATICAL TABLES.—*Continued.*

Circumference and area of circles, squares, cubes, square and cube roots.

n	πn ◯	$\pi \dfrac{n^2}{4}$ ●	n^2	n^3	$\sqrt{n}$	$\sqrt[3]{n}$
8·5	26·704	56·745	72·25	614·125	2·9155	2·0408
8·6	27·018	58·088	73·96	636·056	2·9326	2·0488
8·7	27·332	59·447	75·69	658·508	2·9496	2·0567
8·8	27·646	60·821	77·44	681·472	2·9665	2·0646
8·9	27·960	62·211	79·21	704·969	2·9833	2·0724
9·0	28·274	63·617	81·00	729·000	3·0000	2·0801
9·1	28·588	65·039	82·81	753·571	3·0166	2·0878
9·2	28·908	66·476	84·64	778·688	3·0332	2·0954
9·3	29·217	67·929	86·49	804·357	3·0496	2·1029
9·4	29·531	69·398	88·36	830·584	3·0659	2·1105
9·5	29·845	70·882	90·25	857·375	3·0822	2·1179
9·6	30·159	72·382	92·16	884·736	3·0984	2·1253
9·7	30·473	73·898	94·09	912·673	3·1145	2·1327
9·8	30·788	75·430	96·04	941·192	3·1305	2·1400
9·9	31·102	76·977	98·01	970·299	3·1464	2·1472
10·0	31·416	78·540	100·00	1000·000	3·1623	2·1544
10·1	31·780	80·119	102·01	1030·301	3·1780	2·1616
10·2	32·044	81·718	104·04	1061·208	3·1937	2·1687
10·3	32·358	83·323	106·09	1092·727	3·2094	2·1757
10·4	32·673	84·949	108·16	1124·863	3·2249	2·1828
10·5	32·987	86·590	110·25	1157·625	3·2404	2·1897
10·6	33·301	88·247	112·36	1191·016	3·2558	2·1967
10·7	33·615	89·920	114·49	1225·043	3·2711	2·2036
10·8	33·929	91·609	116·64	1259·712	3·2863	2·2104
10·9	34·243	93·318	118·81	1295·029	3·3015	2·2172
11·0	34·558	95·088	121·00	1331·000	3·3166	2·2239
11·1	34·872	96·769	123·21	1367·631	3·3317	2·2307
11·2	35·186	98·520	125·44	1404·928	3·3466	2·2374
11·3	35·500	100·29	127·69	1442·897	3·3615	2·2441
11·4	35·814	102·07	129·96	1481·544	3·3754	2·2506
11·5	36·128	103·87	132·25	1520·875	3·3912	2·2572
11·6	36·442	105·68	134·56	1560·896	3·4059	2·2637
11·7	36·757	107·51	136·89	1601·613	3·4205	2·2702
11·8	37·071	109·36	139·24	1643·032	3·4351	2·2766
11·9	37·385	111·22	141·61	1685·159	3·4496	2·2831
12·0	37·699	113·10	144·00	1728·000	3·4641	2·2894
12·1	38·013	114·99	146·41	1771·561	3·4785	2·2957
12·2	38·327	116·90	148·84	1815·848	3·4928	2·3021

TABLE 27.—MATHEMATICAL TABLES.—*Continued.*

Circumference and area of circles, squares, cubes, square and cube roots.

n	πn O	$\pi \dfrac{n^2}{4}$ ●	n^3	n^3	$\sqrt{n}$	$\sqrt[3]{n}$
12·3	38·642	118·82	151·29	1860·867	3·5071	2·3084
12·4	38·956	120·76	153·76	1906·624	3·5214	2·3146
12·5	39·270	122·72	156·25	1953·125	3·5355	2·3208
12·6	39·584	124·69	158·76	2000·376	3·5496	2·3270
12·7	39·898	126·68	161·29	2048·383	3·5637	2·3334
12·8	40·212	128·68	163·84	2097·152	3·5777	2·3392
12·9	40·527	130·70	166·41	2146·689	3·5917	2·3453
13·0	40·841	132·73	169·00	2197·000	3·6056	2·3513
13·1	41·155	134·78	171·61	2248·091	3·6194	2·3573
13·2	41·469	136·85	174·24	2299·968	3·6332	2·3633
13·3	41·783	138·93	176·89	2352·637	3·6469	2·3693
13·4	42·097	141·03	179·56	2406·104	3·6606	2·3752
13·5	42·412	143·14	182·25	2460·375	3·6742	2·3811
13·6	42·726	145·27	184·96	2515·456	3·6878	2·3870
13·7	43·040	147·41	187·69	2571·353	3·7013	2·3928
13·8	43·354	149·57	190·44	2628·072	3·7148	2·3986
13·9	43·668	151·75	193·21	2685·619	3·7288	2·4044
14·0	43·892	153·94	196·00	2744·000	3·7417	2·4101
14·1	44·296	156·15	198·81	2803·221	3·7550	2·4159
14·2	44·611	158·37	201·64	2863·288	3·7683	2·4216
14·3	44·925	160·61	204·49	2924·207	3·7815	2·4272
14·4	45·239	162·86	207·86	2985·984	3·7947	2·4329
14·5	45·553	165·13	210·25	3048·625	3·8079	2·4385
14·6	45·867	167·42	213·16	3112·136	3·8210	2·4411
14·7	46·181	169·72	216·09	3176·523	3·8341	2·4497
14·8	46·496	172·03	219·04	3241·792	3·8471	2·4552
14·9	46·810	174·87	222·01	3307·949	3·8600	2·4607
15·0	47·124	176·72	225·00	3375·000	3·8730	2·4662
15·1	47·438	179·08	228·09	3442·951	3·8859	2·4717
15·2	47·752	181·46	231·04	3511·808	3·8987	2·4772
15·3	48·066	183·85	234·09	3581·577	3·9115	2·4825
15·4	48·381	186·27	237·16	3652·264	3·9243	2·4879
15·5	48·695	188·69	240·25	3723·875	3·9370	2·4933
15·6	49·009	191·13	243·36	3796·416	3·9497	2·4986
15·7	49·323	193·59	246·49	3869·893	3·9623	2·5039
15·8	49·637	196·07	249·64	3944·312	3·9749	2·5092
15·9	49·951	198·56	252·81	4019·679	3·9875	2·5146

TABLE 27.—MATHEMATICAL TABLES.—*Continued.*

Circumference and area of circles, squares, cubes, square and cube roots.

n	πn ◯	$\pi \dfrac{n^2}{4}$ ◉	n^2	n^3	$\sqrt{n}$	$\sqrt[3]{n}$
16·0	50·265	201·06	256·00	4096·000	4·0000	2·5198
16·1	50·580	203·58	259·21	4173·281	4·0125	2·5251
16·2	50·894	206·13	262·44	4251·528	4·0249	2·5303
16·3	51·208	208·67	265·69	4330·747	4·0373	2·5355
16·4	51·522	211·24	268·56	4410·944	4·0497	2·5406
16·5	51·836	213·83	272·25	4492·125	4·0620	2·5458
16·6	52·150	216·42	275·56	4574·296	4·0743	2·5509
16·7	52·465	219·04	278·89	4657·463	4·0866	2·5561
16·8	52·779	221·67	282·24	4741·632	4·0988	2·5612
16·9	53·093	224·32	285·61	4826·809	4·1110	2·5663
17·0	53·407	226·98	299·00	4913·000	4·1231	2·5713
17·1	53·721	229·66	292·41	5000·211	4·1352	2·5763
17·2	54·035	232·35	295·84	5988·448	4·1473	2·5813
17·3	54·350	235·06	299·29	5177·717	4·1593	2·5863
17·4	54·664	237·79	302·76	5268·024	4·1713	2·5913
17·5	54·978	240·53	306·25	5359·375	4·1833	2·5963
17·6	55·292	243·29	309·76	5451·776	4·1952	2·6012
17·7	55·606	246·06	313·29	5545·233	4·2071	2·6061
17·8	55·920	248·85	316·84	5639·752	4·2190	2·6109
17·9	56·235	251·65	320·41	5735·339	4·2308	2·6158
18·0	56·549	254·47	324·00	5832·000	4·2426	2·6207
18·1	56·863	257·30	327·61	5929·711	4·2544	2·6256
18·2	57·177	260·16	331·24	6028·568	4·2661	2·6304
18·3	57·491	263·02	334·89	6128·487	4·2778	2·6352
18·4	57·805	265·90	338·56	6229·504	4·2895	2·6401
18·5	58·119	268·80	342·25	6331·625	4·3012	2·6448
18·6	58·434	271·72	345·96	6434·856	4·3128	2·6495
18·7	58·748	274·65	349·69	6539·203	4·3243	2·6543
18·8	59·062	277·59	353·44	6644·672	4·3159	2·6590
18·9	59·376	280·55	357·21	6751·269	4·3474	2·6687
19·0	59·690	283·53	361·00	6859·000	4·3589	2·6684
19·1	60·004	286·52	364·81	6967·871	4·3708	2·6731
19·2	60·319	289·53	368·64	7077·888	4·3818	2·6777
19·3	60·633	292·55	372·49	7189·057	4·3942	2·6824
19·4	60·947	295·59	376·36	7301·384	4·4045	2·6869
19·5	61·261	298·65	380·25	7414·875	4·4159	2·6916
19·6	61·575	301·72	384·16	7529·566	4·4272	2·6962
19·7	61·889	304·81	388·09	7645·373	4·4385	2·7008

TABLE 27.—MATHEMATICAL TABLES.—*Continued.*

Circumference and area of circles, squares, cubes, square and cube roots.

n	πn $\bigcirc$	$\dfrac{\pi \dfrac{n^2}{4}}{}$ $\bullet$	n^2	n^3	$\sqrt{n}$	$\sqrt[3]{n}$
19·8	62·204	307·91	392·04	7762·392	4·4497	2·7053
19·9	62·518	311·03	396·01	7880·599	4·4609	2·7098
20·0	62·832	314·16	400·00	8000·000	4·4721	2·7144
20·1	63·146	317·31	404·01	8120·601	4·4833	2·7189
20·2	63·460	320·47	408·04	8242·408	4·4944	2·7234
20·3	63·774	323·66	412·09	8365·427	4·5055	2·7279
20·4	64·088	326·85	416·16	8489·664	4·5166	2·7324
20·5	64·403	330·06	420·25	8615·125	4·5277	2·7368
20·6	64·717	333·29	424·36	8741·816	4·5387	2·7413
20·7	65·031	336·54	428·49	8869·743	4·5497	2·7457
20·8	65·345	339·80	432·64	8998·912	4·5607	2·7502
20·9	65·659	343·07	436·81	9129·329	4·5716	2·7545
21·0	65·973	346·36	441·00	9261·000	4·5826	2·7589
21·1	66·288	349·67	445·21	9393·931	4·5935	2·7633
21·2	66·602	352·99	449·44	9528·128	4·6043	2·7676
21·3	66·916	356·33	453·69	9663·597	4·6152	2·7720
21·4	67·230	359·68	457·96	9800·344	4·6260	2·7763
21·5	67·544	363·05	462·25	9938·375	4·6368	2·7806
21·6	67·858	366·44	466·56	10077·696	4·6476	2·7849
21·7	68·173	369·84	470·89	10218·313	4·6583	2·7893
21·8	68·487	373·25	475·24	10360·232	4·6690	2·7935
21·9	68·801	376·69	479·41	10503·459	4·6797	2·7978
22·0	69·115	380·13	484·00	10648·000	4·6904	2·8021
22·1	69·429	383·60	488·41	10793·861	4·7011	2·8063
22·2	69·743	387·08	492·84	10941·048	4·7117	2·8105
22·3	70·058	390·57	497·29	11089·567	4·7223	2·8147
22·4	70·372	394·08	501·76	11239·424	4·7329	2·8189
22·5	70·686	397·61	506·25	11390·625	4·7434	2·8231
22·6	71·000	401·15	510·76	11543·176	4·7539	2·8273
22·7	71·314	404·71	515·29	14697·083	4·7644	2·8314
22·8	71·628	408·28	519·84	11852·352	4·7749	2·8356
22·9	71·942	411·87	524·41	12008·989	4·7854	2·8397
23·0	72·257	415·48	529·00	12167·000	4·7958	2·8438
23·1	72·571	419·10	533·61	12326·891	4·8062	2·8479
23·2	72·885	422·73	538·24	12487·168	4·8166	2·8521
23·3	73·199	426·39	542·89	12649·337	4·8270	2·8562
23·4	73·513	430·05	547·56	12812·904	4·8373	2·8603

TABLE 27.—MATHEMATICAL TABLES.—*Continued.*

Circumference and area of circles, squares, cubes, square and cube roots.

n	πn $\bigcirc$	$\pi \dfrac{n^2}{4}$ $\bullet$	n^2	n^3	$\sqrt{n}$	$\sqrt[3]{n}$
23·5	73·827	433·74	552·25	12977·875	4·8477	2·8643
23·6	74·142	437·44	556·96	13144·256	4·8580	2·8684
23·7	74·456	441·15	561·69	13312·053	4·8683	2·8724
23·8	74·770	444·88	566·44	13481·272	4·8785	2·8765
23·9	75·084	448·63	471·21	13651·919	4·8888	2·8805
24·0	75·398	452·39	576·00	13824·000	4·8990	2·8845
24·1	75·712	456·17	580·81	13997·521	4·9092	2·8885
24·2	76·027	459·96	585·64	14172·488	4·9192	2·8925
24·3	76·341	463·77	590·49	14348·907	4·9295	2·8965
24·4	76·655	467·60	595·36	14526·784	4·9396	2·9004
24·5	76·969	471·44	600·25	14706·125	4·9497	2·9044
24·6	77·283	475·29	605·16	14886·936	4·9598	2·9083
24·7	77·597	479·16	610·09	15669·223	4·9699	2·9123
24·8	77·911	483·05	615·04	15252·992	4·9799	2·9162
24·9	78·226	486·96	620·01	15438·249	4·9899	2·9201
25·0	78·540	490·87	625·00	15625·000	5·0000	2·9241
25·1	78·854	494·81	630·01	15813·251	5·0099	2·9279
25·2	79·168	498·76	635·04	16008·008	5·0199	2·9318
25·3	79·482	502·73	640·09	16194·277	5·0299	2·9356
25·4	79·796	506·71	645·16	16387·064	5·0398	2·9395
25·5	80·111	510·71	650·25	16581·375	5·0497	2·9434
25·6	80·425	514·72	655·36	16777·216	5·0596	2·9472
25·7	80·739	518·75	660·49	16974·593	5·0695	2·9510
25·8	81·053	522·79	665·64	17173·512	5·0793	2·9549
25·9	81·367	526·85	670·81	17373·979	5·0892	2·9586
26·0	81·681	530·93	676·00	17576·000	5·0990	2·9624
26·1	81·996	535·02	681·21	17779·581	5·1088	2·9662
26·2	82·310	539·13	686·44	17984·728	5·1185	2·9701
26·3	82·624	543·25	691·69	18191·447	5·1283	2·9738
26·4	82·938	547·39	696·96	18399·744	5·1380	2·9776
26·5	83·252	551·55	702·25	18609·625	5·1478	2·9814
26·6	83·566	555·72	707·56	18821·096	5·1575	2·9851
26·7	83·881	559·90	712·89	19034·163	5·1672	2·9888
26·8	84·195	561·10	718·24	19248·832	5·1768	2·9926
26·9	84·509	568·32	723·61	19465·109	5·1865	2·9963
27·0	84·823	572·56	729·00	19683·000	5·1962	3·0000
27·1	85·137	576·80	734·41	19902·511	5·2057	3·0037
27·2	85·451	581·07	739·84	20123·648	5·2153	3·0074

TABLE 27.—MATHEMATICAL TABLES.—*Continued*.

Circumference and area of circles, squares, cubes, square and cube roots.

n	πn ◯	$\dfrac{n^2}{4}$ ●	n^2	n^3	$\sqrt{n}$	$\sqrt[3]{n}$
27·3	85·765	585·35	745·29	20346·417	5·2249	3·0111
27·4	86·080	589·65	750·76	20570·824	5·2345	3·0147
27·5	86·394	593·96	756·25	20796·875	5·2440	3·0184
27·6	86·708	598·29	761·76	21024·576	5·2535	3·0221
27·7	87·022	602·63	767·29	21253·933	5·2630	3·0257
27·8	87·336	606·99	772·84	21484·952	5·2725	3·0293
27·9	87·650	611·36	778·41	21717·639	5·2820	3·0330
28·0	87·965	615·75	784·00	21952·000	5·2915	3·0366
28·1	88·279	620·16	789·61	22188·041	5·3009	3·0402
28·2	88·593	624·58	795·24	22425·768	5·3103	3·0438
28·3	88·907	629·02	800·89	22665·187	5·3197	3·0474
28·4	89·221	633·47	806·56	22906·304	5·3291	3·0510
28·5	89·535	637·94	812·25	23149·125	5·3385	3·0546
28·6	89·850	642·42	817·96	23393·656	5·3478	3·0581
28·7	90·164	646·93	823·69	23639·903	5·3572	3·0617
28·8	90·478	651·44	829·44	23887·872	5·3665	3·0652
28·9	90·792	655·97	835·21	24137·569	5·3758	3·0688
29·0	91·106	660·52	841·00	24389·000	5·3852	3·0723
29·1	91·420	665·08	846·81	24642·171	5·3944	3·0758
29·2	91·735	669·66	852·64	24897·088	5·4037	3·0794
29·3	92·049	674·26	858·49	25153·757	5·4129	3·0829
29·4	92·363	678·87	864·36	25412·184	5·4221	3·0864
29·5	92·677	683·49	870·25	25672·875	5·4313	3·0899
29·6	92·991	688·13	876·16	25934·336	5·4405	3·0934
29·7	93·305	692·79	882·09	26198·073	5·4497	3·0968
29·8	93·619	697·47	888·04	26463·592	5·4589	3·1003
29·9	93·934	702·15	894·01	26730·899	5·4680	3·1038
30·0	94·248	706·86	900·00	27000·000	5·4772	3·1072
30·1	94·562	711·58	906·01	27270·901	5·4863	3·1107
30·2	94·876	716·32	912·04	27543·608	5·4954	3·1141
30·3	95·190	721·07	918·09	27818·127	5·5045	3·1176
30·4	95·504	725·83	924·16	28094·464	5·5136	3·1210
30·5	95·819	730·62	930·25	28372·625	5·5226	3·1244
30·6	96·133	735·42	936·36	28652·616	5·5317	3·1278
30·7	96·447	740·23	942·49	28934·443	5·5407	3·1312
30·8	96·761	745·06	948·64	29218·112	5·5497	3·1346
30·9	97·075	749·91	954·81	29503·629	5·5587	3·1380

63

TABLE 27.—MATHEMATICAL TABLES.—*Continued.*

Circumference and area of circles, squares, cubes, square and cube roots.

n	πn $\circ$	$\pi \dfrac{n^2}{4}$ $\bullet$	n^2	n^3	$\sqrt{n}$	$\sqrt[3]{n}$
31·0	97·389	754·77	961·00	29791·000	5·5678	3·1414
31·1	97·704	759·65	967·21	30080·231	5·5767	3·1448
31·2	98·018	764·54	673·44	30371·328	5·5857	3·1481
31·3	98·332	769·45	979·69	30664·297	5·5946	3·1515
31·4	98·646	774·37	985·96	30959·144	5·6035	3·1549
31·5	98·960	779·31	992·25	31255·875	5·6124	3·1582
31·6	99·274	784·27	998·56	31554·496	5·6213	3·1615
31·7	99·588	789·24	1004·89	31855·013	5·6302	3·1648
31·8	99·908	794·23	1011·24	32157·432	5·6391	3·1681
31·9	100·22	799·23	1017·61	32461·759	5·6480	3·1715
32·0	100·58	804·25	1024·00	32768·000	5·6569	3·1748
32·1	100·85	809·28	1030·41	33076·161	5·6656	3·1781
32·2	101·16	814·33	1036·84	33386·248	5·6745	3·1814
32·3	101·47	819·40	1043·29	33698·267	5·6833	3·1847
32·4	101·79	824·49	1049·76	34012·224	5·6921	3·1880
32·5	102·10	829·58	1056·25	34328·125	5·7008	3·1918
32·6	102·42	834·69	1062·76	34615·976	5·7056	3·1945
32·7	102·78	839·82	1069·29	34965·783	5·7183	3·1978
32·8	103·04	844·96	1075·84	35287·552	5·7271	3·2010
32·9	103·36	850·12	1082·41	35611·289	5·7358	3·2043
33·0	103·67	855·30	1089·00	35937·000	5·7447	3·2075
33·1	103·99	860·49	1095·61	36264·691	5·7532	3·2108
33·2	104·30	865·70	1102·24	36594·368	5·7619	3·2140
33·3	104·62	870·92	1108·89	36925·037	5·7706	3·2172
33·4	164·93	876·19	1115·56	37259·704	5·7792	3·2204
33·5	105·24	881·41	1122·25	37595·375	5·7879	3·2237
33·6	105·56	886·68	1128·96	37933·056	5·7965	3·2269
33·7	105·87	891·97	1135·69	38272·753	5·8051	3·2301
33·8	106·19	897·27	1142·44	38614·472	5·8137	3·2332
33·9	106·50	902·59	1149·21	38958·219	5·8223	3·2364
34·0	106·81	907·92	1156·00	39304·000	5·8310	3·2396
34·1	107·18	913·27	1162·81	39651·821	5·8395	3·2424
34·2	107·44	918·63	1160·64	40001·688	5·8480	3·2460
34·3	107·76	924·01	1176·49	40353·607	5·8566	3·2491
34·4	108·07	929·41	1183·36	40707·584	5·8751	3·2522
34·5	108·38	934·82	1190·25	41063·525	5·8736	3·2554
34·6	108·70	940·25	1197·16	41421·736	5·8821	3·2586
34·7	109·01	945·69	1204·09	41781·923	5·8906	3·2617

F

TABLE 27.—MATHEMATICAL TABLES.—*Continued.*

Circumference and area of circles, squares, cubes, square and cube roots.

n	πn $\bigcirc$	$\pi \dfrac{n^2}{4}$ ●	n^2	n^3	$\sqrt{n}$	$\sqrt[3]{n}$
34·8	109·33	951·15	1211·04	42144·192	5·8991	3·2618
34·9	109·64	956·62	1218·01	42508·549	5·9076	3·2679
35·0	109·96	962·11	1225·00	42875·000	5·9161	3·2710
35·1	110·27	967·62	1232·01	43243·551	5·9245	3·2742
35·2	110·58	973·14	1239·04	43614·208	5·9326	3·2773
35·3	110·90	978·68	1246·09	43986·977	5·9413	3·2804
35·4	111·21	984·23	1253·16	44361·864	5·9497	3·2835
35·5	111·53	989·80	1260·25	44738·875	5·9581	3·2866
35·6	111·84	995·38	1267·36	45118·016	5·9665	3·2897
35·7	112·15	1000·98	1274·49	45499·293	5·9749	3·2927
35·8	112·47	1006·60	1281·64	45882·712	5·9833	3·2958
35·9	112·78	1012·23	1288·81	46268·279	5·9916	3·2989
36·0	113·10	1017·88	1296·00	46656·000	6·0000	3·3019
36·1	113·41	1023·54	1303·21	47045·881	6·0083	3·3050
36·2	113·73	1029·22	1310·44	47437·928	6·0166	3·3080
36·3	114·04	1034·91	1317·69	47832·147	6·0249	3·3111
36·4	114·35	1040·62	1324·96	48228·544	6·0332	3·3141
36·5	114·67	1046·35	1332·25	48627·125	6·0415	3·3171
36·6	114·98	1052·09	1339·56	49017·896	6·0497	3·3202
36·7	115·30	1057·84	1346·89	49430·863	6·0580	3·3232
36·8	115·61	1063·62	1354·24	49836·032	6·0663	3·3262
36·9	115·92	1069·41	1361·61	50243·409	6·0745	3·3292
37·0	116·24	1075·21	1369·00	50653·000	6·0827	3·3322
37·1	116·55	1081·03	1376·41	51064·811	6·0909	3·3352
37·2	116·87	1086·87	1383·84	51478·848	6·0991	3·3382
37·3	117·18	1092·72	1391·29	51895·117	6·1078	3·3412
37·4	117·50	1098·58	1398·76	52313·624	6·1155	3·3442
37·5	117·81	1104·47	1406·25	52734·375	6·1237	3·3472
37·6	118·12	1110·36	1413·76	53157·376	6·1318	3·3501
37·7	118·44	1116·28	1421·29	53582·633	6·1400	3·3531
37·8	118·75	1122·21	1428·84	54010·152	6·1481	3·3561
37·9	119·07	1128·15	1436·41	54439·939	6·1563	3·3590
38·0	119·38	1134·11	1444·00	54872·000	6·1644	3·3620
38·1	119·69	1140·09	1451·61	55806·341	6·1725	3·3649
38·2	120·01	1146·08	1459·24	55742·968	6·1806	3·3679
38·3	120·32	1152·09	1466·89	56181·887	6·1887	3·3708
38·4	120·64	1158·12	1474·56	96623·104	6·1967	3·3737

TABLE 27.—MATHEMATICAL TABLES.—*Continued*.

Circumference and area of circles, squares, cubes, square and cube roots.

n	πn $\circ$	$\pi\dfrac{n^2}{4}$ ●	n^2	n^3	$\sqrt{n}$	$\sqrt[3]{n}$
38·5	120·95	1164·16	1482·25	57066·625	6·2048	3·3767
38·6	121·27	1170·21	1489·96	57512·456	6·2129	3·3797
38·7	121·58	1176·28	1497·69	57960·603	6·2209	3·3825
38·8	121·80	1182·37	1505·44	58411·072	6·2289	3·3854
38·9	122·21	1188·47	1513·21	58863·869	6·2370	3·3883
39·0	122·52	1194·59	1521·00	59319·000	6·2450	3·3912
39·1	122·84	1200·72	1528·81	59776·471	6·2530	3·3941
39·2	123·15	1206·87	1536·64	60236·288	6·2610	3·3970
39·3	123·46	1213·04	1544·49	60698·457	6·2689	3·3999
39·4	123·78	1219·22	1552·36	61162·984	6·2769	3·4028
39·5	124·09	1225·42	1560·25	61629·875	6·2849	3·4056
39·6	124·41	1231·63	1568·16	62099·136	6·2928	3·4085
39·7	124·72	1237·86	1576·09	62570·773	6·3008	3·4114
39·8	125·04	1244·10	1584·04	63044·792	6·3087	3·4142
39·9	125·35	1250·36	1592·01	63521·199	6·3166	3·4171
40·0	125·66	1264·64	1600·00	64000·000	6·3245	3·4200
40·1	125·98	1293·93	1608·01	64481·201	6·3325	3·4228
40·2	126·29	1223·23	1616·04	64964·808	6·3404	3·4256
40·3	126·61	1256·56	1624·09	65450·827	6·3482	3·4285
40·4	126·92	1297·90	1632·16	65939·264	6·3561	3·4313
40·5	127·23	1288·25	1640·25	66430·126	6·3639	3·4341
40·6	127·55	1294·62	1648·36	66923·416	6·3718	3·4370
40·7	127·86	1301·00	1656·49	67419·143	6·3796	3·4398
40·8	128·18	1307·41	1664·64	67911·312	6·3875	3·4426
40·9	128·49	1313·82	1672·81	68417·929	6·3953	3·4454
41·0	128·81	1320·25	1681·00	68921·000	6·4031	3·4482
41·1	129·12	1326·70	1689·21	69426·531	6·4109	3·4510
41·2	129·43	1333·17	1697·44	69934·528	6·4187	3·4538
41·3	129·75	1339·65	1705·69	70444·997	6·4265	3·4566
41·4	130·06	1346·14	1713·96	70957·944	6·4343	3·4594
41·5	130·38	1352·65	1722·25	71473·375	6·4421	3·4622
41·6	130·69	1359·18	1730·56	71991·296	6·4498	3·4650
41·7	131·00	1365·72	1738·89	72511·719	6·4575	3·4677
41·8	131·32	1372·28	1747·24	73034·682	6·4653	3·4705
41·9	131·63	1378·85	1755·61	73560·059	6·4730	3·4733
42·0	131·95	1385·44	1764·00	74088·000	6·4807	3·4760
42·1	132·26	1392·05	1772·41	74618·461	6·4884	3·4788
42·2	132·58	1398·67	1780·84	75151·448	6·4961	3·4815

TABLE 27.—MATHEMATICAL TABLES.—*Continued.*

. Circumference and area of circles, squares, cubes, square and cube roots.

n	πn $\bigcirc$	$\dfrac{n^2}{\pi \ 4}$ ●	n^2	n^3	$\sqrt{n}$	$\sqrt[3]{n}$
42·3	132·89	1405·31	1789·29	75686·967	6·5038	3·4813
42·4	133·20	1411·96	1797·76	76225·024	6·5115	3·4870
42·5	133·52	1418·63	1806·25	76765·625	6·5192	3·4898
42·6	133·83	1425·31	1814·76	77308·776	6·5268	3·4925
42·7	134·15	1432·01	1823·29	77854·483	6·5345	3·4952
42·8	134·46	1438·72	1831·84	78402·752	6·5422	3·4980
42·9	134·77	1445·45	1840·41	78953·589	6·5498	3·5007
43·0	135·09	1452·20	1849·00	79507·000	6·5574	3·5034
43·1	135·40	1458·96	1857·61	80062·991	6·5651	3·5061
43·2	135·72	1465·74	1866·24	80621·568	6·5727	3·5088
43·3	136·03	1472·54	1874·89	81182·737	6·5803	3·5115
43·4	136·35	1479·34	1883·56	81746·504	6·5879	3·5142
43·5	136·66	1486·17	1892·25	82312·875	6·5954	3·5169
43·6	136·97	1493·01	1900·96	82881·856	6·6030	3·5196
43·7	137·29	1499·87	1909·69	83453·453	6·6106	3·5223
43·8	137·60	1506·74	1918·44	84027·672	6·6182	3·5250
43·9	137·92	1513·63	1927·21	84604·519	6·6257	3·5277
44·0	138·23	1520·53	1936·00	85184·000	6·6333	3·5303
44·1	138·54	1527·45	1944·81	85766·121	6·6408	3·5330
44·2	138·86	1534·39	1953·64	86350·888	6·6483	3·5357
44·3	139·17	1541·34	1962·49	86938·307	6·6558	3·5384
44·4	139·49	1541·80	1971·36	87528·384	6·6633	3·5410
44·5	139·80	1555·28	1980·25	88121·125	6·6708	3·5437
44·6	140·12	1562·28	1989·16	88716·536	6·6783	3·5463
44·7	140·43	1569·30	1998·09	89314·623	6·6858	3·5490
44·8	140·74	1576·33	2007·04	89915·392	6·6933	3·5516
44·9	141·06	1583·37	2016·01	90518·849	6·7007	3·5543
45·0	141·37	1590·43	2025·00	91125·000	6·7082	3·5569
45·1	141·69	1597·51	2034·01	91733·851	6·7156	3·5595
45·2	142·00	1604·60	2043·04	92345·408	6·7231	3·5621
45·3	142·31	1611·71	2052·09	92959·677	6·7305	3·5648
45·4	142·63	1618·83	2061·16	93576·664	6·7379	3·5674
45·5	142·94	1625·97	2070·25	94196·375	6·7454	3·5700
45·6	143·26	1633·13	2079·36	94818·816	6·7528	3·5726
45·7	143·57	1640·30	2088·49	95443·993	6·7602	3·5752
45·8	143·88	1647·48	2097·64	96071·912	6·7676	3·5778
45·9	144·20	1654·63	2106·81	96702·579	6·7749	3·5805

TABLE 27.—MATHEMATICAL TABLES.—*Continued*.

Circumference and area of circles, squares, cubes, square and cube roots.

n	πn $\bigcirc$	$\pi \dfrac{n^2}{4}$ ●	n^2	n^3	$\sqrt{n}$	$\sqrt[3]{n}$
46·0	144·51	1661·90	2116·00	97336·000	6·7823	3·5830
46·1	144·83	1669·14	2125·21	97972·181	6·7897	3·5856
46·2	145·14	1676·39	2134·44	98611·128	6·7971	3·5882
46·3	145·46	1683·05	2143·69	99252·847	6·8044	3·5908
46·4	145·77	1690·98	2152·96	99897·344	6·8117	3·5984
46·5	146·08	1698·28	2162·25	100544·625	6·8191	3·5960
46·6	146·40	1705·54	2171·56	101194·696	6·8264	3·5986
46·7	146·71	1712·87	2180·89	101847·563	6·8337	3·6011
46·8	147·03	1720·21	2190·24	102503·232	6·8410	3·6037
46·9	147·34	1727·57	2199·61	103161·709	6·8484	3·6063
47·0	147·65	1734·94	2209·00	103823·000	6·8556	3·6088
47·1	147·97	1742·34	2218·41	104487·111	6·8629	3·6114
47·2	148·28	1749·74	2227·84	105154·048	6·8702	3·6139
47·3	148·60	1757·16	2237·29	105823·817	6·8775	3·6165
47·4	148·91	1764·60	2246·76	106496·424	6·8847	3·6190
47·5	149·23	1772·05	2256·25	107171·875	6·8920	3·6216
47·6	149·54	1779·52	2265·76	107850·176	6·8993	3·6241
47·7	149·85	1787·01	2275·29	108531·333	6·9065	3·6267
47·8	150·17	1794·51	2284·84	109215·352	6·9137	3·6292
47·9	150·48	1802·03	2294·41	109902·239	6·9209	3·6317
48·0	150·80	1809·56	2304·00	110592·000	6·9282	3·6342
48·1	151·11	1817·11	2313·61	111284·641	6·9354	3·6368
48·2	151·42	1824·67	2323·24	111980·168	6·9426	3·6393
48·3	151·74	1832·25	2332·89	112678·587	6·9498	3·6418
48·4	152·05	1839·84	2342·56	113379·904	6·9570	3·6443
48·5	152·37	1847·45	2352·25	114084·125	6·9642	3·6468
48·6	152·68	1855·08	2361·96	114791·256	6·9714	3·6493
48·7	153·00	1862·72	2371·69	115501·303	6·9785	3·6518
48·8	153·31	1870·38	2381·44	116214·272	6·9857	3·6543
48·9	153·62	1878·05	2391·21	116930·169	6·9928	3·6568
49·0	153·94	1885·74	2401·00	117649·000	7·0000	3·6593
49·1	154·25	1893·45	2410·81	118370·771	7·0071	3·6318
49·2	154·57	1901·17	2420·64	119095·488	7·0143	3·6643
49·3	154·88	1908·90	2430·49	119823·157	7·0214	3·6668
49·4	155·19	1916·65	2440·36	120558·784	7·0285	3·6692
49·5	155·51	1924·42	2450·25	121287·875	7·0356	3·6717
49·6	155·82	1932·21	2460·16	122023·936	7·0427	3·6742
49·7	156·14	1940·00	2470·09	122763·473	7·0498	3·6767

TABLE 27.—MATHEMATICAL TABLES.—*Continued.*

Circumference and area of circles, squares, cubes, square and cube roots.

n	πn ○	$\pi\dfrac{n^2}{4}$ ●	n^2	n^3	$\sqrt{n}$	$\sqrt[3]{n}$
49·8	156·45	1947·82	2480·04	123505·992	7·0569	3·6791
49·9	156·77	1955·65	2490·01	124251·499	7·0640	3·6816
50·0	157·08	1963·50	2500·00	125000·000	7·0711	3·6340
51·0	160·22	2042·82	2601·00	132651·000	7·1414	3·7084
52·0	163·36	2123·72	2704·00	140608·000	7·2111	3·7325
53·0	166·50	2206·19	2809·00	148877·000	7·2801	3·7563
54·0	169·64	2290·22	2916·00	157464·000	7·3485	3·7798
55·0	172·78	2375·83	3025·00	166375·000	7·4162	3·8030
56·0	175·93	2463·01	3136·00	175616·000	7·4833	3·8259
57·0	179·07	2551·76	3249·00	185193·000	7·5498	3·8485
58·0	182·21	2642·08	3364·00	195112·000	7·6158	3·8709
59·0	185·35	2733·97	3481·00	205379·000	7·6811	3·8930
60·0	188·49	2827·44	3600·00	210000·000	7·7460	3·9149
61·0	191·68	2922·47	3721·00	226981·000	7·8102	3·9365
62·0	194·77	3019·07	3844·00	238328·000	7·8740	3·9579
63·0	197·92	3117·25	3969·00	250047·000	7·9373	3·9791
64·0	201·06	3216·99	4096·00	262144·000	8·0000	4·0000
65·0	204·20	3318·31	4225·00	274625·000	8·0623	4·0207
66·0	207·34	3421·20	4356·09	287496·000	8·1240	4·0112
67·0	210·48	3525·66	4489·00	300763·000	8·1854	4·0615
68·0	213·63	3631·69	4624·00	314432·000	8·2462	4·0817
69·0	216·77	3739·29	4761·00	328509·000	8·3066	4·1016
70·0	219·91	3848·46	4900·00	343000·000	8·3666	4·1213
71·0	223·05	3959·20	5041·00	357911·000	8·4261	4·1408
72·0	226·19	4071·51	5184·00	373248·000	8·4853	4·1602
73·0	229·33	4185·39	5329·00	389017·000	8·5440	4·1793
74·0	232·47	4300·85	5476·00	405224·000	8·6023	4·1983
75·0	235·62	4417·87	5625·00	421875·000	8·6603	4·2172
76·0	238·76	4536·47	5776·00	438976·000	8·7178	4·2358
77·0	241·90	4656·63	5929·00	456533·000	8·7750	4·2543
78·0	245·04	4778·37	6084·00	474552·000	8·8318	4·2727
79·0	248·18	4901·68	6241·00	493039·000	8·8882	4·2908
80·0	251·32	5026·56	6400·00	512000·000	8·9443	4·3089
81·0	254·47	5158·01	6561·00	531441·000	9·0000	4·3267
82·0	257·61	5281·03	6724·00	551368·000	9·0554	4·3445
83·0	260·75	5410·62	6889·00	571787·000	9·1104	4·3621
84·0	263·89	5541·78	7056·00	592704·000	9·1652	4·3795

TABLE 27.—MATHEMATICAL TABLES.—*Continued.*

Circumference and area of circles, squares, cubes, square and cube roots.

n	πn ○	$\pi \dfrac{n^2}{4}$ ●	n^2	n^3	$\sqrt{n}$	$\sqrt[3]{n}$
85·0	267·03	5674·50	7225·00	614125·000	9·2195	4·3968
86·0	270·17	5808·81	7396·00	636056·000	9·2736	4·4140
87·0	273·32	5944·69	7569·00	658503·000	9·3274	4·4310
88·0	276·46	6082·13	7744·00	681472·000	9·3808	4·4480
89·0	279·60	6221·13	7921·00	704969·000	9·4330	4·4647
90·0	282·74	6361·74	8100·00	729000·000	9·4868	4·4814
91·0	285·88	6503·89	8281·00	753571·000	9·5894	4·4979
92·0	289·02	6647·62	8464·00	778688·000	9·5917	4·5144
93·0	292·17	6792·92	8649·00	804357·000	9·6437	4·5307
94·0	295·31	6939·78	8836·00	830584·000	9·6954	4·5468
95·0	298·45	7088·23	9025·00	857375·000	9·7468	4·5629
96·0	301·59	7238·24	9216·00	884736·000	9·7980	4·5789
97·0	304·73	7389·83	9409·00	912673·000	9·8489	4·5947
98·0	307·87	7542·98	9601·00	941192·000	9·8995	4·6104
99·0	311·02	7697·68	9801·00	970299·000	9·9499	4·6261
100·0	314·16	7854·00	100000·00	1000000·000	10·0000	4·6416

Approximately $\sqrt{a^2 \pm b} = a \pm \dfrac{b}{2a}$ and $\sqrt[3]{a^3 \pm b} = a \pm \dfrac{b}{3a^2}$

TABLE 28.—FORMULÆ FOR MENSURATION OF AREAS AND SOLID CONTENTS.

1.—TRIANGLE.

Area $= \dfrac{1}{2} \times$ base $\times$ height.

If all the sides, a, b, c are known and half their sum is represented by s, so that $s = \dfrac{a+b+c}{2}$ then

$$A = \sqrt{s(s-a)(s-b)(s-c)}$$

2.—CIRCLE.

Area of circle, if $d =$ diameter $r =$ radius and $\pi = 3.14159$

$$A = \frac{\pi}{4}d^2 = r^2 \pi \ldots \left(\frac{\pi}{4} = 0.7854\right)$$

$$d = 1.12838\sqrt{A}$$

Area of segment of circle of an arc of a°

$$A = \left(\frac{a}{180}\pi - \sin a\right)\frac{r^2}{2}$$

Or if d is the diameter and h the height of segment, calculate $\dfrac{h}{d}$ and find the value x in the following table corresponding to $\dfrac{h}{d}$; multiply the square of the diameter by x, the result is the area of the segment.

Area of segment $= xd^2$.

$\dfrac{h}{d}$	x	$\dfrac{h}{d}$	x	$\dfrac{h}{d}$	x	$\dfrac{h}{d}$	x	$\dfrac{h}{d}$	x
·01	·00133	·11	·04701	·21	·11990	·31	·20737	·41	·30319
·02	·00375	·12	·05338	·22	·12811	·32	·21667	·42	·31304
·03	·00687	·13	·06000	·23	·13646	·33	·22603	·43	·32293
·04	·01054	·14	·06688	·24	·14495	·34	·23547	·44	·33284
·05	·01468	·15	·07387	·25	·15355	·35	·24498	·45	·34278
·06	·01924	·16	·08111	·26	·16226	·36	·25455	·46	·35274
·07	·02417	·17	·08854	·27	·17109	·37	·26418	·47	·36272
·08	·02944	·18	·09613	·28	·18002	·38	·27386	·48	·37270
·09	·03501	·19	·10390	·29	·18905	·39	·28359	·49	·38270
·10	·04087	·20	·11182	·30	·19817	·40	·29337	·50	·39270

3.—CONE AND PYRAMID.

Solid content: $S = \dfrac{1}{3}$ base $\times$ height.

Area of convex surface of right cone: When $s = $ side of cone $= \sqrt{r^2 \times h^2}$, where $r = $ radius of base and $h = $ height of cone, the area of convex surface will be

$$A = \pi r s.$$

4.—CYLINDER.

Area of convex surface $A = 2\pi r h$.
Content of cylinder $\quad S = $ base $\times$ height.

5.—SPHERE.

Convex surface $\quad A = 4\pi r^2$
Surface of segment $\quad A = 2\pi rh$, $h = $ height of segment
Solid content of sphere $\quad S = \dfrac{4}{3} r^3 \pi = 4{\cdot}1888 r^3$

Solid content of sphere $S = \dfrac{1}{6}\pi d^3 = 0{\cdot}5236 d^3$

Radius $\quad r = 0{\cdot}62035 \sqrt[3]{\text{content}}$

Content of segment of sphere: If a is the radius of the sectional area, h the height of the segment, and r the radius of the sphere,

$$S = \dfrac{1}{6}\pi h (3a^2 + h^2)$$

$$= \dfrac{1}{3}\pi h^2 (3r - h)$$

Solid content of spherical zone : If a and b are the respective radii of the two terminal surfaces, and h the height,

$$S = \frac{1}{6}\,\pi h\,(3a^2 + 3b^2 + h^2)$$

TABLE 29.—WEIGHTS AND MEASURES OF DIFFERENT COUNTRIES.

1. METRIC SYSTEM (compulsory in France, Germany, Austria, the Netherlands, Belgium, Luxembourg, Switzerland, Italy, Greece, Turkey, Roumania, Spain, Portugal, and most of the South American Republics; optional in Great Britain and the United States.

    1 metre (m.)=443·296 Paris lignes = 3·280899 English feet=3·18620 Prussian feet=1·00000301 metre des archives.

    1 kilometre (km.)=10 hectometre (hm.)=0·6214 English mile=0·1328 Prussian mile=0·9375 Russian verst=0·5390 nautical mile=0·1347 geographical mile (15 to 1 degree of longitude).

    1 lieue (France)=1 myriametre=10 km.

    1 German meile=7½ km.=0·996 Prussian mile=4·66 English miles.

    1 hectare (ha.)=100 ares (a.)=10,000 qm.=0·01 qkm.=2·471 English acres.

    1 litre (l.)=0·001 cbm.=1,000 ccm.=0·2201 gallons.

    1 hectolitre (hl.)=0·1 cbm.=100 l.=22·01 gallons.

    1 kilogramme (kg.)=1,000 g.=weight of 1 litre of water at+4° C.=2 German and Swiss pounds (zollpfund)=0·999999842 kilogramme prototype=2·2046 pound avoirdupois = 1·7857 Austrian pound = 2·3511 Swedish pounds=2·4419 Russian pounds.

    1 gramme (g.)=15·432 grains (English).

    1 quintal=100 kg.=196·84lb. avoirdupois=1cwt. 3qr. 0·84lb.

    1 metrical ton=1,000 kg.=0·9842 English ton=1·1023 American short ton (at 2,000lb).

2. GREAT BRITAIN AND IRELAND.

    1 foot=0·3047943 m.

    1 inch=25·3995 mm.

    1 yard=0·9143835 m.

    1 fathom=2 yards.

    1 rod (pole, perch)=5½ yards=5·029109 m.

    1 statute mile=8 furlongs=320 poles=1,760 yards=5,280 feet=1·6093 kilometre (km.).

    1 nautical mile=$\frac{1}{15}$th degree (at the equator).

      6,082·66 feet=1854·96 m.

    1 acre=4 roods=160 poles=0·40467 ha.

    1 square mile=640 acres.

    1 gallon=4 quarts=8 pints=277·274 cubic inches=4·536 litres.

    1 cubic foot=28·3153 l.

    1 cubic inch=16·3862 ccm.

    1 quarter=8 bushels=32 pecks=64 gallons=2·903 hl.

    1 bushel=8 gallons=0·3628 hl.

    1 fluid ounce=$\frac{1}{20}$th pint=28·35 ccm.

    1 pound avoirdupois (lb.)=16 ounces (oz.)=7,000 grains=0·4535926 kg.

    1 ounce avoirdupois=437½ grains=28·35 g.

    1 gallon=10 lb. water=70,000 grains.

    1 hundredweight (cwt.)=4 quarters (qr.)=8 stones=112 lb.=50·8024 kg.

1 ton=20 cwt.=2,240 lb.=1016·648 kg.
Apothecaries' Weight.
1 pound troy=12 ounces troy=96 drams=288 scruples=5,760 grains=
373·24195 g.
1 ounce troy=8 drams=24 scruples=480 grains=31·1035 g.
1 ounce troy (for gold and precious stones)=20 pennyweight (dwt.)=480
grains.
1 grain (common to avoirdupois and troy weight)=0·06479895 g.

3. Austria (old measures and weights now abolished for the metric system).
1 foot=0·316102 m., at 12 inches of 12 lines each.
3 ruthen=5 klafter=30 feet=360 zoll.
1 meile=4,000 klafter=7586·455 m.
1 maass=1·415 l.
1 eimer=40 maass=160 seidel.
1 metze=61·4995 l.
1 Wiener pfund=560·012 g.
1 centner=5 stein=100 pfund=3200 loth.

4. Denmark and Norway employ as unit of measure the Prussian foot, as
unit of weight the units of the metrical system, viz., kilos, etc.

5. Prussia (old system, now abolished for the metric system).
1 foot (Rhenish foot)=12 zoll (inches)=144 linien=0·313853 m.
1 ruthe=12 fuss=3·76624 m.
1 lachter (fathom)=80 zoll=2·09326 m.
1 meile=24,000 fuss=7,532·5 m.
1 morgen=180 square ruthen=0·2553 ha.
1 quart=64 cubic inches=$\frac{1}{27}$ cubic foot=1·14503 l.
1 scheffel=16 Metzen=48 quarts=0·54961 hl.
1 tonne=4 scheffel=2·19846 hl.
1 klafter=108 cubic fuss=3·3389 cbm.
1 schachtruthe=144 cubic fuss=4·4519 cbm.
1 pfund=30 loth=300 quentchen=500 g.
1 centner=100 pfund=50 kg. (Formerly 1 pfund=32 loth=467·711 g;
1 centner=110 pfund.)

6. Russia.
1 foot=1 English foot.
1 sashehn=7 feet=3 arshin=12 tchetvert=48 vershok=2·13357 m.
1 verst=500 sashehn=1066·78 m.
1 dessatine=2400 square sashehns=10925 m.
1 vedro=10 krushky (stoof)=12·299 l.
1 tchetvert=1 osmini=4 payok=8 tchetverik=209·9 l.
1 pound=32 loth=96 solotnik=9216 doli=0·9028 Eng. lb.=409·531 g.
1 berkovets=10 pud=400 pounds=163·81 kg.
1 pud=40 pounds=36·112 Eng. lbs.=16·3805 kg.

7. Sweden.
1 foot=10 zoll (inches)=100 lines=0·97408 Eng. foot=0·296901 m.
1 famn (fathom)=3 alnar (ells)=6 feet=5·58445 Eng. feet=1·7814 m.
1 mile=6000 fathoms=6·6417 Eng. statute miles=10·6884 km.
1 kanne=100 cubic inches=0·57694 Eng. gallon=2·617 l.
1 skalpund=100 korn (at 100 art)=0·9378 Eng. lb.=425·3395 g.
1 centner=100 skalpund.
1 skipspund=20 liespund=400 skalpund.

8. SWITZERLAND. Metrical measure and weight. Sometimes there is still
employed:
1 fuss=0·3000 m.=0·9843 Eng. ft.
1 juchart=36 are=0·88956 Eng. acre.
1 maass=1·51 l.
1 saum=100 maass=151 l.

9. UNITED STATES. Weights and measures as in Great Britain, but along-
side the "long ton" (gross ton) of 2,240 lbs. more frequently the
"short ton" (net ton) of 2,000 lbs.=907·1852 kg.=0·89285 long ton is
employed.

SQUARE FEET, SQUARE METRE.
1 square metre (qm.)=10·764 square feet (English and Russian)=10·008
square feet (Austrian)=10·152 square feet (Prussian and Danish)=
11·344 square feet (Swedish).
1 square foot (English and Russian)=0·09290 square metre.

CUBIC FEET, CUBIC METRE.
1 cubic metre (cbm.)=35·316 cubic feet (English and Russian).
1   „   „   =31·66   „   (Austrian).
1   „   „   =32·346   „   (Prussian and Danish).
1   „   „   =38·209   „   (Swedish).
1 cubic foot (English and Russian)=0·028315 cubic metre.

1 KILOGRAMME PER RUNNING METRE
=0·6719 English pound per running foot.
=0·6277 zollpfund per Prussian foot.

1 KILOGRAMME PER SQUARE CENTIMETRE.
(for steam pressure)
=14·233 English pounds per square inch.
=13·681 zollpfund per Prussian square inch.
=13·878 zollpfund per Austrian square inch.

HORSE POWERS (per second).

kg-m.	Austria. foot-pounds.	Prussia. foot-pounds.	England. foot-pounds.	Sweden. foot-pounds.	Russia. foot-pounds.
75	474·53	477·93	542·47	598·90	600·85
76·011	481·11	481·56	550	602·14	609·19

75 kilogram-metres taken as unit.
550 English foot-pounds taken as unit.
=1 Admiralty horse power per second;
or, 33,000 foot-pounds per minute.

TABLE 30.—TABLES FOR REDUCING ENGLISH TO METRICAL WEIGHTS AND MEASURES, AND VICE VERSA.

REDUCTION OF METRICAL MEASURE TO ENGLISH MEASURE.

Meter. Sqr.-M. Cub.-M.	Feet.	Inches.	Square Feet.	Square Inches.	Cubic Feet.	Cubic Inches.
1	3·2809	89·8706	10·7642	1550·05	35·3161	61026·2
2	6·5618	78·7412	21·5284	3100·09	70·6322	122052·4
3	9·8427	118·1118	32·2926	4650·13	105·9483	183078·6
4	13·1235	157·4824	43·0568	6200·18	141·2644	244104·9
5	16·4044	196·8530	53·8210	7750·23	176·5805	305131·1
6	19·6853	236·2237	64·5852	9300·27	211·8966	366157·3
7	22·9662	275·5943	75·3494	10850·31	247·2126	427183·5
8	26·2471	314·9649	86·1136	12400·36	282·5287	488209·7
9	29·5280	354·8355	96·8778	13950·40	317·8448	549235·9

ENGLISH FEET=METRES.

Ft.	0	1	2	3	4	5	6	7	8	9
0	0·0000	0·3048	0·6096	0·9144	1·2192	1·5240	1·8288	2·1336	2·4384	2·7432
10	3·0479	3·3527	3·6575	3·9623	4·2671	4·5719	4·8767	5·1815	5·4863	5·7911
20	6·0959	6·4007	6·7055	7·0103	7·3151	7·6199	7·9247	8·2295	8·5342	8·8390
30	9·1438	9·4486	9·7534	10·058	10·363	10·668	10·973	11·277	11·582	11·887
40	12·192	12·497	12·801	13·106	13·411	13·716	14·021	14·325	14·630	14·935
50	15·240	15·545	15·849	16·154	16·459	16·764	17·068	17·373	17·678	17·983
60	18·288	18·592	18·897	19·202	19·507	19·812	20·116	20·421	20·726	21·031
70	21·336	21·640	21·945	22·250	22·555	22·860	23·164	23·469	23·774	24·079
80	24·384	24·688	24·993	25·298	25·603	25·908	26·211	26·517	26·882	27·127
90	27·432	27·736	28·041	28·346	28·651	28·955	29·260	29·565	29·870	30·175
100	30·479	30·784	31·089	31·394	31·699	32·003	32·308	32·613	32·918	33·223
110	33·527	33·832	34·137	34·442	34·747	35·051	35·356	35·661	35·966	36·271
120	36·575	36·880	37·185	37·490	37·795	38·099	38·404	38·709	39·014	39·318
130	39·623	39·928	40·233	40·538	40·842	41·147	41·452	41·757	42·062	42·366
140	42·671	42·976	43·281	43·586	43·890	44·195	44·500	44·805	45·110	45·414
150	45·719	46·024	46·329	46·634	46·938	47·243	47·548	47·853	48·158	48·462
160	48·767	49·072	49·377	49·642	49·986	50·291	50·596	50·901	51·205	51·510
170	51·815	52·120	52·425	52·729	53·034	53·339	53·664	53·943	54·253	54·558
180	54·863	55·168	55·473	55·777	56·082	56·387	56·692	56·997	57·301	57·606
190	57·911	58·216	58·521	58·825	59·130	59·435	59·740	60·045	60·349	60·654

ENGLISH INCHES=MILLIMETERS.

Inches.	Millimeters.	Inches.	Millimeters.	Inches.	Millimeters.
1/64	0·39	1	25·4	7	177·8
1/32	0·79	2	50 8	8	203·2
1/16	1·59	3	76·2	9	228·6
1/8	3·17	4	101·6	10	254·0
1/4	6·35	5	127·0	11	279·4
1/2	12·70	6	152·4	12	304·8

ENGLISH SQUARE FEET=SQUARE METRES.

Sq. Feet.	0	1	2	3	4	5	6	7	8	9
0	0·0000	0·0929	0·1858	0·2787	0·3716	0·4645	0·5574	0·6503	0·7432	0·8361
10	0 9290	1·0219	1·1148	1·2077	1·3006	1·3935	1·4864	1·5793	1·6722	1·7651
20	1·8580	1·9509	2·0438	2·1367	2·2296	2·3225	2·4154	2·5083	2·6012	2·6941
30	2·7870	2·8799	2·9728	3·0657	3·1586	3·2515	3·3444	3·4373	3·5302	3·6231
40	3·7160	3·8089	3·9018	3·9947	4·0876	4·1805	4·2734	4·3663	4·4592	4·5521
50	4·6450	4·7379	4·8308	4·9237	5·0166	5·1095	5·2024	5·2953	5·3882	5·4811
60	5·5740	5·6669	5·7598	5·8527	5·9456	6·0385	6·1314	6·2243	6·3172	6·4101
70	6·5030	6·5959	6·6888	6·7817	6·8746	6·9675	7·0604	7·1533	7·2462	7·3391
80	7·4320	7·5249	7·6178	7·7107	7·8036	7·8965	7·9894	8·0823	8·1752	8·2681
90	8·3610	8·4539	8·5468	8·6397	8·7326	8·8255	8·9184	9·0113	9·1042	9·1971

ENGLISH SQUARE INCHES=SQUARE CENTIMETRES.

Sq. Ins.	0	1	2	3	4	5	6	7	8	9
0	0·0000	6·4514	12·903	19·354	25·805	32·257	38·708	45·160	51·611	58·062
10	64·514	70·965	77·416	83·868	90·319	96·771	103·22	109·67	116·12	122·58
20	129·03	135·48	141·93	148·38	154·83	161·28	167·74	174·19	180·64	187·09
30	193·54	199·99	206·44	212·90	219·35	225·80	232·25	238·70	245·15	251·60
40	258·05	264·51	270·96	277·41	283·86	290·31	296·76	303·21	309·67	316·12
50	322·57	329·02	335·47	341·92	348·37	354·83	361·28	367·73	374·18	380·63
60	387·08	393·53	399·98	406·44	412·89	419·34	425·79	432·24	438·69	445·14
70	451·60	458·05	464·50	470·95	477·40	483·85	490·30	496·76	503·21	509·69
80	516·11	522·56	525·01	535·46	541·91	548·37	554·82	561·27	567·72	574·17
90	580·62	587·07	593·53	599·98	606·43	612·88	619·33	625·78	632·23	638·66

ENGLISH CUBIC FEET = CUBIC METRES.

Cub. Feet	0	1	2	3	4	5	6	7	8	9
0	0·0000	0·0283	0·0566	0·0849	0·1133	0·1416	0·1699	0·1982	0·2265	0·2548
10	0·2832	0·3115	0·3398	0·3681	0·3964	0·4247	0·4530	0·4814	0·5097	0·5380
20	0·5663	0·5946	0·6229	0·6513	0·6796	0·7079	0·7362	0·7645	0·7928	0·8211
30	0·8494	0·8778	0·9061	0·9344	0·9627	0·9910	1·0194	1·0477	1·0760	1·1043
40	1·1326	1·1609	1·1892	1·2176	1·2459	1·2742	1·3025	1·3308	1·3591	1·3875
50	1·4158	1·4441	1·4724	1·5007	1·5290	1·5573	1·5857	1·6140	1·6423	1·6706
60	1·6989	1·7272	1·7555	1·7839	1·8122	1·8405	1·8688	1·8971	1·9254	1·9538
70	1·9821	2·0104	2·0387	2·0670	2·0953	2·1236	2·1520	2·1803	2·2086	2·2369
80	2·2652	2·2935	2·3219	2·3502	2·3785	2·4068	2·4351	2·4634	2·4917	2·5201
90	2·5484	2·5767	2·6050	2·6333	2·6616	2·6900	2·7183	2·7466	2·7749	2·8032

ENGLISH CUBIC INCHES = CUBIC CENTIMETRES.

Cub. Inch	0	1	2	3	4	5	6	7	8	9
0	0·0000	16·386	32·772	49·159	65·545	81·931	98·317	114·70	131·09	147·48
10	163·86	180·25	196·63	213·02	229·41	245·79	262·18	278·56	294·95	311·34
20	327·72	344·11	360·50	376·88	393·27	409·65	426·04	442·43	458·81	475·20
30	491·59	507·97	524·36	540·74	557·13	573·52	589·90	606·29	622·67	639·06
40	655·45	671·83	688·22	704·61	720·99	737·38	753·76	770·15	786·54	802·92
50	819·31	835·69	852·08	868·47	884·85	901·24	917·63	934·01	950·40	966·78
60	983·17	999·56	1015·9	1032·3	1048·7	1065·1	1081·5	1097·9	1114·3	1130·6
70	1147·0	1163·4	1179·8	1196·2	1212·6	1229·0	1245·3	1261·7	1278·1	1294·5
80	1310·9	1327·3	1343·7	1360·1	1376·4	1392·8	1409·2	1425·6	1440·9	1458·4
90	1474·8	1491·1	1507·5	1523·9	1540·3	1556·7	1573·1	1589·5	1605·8	1622·2

ENGLISH POUNDS = KILOGRAMMES.

Lbs.	0	1	2	3	4	5	6	7	8	9
0	0·0000	0·4536	0·9072	1·3608	1·8144	2·2680	2·7216	3·1751	3·6287	4·0823
10	4·5359	4·9895	5·4431	5·8967	6·3503	6·8039	7·2575	7·7111	8·1647	8·6183
20	9·0719	9·5254	9·9790	10·433	10·886	11·340	11·793	12·247	12·701	13·154
30	13·608	14·061	14·515	14·969	15·422	15·876	16·329	16·783	17·237	17·690
40	18·144	18·597	19·051	19·504	19·958	20·412	20·865	21·319	21·772	22·226
50	22·680	23·133	23·587	24·040	24·494	24·948	25·401	25·855	26·308	26·762
60	27·216	27·669	28·123	28·576	29·030	29·484	29·937	30·391	30·844	31·296
70	31·751	32·205	32·659	33·112	33·566	34·019	34·473	34·927	35·380	35·834
80	36·287	36·741	37·195	37·648	38·102	38·555	39·009	39·463	39·916	40·370
90	40·823	41·277	41·731	42·184	42·638	43·091	43·545	43·998	44·452	44·906

ENGLISH TONS = KILOGRAMMES.

Tons.	0	1	2	3	4	5	6	7	8	9
0	0·0000	1016	2032	3048	4064	5080	6096	7112	8129	9145
10	10161	11177	12193	13209	14225	15241	16257	17273	18289	19305
20	20321	21337	22353	23369	24386	25402	26418	27434	28450	29466
30	30482	31498	32514	33530	34546	35562	36578	37594	38610	39627
40	40643	41659	42675	43691	44707	45723	46739	47755	48771	49787
50	50803	51819	52835	53851	54868	55884	56900	57916	58932	59948
60	60964	61980	62996	64012	65028	66044	67060	68076	69092	70108
70	71125	72141	73157	74173	75189	76205	77221	78237	79253	80269
80	81285	82302	83317	84333	85346	86366	87382	88398	89414	90430
90	91446	92246	93478	94494	95510	96526	97542	98558	99574	100590

ENGLISH GRAINS = GRAMMES.

Grains.	0	1	2	3	4	5	6	7	8	9
—	0	·065	·1296	·194	·259	·324	·389	·454	·518	·583
10	·648	·713	·778	·842	·907	·972	1·037	1·102	1·166	1·231
20	1·296	1·361	1·426	1·490	1·555	1·620	1·685	1·749	1·814	1·879
30	1·944	2·009	2·074	2·138	2·203	2·268	2·333	2·397	2·462	2·527
40	2·592	2·657	2·721	2·786	2·851	2·916	2·981	3·045	3·110	3·175
50	3·240	3·305	3·369	3·434	3·499	3·564	3·629	3·693	3·758	3·823
60	3·888	3·953	4·018	4·082	4·147	4·212	4·277	4·341	4·406	4·471
70	4·536	4·601	4·666	4·730	4·795	4·860	4·925	4·989	5·054	5·119
80	5·184	5·249	5·314	5·378	5·443	5·508	5·573	5 637	5·702	5·767
90	5·832	5·897	5·962	6·026	6·091	6·156	6·221	6·286	6·350	6·415

GRAMMES = ENGLISH GRAINS.

Grammes.	0	·1	·2	·3	·4	·5	·6	·7	·8	·9
0	0	1·543	3·086	4·629	6·172	7·716	9·259	10·802	12·345	13·808
1	15·432	16·975	18·518	20·061	21·604	23·148	24·691	26·234	27·777	29·320
2	30·864	32·407	33·950	35·493	37·036	38·580	40·123	41·666	43·209	44·752
3	46·296	47·839	49·382	50·925	52·468	54·012	55·555	57·098	58·641	60·184
4	61·728	63·271	64·814	66·375	67·900	69·444	70·987	72·530	74·073	75·616
5	77·160	78·703	80·243	81·789	83·332	84·876	86·419	87·962	89·505	91·048

TABLE 31.—WEIGHT OF SHEET METALS.

WEIGHT OF A SUPERFICIAL FOOT.

Thick-ness.	Wrought Iron.	Cast Iron.	Steel.	Copper.	Brass.	Lead.	Zinc.
Inches.	Lb.	Lb.	Lb.	Lb.	Lb.	Lb.	Lb.
1/16	2·53	2·34	2·55	2·89	2·78	3·71	2·31
1/8	5·05	4·69	5·10	5·78	5·47	7·42	4·69
3/16	7·58	7·03	7·66	8·67	8·20	11·13	7·03
1/4	10·10	9·38	10·21	11·76	10·94	14·83	9·38
5/16	12·63	11·72	12·76	14·45	13·67	18·54	11·72
3/8	15·16	14·06	15·31	17·34	16·41	22·25	14·06
7/16	17·68	16·41	17·87	20·23	19·14	25·96	16·41
1/2	20·21	18·75	20·42	23·13	21·88	29·67	18·75
9/16	22·73	21·09	22·97	26·02	24·61	33·33	21·09
5/8	25·27	23·44	25·52	28·91	27·34	37·08	23·44
11/16	27·79	25·78	28·07	31·80	30·08	40·79	25·78
3/4	30·31	28·13	30·68	34·69	32·81	44·50	28·13
13/16	32·84	30·47	33·18	37·58	35·55	48·21	30·47
7/8	35·87	32·81	35·73	40·47	38·28	51·92	32·81
15/16	37·90	35·16	38·28	43·36	41·02	55·63	35·16
1	40·42	37·50	40·83	46·25	43·75	59·33	37·50

TABLE 32.—COINAGE OF DIFFERENT COUNTRIES.

	Exact Value in		
	£	s.	d.
AUSTRIA—			
1 Vereins Thaler (=1 former Prussian Thaler)	0	2	11·24
1 Gulden=100 Neukreuzer	0	1	11·49
1 Maria Theresia Thaler	0	4	1·46
1 Dukaten...	0	9	4·78
4 Gulden Gold=10 Francs ; 8 Gulden Gold=20 Francs			
BELGIUM=France.			
BRAZIL—			
1 Milreis=1,000 Reales.....................................	0	2	8·48
CHILI—			
1 Peso=100 Centavos.......................................	0	3	11·58
DENMARK—			
1 Rigsbankdaler=6 Marks=90 Skillings	0	2	2·67
1 Krone=100 Oere	0	1	0·83
EAST INDIA—			
1 Rupee=16 Annas...	0	2	0
EGYPT—			
1 Bag of Gold=80,000 Piastres	278	2	10
1 Piastre=40 Para...	0	0	2·5

TABLE 82.—COINAGE OF DIFFERENT COUNTRIES.—*Continued.*

	Exact Value in		
	£	s.	d.
FRANCE—			
1 Franc=100 Centimes	0	0	9·516
The 20-Franc piece contains 5·8065 g. fine gold	0	15	10·31
The 5-Franc piece contains 22·5 g. fine silver	0	8	11·58
GERMAN EMPIRE—			
1 Mark=100 Pfennig..........................	0	0	11·748
The 20-Mark piece contains 7·1685 g. fine gold	0	19	6·96
The 5-Mark piece contains 25 g. fine silver			
GREAT BRITAIN—			
1 Pound Sterling contains 7·3224 g. fine gold...........	1	0	0
1 Shilling contains 5·231 grms. fine silver	0	1	0
GREECE—			
1 Drachma=100 Lepta=1 Franc (=France)	0	0	9·516
ITALY—			
1 Lira=1 Franc (=France)	0	0	9·516
JAPAN—			
1 Silver Itzebue=100 Cents................................	0	1	7
1 Gold Yen	0	4	1
1 Silver Yen=100 Sen	0	4	3·8
MEXICO—			
1 Piastre (Peso. Mexican Dollar)=8 Reales=100 Cents	0	4	3·5
1 Doblon=16 Piastres	3	8	8
NETHERLANDS—			
1 Guilder=100 Cents.....................................	0	1	8
1 Willems d'Or..	0	16	6·4
1 Ducat	0	9	4·5
NORWAY—			
1 Krone=100 Oere	0	1	0·83
1 Species Daler=120 Skillings	0	4	5·48
PERSIA—			
1 Toman=10 Keran	0	9	0·31
1 Rupee Silver..	0	1	6·2
PERU—			
1 Sol (Peso)=10 Dineros=100 Centavos	0	3	11·58
PORTUGAL—			
1 Milreis (in accounts)	0	4	6·75
1 Milreis (silver)	0	4	0·46
1 Tostao=100 Reis......................................	0	0	4·8
ROUMANIA—			
1 Piastre=1 Franc (France)	0	0	9·516
RUSSIA—			
1 Silver Rouble=100 Kopeks	0	3	2·06
1 Half-Imperial=5 Rouble Gold=5·9987 g. fine gold	0	16	4·61
1 Paper Rouble	0	2	7·7
SERVIA—			
1 Dinar=1 Franc (=France)	0	0	9·516
SPAIN—			
1 Peseta=1 Franc (=France)	0	0	9·516
1 Duro (Spanish Dollar)=2 Escudos=5 Pesetas=20 Reales	0	3	11·58
SWEDEN—			
1 Kronor=100 Oere	0	1	0·83

TABLE 82.—COINAGE OF DIFFERENT COUNTRIES.—*Continued*.

	Exact Value in		
	£	s.	d.
SWITZERLAND=France.			
TURKEY—			
1 Piastre=40 Para=120 Asper	0	0	2·1
1 Turkish Pound (Yuslik)	0	18	1
UNITED STATES—			
1 Dollar=10 Dimes=100 Cents	0	4	1·15
1 Eagle=10 Dollars=15·0463 g. fine gold...................	2	1	1·16

TABLE 33.—AIR-COMPRESSION.

The following table is compiled with a view to facilitate calculations of problems connected with the application of compressed gases. The table is strictly correct for air only, but is applicable also to other gases, such as lime-kiln gases. The table relates to 1 cub. foot of atmospheric air measured at 60° F. and 29·92 inches barometric pressure, and shows the volume, temperature and pressure after adiabatic compression; also the height of a column of water which the compressed gas will just balance, and the power required to compress the air in foot-pounds (33,000 ft.-lbs. per minute =1 indicated horse power), and the mean pressure on the air piston.

Final Pressure lbs. per sq. in. above Atmosphere. lbs.	Column of Water the gas will balance. feet.	Volume of compressed Air. cub. feet.	Temperature after compression. F.°	Mean pressure on piston. lbs. per sq. in.	Foot-pounds of work per cub. foot atmosph. air.
10	23·12	0·692	144·5	8·23	1186·3
12	27·75	·655	158·1	9·58	1387
14	32·37	·622	171·0	10·86	1564
16	37·00	·593	184·0	12·08	1739
18	41·62	·567	196·0	13·23	1907
20	46·25	·544	207·3	14·35	2066
22	50·87	·528	218·3	15·42	2220
24	55·50	·504	228·6	16·45	2363
26	60·12	·486	239·0	17·43	2510
28	64·75	·469	249·0	18·39	2647
30	69·37	·454	258·2	19·32	2782
32	74·00	·440	267·5	20·21	2910
34	78·62	·428	276·4	21·07	3034
36	83·25	·416	285·3	21·92	3156
38	87·87	·404	293·5	22·74	3275
40	92·50	·394	301·8	23·58	3389

SPECIAL PART.

1.- FUEL AND FURNACES.

A.—FUEL.

Should be tested in the case of lignite, peat, coal, coke. Refer to the Appendix as to sampling.

1. *Moisture.*—Heat 100 to 200 grms. of coal to 105° C. (not above), for two hours, preventing access of air as much as possible. At a higher temperature the result might be too high, owing to escape of volatile matters, or too low, owing to a partial oxidation. The moisture sample should be broken up quickly into pieces not smaller than a bean, otherwise too much water would evaporate during the process. Lignite and peat are heated to 100°C. for five or six hours, and repeatedly weighed, till no further diminution of weight takes place. Coke is heated to 110° C. for two hours.

2. *Residual Coke (Fixed Carbon).*—One grm. of finely-powdered coal is placed in a platinum crucible at least 1¼in. deep, provided with a tightly fitting cover. The crucible should then be heated by means of an ordinary Bunsen burner, the flame of which should not be less than 7 in. high. The crucible should be supported on a triangle of thin wire, and it should be so placed that the space between the bottom and the top of the burner is not more than 1¼ in. The heating ought not to last longer than a few minutes, but must be continued as long as any appreciable quantity of inflammable matter escapes. If the flame be smaller, or the crucible be supported by a

Fig. 1.

stout wire triangle, the yield of coke will be too high. The results should always be calculated upon coal or coke free from ash, in order to render them comparative. Good coal for reverberatory furnaces should yield from 60 to 70 per cent. of coke.

3. *Ash.*—This estimation is very simple for lignite or peat; coke requires a very high temperature; coal which cakes presents most difficulties. The latter must be powdered very finely, and heated up gradually, so that the volatile matters may escape before the powder can form a cake. If an analysis is only occasionally required, 1 to 3 grms. of finely-ground coal is heated in a platinum crucible, which is fitted in a hole into a stoneware slab, or better, in asbestos board. (Fig. 1.) This is placed in a slanting position on a tripod stand. The slab serves to separate the air required for oxidation from the gases of the burner, and greatly hastens the combustion, which is thus completed in two hours, whereas without the slab it frequently remains incomplete even after 8 or 10 hours' heating. It is not advisable to use a blow-pipe, because the chance of mechanical loss is thereby greatly in-

creased. If determinations have to be made frequently, it is preferable to effect the combustion in a muffle furnace, or still more quickly in a platinum boat placed in a heated porcelain tube, through which a current of oxygen is passed. When using the latter, the coal or coke should be broken in small pieces, and not ground fine, or else the oxygen does not come sufficiently into contact with the lower strata.

B.—FURNACES.

1. *Chimney Gases.*—In these, CO_2, O, CO, and N (the latter by difference) are most conveniently estimated by means of Orsat's apparatus, consisting of a gas burette divided into 100 cub. centim., from which the gas can be forced by raising a water bottle connected by an indiarubber tube with the lower end of the burettes into three separate U-tubes, closed by glass taps at one end and open to the atmosphere, or preferably closed by a thin india-cubber ball at the other end. These U-tubes are filled with different absorbing reagents; for CO_2 with solution of caustic potash, of spec. grav. 1·20—1·28; for O with very thin sticks of phosphorus, obtained by sucking phosphorus, melted under water, into a glass tube ⅛in. wide, or with very small and irregular pieces of phosphorus obtained by shaking up melted phosphorus under water—the whole to be always kept under water, protected from light, from any tarry matters, etc., and never to be employed below a temperature of 18° C. (if the temperature of the working room is below this, the absorption is too slow, but can be started at once by cautiously warming the tube with a spirit flame). For CO serves a mixture of 10 grms. cupric chloride, 90 cub. cent. concentrated hydrochloric acid, 20 cub. cent. of water, and sheet copper sufficient to reduce it, the whole brought together at least 24 hours before using it. This reagent also absorbs any ethylene present, which would thus be estimated as CO; but this is quite immaterial in chimney gases, in which it is usually quite sufficient to estimate only the CO_2. It should be frequently renewed.[*]

2. *Gas from Producers (Generators).*—As a rule only CO_2 and CO are estimated by means of Orsat's apparatus (see preceding paragraph). Any C_2H_4 present would be absorbed and estimated together with the CO. It can be estimated in the residue by mixing it with a measured volume of air, and passing the mixture over gently-heated platinum or palladium asbestos,[†] most conveniently in Lunge's modification of Orsat's apparatus, fitted with a capillary tube for receiving the asbestos, a small spirit lamp turning on a pivot, and an extra U-tube filled with water, into which the gas is forced through the capillary tube containing the asbestos, and from which it is drawn back again into the gas burette. The gas freed from CO_2, CO, C_2H_4, and from O, if present, is mixed with as much air as the gas burette will admit of. This will suffice for a quantity of hydrogen corresponding to $\frac{1}{10}$ of the employed volume of air (*i.e.*, twice the volume of oxygen contained in that air). If more H be present, which will only occur with "water gas," either less than 100 ccm. of gas must be employed at the

---

[*] A formula for calculating the efficiency of fire-places from estimations of the percentage of CO_2 in the chimney-gases is given on p. 181.

[†] This can be obtained ready made from Mawson & Swan, at Newcastle-on-Tyne, or is prepared by soaking a few threads of long soft asbestos in a strong solution of platinum or palladium chloride, mixed with a saturated solution of sodium formiate and enough sodium carbonate to produce alkaline reaction. After one hour's soaking the asbestos is dried completely in a water bath, whereby the metal is precipitated in an extremely minute state of division. The soluble salts are then washed out by hot water and the asbestos dried again.

commencement for the analyses, or the residual gas is mixed with oxygen instead of with air. The capillary tube is heated very gently and the gaseous mixture is quickly passed once through it and back again, when one end of the platinum asbestos should become red hot. The residual gas is measured once more, and $\frac{2}{3}$ of the diminution in volume calculated as hydrogen. If methane (marsh gas, CH_4) is to be estimated, the residue from the last operation is mixed with more air and burnt by means of an electrically-glowing palladium or platinum wire, enclosed in a capillary tube. If a capillary platinum tube is employed, filled with a few platinum wires, so as to leave a very small space for the gases to pass through, the electric heating may be replaced by a broad gas flame, producing a strong red heat.

3. *Speed of Draught.*—A convenient apparatus for measuring this in chemical works, where any fine mechanism would soon be ruined, is Fletcher's anemometer, based upon the movement of a column of ether in a U-tube (described in "Lunge's Sulphuric Acid and Alkali," I. 330; III., 861). Fig. 2 shows this in the simpler form, leaving out the microscopes, which

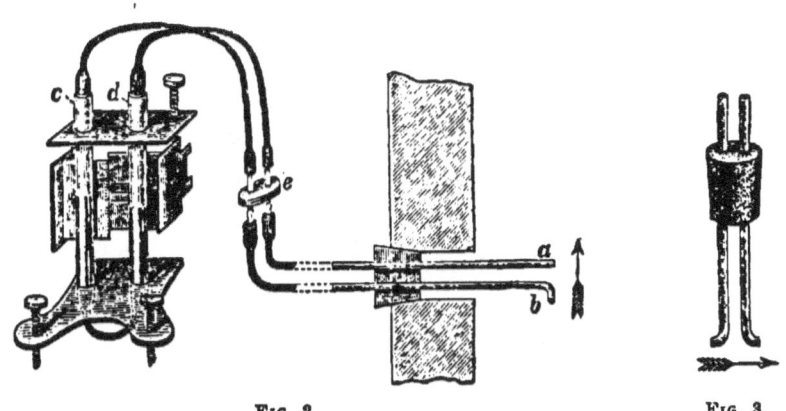

Fig. 2.   Fig. 3.

are quite unnecessary for reading the divisions of the scale or the vernier. The ends of the glass tubes *a b* should be placed rather less than one-sixth of the diameter of the flue from its inner wall. The straight end of *a* ought to be as exactly parallel as possible to the direction of the draughts; the end of *b* ought to be exactly at a right angle to this, and so that the current would blow into it. Without this precaution a mistake is made, which is avoided by the arrangement shown in Fig. 3, and proposed by Hurter, viz., employing tubes with ends bent in opposite directions. The tubes *a b* communicate with the ether tube *c d*; the draught causes the ether to rise in *a* by aspiration, to fall in *b* by the pressure of the air blowing into the tube. The difference of level between *c* and *d* is read off by means of the scale and vernier. Now the sliding disc *e* is turned 180°, whereby the currents are reversed. There will now be a difference of levels in the opposite direction, but equal in amount to the first, if the observation is correct. The sum of these two differences is meant by the "anemometer readings" in the tables.

The following tables show the application of the readings of the Anemometer for calculating the speed of draughts, both for instruments graduated on the inch scale and for those on the metrical scale.

a.—TABLE TO SHOW THE SPEED OF CURRENTS OF AIR,

At a temperature of 15° C.=60° F.; Barometer, 760mm.=29·92 inches.

A.—READINGS IN INCHES.

Anemometer Reading Inches.	Speed Feet per Second.	Anemometer Reading Inches.	Speed Feet per Second.	Anemometer Reading Inches.	Speed Feet per Second.	Anemometer Reading Inches.	Speed Feet per Second.
·01	2·855	·16	11·42	·32	16·15	·95	27·83
·02	4·038	·17	11·77	·34	16·65	1·00	28·55
·03	4·945	·18	12·11	·36	17·13	1·25	31·93
·04	5·710	·19	12·45	·38	17·60	1·50	34·97
·05	6·384	·20	12·77	·40	18·06	1·75	37·77
·06	6·993	·21	13·08	·45	19·15	2·00	40·37
·07	7·554	·22	13·39	·50	20·18	...	...
·08	8·075	·23	13·70	·55	21·17	...	...
·09	8·565	·24	13·99	·60	22·12	...	...
·10	9·028	·25	14·28	·65	23·02	...	...
·11	9·469	·26	14·56	·70	23·89	...	...
·12	9·891	·27	14·84	·75	24·73	...	...
·13	10·29	·28	15·11	·80	25·54	...	...
·14	10·68	·29	15·38	·85	26·32	...	...
·15	11·06	·30	15·64	·90	27·08	...	...

B.—READINGS IN MILLIMETERS.

Reading. mm.	Speed. m.	Read ing. mm.	Speed. m.	Read ing. mm.	Speed. m.	Read ing. mm.	Speed. m.	Reading. mm.	Speed. m.	Read ing. mm.	Speed. m.
0·1	0·575	1·4	2·040	2·7	2·833	5·0	3·855	10·0	5·452	19·0	7·515
0·2	0·771	1·5	2·111	2·8	2·885	5·2	3·931	10·5	5·586	20·0	7·710
0·3	0·944	1·6	2·181	2·9	2·935	5·4	4·006	11·0	5·718	21	7·900
0·4	1·090	1·7	2·248	3·0	2·986	5·6	4·080	11·5	5·846	22	8·086
0·5	1·205	1·8	2·313	3·2	3·077	5·8	4·152	12·0	5·972	23	8·268
0·6	1·341	1·9	2·376	3·4	3·179	6·0	4·223	12·5	6·095	24	8·446
0·7	1·412	2·0	2·438	3·6	3·271	6·5	4·395	13·0	6·216	25	8·620
0·8	1·560	2·1	2·498	3·8	3·361	7·0	4·561	13·5	6·334	30	9·443
0·9	1·636	2·2	2·557	4·0	3·418	7·5	4·721	14·0	6·450	35	10·199
1·0	1·724	2·3	2·615	4·2	3·469	8·0	4·876	15·0	6·667	40	10·903
1·1	1·808	2·4	2·671	4·4	3·616	8·5	5·026	16·0	6·896	45	11·565
1·2	1·889	2·5	2·726	4·6	3·698	9·0	5·172	17·0	7·108	50	12·190
1·3	1·966	2·6	2·779	4·8	3·777	9·5	5·314	18·0	7·314		

β.—CORRECTIONS FOR TEMPERATURE.

Column a shows the temperature of the chimney or flue, column b the factor for multiplying the figure found in Table a in order to arrive at the real speed of the current of gas.

A.—READINGS IN DEGREES FAHRENHEIT.

Fair. a	b	a	b	a	b	a	b
0	1·0634	90	0·9723	180	0·9012	380	0·7865
5	1·0577	95	0·9679	185	0·8977	400	0·7763
10	1·0520	100	0·9636	190	0·8943	425	0·7663
15	1·0464	105	0·9593	195	0·8909	450	0·7556
20	1·0409	110	0·9551	200	0·8875	475	0·7454
25	1·0355	115	0·9509	210	0·8808	500	0·7356
30	1·0302	120	0·9468	220	0·8743	525	0·7261
35	1·0250	125	0·9428	230	0·8680	550	0·7171
40	1·0198	130	0·9388	240	0·8614	575	0·7085
45	1·0148	135	0·9348	250	0·8557	600	0·7000
50	1·0098	140	0·9309	260	0·8497	650	0·6841
55	1·0049	145	0·9270	270	0·8438	700	0·6691
60	1·0000	150	0·9232	280	0·8380	750	0·6552
65	0·9952	155	0·9194	290	0·8324	800	0·6420
70	0·9905	160	0·9156	300	0·8269	850	0·6297
75	0·9858	165	0·9119	320	0·8163	900	0·6181
80	0·9812	170	0·9083	340	0·8060	950	0·6070
85	0·9767	175	0·9047	360	0·7960	1000	0·5964

B.—READINGS IN DEGREES CENTIGRADE.

a t°C	b	a t°C	b	a t°C	b	a t°C	b	a t°C	b	a t°C	b
−10	1·046	18	0·905	42	0·956	66	0·922	140	0·835	260	0·735
− 5	1·036	20	0·991	44	0·953	68	0·919	150	0·825	270	0·728
0	1·027	22	0·988	46	0·950	70	0·916	160	0·815	280	0·721
2	1·023	24	0·985	48	0·947	75	0·909	170	0·806	290	0·715
4	1·020	26	0·981	50	0·944	80	0·903	180	0·797	300	0·709
6	1·016	28	0·978	52	0·941	85	0·897	190	0·788	320	0·697
8	1·012	30	0·975	54	0·938	90	0·890	200	0·780	340	0·685
10	1·009	32	0·972	56	0·935	95	0·884	210	0·772	360	0·676
12	1·005	34	0·968	58	0·933	100	0·878	220	0·764	400	0·654
14	1·003	36	0·965	60	0·930	110	0·867	230	0·756	450	0·631
15	1·000	38	0·962	62	0·927	120.	0·856	240	0·749	500	0·608
16	0·998	40	0·959	64	0·924	130	0·845	250	0·742		

A very simple and cheaper instrument is also Seger's Differential Anemometer, Fig. 4. The U tube A is surmounted by two enlargements, B and C. D is a sliding scale, adjustable by slits aa and screw-pins bb. The tube is filled with two not mixable liquids; for instance paraffin oil and dilute spirits of wine (coloured), of nearly equal specific gravity. The line of contact, at X, is marked by the zero point of the scale D. If an aspirating force is acting on the surface of the liquid in C, the level of the liquid will be raised in C, and the point X will be lowered at a multiplied ratio, corresponding to the difference in the sectional area of the narrow part of A and the enlargements in C, say 1:20.

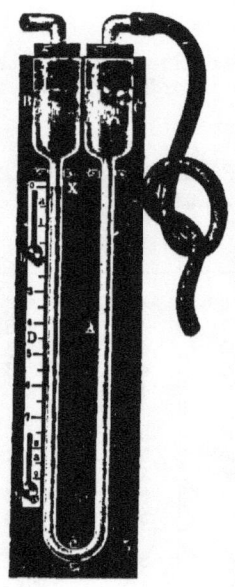

FIG. 4.

C.—TEMPERATURE.

None of the ordinary pyrometers are reliable for any length of time, not even that of Siemens, whose high price and inconvenient shape prevent its general use. We mention, of more recent pyrometers—

1. *Gauntlett's* metal pyrometer, manufactured by Schäffer and Budenberg (Magdeburg and Manchester). This can be used up to 900° C., or 1,600° F., but the metallic parts must be well protected.

2. *Steinle and Hartung's* (of Quedlinburg, Germany) *graphite pyrometer,* graduated up to 1,200° C. (say 2,000° F.) This, as well as Gauntlett's or other pyrometers, must be controlled from time to time, preferably by a calorimeter.

3. *Fischer's Calorimetric Pyrometer* consists (1) of a wrought-iron box fitted with a lid, and welded to the end of a long rod, by means of which it can be placed in the space whose temperature has to be taken; (2) of a small cylinder of wrought iron, copper,* or platinum, say 2c. long by 1c. diameter, which is accurately weighed and exposed to the heat of the furnace, etc., within the above iron box; (3) of the calorimeter itself, viz., a vessel made of thin sheet copper, about 6c. wide by 15c. deep. This is surrounded by a thick wooden jacket (preferably having a space in between which can be filled up with loose wool, fur, and the like), and can be manipulated by a wooden handle without grasping the jacket itself. The vessel is fitted with a brass cover provided with two holes, one allowing a fine thermometer (graduated in tenths of degrees) to pass through, the other, 2c. wide, for dropping in the hot metal cylinder. Through this hole also passes the wire handle of a copper disc, a little less in diameter than that of the calorimeter, which serves as a stirrer. This vessel is filled two-thirds with an accurately weighed or measured quantity of water. The operation is performed by exposing the metal cylinder No. 2, enclosed within the box No. 1, long enough to assume the temperature of the furnace at least for 20 minutes; then quickly take out the box, remove the lid by a forceps, and

---

* Copper does not, however, last well, scales of CuO forming the first time it is used, while iron can be used daily for three months without great error.

drop the hot cylinder into the calorimeter No. 3, whose temperature=t^0 has been ascertained just before. The cylinder falls upon the disc of the stirrer, which is rapidly moved up and down, constantly observing the thermometer. When this is at its maximum, it is read off. This temperature we will call t^1. We must further know the weight of the metal cylinder=p; its specific heat=c (this is 0·094 for copper, 0·114 for wrought iron, 0·032 for platinum, but increases with the temperature, so that there is here a source of inaccuracy); the weight of the water within the calorimeter, added to the water-weight of the copper vessel and stirrer itself=p^1 (water-weight means the actual weight multiplied by the specific heat, *i.e.*, 0·094 for copper; the thermometer, if very slender, may be left out of the calculation). The temperature of the hot cylinder T is found by the formula—

$$T = t^1 + \frac{p^1(t^1-t^0)}{pc}$$

If p^1 and p are constant, the magnitude

$$\frac{p^1}{pc}$$

can be converted into a factor, by which the difference of thermometer readings is multiplied, thus at once yielding the temperature sought, after the first temperature t^1 has been added to the product. For practical purposes it is convenient to choose the quantities so that this factor becomes a simple number. For very high temperatures the value

$$\frac{p^1}{pc}$$

should not be less that 50. For lower ones it will be sufficient if it is 25, but it should not be chosen less than 25. The same factor will,. with the same apparatus, yield Fahrenheit degrees if a Fahrenheit thermometer is used instead of a Centigrade one. The mean specific heat of iron between 0° C. and t° C. is G=0·1053+0·000071 t^0 (Bède). By means of this value for the mean specific heat of iron, the temperature can be calculated according to the following formula :—

$$T= \sqrt{\left(\frac{p^1(t^1-t^0)+pt^1(0.1053+0.000071\ t^1)}{0.000071p}+549822\right)} -741.47$$

Siemens' copper pyrometer, which is on the same principle, gives the degrees corresponding to the readings of the thermometer without any calculations by means of a special scale; but the indications of this instrument are very rough.

2.—SULPHURIC ACID MANUFACTURE.

A.—BRIMSTONE.

1. *Moisture.*—In order to prevent the evaporation of moisture during grinding, an average sample of the unground or only roughly-crushed materials weighing 100grms. is dried at 100° C. for some hours in an oven or water-bath.

2. *Ashes.*—10grms. are burnt in a tared porcelain dish, and the residue weighed.

3. *Direct Estimation of Sulphur.*—(Macagno, *Chem. News*, v. 43, p. 192). 50grms. of the finely-ground brimstone are dissolved in 200c.c. carbon

bisulphide by digesting in a stoppered bottle at the ordinary temperature, and the specific gravity of the liquid=s is estimated. This must be reduced to the specific gravity at 15° C.=S by means of the formula (valid up to 25° C.) $S = s + 0.0014 (t - 15°)$. The following table gives for each value of S the percentage in this solution, which number must be multiplied by 4 to indicate the percentage of sulphur in the sample of brimstone :—

SPECIFIC GRAVITIES OF SOLUTIONS OF SULPHUR IN CARBON BISULPHIDE.

Spec. Grav.	% S	Spec. Grav.	% S	Spec. Grav.	% S	Spec. Grav.	% S	Spec. Grav.	% S	Spec. Grav.	% S
1·271	0	1·292	5·0	1·313	10·2	1·334	15·2	1·355	20·4	1·376	28·1
1·272	0·2	1·293	5·3	1·314	10·4	1·335	15·4	1·356	20·6	1·377	28·5
1·273	0·4	1·294	5·6	1·315	10·6	1·336	15·6	1·357	21·0	1·378	29·0
1·274	0·6	1·295	5·8	1·316	10·9	1·337	15·9	1·358	21·2	1·379	29·7
1·275	0·9	1·296	6·0	1·317	11·1	1·338	16·1	1·359	21·5	1·380	30·2
1·276	1·2	1·297	6·3	1·318	11·3	1·339	16·4	1·360	21·8	1·381	30·8
1·277	1·4	1·298	6·5	1·319	11·6	1·340	16·6	1·361	22·1	1·382	31·4
1·278	1·6	1·299	6·7	1·320	11·8	1·341	16·9	1·362	22·3	1·383	31·9
1·279	1·9	1·300	7·0	1·321	12·1	1·342	17·1	1·363	22·7	1·384	32·6
1·280	2·1	1·301	7·2	1·322	12·3	1·343	17·4	1·364	23·0	1·385	33·2
1·281	2·4	1·302	7·5	1·323	12·6	1·344	17·6	1·365	23·2	1·386	33·8
1·282	2·6	1·303	7·8	1·324	12·8	1·345	17·9	1·366	23·6	1·387	34·5
1·283	2·9	1·304	8·0	1·325	13·1	1·346	18·1	1·367	24·0	1·388	35·2
1·284	3·1	1·305	8·2	1·326	13·3	1·347	18·4	1·368	24·3	1·389	36·1
1·285	3·4	1·306	8·5	1·327	13·5	1·348	18·6	1·369	24·8	1·390	36·7
1·286	3·6	1·307	8·7	1·328	13·8	1·349	18·9	1·370	25·1	1·391	37·2
1·287	3·9	1·308	8·9	1·329	14·0	1·350	19·0	1·371	25·6	(saturated)	
1·288	4·1	1·309	9·2	1·330	14·2	1·351	19·3	1·372	26·0		
1·289	4·4	1·310	9·4	1·331	14·5	1·352	19·6	1·373	26·5		
1·290	4·6	1·311	9·7	1·332	14·7	1·353	19·9	1·374	26·9		
1·291	4·8	1·312	9·9	1·333	15·0	1·354	20·1	1·375	27·4		

B.—SPENT OXIDE OF GASWORKS.

This is contaminated with saw-dust, tarry matters, and variable quantities of lime, etc., which latter retain part of the sulphur in burning, hence a method is employed which estimates only the recoverable portion of the sulphur (Zulkowsky, *Dingler's Journal*, v. 241, p. 52). The sulphur of the spent oxide is burnt with the aid of platinized asbestos (comp. p. 86), the gases are passed into a solution of caustic potash and potassium hypobromite, and the sulphuric acid there condensed or formed is estimated by precipitation with $BaCl_2$. The combustion takes place in a combustion tube (Fig. 5) 2ft. long, narrowed at a, and drawn out at the end into a long tube, not too thin, and bent downwards. Between a and b there is a layer of asbestos 8in. to 10in. long, and at a distance of 3in. from this a porcelain boat with about 0·4grm. spent oxide. The end of the tube at k is connected with an oxygen gasholder. The absorption takes place in the two 3-bulb tubes c and d (5½in. high) and the tube e, filled with glass-wool. The absorbing liquid is made by dissolving 180grms. caustic potash (purified with alcohol from sulphate) in water, adding 100grms. bromine, taking care to keep the mixture cool, and diluting to 1,000c.c. 80c.c. of this suffice for estimating 0·5grm. sulphur. The tube *e* ought also to be moistened with it. First heat the portion of the tube between *a* and *b*, passing moist oxygen through it at the same time; then heat the boat from the right to the left, lastly the tube, up to the place *f*. The current of gas must be much stronger than for an organic analysis, lest any sulphur should escape unburnt, but not so strong as to draw off any SO_3 unabsorbed. So long as

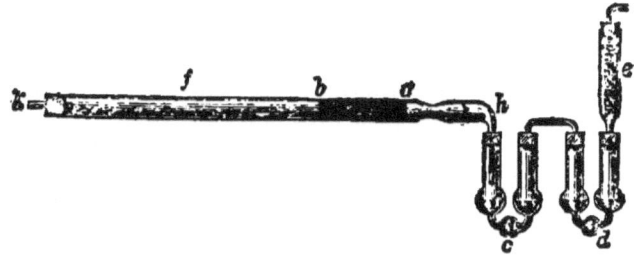

Fig. 5.

any dew appears at *h* it must be driven into the receiver with a Bunsen burner. When this ceases (usually in about an hour) the experiment is finished. The receivers are then taken off, washed out, and the acid remaining in *h* is recovered by aspirating several times water through it. All the liquids are united, supersaturated with HCl in order to decompose the potassium hydrate and hypobromite, heated, concentrated if necessary, and the sulphuric acid is precipitated with $BaCl_2$, as directed in the following paragraph (C 2).

In lieu of the bromine solution proposed by Zulkowsky, hydrogen peroxide can be used; but it must be free from sulphuric acid, or else the sulphuric acid contained in it must be allowed for. In this case the analysis may be performed volumetrically by means of caustic soda solution.

C.—PYRITES.

1. *Moisture.*—The ground pyrites is dried at 105° C. till the weight remains constant. For the following tests the pyrites is not employed in the dried state, but the finely-ground average sample, as it is kept in a well-sealed bottle. Compare the Appendix as to drawing and reducing an average sample.

2. *Sulphur.*—About 0·5grm. of pyrites is treated with about 10c.c. of a mixture of 3 vols. nitric acid (specific gravity 1·4) and 1 vol. strong hydrochloric acid, both ascertained to be absolutely free from sulphuric acid. Avoid all spurting. Heat up the mixture now and then, evaporate to dryness in a water-bath, add 5c.c. hydrochloric acid, evaporate once more (no nitrous fumes ought to escape now), add 1c.c. concentrated hydrochloric acid and 100c.c. hot water, filter through a small filter, and wash with hot water. The insoluble residue may be dried, ignited, and weighed. It may contain, besides silicic acid and silicates, the sulphates of barium, lead, and even calcium, whose sulphur, as being useless, is purposely neglected. The filtrate and washings are saturated with ammonia, avoiding much excess of it and keeping the hot liquid about 10 or 15 minutes before filtration, but *not* boiling till all the ammonia is expelled (in which case the preci-

pitate contains some basic sulphate). The precipitated ferric hydrate is filtered and washed. This can be done in from half to one hour, by employing the following precautions: (1) Filter hot, and wash on the filter with hot water, avoiding channels in the mass, but so that the whole precipitate is thoroughly churned up with the water each time (washing by decantation would produce too great a bulk of liquid); (2) employ sufficiently dense but rapidly-filtering paper; (3) use funnels, made at an angle of exactly 60°, whose tube is not too wide, and is *completely filled* by the liquid running through. A filter pump may also be employed with the usual precautions. Wash till about 1c.c. of the washings on adding BaCl$_2$ shows no opalescence even after a few minutes. The filtrate and washings should not exceed 200c.c., or else should be concentrated by evaporation. Acidulate with pure HCl in *very slight excess*, heat to boiling, remove the burner, and add a solution of BaCl$_2$ previously heated to boiling. (A large excess of BaCl$_2$ must be decidedly avoided.) For 0·5grm. pyrites, 20c.c. of a 10 per cent. solution of BaCl$_2$ is always more than sufficient. This is roughly measured off in a test-tube provided with a mark, and heated in the same tube. After precipitation the liquid is left to stand for half an hour, when the precipitate should be completely settled. Decant the clear portion as well as possible through a filter, pour 100c.c. boiling water on the precipitate, and stir up. Wait two or three minutes, when the liquid ought to have settled completely, and decant again. Repeat the treatment with boiling water, and the decantation three or four times, till the liquid has lost its acid reaction. Wash the precipitate on to the filter, dry, and ignite. It should be a perfectly white and loose powder. One part of it is equal to 0·13734 sulphur (factors on pp. 14, 15).

3. *Copper (Process employed at the Duisburg Copper Extraction Works).*— 1grm. of pyrites, finely powdered and dried at 100° C., is treated with concentrated nitric acid, and then evaporated to dryness. Pour concentrated sulphuric acid over the residue, and heat on a sand-bath till the free acid is driven off. Let it cool down, boil up the mass with water, allow it to cool, add quarter of the bulk of spirit of wine, let stand for 12 hours, and filter. The residue on the filter is washed with a mixture of 1 part alcohol and 2 parts water till no more copper can be found. The dilute filtrate is saturated with H$_2$S and allowed to stand for some hours. The precipitate (containing the sulphides of copper, arsenic, antimony, and bismuth) is washed with a solution of H$_2$S containing a little sulphuric acid, dried, mixed with the ashes of the filter and with pure sulphur (recrystallized from CS$_2$), ignited in a Rose's crucible in a current of hydrogen or coal gas, and weighed. In this operation arsenic is completely volatilised; antimony and bismuth remain along with the copper. Spanish pyrites contains an almost constant quantity of 0·05 per cent. Sb and Bi, of which 0·0005grm., together with the weight of the filter ashes, is deducted from the Cu$_2$S (1 part Cu$_2$O=0·79874 Cu).[*]

4. *Zinc* is sometimes estimated in pyrites, because the sulphur combined with it is hardly recoverable for acid making. The following method (Schaffner's modified) is employed at the Vieille Montagne and the Rhenish

---

[*] The electrolytical method has not been adopted at Duisburg, because copper precipitated the first time is not pure, and two precipitations cause more trouble than the above-described method. But at the copper works the purity of the Cu$_2$S is checked by the electrolytical method. The Duisburg method, as given in text, is open to the objection of being rather lengthy, and of deducting a constant quantity of Sb and Bi, which cannot be quite correct in all cases; but as it is accepted as binding upon buyers and sellers in Germany, we have given it as it stands.

Zincworks: 0·5grm. of the ore is dissolved as described on p. 94. All nitric acid is destroyed in the same way. Any metals precipitable by H_2S from an acid solution are removed by this reagent. The filtrate is freed from H_2S by boiling, and oxidized by a little aqua regia. The ferric oxide is precipitated with 30c.c. of liquor ammoniæ (if Mn is present, the liquor is allowed to stand for six hours, when the Mn will be precipitated as well), filtered, dissolved on the filter (as it always contains zinc) in a little HCl, without previous washing, precipitated once more with NH_3, and filtered again. Both filtrates are united, diluted to half a litre, and titrated in a tall beaker by a solution of pure crystallized sodium sulphide, of which 1c.c. ought to be as nearly as possible=0·01 Zn. With more dilute liquors the results are not so good. Add the liquid, constantly stirring, till a paper soaked with a basic solution of ferric chloride, half dipping into the liquid, is blackened. The paper is either attached to the side of the beaker or suspended from platinum wire. The Na_2S solution is standardized exactly in the same way by weighing off pure zinc, dissolving, and supersaturating with NH_3. But exactly the same dilution and excess of ammonia must be used as in the former operation, in order to employ the same excess of Na_2S for blackening the iron paper in both cases, and the degree of blackening should also be the same. The solution of sodium sulphide should not be more than a fortnight old.

Fig. 6.

5. *Carbonic Acid* (calcium carbonate, etc.) is sometimes estimated, because the bases combined with it make a corresponding quantity of sulphur useless in the form of sulphates. As the quantity is always small, the CO_2 is estimated gravimetrically by expelling it by strong acids and absorbing it in soda lime in the apparatus, Fig. 6. The flask a, holding 200c.c., is closed with an indiarubber cork. Through this passes the swan-neck tube b, reaching down to the bottom of a and connected outside by means of a pinch-cock joint, either with a small funnel or (at the end of the operation) with a U tube filled with soda lime. In a second perforation of the cork is fixed the delivery tube c, cut obliquely at the lower end, and enlarged above the cork into a bulb. The latter is connected with a series of U tubes, which are once for all put together and hung with wire loops from a carrying rod fixed in a stand, so that the whole is ready for use at any time. The tube No. 1 (7in. long, ⅜in. wide inside) contains only a little calcium chloride (absolutely free from alkaline reaction) in its bend. No. 2 (same size) is filled with calcium chloride. No. 3 (same size) with pumice, boiled with a concentrated solution of copper sulphate, dried, and heated to the point

where all water is driven off for the absorption of H_2S and HCl.[*] The tubes Nos. 4 to 7 are $4\frac{1}{2}$in. long and $\frac{1}{2}$in. wide. No. 4 contains calcium chloride; Nos. 5 and 6 about 20grms. granular soda lime, except the upper third of the *second* limb, which is filled with granular calcium chloride: No. 7, in the first limb calcium chloride, and in the second soda lime. Nos. 1 to 4 serve for removing from the gas its moisture and HCl; Nos. 5 and 6 for absorbing the CO_2, the $CaCl_2$ preventing any escape of moisture from the soda lime. No. 7 is a guard-tube against CO_2 and H_2O entering from without. Only Nos. 5 and 6 are weighed (both together) before and after the experiment. The contents of No. 1 must generally be renewed after each experiment; those of No. 5 pretty frequently, according to the CO_2 present; those of No. 6 very rarely. The apparatus is tested in the usual way for its gas-tightness, and serves for all estimations of CO_2 by weight. For making a test, put the weighed substance into the flask a, along with 50c.c. of water; gradually run in through b a sufficient quantity of dilute HCl or SO_4H_2 (compare footnote), take away the funnel, connect b with the soda-lime guard-tube, and aspirate from the other end, at the $\bigcup$ tube No. 7, a steady current of air, free from CO_2, through a, whose contents are at the same time heated, but not to the boiling point. The process of absorption can be followed by the progressive rise of temperature in the soda-lime tube No. 5. When this has become quite cold, the current of air is passed through another 20 minutes, after which the experiment is finished. The contents of a ought never to be heated strongly enough to make the calcium chloride in No. 1 deliquesce. (This estimation requires a great deal of practice and care to avoid errors. An easier, quicker, and more reliable method of estimating CO_2 by the volume of the gas has been worked out by Lunge and Marchlewski, Zeitsch. f. angew. Chem., April, 1891, p. 229).

D.—BURNT PYRITES (CINDERS).

1. *Sulphur* is estimated by John Watson's method (S.C.I., 1888, pp. 305. 730). Place exactly 2 grams bicarbonate of soda of known alkalinity in a nickel or platinum crucible; add 3·200 grams of the powdered sample of burnt ore; mix intimately with a flattened glass rod; heat gently over a low Bunsen flame for five or ten minutes; stir up the mixture again; continue the heating over a stronger flame for ten or fifteen minutes longer; wash the contents of the crucible into a beaker; boil for ten minutes; filter and wash the insoluble portion, till all alkaline reaction has ceased; allow the washings to cool; add methyl-orange and titrate with normal hydrochloric acid; each c.c. of which saturates 0·053 Na_2CO_3, and indicates 0·016 S. If we call the number of c.c. of that acid, consumed by 2 grams of the bicarbonate employed, a, and the number of c.c., consumed on retitrating after the test, b, the number $2(a-b)$ expresses the percentage of sulphur in the burnt ore.

2. *Copper* is estimated as on page 94, but the solution of the sample (1 grm.) is made by means of hydrochloric acid, with a few drops of nitric acid. A deduction of 0·07 per cent. for Bi and Sb is made from the percentage of Cu found.

---

[*] If the carbonates can be decomposed by dilute sulphuric acid, and if at the same time no sensible quantity of H_2S can escape (*e.g.*, in estimating CO_2 in caustic soda), it is preferable to employ dilute sulphuric acid for driving off the CO_2 in the flask a, and to leave out the tube No. 3, which omission will lessen the chance of error caused by any trace of water left in the copper sulphate.

E.—GASES.

1. *Burner Gases.*—SO_2 is estimated by Reich's method (*Lunge's Sulphuric Acid and Alkali*, vol. i., p. 251; vol. iii., p. 352). The gas is aspirated through a solution of iodine, contained in a wide-necked 200c.c. bottle, and coloured blue by starch solution, till the colour has been just discharged. This bottle is connected with a larger bottle, converted into an aspirator by a tap near its bottom, or by a siphon fitted with a pinch-cock. Water is run from this into a graduated 250c.c. jar. All this time the iodine bottle is shaken up, and at the moment when the colour is discharged the tap of the aspirator is closed, and the volume of water in the jar is read off. It is equal to that of the gas aspirated through when increased by that of the SO_2 absorbed. The absorbing bottle is charged with 10c.c. of a decinormal solution of iodine (12·7 grms. iodine per litre, preparation and examination in the Appendix), along with about 50c.c. of water, a little starch solution, and a little sodium bicarbonate. The above quantity of iodine is=0·082grm. SO_2=11·14c.c. at 0° C. and a pressure of 760mm. The latter figure, multiplied by 100 and divided by 11c.c.+the volume of the water run out, yields the percentage of SO_2 in the gas by volume.

This calculation is saved by the following table, in which the 11c.c. are already taken into account.

c.c. Water in the Measuring Jar.	Per cent. SO_2 by Volume.	c.c. Water in the Measuring Jar.	Per cent. SO_2 by Volume.
82	12·0	128	8·0
86	11·5	138	7·5
90	11·0	148	7·0
95	10·5	160	6·5
100	10·0	175	6·0
106	9·5	192	5·5
113	9·0	212	5·0
120	8·5	—	—

In this no notice is taken of temperature and barometer. If these are to be observed, the volume read off is reduced to 0° and 760mm. by the tables 20 and 21 or 21B, and then looked up in the above table.

Total Acids (SO_2+SO_3) are estimated in exactly the same way, and calculated as SO_2, by employing, in lieu of iodine and starch, a decinormal caustic soda solution, coloured by phenolphthalein, and passing gas through it with constant agitation, until the liquid is just decolorized. A very suitable form of apparatus is that in which the inlet gas-tube is closed at the lower end, and is provided, below the level of the liquid, with many pinhole openings, which break up the current of gas into as many fine streams.

2. *Chamber Gases.*—These are analysed like No. 3.

3. *Chamber Exit Gases as Oxygen.*—Before estimating this the acids are removed from the gas by washing with a solution of potash or soda. Single samples can be taken at odd times during the day, but it is recommended to take an average sample for the whole day, by aspirating at least 10 or 20 litres of gas, and analysing a portion of this. The estimation of oxygen is best made by moist phosphorus in an Orsat apparatus (page 86) with two absorbing tubes, one of which is filled with potash solution for removing the acids, the other with small pieces of phosphorus. The manipulation is exactly as in testing fire gases, but it should be observed that the temperature must be at least 16°, better 18° C., otherwise the tube must be warmed a little.

4. *Sulphur and Nitrogen Acids.*—The different acid compounds of sulphur

H

are estimated together, as well as those of nitrogen, whatever degree of oxidation they may possess. The following prescriptions agree in the main with those published by the British Alkali Makers' Association in 1878. A continuous test over 24 hours is taken of the gases escaping from the exit pipes of the Gay-Lussac towers, aspirating at least one cubic foot per hour by means of any aspirator acting at a constant rate and recording the volume of gas $= V$ by means of gauging the aspirator or by a gas meter. The volume V is reduced to 0° C. and 760mm. pressure ($=32°$ F. and 29·92 inches*) by the tables 20 and 21 or 21a, and is now called V^1. In order to allow comparisons, the number of cubic feet of chamber space per pound of sulphur burnt and passing into the chambers is recorded, excluding towers, but including tunnels, the amount of sulphur being taken by the weekly average, each firm to state the distance of the testing hole from the point at which the gases leave the Gay-Lussac towers. The absorption apparatus consists of four bottles or tubes, containing not less than 100c.c. of absorbing liquid, with a depth of at least 3in. in each bottle, the aperture of inlet tubes not to exceed $\frac{1}{50}$in. in diameter, and to be measured by a standard wire. The first three bottles contain each 100c.c. of normal caustic soda solution (31 grms. per litre), the fourth 100c.c. distilled water. The caustic soda used must be free from nitrogen acids. The gases are tested (1) for total acidity, stated in grains of SO_3 per cubic foot of gas, elsewhere in grammes per cubic metre. (2) Sulphur acids. (3) Nitrogen acids, both stated in grains of S and N per cubic foot (or grammes per cubic metre). The analysis is carried out as follows: The contents of the four bottles are united, taking care not to unnecessarily augment the bulk of the liquids, and are divided into three equal parts, one of which is reserved for accidents, etc. The first part is titrated with normal sulphuric acid (49 grms. SO_4H_2 per litre), to ascertain total acidity. The number of cubic centimetres of acid necessary for neutralization is called x. The second part of the liquid is gradually poured into a warm solution of potassium permanganate, strongly acidified with pure sulphuric acid. A small excess of permanganate must be present, and must be afterwards reduced by the addition of a few drops of sulphurous acid solution, until only a faint red tint is visible. Now all Nitrogen acids are present as HNO_3, but no excess of SO_2. The HNO_3 is estimated by its action on $Fe SO_4$. 25c.c. of a solution, containing per litre 100 grms. crystallized ferrous sulphate and 100 grms. pure sulphuric acid (the same solution which is used for estimating MnO_2) are put into a flask, 20c.c. to 25c.c. pure concentrated sulphuric acid is added, the mixture is allowed to cool, and the other mixture, treated with permanganate, etc., is added. The flask is closed by a cork with glass tubes. A current of CO_2 passes through and issues beneath the surface of some water, to prevent entrance of air. First, all the air is expelled in this way by means of an apparatus evolving CO_2 with constant action; then the solutions are introduced, and the contents of the flask are heated to boiling, till the dark colour produced by the formation of NO has changed to a clear light yellow. This lasts a quarter of an hour to one hour, according to the quantity of NO_3H present and that of the sulphuric acid added. The unoxidized ferrous sulphate is titrated by a seminormal permanganate solution (yielding 0·004 grm. oxygen per cubic centimetre—compare Appendix). The cubic centimetres used $= y$. Since the titre of the iron solution changes pretty quickly, it should be tested

---

* The law prescribes the cubic feet to be measured at 60° F. and 30 inches, which necessitates the use of other tables or factors than those mentioned in the text, but the difference should be hardly perceptible, and certainly within the limits of experimental error.

daily by taking out 25c.c. with the same pipette as serves for the above-described operation, and ascertaining the amount of permanganate required for oxidizing it=z c.c. The magnitudes sought are found by the following equations:—

1. *Total Acidity* in grammes per cubic metre=
$$SO_3 = \frac{0.120(100-x)}{V^1}$$

1. *Total Acidity* in grains per cubic foot=
$$SO_3 = \frac{1.852(100-x)}{V^1}$$

2. *Sulphur* in grammes per cubic metre=
$$S = \frac{0.008(600-6x-z+y)}{V^1}$$

2. *Sulphur* in grains per cubic foot=
$$S = \frac{0.12346(600-6x-z+y)}{V^1}$$

3. *Nitrogen* in grammes per cubic metre=
$$N = \frac{0.007(z-y)}{V^1}$$

3. *Nitrogen* in grains per cubic foot=
$$N = \frac{0.10808(z-y)}{V^1}$$

The legal limit for total acidity is 4 grains of SO_3 per cubic foot.*

For the purposes of the Alkali Act, it is sufficient, in lieu of the just-described separate process, to estimate *total acidity* only by the test described on p. 97, employing decinormal soda solution and phenolphthalein.

5. *Nitric Oxide* (NO) can be present in the exit gases after passing through the absorbing bottles. If it is to be estimated, an absorption tube (Fig. 7)† is interposed between the tubes of the last-described apparatus and the

Fig. 7.

aspirator. This tube contains 30c.c. of semi-normal permanganate and 1c.c. of sulphuric acid, specific gravity 1·25. The gas is passed through for 24 hours, and the tube emptied and washed out. Now add 50c.c ferrous sulphate solution, corresponding to 2z permanganate (compare last paragraph), and retitrate the decolorized liquid with permanganate. The quantity of the latter now used is called u. The NO has consumed (30+u−2z)c.c. permanganate, which is equal—

In grammes of nitrogen per cubic metre of the volume V^1.
$$N = \frac{0.007(30+u-2z)}{3V^1}$$

In grains of nitrogen per cubic foot.
$$N = \frac{0.10808(30+u-2z)}{3V^1}$$

---

* Alkali Act, 1881, Sec. 8.
† This shape of bulb-tubes has been found to be far superior to any other form of absorption-tubes tried.

F.—SULPHURIC ACID.

1. SPECIFIC GRAVITY OF SULPHURIC ACID AT 60° F.

(Lunge & Isler.)

Twaddell.	100 parts by weight contain		Kilo per litre	1 Cubic Foot of Acid 60° F.		
				weighs lb. avd.	contains lb. avd.	yields lb. avd.
	SO₃	H₂SO₄	H₂SO₄		H₂SO₄	Na₂SO₄
40	22·30	27·82	0·328	74·82	20·44	29·62
41	22·82	27·95	0·337	75·14	21·00	33·48
42	23·33	28·58	0·346	75·45	21·57	31·25
43	23·84	29·21	0·355	75·76	22·14	32·08
44	24·36	29·84	0·364	76·07	22·71	32·90
45	24·88	30·48	0·373	76·38	23·28	33·73
46	25·39	31·11	0·382	76·69	23·85	34·55
47	25·88	31·70	0·391	77·00	24·41	35·37
48	26·35	32·28	0·400	77·32	24·97	36·18
49	26·83	32·86	0·409	77·63	25·54	37·01
50	27·29	33·48	0·418	77·94	26·10	37·82
51	27·76	34·00	0·426	78·25	26·66	38·63
52	28·22	34·57	0·435	78·56	27·23	39·45
53	28·69	35·14	0·444	78·87	27·79	40·27
54	29·15	35·71	0·454	79·19	28·35	41·08
55	29·62	36·29	0·462	79·50	28·92	41·90
56	30·10	36·87	0·472	79·81	29·48	42·72
57	30·57	37·45	0·481	80·12	30·04	43·53
58	31·04	38·08	0·490	80·43	30·60	44·34
59	31·52	38·61	0·500	80·74	31·17	45·16
60	31·99	39·19	0·510	81·06	31·74	45·99
61	32·46	39·77	0·519	81·37	32·32	46·83
62	32·94	40·35	0·529	81·68	32·89	47·65
63	33·41	40·98	0·538	81·99	33·46	48·48
64	33·88	41·50	0·548	82·30	34·03	49·31
65	34·35	42·08	0·557	82·62	34·60	50·13
66	34·80	42·66	0·567	82·93	35·18	50·98
67	35·27	43·20	0·577	83·24	35·79	51·86
68	35·71	43·74	0·586	83·55	36·40	52·74
69	36·14	44·28	0·596	83·86	37·01	53·63
70	36·58	44·82	0·605	84·17	37·63	54·52
71	37·02	45·35	0·614	84·49	38·24	55·41
72	37·45	45·88	0·624	84·80	38·85	56·29
73	37·89	46·41	0·633	85·11	39·46	57·18
74	38·32	46·94	0·643	85·42	40·07	58·05
75	38·75	47·47	0·653	85·73	40·68	58·94
76	39·18	48·00	0·662	86·04	41·29	59·83
77	39·62	48·58	0·672	86·36	41·91	60·72
78	40·05	49·06	0·682	86·67	42·52	61·61
79	40·48	49·59	0·692	86·98	43·13	62·50
80	40·91	50·11	0·702	87·29	43·74	63·38

1. SPECIFIC GRAVITY OF SULPHURIC ACID AT 60° F.—*Continued.*

Twaddell.	100 parts by weight contain		Kilo per litre	1 Cubic Foot of Acid 60° F.		
	SO$_3$	H$_2$SO$_4$	H$_2$SO$_4$	weighs lb. avd.	contains lb. avd. H$_2$SO$_4$	yields lb. avd: Na$_2$SO$_4$
81	41·33	50·63	0·711	87·60	44·36	64·27
82	41·76	51·15	0·721	87·92	44·97	65·13
83	42·17	51·66	0·730	88·23	45·58	66·02
84	42·57	52·15	0·740	88·54	46·18	66·90
85	42·96	52·63	0·750	88·85	46·78	67·78
86	43·36	53·11	0·759	89·16	47·38	68·65
87	43·75	53·59	0·769	89·47	47·99	69·53
88	44·14	54·07	0·779	89·79	48·59	70·41
89	44·53	54·55	0·789	90·10	49·19	71·28
90	44·92	55·03	0·798	90·41	49·79	72·15
91	45·31	55·50	0·808	90·72	50·39	73·01
92	45·69	55·97	0·817	91·03	50·99	73·88
93	46·07	56·43	0·827	91·35	51·59	74·76
94	46·45	56·90	0·837	91·66	52·19	75·62
95	46·88	57·37	0·846	91·97	52·79	76·49
96	47·21	57·83	0·856	92·28	53·39	77·36
97	47·57	58·28	0·866	92·59	54·00	78·25
98	47·95	58·74	0·876	92·90	54·60	79·12
99	48·34	59·22	0·886	93·22	55·20	79·98
100	48·73	59·70	0·896	93·53	55·84	80·92
101	49·12	60·18	0·906	93·84	56·47	81·82
102	49·51	60·65	0·916	94·15	57·10	82·74
103	49·89	61·12	0·926	94·46	57·73	83·65
104	50·28	61·59	0·936	94·77	58·36	84·56
105	50·66	62·06	0·946	95·09	59·00	85·50
106	51·04	62·53	0·957	95·40	59·62	86·39
107	51·43	63·00	0·967	95·71	60·26	87·32
108	51·78	63·43	0·977	96·02	60·89	88·23
109	52·12	63·85	0·987	96·33	61·52	89·15
110	52·46	64·26	0·996	96·65	62·15	90·06
111	52·79	64·67	1·006	96·96	62·78	90·97
112	53·12	65·08	1·015	97·27	63·42	91·90
113	53·46	65·49	1·025	97·58	64·05	92·81
114	53·80	65·90	1·035	97·89	64·68	93·72
115	54·13	66·30	1·044	98·20	65·31	94·64
116	54·46	66·71	1·054	98·52	65·94	95·54
117	54·80	67·13	1·064	98·83	66·58	96·48
118	55·18	67·59	1·075	99·14	67·21	97·40
119	55·55	68·05	1·085	99·45	67·84	98·30
120	55·93	68·51	1·096	99·76	68·47	99·22
121	56·30	68·97	1·107	100·07	69·10	100·15
122	56·68	69·43	1·118	100·39	69·74	101·05
123	57·05	69·89	1·128	100·70	70·37	101·95
124	57·40	70·32	1·139	101·01	71·07	102·96
125	57·75	70·74	1·150	101·32	71·77	104·00

1. SPECIFIC GRAVITY OF SULPHURIC ACID AT 60° F.—*Continued.*

Twaddell.	100 parts by weight contain		Kilo per litre	1 Cubic Foot of Acid 60° F.		
	SO_3	H_2SO_4	H_2SO_4	weighs lb. avd.	contains lb. avd. H_2SO_4	yields lb. avd. Na_2SO_4
126	58·09	71·16	1·160	101·64	72·46	105·00
127	58·43	71·57	1·170	101·95	73·16	106·00
128	58·77	71·99	1·181	102·26	73·85	107·00
129	59·10	72·40	1·192	102·57	74·55	108·00
130	59·45	72·87	1·202	102·88	75·25	109·05
131	59·78	73·23	1·212	103·19	75·94	110·04
132	60·11	73·64	1·222	103·50	76·64	111·05
133	60·46	74·07	1·233	103·82	77·33	112·05
134	60·82	74·51	1·244	104·13	78·03	113·05
135	61·20	74·97	1·256	104·44	78·73	114·10
136	61·57	75·42	1·267	104·75	79·42	115·10
137	61·93	75·86	1·278	105·07	80·12	116·10
138	62·29	76·30	1·289	105·38	80·81	117·10
139	62·64	76·73	1·301	105·69	81·51	118·10
140	63·00	77·17	1·312	106·00	82·21	119·15
141	63·35	77·60	1·323	106·31	82·90	120·15
142	63·70	78·04	1·334	106·62	83·60	121·15
143	64·07	78·48	1·346	106·94	84·29	122·15
144	64·43	78·92	1·357	107·25	84·99	123·15
145	64·78	79·36	1·369	107·56	85·69	124·20
146	65·14	79·80	1·381	107·87	86·83	125·20
147	65·50	80·24	1·392	108·18	87·08	126·20
148	65·86	80·68	1·404	108·49	87·77	127·20
149	66·22	81·12	1·416	108·80	88·47	128·20
150	66·58	81·56	1·427	109·12	89·17	129·20
151	66·94	82·00	1·439	109·43	89·86	130·20
152	67·30	82·44	1·451	109·74	90·56	131·20
153	67·65	82·88	1·463	110·05	91·25	132·25
154	68·02	83·32	1·475	110·36	91·95	133·25
155	68·49	83·90	1·489	110·68	92·88	134·60
156	68·98	84·50	1·504	110·99	93·81	135·90
157	69·47	85·10	1·519	111·30	94·74	137·30
158	69·96	85·70	1·534	111·61	95·67	138·50
159	70·45	86·30	1·549	111·92	96·60	140·00
160	70·94	86·90	1·564	112·23	97·52	141·30

2. SPECIFIC GRAVITY OF HIGHLY CONCENTRATED SULPHURIC ACID AT 60° F. (LUNGE & ISLER.)

Twaddell.	Specific Gravity.	100 Parts by Weight contain		Kilo per litre H_2SO_4.
		SO_3	H_2SO_4.	
160	1·800	70·94	86·90	1·564
161	1·805	71·50	87·60	1·581
162	1·810	72·08	88·30	1·598
163	1·815	72·69	89·05	1·621
164	1·820	73·51	90·05	1·639
...	1·821	73·63	90·20	1·643
...	1·822	73·80	90·40	1·647
...	1·823	73·96	90·60	1·651
...	1·824	74·12	90·80	1·656
165	1·825	74·29	91·00	1·661
...	1·826	74·49	91·25	1·666
...	1·827	74·69	91·50	1·671
...	1·828	74·86	91·70	1·676
...	1·829	75·03	91·90	1·681
166	1·830	75·19	92·10	1·685
...	1·831	75·35	92·30	1·690
...	1·832	75·53	92·52	1·695
...	1·833	75·72	92·75	1·700
...	1·834	75·96	93·05	1·706
167	1·835	76·27	93·43	1·713
...	1·836	76·57	93·80	1·722
...	1·837	76·90	94·20	1·730
...	1·838	77·23	94·60	1·739
...	1·839	77·55	95·00	1·748
168	1·840	78·04	95·60	1·759
...	1·8405	78·33	95·95	1·765
...	1·8410	79·19	97·00	1·786
...	1·8415	79·76	97·70	1·799
...	1·8410	80·16	98·20	1·808
...	1·8405	80·57	98·70	1·816
...	1·8400	80·98	99·20	1·825
...	1·8395	81·18	99·45	1·830
...	1·8390	81·39	99·70	1·834
...	1·8385	81·59	99·95	1·838

3.—SPECIFIC GRAVITIES AND PERCENTAGE OF FUMING (NORDHAUSEN) OIL OF VITRIOL AT DIFFERENT TEMPERATURES.

Density at					SO_3 Per Cent.
15°	20°	25°	30°	35°C.	
1·8417	1·8371	1·8323	1·8287	1·8240	76·67
1·8427	1·8378	1·8333	1·8295	1·8249	77·49
1·8428	1·8388	1·8351	1·8302	1·8255	78·34
1·8437	1·8390	1·8346	1·8300	1·8257	79·04
1·8427	1·8386	1·8351	1·8297	1·8250	79·99
1·8420	1·8372	1·8326	1·8281	1·8234	80·46
1·8398	1·8350	1·8305	1·8263	1·8218	80·94
1·8416	1·8400	1·8353	1·8307	1·8262	81·37
1·8509	1·8466	1·8418	1·8371	1·8324	81·91
1·8571	1·8522	1·8476	1·8432	1·8385	82·17
1·8697	1·8647	1·8595	1·8545	1·8498	82·94
1·8790	1·8742	1·8687	1·8640	1·8592	83·25
1·8875	1·8823	1·8767	1·8713	1·8661	83·84
1·8942	1·8888	1·8833	1·8775	1·8722	84·12
1·8990	1·8940	1·8890	1·8830	1·8772	84·38
1·9031	1·8984	1·8930	1·8874	1·8820	84·67
1·9072	1·9021	1·8950	1·8900	1·8845	84·82
1·9095	1·9042	1·8986	1·8932	1·8866	84·99
1·9121	1·9053	1·8993	1·8948	1·8892	85·14
1·9250	1·9198	1·9135	1·9082	1·9023	85·54
1·9290	1·9236	1·9183	1·9129	1·9073	85·68
1·9368	1·9310	1·9250	1·9187	1·9122	85·88
1·9447	1·9392	1·9331	1·9279	1·9222	86·51
1·9520	1·9465	1·9402	1·9338	1·9278	86·72
1·9584	1·9528	1·9466	1·9406	1·9340	87·08
1·9632	1·9573	1·9518	1·9457	1·9398	87·46
cryst.	cryst.	1·9740	1·9666	1·9740	88·00

The above table is only intended for controlling the works, but not for commercial purposes, because the specific gravity is anything but a certain guide for the percentage of Nordhausen acid, and altogether fails as such for the strengths just below the monohydrate. The table was not made for chemically pure acids, but for commercial acid.

4.—TABLE FOR REDUCING THE SPECIFIC GRAVITIES OF SULPHURIC ACID OF VARIOUS STRENGTHS TO ANY OTHER TEMPERATURE (DEGREES C.).

0°	5°	10°	15°	20°	25°	30°	35°	40°	45°	50°
1·857	1·852	1·846	1·840	1·835	1·830	1·825	1·821	1·816	1·811	1·806
1·847	1·841	1·836	1·830	1·825	1·820	1·815	1·810	1·805	1·800	1·795
1·837	1·831	1·825	1·820	1·815	1·809	1·804	1·799	1·794	1·789	1·784
1·827	1·821	1·815	1·810	1·805	1·799	1·793	1·788	1·783	1·778	1·773
1·817	1·811	1·805	1·800	1·794	1·788	1·783	1·777	1·772	1·766	1·761
1·807	1·801	1·796	1·790	1·784	1·778	1·773	1·767	1·762	1·756	1·751
1·797	1·791	1·786	1·780	1·774	1·768	1·763	1·757	1·752	1·746	1·741
1·786	1·781	1·776	1·770	1·765	1·759	1·754	1·748	1·743	1·737	1·732
1·776	1·770	1·765	1·760	1·755	1·749	1·744	1·738	1·733	1·728	1·723
1·765	1·760	1·755	1·750	1·745	1·740	1·735	1·730	1·725	1·720	1·715
1·754	1·750	1·745	1·740	1·735	1·730	1·726	1·721	1·716	1·711	1·706
1·744	1·740	1·735	1·730	1·725	1·720	1·716	1·711	1·706	1·701	1·696
1·734	1·730	1·725	1·720	1·715	1·710	1·706	1·701	1·696	1·691	1·686
1·724	1·720	1·715	1·710	1·705	1·700	1·696	1·691	1·686	1·681	1·676
1·714	1·710	1·705	1·700	1·695	1·690	1·686	1·681	1·676	1·671	1·667
1·704	1·700	1·695	1·690	1·685	1·680	1·676	1·671	1·666	1·661	1·656
1·694	1·690	1·685	1·680	1·675	1·670	1·666	1·661	1·656	1·651	1·646
1·684	1·680	1·675	1·670	1·665	1·660	1·656	1·651	1·646	1·641	1·637
1·674	1·670	1·665	1·660	1·655	1·650	1·646	1·641	1·636	1·632	1·628
1·664	1·660	1·655	1·650	1·645	1·640	1·636	1·632	1·627	1·622	1·618
1·654	1·650	1·645	1·640	1·635	1·631	1·626	1·622	1·617	1·612	1·608
1·644	1·640	1·635	1·630	1·625	1·621	1·616	1·612	1·607	1·602	1·598
1·634	1·630	1·625	1·620	1·615	1·611	1·606	1·602	1·597	1·592	1·588
1·624	1·620	1·615	1·610	1·605	1·601	1·596	1·592	1·587	1·582	1·578
1·614	1·610	1·605	1·600	1·595	1·591	1·586	1·582	1·577	1·572	1·568
1·604	1·600	1·595	1·590	1·585	1·581	1·576	1·572	1·567	1·562	1·558
1·594	1·589	1·584	1·580	1·575	1·570	1·566	1·562	1·558	1·553	1·548
1·584	1·579	1·574	1·570	1·566	1·561	1·556	1·552	1·548	1·543	1·539
1·574	1·569	1·564	1·560	1·556	1·552	1·547	1·543	1·539	1·534	1·530
1·563	1·554	1·551	1·550	1·546	1·542	1·538	1·534	1·530	1·525	1·521
1·552	1·548	1·544	1·540	1·536	1·532	1·528	1·524	1·520	1·516	1·512
1·542	1·538	1·534	1·530	1·526	1·522	1·518	1·514	1·510	1·506	1·502
1·532	1·528	1·524	1·520	1·516	1·512	1·508	1·504	1·500	1·497	1·492
1·522	1·518	1·514	1·510	1·506	1·502	1·498	1·494	1·490	1·486	1·482
1·512	1·508	1·504	1·500	1·496	1·492	1·488	1·484	1·480	1·476	1·472
1·502	1·498	1·494	1·490	1·486	1·482	1·478	1·474	1·470	1·466	1·462
1·492	1·488	1·484	1·480	1·476	1·472	1·468	1·465	1·461	1·457	1·453
1·482	1·478	1·474	1·470	1·466	1·462	1·458	1·455	1·451	1·447	1·443
1·472	1·468	1·464	1·460	1·456	1·452	1·448	1·445	1·442	1·438	1·434
1·462	1·458	1·454	1·450	1·446	1·442	1·438	1·435	1·432	1·429	1·425
1·452	1·448	1·444	1·440	1·436	1·432	1·429	1·426	1·423	1·420	1·416
1·442	1·438	1·434	1·430	1·426	1·422	1·419	1·416	1·413	1·409	1·405
1·432	1·428	1·424	1·420	1·416	1·413	1·410	1·406	1·402	1·398	1·394
1·422	1·418	1·414	1·410	1·406	1·403	1·399	1·396	1·392	1·388	1·384
1·412	1·408	1·404	1·400	1·396	1·393	1·389	1·386	1·382	1·378	1·374
1·402	1·398	1·394	1·390	1·386	1·383	1·379	1·372	1·372	1·368	1·364
1·392	1·388	1·384	1·380	1·376	1·373	1·370	1·362	1·362	1·359	1·355
1·382	1·378	1·374	1·370	1·366	1·363	1·360	1·352	1·352	1·349	1·346
1·372	1·368	1·364	1·360	1·356	1·353	1·350	1·344	1·344	1·340	1·336
1·362	1·358	1·354	1·350	1·346	1·343	1·340	1·334	1·334	1·330	1·326

4.—TABLE FOR REDUCING THE SPECIFIC GRAVITIES OF SULPHURIC ACID OF VARIOUS STRENGTHS TO ANY OTHER TEMPERATURE (DEGREES C.).—*Continued.*

55°	60°	65°	70°	75°	80°	85°	90°	95°	100°
1·801	1·796	1·792	1·787	1·782	1·778	1·774	1·770	1·766	1·762
1·790	1·787	1·781	1·776	1·770	1·766	1·762	1·757	1·752	1·748
1·779	1·774	1·769	1·764	1·759	1·754	1·749	1·744	1·739	1·734
1·767	1·762	1·757	1·752	1·747	1·741	1·736	1·731	1·726	1·721
1·755	1·750	1·744	1·739	1·734	1·729	1·724	1·719	1·714	1·708
1·746	1·741	1·735	1·730	1·725	1·720	1·715	1·710	1·705	1·700
1·736	1·731	1·726	1·721	1·716	1·712	1·707	1·702	1·697	1·692
1·727	1·722	1·717	1·712	1·707	1·702	1·697	1·693	1·688	1·683
1·718	1·713	1·708	1·703	1·698	1·693	1·688	1·684	1·679	1·674
1·710	1·705	1·700	1·695	1·699	1·685	1·681	1·676	1·671	1·667
1·702	1·697	1·692	1.688	1·683	1·678	1·674	1·669	1·664	1·660
1·692	1·687	1·683	1·678	1·673	1·668	1·664	1·659	1·654	1·650
1·682	1·677	1·673	1·668	1·663	1·659	1·654	1·649	1·644	1·640
1·672	1·667	1·663	1·658	1·653	1·649	1·644	1·639	1·635	1·630
1·662	1·657	1·653	1·648	1·644	1·639	1·634	1·630	1·625	1·620
1·652	1·647	1·642	1·638	1·634	1·630	1·625	1·620	1·615	1·610
1·642	1·637	1·632	1·628	1·624	1 620	1·615	1·611	1·606	1·602
1·633	1·628	1·623	1·619	1·615	1·611	1·606	1·602	1·597	1·593
1·623	1·619	1·614	1·610	1·606	1·602	1·597	1·593	1·588	1·584
1·614	1·610	1·605	1·600	1·596	1·592	1·588	1·583	1·579	1·575
1·604	1·600	1·595	1·591	1·586	1·582	1·578	1·574	1·570	1·565
1·594	1·590	1·585	1·581	1·577	1·573	1·569	1 565	1·561	1·556
1·584	1·580	1·576	1·572	1·568	1·564	1·560	1·556	1·552	1·517
1·574	1·570	1·566	1·562	1·558	1·554	1·550	1·546	1 542	1·537
1·564	1·560	1·556	1·552	1·548	1·544	1·540	1·536	1·531	1·527
1·554	1·550	1·545	1·541	1·537	1·533	1·529	1·525	1·521	1·516
1·544	1·539	1·535	1·531	1·527	1·523	1·519	1·515	1·510	1·503
1·535	1·531	1·526	1·522	1·518	1·513	1·509	1·505	1·501	1·496
1·526	1·522	1·517	1·513	1·509	1·504	1·500	1·496	1·492	1·487
1·517	1·513	1·509	1·504	1·500	1·495	1·491	1·487	1·483	1·478
1·508	1·504	1·500	1·495	1·491	1·486	1·482	1·478	1·473	1·469
1·498	1·494	1·490	1·485	1·481	1·476	1·472	1·468	1·463	1·459
1·488	1·484	1·480	1·476	1·472	1·467	1·462	1·458	1·453	1·449
1·478	1·474	1·470	1·466	1·462	1·457	1·452	1·448	1·443	1·438
1·468	1·464	1·460	1·455	1·451	1·446	1·442	1·438	1·433	1·428
1·458	1 454	1·450	1·442	1·441	1·437	1·433	1·429	1·424	1·419
1·449	1·445	1·441	1·436	1·432	1·428	1·424	1·419	1·414	1·410
1·439	1·435	1·431	1·427	1·423	1·418	1·414	1·409	1·405	1·401
1·430	1·426	1·422	1·418	1·413	1·409	1·405	1·400	1·396	1·392
1·421	1·417	1·413	1·409	1·404	1·400	1·396	1·391	1·387	1·383
1·412	1·407	1·403	1·399	1·395	1·391	1·386	1·382	1·378	1·374
1·401	1·397	1·393	1·389	1·385	1·380	1·376	1·372	1·368	1·364
1·390	1·386	1·382	1·378	1·374	1·370	1·366	1·362	1·358	1·353
1·380	1·376	1·372	1·368	1·364	1·360	1·356	1·352	1·348	1·343
1·370	1·366	1·362	1·358	1·354	1·350	1·346	1·342	1·338	1·333
1·360	1·356	1·352	1·348	—	—	—	—	—	—
1·351	1·346	1·342	1·338	—	—	—	—	—	—
1·342	1·337	1·334	1·329	—	—	—	—	—	—
1·332	1·327	1·323	1·319	—	—	—	—	—	—
1·322	1·317	1·314	·1·310	—	—	—	—	—	—

4.—TABLE FOR REDUCING THE SPECIFIC GRAVITIES OF SULPHURIC ACID OF VARIOUS STRENGTHS TO ANY OTHER TEMPERATURE (DEGREES C.).—Continued.

0°	5°	10°	15°	20°	25°	30°	35°	40°	45°	50°
1·352	1·848	1·344	1·340	1·336	1·333	1·330	1·327	1·324	1·320	1·316
1·341	1·337	1·333	1·330	1·327	1·324	1·321	1·318	1·314	1·310	1·306
1·330	1·326	1·323	1·320	1·317	1·314	1·311	1·308	1·304	1·301	1·297
1·320	1·316	1·313	1·310	1·307	1·304	1·301	1·298	1·294	1·291	1·2b7
1·310	1·306	1·303	1·300	1·297	1·294	1·291	1·288	1·284	1·281	1·277
1·300	1·296	1·293	1·290	1·287	1·284	1·280	1·277	1·274	1·270	1·267
1·290	1·286	1·283	1·280	1·277	1·274	1·270	1·267	1·264	1·260	1·256
1·280	1·276	1·273	1·270	1·267	1·264	1·260	1·257	1·254	1·250	1·246
1·270	1·266	1·263	1·260	1·257	1·254	1·251	1·248	1·245	1·241	1·237
1·260	1·256	1·253	1·250	1·247	1·244	1·241	1·238	1·235	1·231	1·227
1·250	1·246	1·243	1·240	1·237	1·234	1·230	1·227	1·224	1·220	1·217
1·240	1·236	1·233	1·230	1·227	1·224	1·220	1·217	1·214	1·210	1·207
1·230	1·226	1·223	1·220	1·217	1·214	1·210	1·207	1·204	1·200	1·197
1·220	1·216	1·213	1·210	1·206	1·204	1·200	1·197	1·194	1·190	1·187
1·210	1·206	1·203	1·200	1·196	1·193	1·190	1·186	1·183	1·180	1·176
1·200	1·196	1·193	1·190	1·186	1·183	1·180	1·176	1·173	1·169	1·165
1·190	1·186	1·183	1·180	1·176	1·173	1·170	1·166	1·163	1·159	1·155
1·180	1·176	1·173	1·170	1·166	1·163	1·160	1·156	1·153	1·149	1·146
1·169	1·166	1·163	1·160	1·157	1·153	1·150	1·147	1·144	1·141	1·138
1·159	1·156	1·153	1·150	1·147	1·143	1·140	1·137	1·134	1·131	1·128
1·149	1·146	1·143	1·140	1·137	1·134	1·131	1·128	1·125	1·122	1·119
1·138	1·135	1·133	1·130	1·127	1·125	1·122	1·119	1·116	1·113	1·110
1·128	1·125	1·123	1·120	1·118	1·115	1·112	1·110	1·107	1·104	1·102
1·118	1·115	1·113	1·110	1·108	1·105	1·102	1·100	1·097	1·094	1·092
1·108	1·105	1·103	1·100	1·097	1·094	1·092	1·090	1·087	1·084	1·082
1·098	1·095	1·093	1·090	1·087	1·084	1·082	1·080	1·077	1·074	1·072
1·088	1·085	1·083	1·080	1·077	1·074	1·072	1·070	1·067	1·064	1·062
1·078	1·075	1·073	1·070	1·067	1·064	1·062	1·060	1·057	1·054	1·052
1·068	1·065	1·063	1·060	1·057	1·054	1·052	1·050	1·048	1·044	1·042
1·058	1·055	1·053	1·050	1·047	1·044	1·042	1·040	1·038	1·034	1·032
1·048	1·045	1·043	1·040	1·037	1·034	1·032	1·030	1·028	1·024	1·022
1·038	1·035	1·033	1·030	1·027	1·024	1·022	1·020	1·018	1·014	1·012
1·028	1·025	1·023	1·020	1·017	1·014	1·012	1·010	1·008	1 004	1·002
1·018	1·015	1·013	1·010	1·007	1·004	1·002	1 000	0·998	0·994	0·992

5.—FREEZING AND MELTING POINTS OF SULPHURIC ACID.*

Spec. Grav. at 15°.	Freezing point.	Melting point.
1·671	Liquid at − 20°	—
1·691	Liquid at − 20°	—
1·712	Liquid at − 20°	—
1·727	− 7·5°	− 7·5°
1·732	− 8·5	− 8·5
1·749	− 0·2	+ 4·5
1·767	+ 1·6	+ 6·5
1·778	+ 8·5	+ 8·5
1·790	+ 4·5	+ 8·0
1·807	− 9·0	− 6·0
1·822	Liquid at − 20°	—
1·840	Liquid at − 20°	—

* Lunge, Berichte d. deutsch. chem. Ges. 1891 S.

4.—TABLE FOR REDUCING THE SPECIFIC GRAVITIES OF SULPHURIC ACID OF VARIOUS STRENGTHS TO ANY OTHER TEMPERATURE (DEGREES C.).—Continued.

55°	60°	65°	70°	75°	80°	85°	90°	95°	100°
1·312	1·308	1·304	1·300	—	—	—	—	—	—
1·302	1·298	1·294	1·290	—	—	—	—	—	—
1·293	1·289	1·284	1·280	—	—	—	—	—	—
1·283	1·279	1·274	1·270	—	—	—	—	—	—
1·273	1·269	1·265	1·260	—	—	—	—	—	—
1·263	1·259	1·255	1·250	—	—	—	—	—	—
1·252	1·248	1·244	1·240	—	—	—	—	—	—
1·242	1·238	1·234	1·230	—	—	—	—	—	—
1·233	1·224	1·224	1·220	—	—	—	—	—	—
1·223	1·214	1·214	1·210	—	—	—	—	—	—
1·210	1·209	1·204 ·	1·200	—	—	—	—	—	—
1·204	1·200	1·195	1·190	—	—	—	—	—	—
1·194	1·190	1·185	1·180	—	—	—	—	—	—
1·183	1·179	1·175	1·170	—	—	—	—	—	—
1·172	1·168	1·164	1·160	—	—	—	—	—	—
1·162	1·158	1·154	1·150	—	—	—	—	—	—
1·152	1·148	1·144	1·140	—	—	—	—	—	—
1·143	1·139	1·135	1·131	—	—	—	—	—	—
1·135	1·131	1·127	1·123	—	—	—	—	—	—
1·125	1·122	1·118	1·114	—	—	—	—	—	—
1·116	1·113	1·109	1·106	—	—	—	—	—	—
1·107	1·104	1·100	1·097	—	—	—	—	—	—
1·099	1·096	1·092	1·088	—	—	—	—	—	—
1·089	1·086	1·082	1·078	—	—	—	—	—	—
1·079	1·075	1·072	1·068	—	—	—	—	—	—
1·069	1·065	1·062	1·058	—	—	—	—	—	—
1·059	1·055	1·052	1·048	—	—	—	—	—	—
1·049	1·045	1·042	1·038	—	—	—	—	—	—
1·036	1·035	1·032	1·028	—	—	—	—	—	—
1·039	1·025	1·022	1·018	—	—	—	—	—	—
1·019	0·015	1·012	1·008	—	—	—	—	—	—
1·009	1·005	1·002	0·998	—	—	—	—	—	—
0·999	1·995	0·992	0·988	—	—	—	—	—	—
0·989	0·985	0·982	0·978	—	—	—	—	—	—

6.—BOILING POINTS OF SULPHURIC ACID.
(Lunge, *Ber. d. d. chem. Ges.* 11, 370.)

Proc. SO_4H_2	Spec. Gr.	Boil. Point.	Proc. SO_4H_2	Spec. Gr.	Boil. Point.	Proc. SO_4H_2	Spec. Gr.	Boil. Point.
5	1·031	101°	56	1·459	133°	82	1·758	218·5°
10	1·069	102	60	1·503	141·5	84	1·773	227
15	1·107	103·5	62·5	1·530	147	86	1·791	238·5
20	1·147	105	65	1·557	153·5	88	1·807	251·5
25	1·184	106·5	67·5	1·585	161	90	1·818	262·5
30	1·224	108	70	1·615	170	91	1·824	268
35	1·265	100	72	1·639	174·5	92	1·830	274·5
40	1·307	114	74	1·661	180·5	93	1·834	281·5
45	1·352	118·5	76	1·688	189	94	1·837	288·5
50	1·399	124	78	1·710	199	95	1·840	295
53	1·428	128·5	80	1·733	207			

Monohydrate (100%) boils at 338° (Marignac).

7.—PERCENTAGE OF SO₃ IN NORDHAUSEN OIL OF VITRIOL.

Found by Titrating SO₃	Contains per cent. SO₄H₂	SO₃	Found by Titrating SO₃	Contains per cent. SO₄H₂	SO₃	Found by Titrating SO₃	Contains per cent. SO₄H₂	SO₃
81·6326	100	0	87·8775	66	34	93·9387	33	67
81·8163	99	1	88·0612	65	35	94·1224	32	68
82·0000	98	2	88·2448	64	36	94·3061	31	69
82·1836	97	3	88·4285	63	37	94·4897	30	70
82·3674	96	4	88·6122	62	38	94·6734	29	71
82·5510	95	5	88·7959	61	39	94·8571	28	72
82·7346	94	6	88·9795	60	40	95·0408	27	73
82·9183	93	7	89·1632	59	41	95·2244	26	74
83·1020	92	8	89·3469	58	42	95·4081	25	—
83·2857	91	9	89·5806	57	43	95·5918	24	—
83·4693	90	10	89·7142	56	44	95·7755	23	—
83·6530	89	11	89·8979	55	45	95·9591	22	—
83·8367	88	12	90·0816	54	46	96·1428	21	—
84·0204	87	13	90·2653	53	47	96·3265	20	—
84·2040	86	14	90·4489	52	48	96·5102	19	—
84·3877	85	15	90·6326	51	49	96·6938	18	—
84·5714	84	16	90·8163	50	50	96·8775	17	—
84·7551	83	17	91·0000	49	51	97·0612	16	—
84·9387	82	18	91·1836	48	52	97·2448	15	—
85·1224	81	19	91·3673	47	53	97·4285	14	—
85·3061	80	20	91·5510	46	54	97·6122	13	—
85·4897	79	21	91·7346	45	55	97·7959	12	—
85·6734	78	22	91·9183	44	56	97·9795	11	—
85·8571	77	23	92·1020	43	57	98·1632	10	—
86·0408	76	24	92·2857	42	58	98·3469	9	—
86·2244	75	25	92·4093	41	59	98·5806	8	—
86·4081	74	26	92·6530	40	60	98·7142	7	—
86·5918	73	27	92·8367	39	61	98·8979	6	—
86·7755	72	28	93·0204	38	62	99·0816	5	—
86·9591	71	29	93·2040	37	63	99·2653	4	—
87·1428	70	30	93·3877	36	64	99·4489	3	—
87·3265	69	31	93·5714	35	65	99·6326	2	—
87·5102	68	32	93·7551	34	66	99·8163	1	—
87·6938	67	33						

7a.—THE QUANTITATIVE ESTIMATION OF FREE SULPHURIC ACID

is made by titrating a *measured* volume by standard soda solution. The results are always expressed in per cent. of monohydrated sulphuric acid (hydrogen sulphate, H_2SO_4) by weight. The specific gravity of the acid is taken with a hydrometer. This is called x. Take 10c.c. of the acid with an accurate pipette, dilute to 100c.c., and take again 10c.c. of this for titration. For very accurate results it is preferable to weigh the quantity of acid to be tested in a glass-cock tube, fig. 8 (comp. *infra*, No. 9), and employ the whole quantity weighed for titration. If the number of cubic centimetres of normal soda solution (=0·031gr. Na_2O per cubic centimetre consumed) is called y, the percentage of the acid is

$$\frac{4\cdot9y}{x}$$

The normal soda solution is standardized with normal hydrochloric acid (0·0365gr. of HCl per cubic centimetre), and the latter with pure sodium carbonate, which thus forms the foundation of alkalimetry and acidimetry. (Compare the Appendix.) If the sulphuric acid to be tested contains an appreciable quantity of nitrous acid, methyl-orange cannot be employed as indicator, unless the nitrous acid is previously oxidized by potassium permanganate.

8.—EXAMINATION OF SULPHURIC ACID FOR OTHER SUBSTANCES.

(*a*) *Nitrous Acid* is titrated with semi-normal permanganate. (Preparation in the Appendix.) This can be done without loss of NO when manipulating, as follows (Lunge, *Berliner Berichte* x. 1075): Put the nitrous vitriol into a burette fitted with a glass tap, and run it slowly into a measured quantity of permanganate, diluted with 5 times its volume of tepid water (30° C. to 40° C.), and constantly agitate, till the colour just vanishes. Each cubic centimetre of the permanganate indicates 0·0095grm. N_2O_3, hence more or less of it is employed, according to whether an acid containing more or less N_2O_3 is titrated. For chamber acid employ at most 5c.c.; for good Gay-Lussac acid up to 50c.c. of permanganate. If the quantity of permanganate is called x, and that of the vitriol consumed for decolorizing it y, the quantity of N_2O_3 present in grammes per litre of acid is

$$\frac{9\cdot5x}{y}$$

Calculated as $\quad\quad NO_3H = \dfrac{15\cdot75x}{y}$

as $\quad\quad\quad\quad NaNO_3 = \dfrac{21\cdot25x}{y}$

The following table saves the calculation for all cases in which $x=50$. The column y gives the number of cubic centimetres of nitrous vitriol used, a the percentage in grammes per litre, and b the percentage by weight for acid of 140° Tw. (For other strengths the percentage by weight is calculated by dividing the figures of column a by 10 × specific gravity.)

TABLE FOR ESTIMATING NITROUS VITRIOL.

Employ 50c.c. of semi-normal permanganate. The results are expressed as NO_3H and NO_3Na. The column y refers to acid of 140° Tw. as unit:—

Acid consumed. y c.c.	NO$_3$H a g. per Litre.	NO$_3$H b Per cent.	NO$_3$Na a g. per Litre.	NO$_3$Na b Per cent.	Acid consumed. y c.c.	NO$_3$H a g. per Litre.	NO$_3$H b Per cent.	NO$_3$Na a g. per Litre.	NO$_3$Na b Per cent.
10	78·8	4·62	106·2	6·22	86	21·9	1·28	29·5	1·73
11	71·6	4·20	96·5	5·65	87	21·3	1·25	28·7	1·68
12	65·7	3·85	88·5	5·18	88	20·7	1·21	28·0	1·64
13	60·6	3·55	81·7	4·78	89	20·2	1·18	27·3	1·60
14	56·2	3·28	75·9	4·44	40	19·7	1·15	26·6	1·56
15	52·5	3·07	70·8	4·14	41	19·2	1·12	25·9	1·52
16	49·3	2·89	66·4	3·91	42	18·8	1·10	25·3	1·48
17	46·3	2·71	62·5	3·65	43	18·3	1·07	24·7	1·45
18	43·7	2·56	59·0	3·45	44	17·9	1·05	24·2	1·42
19	41·5	2·43	55·9	3·27	45	17·5	1·02	23·6	1·38
20	39·3	2·30	53·1	3·11	46	17·1	1·00	23·1	1·35
21	37·5	2·19	50·6	2·96	47	16·8	0·98	22·6	1·32
22	35·7	2·09	48·3	2·82	48	16·4	0·96	22·2	1·30
23	34·2	2·00	46·3	2·71	49	16·1	0·94	21·7	1·27
24	32·8	1·92	44·4	2·60	50	15·8	0·925	21·3	1·25
25	31·5	1·84	42·5	2·49	55	14·4	0·835	19·3	1·13
26	30·3	1·77	40·8	2·39	60	13·1	0·765	17·7	1·04
27	29·1	1·71	39·4	2·30	65	12·1	0·705	16·4	0·96
28	28·1	1·64	38·0	2·22	70	11·2	0·655	15·2	0·89
29	27·1	1·58	36·7	2·15	75	10·5	0·615	14·15	0·827
30	26·3	1·54	35·5	2·08	80	9·85	0·575	13·3	0·778
31	25·5	1·49	34·3	2·01	85	9·2	0·538	12·5	0·730
32	24·6	1·44	33·3	1·95	90	8·7	0·510	11·8	0·692
33	23·9	1·40	32·3	1·89	95	8·3	0·485	11·2	0·655
34	23·2	1·36	31·3	1·84	100	7·9	0·462	10·6	0·620
35	22·5	1·32	30·4	1·78					

N.B.—The figures in column a also indicate 0·01lb. avoirdupois per gallon, or nearly ounces per cubic foot.

(b) *Total Nitrogen Acids.*—These are contained in sulphuric acid as N_2O_3 or more properly as nitroso-sulphuric acid, $SO_2(OH)(ONO)$, and NO_3H. NO can be present only in minute quantity, and not at all when NO_3H is present. N_2O_4 is decomposed by sulphuric acid into nitrosulphuric and nitric acid. The estimation made according to a only indicates N_2O_3. The total of the nitrogen acids is converted into NO by shaking up the nitrous vitriol with mercury; the quantity of NO formed is estimated by volume (Crum's reaction). This is done by Lunge's nitrometer (compare Lunge's "Sulphuric Acid and Alkali," 2nd ed. i., 181). Fill the graduated limb a with mercury by raising the level tube b; put the three-way cock in the position of communicating with none of the openings; run the nitrous acid into the top cups of *a* from a 1c.c. pipette graduated in $\frac{1}{100}$c.c., employing only 0·5c.c. of very strong, but up to 5c.c. of very weak nitrous vitriol; lower the level tube, open the cock carefully so that the vitriol runs down without any air entering; pour 2 or 3c.c. of pure strong sulphuric acid, entirely free from nitrogen compounds, into the cup; let this acid enter the nitrometer, and repeat the washing of the cup with 1 or 2c.c. of pure acid. Start the evolution of gas by taking the tube *a* out of the clamp, inclining it several times almost to the horizontal line, and suddenly righting it again, so that mercury and acid are well mixed; shake one or two minutes till no more gas is evolved. Place the tubes so that the mercury in *b* is as much higher than that in *a* as is required for balancing the acid in *a*; this will take 1mm. of Hg for 6½mm. of acid. An exact test can only be produced when the gas has taken the temperature of the room and all froth has subsided. Read off the volume of the gas, also a thermometer hung up close by, and a barometer. In order to check the levelling, open the cock, when the level of *a* should not change. If it rises, too much pressure has been given, and the reading must be increased a little, say 0·1c.c. If it sinks, the opposite must take place, *i.e.*, always in the opposite sense to the change of level. Another plan is, putting a little acid into the cup before opening the cock. This would be sucked in if the pressure were too low, or raised if too high. With adroit manipulation the experiment can then soon be corrected. After finishing it, lower the graduated tube *a*, lest on opening the tap any air should enter; open the tap, raise the tube *b*, force thus the gas and all acid into the cup, and put the tap so that the acid flows through its key into a vessel held below; the last of it is drawn out by blotting paper. The nitrometer is then ready for the next experiment. A test must always be made to see whether the glass tap is gas-tight. It will hardly remain so without greasing it occasionally with vaseline; but this ought to be done very slightly, so as to avoid any grease getting into the bore; for if the grease comes in contact with acid, troublesome froth is formed. This process is interfered with by the presence of sulphurous acid, the best test for which is the smell. To remove it, the acid is stirred up with a very slight quantity of powdered potassium permanganate. Any great excess of this makes the process very troublesome and inaccurate. The volume of NO read off is reduced to 0° C. and 760mm. (32° F. and .29·92in.) by means of the tables, pages 20 and 21 or 21B and calculated for the nitrogen compounds present by the following table, in which column *a* means milligrammes, *b* per cent. by weight when employing 1c.c. acid of 140° Tw.

per cent. NO	N		NO		N_2O_3		NO_3H		$NaNO_3$	
	a	*b*	*a*	*b*	*a*	*b*	*a*	*b*	*a*	*b*
1	0·627	0·0366	1·343	0·0785	1·701	0·0995	2·820	0·1648	3·805	0·2225
2	1·254	0·0732	2·686	0·1570	3·402	0·1990	5·640	0·3296	7·610	0·4450
3	1·881	0·1098	4·029	0·2355	5·103	0·2985	8·460	0·4944	11·415	0·6675
4	2·508	0·1464	5·372	0·3140	6·804	0·3980	11·280	0·6592	15·220	0·8900
5	3·135	0·1830	6·715	0·3925	8·506	0·4975	14·100	0·8240	19·025	1·1125
6	3·762	0·2196	8·058	0·4710	10·206	0·5970	16·920	0·9888	22·830	1·3350
7	4·389	0·2562	9·401	0·5495	11·907	0·6965	19·740	1·1536	26·635	1·5575
8	5·016	0·2928	10·744	0·6280	13·608	0·7960	22·560	1·3184	30·440	1·7800
9	5·643	0·3294	12·087	0·7065	15·309	0·8955	25·380	1·4832	34·245	2·0025

The reduction to 0° and 760 mm. can be effected without thermometer and barometer, and without the use of any tables, by means of Lunge's Gas-volumeter, Fig. 8. It consists of the gas-measuring tube, A, the reduction-

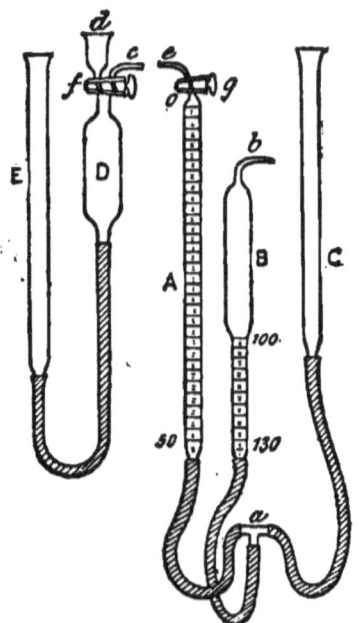

Fig. 8.

tube, B, and the level-tube, C, all connected by very thick elastic tubing, with the three-way tube, a. B and C are held in two arms of the same clamp, so as to be each individually movable in its own arm, or both together by means of the common clamp. Tube B is graduated from 100 to 180 c.c., and contains a volume of air equal to that which 100 c.c. of dry air occupy at 0° and 760 mm. This is obtained by taking, once for all, a reading of the thermometer and the barometer, calculating what would be the volume of 100 c.c. of dry air of 0° and 760 mm. under the atmospheric conditions just observed, pouring mercury into C, till it stands in tube B at the volume just calculated (after introducing one or two drops of strong sulphuric acid into tube B), and sealing the capillary end b, taking care lest the air in B should get heated and expand during this operation. After thus enclosing the before-mentioned exact volume of air in tube B, the instrument is ready for use for an indefinite time. Tube A might be an ordinary nitrometer with three-way tap and funnels; it is, however, best employed merely as a gas-measuring tube, whilst a special reaction vessel, D, with its own level tube, E, serves for treating the nitrous vitriol (or

I

nitrate of soda, etc., as the case may be). D is a vessel, holding about 150 c.c., provided with the three-way tap, funnel, and outlet-tube of the old Lunge's nitrometer. By raising E, the vessel D is completely filled with mercury, till this begins to run out at c. The tap f is shut, the end of c is closed by a glass or indiarubber cap, funnel d is charged with nitrous vitriol ; this is sucked into D, and the decomposition is brought about in the usual manner by shaking the vitriol with the mercury, to evolve all the nitrogen acids in the shape of NO. Now the tubes D and A are brought opposite to each other (A having been previously filled, by raising C, with mercury till it flows out at e); c and e are joined by a short bit of indiarubber tubing, till they touch, so that no air remains in the space between ; C is lowered ; E is raised, and by cautiously opening tap f, the NO contained in D is transferred into A. As soon as all the gas is within A, and the acid following it has filled the narrow tube e, tap g is shut. Now tube C is raised till the mercury in B has risen to the mark 100, and B and C are simultaneously moved up or down, as the case may require it, till the mercurial levels in A and B coincide, that in B being still at 100 c.c. Since the air in B is now compressed to the point which it would occupy in the dry state at 0° and 760 mm., and the gas in A is placed under exactly the same pressure (the temperature of these two parallel tubes being presumably alike), the reading in A shows the NO at once reduced to the same conditions of 0° and 760 mm.

Qualitative Test for Traces of Nitrogen Acid.—This is best done by means of diphenylamine. Dissolve a few grammes of diphenylamine in 100 parts of pure sulphuric acid. This should be completely free from N compounds, and can be obtained, if not at hand, by boiling with a trace of ammonium sulphate. Dilute the acid with $\frac{1}{10}$th volume of water before dissolving the diphenylamine. Pour about 2 c.c. of the vitriol to be tested into a test tube, and run about 1 c.c. of the diphenylamine solution upon it, so that the layers mix only gradually. In the case of dilute acids, or other lighter liquids, proceed in the opposite manner. The slightest traces of nitrogen acids are proved by the appearance of a brilliant blue colour in the area of contact of both liquids.

This test, however, fails in the presence of selenium (which can be recognised by adding to the acid a strong solution of ferrous sulphate, when a brownish-red precipitate will make its appearance, which cannot be confounded with the colour produced by NO). In this case the nitrogen acids must be sought for by adding a solution of brucine sulphate, which in their presence produces a red colour.

(c) *Examination for Lead.*—Dilute the acid, if concentrated, with the same volume of water and twice its volume of alcohol. Allow the mixture to stand for some time, filter any precipitate of $PbSO_4$, wash it with dilute alcohol, and dry and ignite in a porcelain crucible, burning the filter separately. 1gr. $PbSO_4 = 0.68317$gr. Pb.

(d) *Examination for Iron.*—Boil the acid, if free from nitrogen, with a drop of nitric acid to peroxidize the iron. Dilute a little, allow to cool, and add solution of potassium sulphocyanide. A red colour proves the presence of iron. If there is not too little of it, it can be quantitatively estimated in another sample by heating with pure zinc (free from iron), pouring off the zinc, washing the latter, allowing to cool, and titrating with permanganate. This is best employed as $\frac{1}{20}$th normal, indicating 0.0028 gr. Fe per cubic centimetre. Not less than 50 c.c. of acid should be taken for this test, as the acid generally contains very little iron.

9.—ANALYSIS OF FUMING SULPHURIC ACID (NORDHAUSEN ACID, ANHYDRIDE).

This is either weighed in glass bulbs or in a glass-tap tube. The former are very thin bulbs of about 2 cm. diameter, ending each way in a capillary tube. Melt the acid, if solid, till it is just completely homogeneous, and suck 3 grms. to 5 grms. of it into the bulb, which ought to be half filled with it. The sucking is best done by means of a bottle closed with an indiarubber cork, through which passes a tightly-fitting glass tap, connected at its free end with an elastic tube. Suction is applied to the latter, the tap is closed, the elastic tube is drawn over one of the capillary ends of the weighing bulb, and by opening the tap a sufficient quantity of acid is admitted into the bulb. The tube is cleaned, and one of the capillary ends is sealed at the lamp. The other end can be left open without fear of any loss of SO_3 or attraction of moisture during weighing. The weighing is best done on a small platinum crucible with two nicks, on which the ends of the bulb can rest. If the latter should be accidentally broken, the acid runs into the crucible, not on the balance. Put the bulb, after weighing, open end downwards into a small Erlenmeyer flask, into the neck of which it ought to fit exactly (Fig. 9), and which contains so much water that the capillary tube

FIG. 9.

dips pretty far into it, to prevent any loss of SO_3 on mixing the acid with water. Break off the other point, allow the acid to run out, squirt a few drops of water into the upper capillary, and ultimately rinse the whole bulb tube by repeated aspiration of water. Dilute the liquid to 500 c.c. and take 50 c.c. for each test. This is done with $\frac{1}{5}$ normal soda solution (1c. c.= 0·008 grm. SO_3), and litmus or methyl-orange as indicator. The acidity found is diminished by that proceeding from SO_2, and found by titrating another sample with iodine. More convenient than the bulb tube is Lunge & Rey's glass-tap pipette, Fig. 10. Shut the lower tap c, open the upper tap a, apply suction (with the mouth) at d, and shut a whilst sucking. Immerse the point e in the acid to be tested, and open c; the partial vacuum in bulb b suffices for drawing up enough acid, which must not be allowed to reach the tap c. Shut c, clean the point e, put the pipette in the outer glass f, and weigh. Take the pipette out of f, place it point downwards in water, or, in the case of the strongest Nordhausen acids, in a layer of crystallized, coarsely powdered sodium sulphate, and slowly run out the contents. Then squirt some water from above into b, allow to stand for a moment, and rinse thoroughly with water. If only 0·5 grm. to 1 grm. o' acid has been weighed off, titrate directly. This process is more accurate than diluting and titrating only part of the liquid, but this cannot be

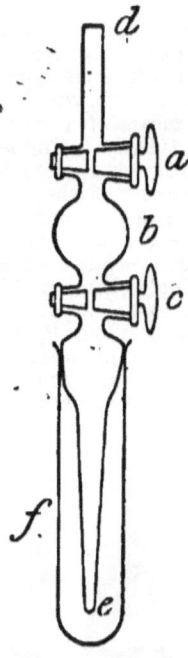

FIG. 10.

avoided when a larger quantity of acid has been weighed. Anhydride, etc., once melted for the purpose of filling the tube remains liquid long enough to complete the weighing and running out without requiring to be heated again. Solid anhydride is best dissolved in monohydrated acid on taking out the samples as will be described in the Appendix.

3.—SALTCAKE AND HYDROCHLORIC ACID.
A.—SALT (COMMON SALT, ROCK-SALT).

1. *Moisture.*—Ignite 5 grms. of salt in a covered platinum crucible (to prevent projections); heat first quite gradually, then for some minutes up to a low red heat.

2. *Insoluble.*—Dissolve 5 grms., filter the insoluble matter, wash, dry, and ignite the same.

3. *Chlorine.*—Weigh off 5·85 grms. of the moist salt, dissolve it, and dilute up to 500 c.c.; take out 25 c.c. by means of a pipette; add so much of a solution of neutral potassium chromate that the liquid is distinctly yellow, and titrate with decinormal silver solution (refer to Appendix). Add the silver solution from a 50 c.c. burette, till the precipitate, even after agitation, shows a distinct but faint pink colour. 0·2 c.c. is deducted from

the number of cubic centimetres of silver solution employed, as being required for producing the colour. The remainder, multiplied by 2, indicates the percentage of NaCl in the salt.

4. *Lime.*—Dissolve 5 grms. of the salt in water, in case of need with the aid of a little HCl. When analyzing impure rock-salt the treatment with dilute HCl must be continued for some time, in order to dissolve all $CaSO_4$. It is also necessary to filter off any clay, etc., but non-argillaceous salt ought to be dissolved completely, excepting any grains of sand and the like. In the clear solution precipitate the lime with ammonia and ammonium oxalate, allow to stand for 12 hours, filter the precipitate through dense filter paper in a well-shaped funnel (compare p. 94), wash, dry, and ignite it in a platinum crucible till it is completely converted into CaO. This is done by first gently heating till the calcium oxalate is decomposed, and then igniting at nearly a white heat for 20 minutes, either over a gas blow-pipe or, more conveniently, in a Hempels gas-stove or over a Muencke patent burner.* 1 part CaO is equal to $2·4286$ $CaSO_4$, and is calculated as such.

B.—SALTCAKE.

(N.B.—Nos. 1 and 2 are sufficient for daily examinations of the produce of works, the others are employed for saltcake bought and sold.)

1. *Free Acid.*—Dissolve 20 grms. saltcake, dilute to 250 c.c., take out 50 c.c. with a pipette, add litmus or methyl-orange, and titrate with standard soda up to the point of neutralization. Each cubic centimetre of the standard alkali is equal to 1 per cent. SO_3. The total acidity is calculated as SO_3, including HCl, $NaHSO_4$, and, in the case of litmus, the salts of iron and alumina which have an acid reaction to litmus. If the latter are present in appreciable quantities, and if it is desirable to exclude them from the result, employ methyl-orange as indicator, or else add the standard alkali without any indicator, till the first flakes of a permanent precipitate appear, which occurs when the free acid and that of the bisulphate is just saturated.

2. *Sodium Chloride.*—Take another 50 c.c. of the solution made for the test No. 1, add the same quantity of standard alkali as used for this test, so that the acid is exactly neutralized, then a little neutral potassium chromate, and titrate with decinormal silver solution, as in A, 3. Each cubic centimetre of silver solution (after deducting $0·2$ from the whole) is equal to $0·146$ per cent. NaCl. Or else employ a solution containing $2·906$ grms. $AgNO_3$ per litre and indicating $0·001$ grm. NaCl per cubic centimetre. This would in the present case indicate $0·025$ per cent. NaCl per cubic centimetre.

3. *Iron.*—Dissolve 10 grms. of sulphate in water, reduce the iron salts to protoxide by a little sulphuric acid, and zinc, and titrate with potassium permanganate. (Details page 114.)

4. *Residue,* insoluble in water, is estimated as usual if present.

5. *Lime.*—Dissolve 10 grms. in water if necessary with a little HCl_1; add NH_4Cl and NH_3, precipitate with ammonium oxalate. Ignite, and weigh as CaO. (Compare A, 4.) If any appreciable quantity of Fe_2O_3 has been found, this must be deducted.

6. *Magnesia* is precipitated in the filtrate from No. 5 by ammonium phosphate; allow to stand for 24 hours; filter, wash with dilute ammonia, dry, ignite and weigh the magnesium pyrophosphate of which 1 part = $0·36036$ MgO.

---

* To be obtained from Dr. Muencke, Luisenstrasse 58, Berlin, or from the English dealers in chemical apparatus.

7. *Alumina.*—The solution of the saltcake is precipitated with ammonia (free from CO_2). The precipitate is ignited and weighed. Deducting the weight of Fe_2O_3 found in No. 3, the remainder $= Al_2O_3$.

8. *Sodium Sulphate (direct estimation).*—Dissolve 1 grm. of the saltcake; precipitate any lime along with ferric oxide, etc., as in No. 5; filter; evaporate the filtrate to dryness after adding a few drops of pure sulphuric acid; ignite; repeat this after adding a small piece of ammonium carbonate, and weigh. Deduct from this weight (1) the NaCl found in test No. 2, calculated for Na_2SO_4 ($1.0000 NaCl = 1.2136 Na_2SO_4$, or each cubic centimetre of decinormal silver solution employed in test No. 2 $= 0.00177$ grm. Na_2SO_4); (2) the MgO found in test No. 6, calculated as $MgSO_4$ (1.000 MgO $= 3.000 MgSO_4$) The remainder is equal to the sodium sulphate actually present in 1 grm. saltcake.

C.—CHIMNEY-TESTING.

Act of Parliament.—By the Alkali Works Regulation Act of 1881 it is enacted that "Every alkali work shall be carried on in such a manner as to secure the condensation to the satisfaction of the chief inspector, derived from his own examination or from that of some other inspector. (*a*) Of the muriatic acid gas evolved in such works to the extent of 95 per centum, and to such an extent that in each cubic foot of air, smoke, or chimney gases escaping from the works into the atmosphere, there is not contained more than *one-fifth part of a grain* of muriatic acid. (*b*) Of the acid gases of sulphur and nitrogen which are evolved in the process of manufacturing sulphuric acid or sulphates in the work to such an extent that the total acidity of such gases in each cubic foot of air, smoke, or gases escaping into the chimney or into the atmosphere does not exceed what is equivalent to *four grains* of sulphuric anhydride." Part I. (3). "Sulphurous acid arising from the combustion of coal is not included." Part III. (29). "In calculating the proportion of acid to a cubic foot of air, smoke, or gases, for the purposes of this Act, such air, smoke, or gases shall be calculated at the temperature of 60 degrees of Fahrenheit's thermometer, and at a barometic pressure of thirty inches." Part III. (21). Methods for ascertaining the total acidity of chamber exits will be found on pages 97 to 99.

Hydrochloric Acid in Chimney.—In order to ascertain the HCl in chimney gases, an aspirator is used known as Fletcher's flexible aspirator, or the bellows. This aspirator is supposed to draw at one aspiration one-tenth of a cubic foot. It is not safe to trust to this intended capacity, and moreover the capacity of a new aspirator varies for some time. To ascertain the real capacity, fill a very large beaker or other cylindrical vessel with water, and invert it under water. Completely fill the aspirator with air, and expel this air into the inverted beaker. Mark the point to which the beaker is filled when the water inside the beaker is level with that outside. Measure the capacity of the beaker to that mark, say it contains V cubic centimetres of water. Then the number of aspirations which must be made with this aspirator in order to draw one cubic foot of air is

$$N = \frac{28290}{V}$$

or if the capacity of the beaker is measured in grains,

$$N = \frac{436485}{V}$$

N will usually be a mixed number, but the nearest integral number is substituted, and it will be safest to substitute the next higher integral number. Thus, if N be found 9·3, it will be safest to consider 10 as the number of aspirations necessary to draw one cubic foot. The aspirator must be air-tight. The gas is withdrawn from the chimney through a glass tube, which should be sufficiently long to reach a considerable distance into the chimney, say 6ft. The glass tube should be of at least ½in. diameter, otherwise the aspiration is tedious. In flues where the temperature is too high for glass, a platinum tube must be employed. The bellows and tube are washed with distilled water until the washings give no reaction with silver nitrate. 100 or 200 cubic centimetres of distilled water free from chloride are then charged into the bellows, and after each aspiration the gas is well washed by shaking the contents of the aspirator violently. When the number N of aspirations has been made, some water is forced into the glass tube, and allowed to flow back into the bellows to wash out any acid which may have condensed in the tube. The liquid is then transferred into a porcelain dish (or into a beaker standing on a porcelain slab). If the liquid is so highly charged with soot that it would be impossible to recognise the change of colour, it must be filtered through a filter previously washed free from chlorides. The liquid is then oxidized with potassium permanganate, and any excess of this reagent removed with a trace of ferrous sulphate, neutralized with pure sodium carbonate, coloured with potassium chromate, and titrated with decinormal silver solution. (See p. 116, A, 3, and Appendix.) Some use a centinormal silver solution. Call the number of cubic centimetres consumed$=x$, then the hydrochloric acid, in grains per cubic foot of gas, will be

$$G = 0{\cdot}05633{\cdot}x \; grains.$$

In order to calculate the percentage escape, the velocity of the gas in the chimney must be ascertained and reduced to 60° F. No notice is usually taken of the barometric pressure, since the measurement by the bellows is otherwise inaccurate. In addition, the diameter of the chimney and the number of tons of salt decomposed per 24 hours in the furnaces connected with the chimney must be known.

If G =number of grains of HCl per cubit foot
If V =velocity at 60° F. in feet per second
If D =diameter of chimney at testing hole in feet
If T =tons of salt decomposed per 24 hours assumed
        to contain 93 per cent. NaCl

the percentage escape will be

$$0{\cdot}7458 \times \frac{GVD^2}{T}$$

HYDROCHLORIC ACID.

Specific Gravity of Hydrochloric Acid at 15°C Compared with Water at 4° and Reduced to Vacuum.

(Lunge & Marchlewski.)

De-grees Twad-dell.	Specific Gravity at $\frac{15°}{4°}$ in vacuo.	100 parts by weight correspond to parts by weight of			1 litre contains grms. HCl.	1 Cub. foot contains lbs. of HCl.
		HCl.	Acid of spec. grav. 1·1425 = 28·°, Tw.	Acid of spec. grav. 1·152 = 30·°, Tw.		
0	1·000	0·16	0·57	0·53	1·6	0·10
1	1·005	1·15	4·08	3·84	12·	0·75
2	1·010	2·14	7·60	7·14	22·	1·37
3	1·015	3·12	11·80	10·41	32·	1·99
4	1·020	4·13	14·67	13·79	42·	2·62
5	1·025	5·15	18·30	17·19	53·	3·30
6	1·030	6·15	21·85	20·53	64·	3·99
7	1·085	7·15	25·40	23·87	74·	4·61
8	1·040	8·16	28·99	27·24	85·	5·30
9	1·045	9·16	32·55	30·58	96·	5·98
10	1·050	10·17	36·14	33·95	107	6·67
11	1·055	11·18	39·73	37·33	118	7·35
12	1·060	12·19	43·32	40·70	129	8·04
13	1·065	13·19	46·87	44·04	141	8·79
14	1·070	14·17	50·35	47·31	152	9·48
15	1·075	15·16	53·87	50·62	163	10·16
16	1·080	16·15	57·39	53·92	174	10·85
17	1·085	17·13	60·87	57·19	186	11·59
18	1·090	18·11	64·35	60·47	197	12·28
19	1·095	19·06	67·78	63·64	209	13·03
20	1·100	20·01	71·11	66·81	220	13·71
21	1·105	20·97	74·52	70·01	232	14·46
22	1·110	21·92	77·89	73·19	243	15·15
23	1·115	22·86	81·23	76·32	255	15·90
24	1·120	23·82	84·64	79·53	267	16·65
25	1·125	24·78	88·06	82·74	278	17·33
26	1·130	25·75	91·50	85·97	291	18·14
27	1·135	26·70	94·88	89·15	303	18·89
28	1·140	27·66	98·29	92·35	315	19·64
29	1·145	28·61	101·67	95·52	328	20·45
30	1·150	29·57	105·08	98·73	340	21·20
31	1·155	30·55	108·58	102·00	353	22·01
32	1·160	31·52	112·01	105·24	366	22·82
33	1·165	32·49	115·46	108·48	379	23·68
34	1·170	33·46	118·91	111·71	392	24·44
35	1·175	34·42	122·32	114·92	404	25·19
36	1·180	35·39	125·76	118·16	418	26·06
37	1·185	36·31	129·08	121·23	430	26·81
38	1·190	37·28	132·30	124·30	443	27·62
39	1·195	38·16	135·61	127·41	456	28·43
40	1·200	39·11	138·98	130·58	469	29·24

2.—INFLUENCE OF TEMPERATURE ON THE SPECIFIC GRAVITY OF HYDROCHLORIC ACID.

0°	5°	10°	15°	20°	25°	30°	35°	40°	45°	50°
1·168	1·165	1·163	1·160	1·157	1·154	1·152	1·149	1·147	1·144	1·142
1·158	1·155	1·153	1·150	1·147	1·145	1·142	1·139	1·137	1·134	1·132
1·148	1·145	1·143	1·140	1·137	1·134	1·132	1·129	1·127	1·125	1·123
1·138	1·135	1·133	1·130	1·127	1·125	1·122	1·119	1·117	1·114	1·112
1·128	1·125	1·123	1·120	1·117	1·115	1·112	1·110	1 108	1·106	1·103
1·118	1·115	1·113	1·110	1·107	1·105	1·103	1·101	1·099	1·097	1·094
1·108	1·105	1·103	1·100	1·097	1·095	1·092	1·090	1·088	1·086	1·084
1·098	1·095	1·093	1·090	1·087	1·085	1·082	1·080	1·077	1·075	1·073
1·088	1·085	1·083	1·080	1·077	1·075	1·073	1·070	1·068	1·066	1·064
1·078	1·075	1·073	1·070	1·068	1·066	1·063	1·061	1·059	1·057	1·055
1·068	1·065	1·063	1·060	1·058	1·055	1·053	1·050	1·048	1·046	1·044
1·058	1·055	1·053	1·050	1·048	1·045	1·043	1·040	1·038	1·035	1·033
1·048	1·045	1·043	1·040	1·037	1·035	1·032	1·030	1·027	1·025	1·022
1·038	1·035	1·033	1·030	1·027	1·024	1·022	1·019	1·017	1·014	1·012
1·028	1·025	1·023	1·020	1·017	1·014	1·012	1·009	1·007	1·004	1·002
1·018	1·015	1·013	1·010	1·007	1·004	1·002	0·999	0·997	0·994	0·992

55°	60°	65°	70°	75°	80°	85°	90°	95°	100°
1·140	1·138	1·136	1·133	1·131	1·129	1·127	1·125	1·123	1·121
1·130	1·128	1·126	1·123	1·121	1·119	1·116	1·114	1·112	1·110
1·120	1·118	1·116	1·113	1·111	1·108	1·106	1·104	1·102	1·099
1·109	1·107	1·104	1·102	1·100	1·097	1·095	1·093	1·090	1·088
1·101	1·099	1·096	1·094	1·091	1·089	1·086	1·084	1·081	1·079
1·093	1·090	1·088	1·085	1·083	1·080	1·078	1·075	1·073	1·070
1·082	1·080	1·078	1·076	1·073	1·071	1·069	1·066	1·064	1·061
1·071	1·069	1·067	1·065	1·063	1·061	1·059	1·057	1·055	1·053
1·062	1·060	1·058	1·056	1·054	1·053	1·051	1·049	1·047	1·045
1·053	1·051	1·049	1·048	1·046	1·044	1·043	1·041	1·039	1·037
1·042	1·040	1·038	1·036	1·034	1·033	1·031	1·029	1·027	1·025
1·031	1·029	1·027	1·025	1·023	1·021	1·019	1·017	1·115	1·013
1·020	1·018	1·016	1·014	1·011	1·009	1·007	1·005	1·003	1·001
1·010	1·008	1·005	1·003	1·001	0·999	0·997	0·995	0·993	0·991
1·000	0·998	0·995	0·993	0·991	0·989	0·987	0·985	0·983	0·981
0·990	0·988	0·985	0·983	0·981	0·979	0·977	0·975	0·973	0·971

3.—ANALYSIS OF HYDROCHLORIC ACID.

1. *Estimation of* HCl.—Measure off, by means of an accurate pipette, 10 c.c. of the acid, whose specific gravity should be known, dilute to 200 c.c., take out 10 c.c. and add sodium carbonate, free from chloride, till the reaction is neutral or faintly alkaline. This point will be hit quickly, and without the loss of many drops for testing, if the percentage of the acid is ascertained from its specific gravity by the table (p. 120) and the corresponding quantity of sodium carbonate solution is run in from a burette. Now add a little neutral potassium chromate, and titrate with decinormal silver solution till a faint pink colour has been produced. (Compare p. 116.) Deduct 0·2 c.c. from the silver solution employed; the remainder, multiplied by 73 and divided by the specific gravity of the acid, indicates its percentage of HCl.*

2. *Estimation of Sulphuric Acid.*—Neutralize the acid almost, but not quite, with sodium carbonate free from sulphate, and precipitate the sulphuric acid by barium chloride, as in p. 93. If the acid be partially saturated with NH_3, or not saturated at all, the result is too low. Each part of $BaSO_4$ is equal to 0·34335 SO_3.

3. *Estimation of Iron.*—Reduce this to protoxide by digesting the acid for a short time with a rod of zinc free from iron, wash the rod, dilute the whole with water, add some manganous chloride or sulphate (in order to counteract the action of HCl on permanganate), and titrate with a twentieth normal solution of potassium permanganate, each cubic centimetre of which indicates 0·0028 grm. Fe.

4.—BLEACHING POWDER AND CHLORATE OF POTASH MANUFACTURE.

A.—NATURAL MANGANESE ORE.

1. *Manganese Dioxide.*—Weigh 1·0875 grm.† of manganese ore, ground as fine as possible, and dried some time at 100° C.; put it into the flask (Fig. 10), closed by an indiarubber (Bunsen) valve; add 75 c.c. (in three pipettesful at 25 c.c. each) of a solution containing 100 grms. pure crystallized ferrous sulphate and 100 c.c. pure concentrated sulphuric acid, diluted to one litre, and standardized on the same day by means of the same 25 c.c. pipette, with decinormal potassium permanganate. Close the flask by its indiarubber cork and valve, and heat till the manganese is completely decomposed, leaving a light-coloured residue. On cooling, the valve must act properly, which will be seen by the collapsing of the indiarubber tube. After complete cooling add 200 c.c. of water, and titrate with potassium permanganate to a faint pink coloration. Deduct the quantity of permanganate now required from that corresponding to the 75 c.c. of iron solution; the remainder indicates for each cubic centimetre 0·02175 grm., equal to 2 per cent. MnO_2.

As a check upon the above process, the analysis may be performed by means of hydrogen peroxide in an acid solution, measuring the oxygen evolved in a Nitrometer or in the Gasvolumeter (p. 118), as described by Lunge in S.C.I., 1890, p. 24.

---

* This test would fail in the presence of metallic chlorides, which are, however, hardly ever present in appreciable quantity in ordinary hydrochloric acid. The free HCl can also be ascertained by estimating the total acidity and deducting therefrom that due to sulphuric acid, making allowance for any sodium sulphate present.

† This corresponds to the real equivalent of MnO_2 equal to 43·5 (molecular weight 87).

2. *Carbon Dioxide* is estimated gravimetrically by expelling it with dilute sulphuric or nitric acid and absorbing it in soda-lime, by means of the apparatus and process described (p. 95).

Fig. 11.

3. *Estimation of the Hydrochloric Acid required for Decomposing the Ore.*—Dissolve 1 grm. of manganese ore in a flask provided with a reflux cooler in 10 c.c. of ordinary strong hydrochloric acid whose titre is known, employing heat as far as necessary. Allow the solution to cool, add standard alkali till reddish-brown flakes of ferric hydroxide appear, which do not redissolve on agitation. Calculate the standard alkali for the strength of acid employed for dissolving the ore, and deduct the quantity thus found from the 10 c.c. first employed.

B.—RECOVERED MANGANESE MUD AND WELDON LIQUORS.

1. MnO_2 *in Weldon Mud.*—Standardize an acid iron solution (100 grms. pure crystallized ferrous sulphate + 100 c.c. pure concentrated sulphuric acid in 1 litre) with seminormal potassium permanganate (refer to Appendix), by diluting 25 c.c. of the former with 100 c.c. or 200 c.c. of cold water, and adding the permanganate from a glass-cock burette, till, on agitating, the pink colour is not discharged immediately, but remains at least for half a minute. Subsequent bleaching is not taken into account. This test should be made once each day. Call the cubic centimetres of permanganate employed x. Now, put again 25 c.c. of the iron solution into a beaker. Take 10 c.c. of manganese mud out of the well-shaken bottle (mere stirring does not ensure a proper mixture) containing it; wash the pipette outside, run its contents into the beaker containing the iron solution, and wash the mud remaining inside into the same beaker. When all has dissolved, on agitating, add 100 c.c. of water, and titrate with potassium permanganate. The number of cubic centimetres now used equals y. The quantity of MnO_2 in grammes per litre of mud equals $2·175 (x-y)$.

2. *Total Manganese of the Mud, Expressed in Grammes of Theoretically Possible MnO_2 per Litre.*—Take 10 c.c. of the mud, with the same precautions as in test No. 1. Boil with strong hydrochloric acid till all chlorine is driven off; saturate the excess of acid by ground marble or precipitated calcium carbonate; add a concentrated filtered solution of bleaching powder; boil a few minutes till the colour turns a strong pink, and the excess of bleaching powder can be smelled, and again destroy the pink by adding alcohol drop

by drop. All manganese is now present as MnO_2; filter and wash this. The filtrate should not produce any brown colour with a bleaching-powder solution, which would prove the presence of Mn in solution. Continue the washing till starch and KJ do not give any reaction. Throw the filter with the precipitate into 25 c.c. of the acid iron solution employed in test No 1. If all MnO_2 is not dissolved, add another 25 c.c. of iron solution; dilute with 100 c.c. of water, and titrate with permanganate. Calculation as in No. 1.

3. *Estimation of the Base, i.e., the Monoxides, etc., of the Mud which absorb HCl without yielding Free Chlorine.*—Dilute 25 c.c., or with a very high base 50 c.c., of normal oxalic acid (63 grms. crystallized oxalic acid in 1 litre) to 100 c.c.; heat to 60—80° C., add 10 c.c. manganese mud by means of a pipette, with the precautions stated in No. 1, and agitate till the colour of the precipitate is no longer yellowish but pure white, which ought to take place very soon at the above-named temperature. Dilute to 202 c.c. (2 c.c. correspond to the bulk of the precipitate, and are marked on the neck of the 200 c.c. flask); pour through a dry filter, and titrate 100 c.c. of the filtrate with standard alkali, employing litmus or corallin as indicator. (Methylorange is not applicable for oxalic acid.) Call the number of cubic centimetres of standard alkali z. The oxalic acid serves (1) for reducing the MnO_2 with formation of MnO and CO_2; (2) for saturating the MnO thus formed; (3) for saturating the monoxides originally present, i.e., the base. The oxalic acid not thus employed is equal to $2z$. The acid used for reducing MnO_2 is equal to that used for neutralizing the MnO formed, and both amounts together are equal to the number $x-y$ obtained by the MnO_2 test, since the oxalic acid is normal and the permanganate half normal. The amount of oxalic acid consumed by the bases of the mud is found by deducting from the total acid used that required for the MnO_2 $(x-y)$, and that which was not neutralized at all by the mud—$2z$, therefore in all $x-y-2z$. The "base" is equal to the ratio of this expression to the item 1, viz.—

$$\frac{x-y}{2}$$

It is therefore, if 25 c.c. of oxalic acid had been employed, equal to

$$\frac{50-2x-4z+2y}{x-y}=\left(\frac{50-4z}{x-y}\right)-2$$

or, if 50 cc. had been employed, equal to

$$\left(\frac{100-4z}{x-y}\right)-2$$

C.—LIMESTONE.

1. *Insoluble.*—Dissolve 1 grm. hydrochloric acid, filter the residue, wash, dry, and ignite. In the presence of appreciable quantities of organic substance weigh the filter after drying at 100°, and ignite afterwards. The difference is taken as organic matter.

2. *Lime.*—Dissolve 1 grm. in 25 c.c. normal hydrochloric acid and titrate with normal alkali. Deduct the latter from 25 and multiply the remainder with 2·8 to find the percentage of CaO, or with 5 to find that of $CaCO_3$. (N.B.—Here MgO is calculated as CaO. This is admissible for most limestones employed in alkali and bleaching powder making, because they contain but little MgO; otherwise the MgO or $MgCO_3$ found as in No. 3 has to be deducted.)

3. *Magnesia* needs to be estimated only in limestone serving for manganese recovery. Dissolve 2 grms. of limestone in HCl, precipitate the CaO with NH_3 and ammonium oxalate, and precipitate the magnesia in the filtrate by sodium phosphate. (Compare p. 118.)

4. *Iron* is usually estimated only in limestone serving for bleaching powder making. Dissolve 2 grms. HCl, reduce by zinc, dilute, add some manganese solution free from iron, and titrate with permanganate. (Compare p. 114.)

D.—QUICKLIME.

1. *Free* CaO.—Weigh 100 grms. of an average sample carefully taken, slake it completely, put the milk into a half-litre flask, fill up to the mark, shake well, take 100 c.c. out, run it into a half-litre flask, fill up, mix well, and employ 25 c.c. of the contents, equal to 1 grm. quicklime, for the test. Titrate with normal oxalic acid and phenolphthalein as an indicator. The colour is changed when all free lime has been saturated and before the $CaCO_3$ is attacked.

2. *Carbon Dioxide.*—Titrate CaO and $CaCO_3$ together by dissolving in an excess of standard hydrochloric acid and titrating back with standard alkali. By deducting the CaO estimated as in No. 1 the quantity of $CaCO_3$ is obtained. For very accurate estimations the CO_2 is expelled by HCl, absorbed in soda-lime and weighed as described; or it is estimated by volume in Lunge and Marchlewski's apparatus (p. 95).

Da.—SLAKED LIME.

1. *Water.*—Weigh about 1 grm. in a stoppered glass tube, and heat it gradually in a platinum crucible, at last to a strong red heat (compare p. 117); allow to cool in the exsiccator and weigh back. The loss of weight is equal to $H_2O + CO_2$.

2. *Carbon Dioxide* is estimated as above.

TABLE SHOWING AMOUNT OF LIME IN MILK OF LIME.
(Calculated from Blattner.)

Degrees Twaddell.	Grms. CaO per litre.	Lb. CaO per cubic foot.	Degrees Twaddell.	Grms. CaO per litre.	Lb. CaO per cubic foot.
2	11·7	0·7	28	177	11·1
4	24·4	1·5	30	190	11·9
6	37·1	2·8	32	208	12·7
8	49·8	3·1	34	216	13·5
10	62·5	3·9	36	229	14·3
12	75·2	4·7	38	242	15·1
14	87·9	5·5	40	255	15·9
16	100	6·3	42	268	16·7
18	113	7·1	44	281	17·6
20	126	7·9	46	294	18·4
22	138	8·7	48	307	19·2
24	152	9·5	50	321	20·0
26	164	10·3			

E.—BLEACHING POWDER.

1. *Available Chlorine.*—Weigh 7·100 grms. of the sample, previously well-mixed; grind it with a little water in a porcelain mortar (whose lip has been greased a little at the lower side) till a completely homogeneous thin paste has been obtained; dilute with more water, wash the whole into a litre flask, fill up to the mark, and take for each test 50 c.c.=0·355 grm. bleaching powder, having shaken up the flask immediately before. Run into the above, with continuous agitation, an alkaline decinormal arsenite solution, containing 4·95 grms. As$_2$O$_3$ per litre (refer to Appendix) till the expected point is not very far off. Then place a drop of the mixture on to a piece of filtering paper, moistened with a starch solution containing iodine. If there is very much chlorine left, a brown spot will be produced; if less chlorine, the spot will be blue. According to the depth of this colour more or less arsenite solution is run in, and the above test is repeated till the paper is coloured hardly perceptibly, or not at all. Each cubic centimetre of the arsenite solution indicates 1 per cent. available chlorine. (For sampling of bleach refer to Appendix.)

Another very accurate method, requiring no standard liquid, consists in decomposing the bleaching powder by hydrogen peroxide in a Nitrometer or Gasvolumeter (Lunge, S.C.I., 1890, 22).

2. *Comparison of the Percentage of Bleaching Powder with the French (Gay-Lussac) Degrees.*—The latter are understood to mean the number of litres of chlorine gas at 0° C. and 760 mm. pressure, which could be given off by 1 kilogramme of bleaching powder. The oxygen given off in the hydrogen peroxide method (compare last paragraph) shows this directly.

French Degrees.	Per cent. Chlorine.	French Degrees.	Per cent. Chlorine.	French Degrees.	Per cent. Chlorine.	French Degrees.	Per cent. Chlorine.
63	20·02	80	25·42	97	30·82	113	35·91
64	20·34	81	25·74	98	31·14	114	36·22
65	20·65	82	26·06	99	31·46	115	36·54
66	20·97	83	26·37	100	31·78	116	36·86
67	21·29	84	26·69	101	32·09	117	37·18
68	21·61	85	27·01	102	32·41	118	37·50
69	21·93	86	27·33	103	32·73	119	37·81
70	22·24	87	27·65	104	33·05	120	38·13
71	22·56	88	27·96	105	33·36	121	38·45
72	22·88	89	28·28	106	33·68	122	38·77
73	23·20	90	28·60	107	34·00	123	39·08
74	23·51	91	28·92	108	34·32	124	39·40
75	23·83	92	29·23	109	34·64	125	39·72
76	24·15	93	29·55	110	34·95	126	40·04
77	24·47	94	29·87	111	35·27	127	40·36
78	24·79	95	30·19	112	35·59	128	40·67
79	25·10	96	30·51				

F.—DEACON PROCESS.

Aspirate 5 litres of gas, issuing from the decomposer, placing the apparatus as closely to the outlet of the decomposer as possible, and absorb the hydrochloric acid and chlorine in a solution of caustic soda of 15°Tw., of which about 250 c.c. are distributed into two or three absorbing bottles. The time of absorption ought to agree with the time occupied by the charge in the saltcake pan. Unite the contents of the several bottles and dilute to 500 c.c.

1. Take 100 c.c. of this solution, and add it gradually to 25 c.c. of an iron solution (prepared and standardized as directed on page 122) in a flask represented by Fig. 11 (page 123), and heat to boiling. Allow to cool, dilute with 200 c.c. of water, and titrate with semi-normal permanganate solution. Say it required y c.c. Suppose that when standardizing the iron solution 25 c.c. of iron solution required x c.c.

2. Take 10 c.c. of the solution to be tested, add thereto some solution of sulphurous acid, acidify with dilute sulphuric acid. If it does not smell of sulphurous acid, add a little more. Heat to boiling. When cool, add, if necessary, a few drops of permanganate to oxidize any sulphurous acid in excess. Neutralize with pure carbonate of soda, dilute with water, and after adding a few drops potassium chromate, titrate with decinormal silver solution. Suppose it consumes z c.c. of silver solution. Then

$$\frac{50x-y}{z}$$

is the percentage of hydrochloric acid decomposed, and

$$42 \cdot 5 + \frac{x-y}{8}$$
$$\overline{\phantom{42 \cdot 5 + \frac{x-y}{8}}}\ z$$

equals the amount of air present for every volume of hydrochloric acid. If any other volume l of gas instead of 5 litres be employed, the constant $42\cdot5$ changes into

$$\frac{l \times 1\cdot55}{50 \times 0\cdot00365}$$

assuming that the other directions are strictly followed, and that 1 litre of hydrochloric acid weighs $1\cdot55$ grm. at $50°$ C. and 760 mm. pressure.

G.—CHLORATE OF POTASH.

1. *Chlorate Liquors* contain calcium chlorate and chloride, but these are calculated as potassium salts for the sake of convenience.

(*a*) *Chlorate* is estimated both in order to check the work and to calculate the necessary addition of KCl. Measure 2 c.c of liquor in an exact pipette, run it into the flask (Fig. 11, p. 123), add a little hot water and one drop of alcohol, boil (without the valve) till all smell of chlorine and the pink colour have disappeared, allow to cool, add 25 c.c. of the strongly acid ferrous sulphate solution (mentioned p. 122, and requiring a c.c. of seminormal permanganate), close the flask with its valve, and boil for 10 minutes. After cooling, titrate with seminormal permanganate. The number of cubic centimetres required to produce a faint pink$=b$. The liquor then contains calcium chlorate equivalent to $5\cdot105$ $(a-b)$ grms. $KClO_3$ per litre, and it will theoretically require an amount of $3\cdot105$ $(a-b)$ grms. of pure KCl per litre.

(*b*) *Chloride* is estimated in order to check the work, and therefore calculated as KCl, although present as $CaCl_2$. Treat 1 c.c. of liquor as above, to destroy the free chlorine and pink colour, allow to cool, add a little neutral potassium chromate, and titrate with decinormal silver nitrate (as described p. 116). Each cubic centimetre of the latter indicates chloride equivalent to $7\cdot45$ grms. KCl per litre.

2. *Commercial Chlorate of Potash* is only tested for any chlorides calculated as KCl. As their quantity is very slight, it is advisable to dissolve 50 grms. of the salt in water absolutely free from chlorine, and to test with decinormal silver nitrate, as in the last number. Each cubic centimetre of this=0·00745 grm. KCl=0·015 per cent. KCl.

5.—SODA-ASH MANUFACTURE.

A.—RAW MATERIALS.

1. SALTCAKE.—(Refer to p. 117.)
2. LIMESTONE or CHALK, for mixing.
   (a) *Insoluble.*—(Refer to p. 124.)
   (b) *Lime* (+MgO).—(p. 124.)
   (c) *Magnesia* (only in limestones containing much of it).—(p. 125.)
3. MIXING COAL (slack).
   (a) *Moisture.*—(p. 85.)
   (b) *Fixed Carbon.*—(p. 85.)
   (c) *Ashes* (p. 85.)—In the case of unknown descriptions of coal it is not sufficient to estimate the total percentage of ashes, but the latter should be analyzed, and silica, alumina, and ferric oxide estimated according to the rules of the analysis of silicates.
   (d) *Sulphur.*—Mix 0·5 grm. to 1 grm. of finely-ground coal with 1½ times the weight of an intimate mixture of two parts well-calcined magnesia and 1 part anhydrous sodium carbonate. This is done by means of a glass rod in a platinum crucible, which is heated without cover, and in a slanting position, so that only its lower half attains red heat, preferably in the perforated asbestos slab (p. 85). The combustion should be assisted by frequent stirring with a platinum wire, and should last hardly longer than an hour, the grey colour of the mixture passing over into yellow, reddish, or brown. Pour hot water over the mass, add bromine-water till the liquid is faintly yellow; boil, decant through a filter, and wash with hot water. Acidulate the filtrate with HCl, boil till all bromine is removed and the liquor has been decolorized, and precipitate with barium chloride (as described p. 94). If the magnesia or sodium carbonate employed contains sulphates, these must be estimated and taken into account. If the gas for burning contains much sulphur, it is best to employ a spirit lamp; but the perforated asbestos slab, as recommended above, will nearly always suffice for keeping away the products of combustion of the gas from the contents of the crucible, and thus admit of employing ordinary illuminating gas and a Bunsen burner.
   (e) *Nitrogen* is estimated by igniting with soda-lime and receiving the ammonia formed in standard sulphuric acid, according to the rules of organic elementary analysis.

B.—BLACK-ASH.

Digest 50 grms. of the finely powdered average sample with 480 c.c. of water at 45° C., which had been previously freed from CO_2 and O by boiling and cooling down in a corked bottle. This will produce 500 c.c. of liquid. Shake at once and afterwards frequently, at least during two hours. The following tests are made partly with the muddy mixture, partly with the clear portion; but the former ones must be made to begin with.

I. TESTS MADE WITH THE MUDDY MIXTURE.—Each time before taking out a sample, the flask is thoroughly shaken up, and, before the deposit settles again, a sample is taken by means of a 5 c.c. pipette, with a short and somewhat wide outlet (to prevent obstruction by the mud). The mud outwardly adhering is washed off, the contents of the pipette are run out into a beaker, and the mud adhering to the inside of the pipette is washed into the same beaker.

1. *Free Lime* (or its equivalent of sodium hydrate) is found by adding to 5 c.c. of the mixture an excess of barium chloride solution, as well as a drop of phenolphthalein solution and titrating with $\frac{1}{2}$-normal oxalic acid, till the red colour has just vanished. Each c.c. of the acid $= 0.0056$ CaO.

2. *Total Lime.*—5 c.c. of the muddy mixture are put into a flask, a few c.c. of concentrated hydrochloric acid are added, and the whole is boiled till all the gases have been expelled. Cool down a little, add a drop of methyl-orange solution, and neutralize exactly with sodium carbonate, *i.e.*, till the red colour has just gone. Now add 30 c.c. of $\frac{1}{2}$-normal sodium carbonate solution, exactly measured, and heat to boiling, to precipitate all the lime as $CaCO_3$ (together with any ferric oxide, alumina and magnesia, whose quantity is too insignificant to be regarded for this test). Wash the whole into a 200 c.c. flask, fill up to the mark, take 100 c.c. of the clear liquid, and titrate back with $\frac{1}{2}$-normal hydrochloric acid. Deduct the c.c. used $\times 2$ from 30; the difference $\times 0.0056 =$ total lime, or $\times 0.0100 =$ calcium carbonate.

(N.B.—These tests cannot be expected to give any very accurate results, owing to the almost insurmountable difficulty of obtaining a real average sample of black-ash ball. This, however, applies to all tests made with black-ash.)

II. TESTS MADE WITH THE CLEAR PORTION.—After having made all the tests described sub I., allow the mixture to settle down in the well-corked flask, and take samples of the supernatant clear liquid for the following tests:—

1. 10 c.c. ($= 1$ grm. black-ash) is titrated cold with hydrochloric acid and methyl-orange. This indicates the total available alkali, *i.e.*, Na_2CO_3, NaOH, and Na_2S. (The small quantity of alumina and silica present causes no appreciable error.) By deducting the quantities found in tests Nos. 2 and 3 the quantity of *sodium carbonate* is found, viz., 0.058 grm. for each cubic centimetre of normal HCl. It is, however, expressed, like all other sodium compounds, in terms of Na_2O, by multiplying each cubic centimetre of normal acid by 0.031.

2. *Caustic Soda* is estimated by adding to 20 c.c. of liquor, contained in a 100 c.c. flask, an excess of barium chloride (10 c.c. of a 10 per cent. solution of $BaCl_2$, $2H_2O$ will always more than suffice for this), adding boiling water up to the mark, shaking up, and corking the flask. After a few minutes the precipitate is settled. Take out 50 c.c. of the clear portion, without filtering,* and titrate with normal hydrochloric acid. When employing methyl-orange as indicator, the liquid must be cooled first. According to Cl. Winkler, the separation of the barium carbonate is unnecessary when oxalic acid is employed as the standard acid. In this case litmus or, better, phenol-phthalein must be employed as indicator. Each cubic centimetre of the standard acid indicates 0.040 grm. of NaOH in 1 grm. of black-ash $= 0.031$ Na_2O, but sodium sulphide is here included as well.

3. *Sodium Sulphide.*—Dilute 10 c.c. of liquor to about 200 c.c., employing water freed from oxygen by boiling, acidulate with acetic acid, and titrate

---

* The filtering paper absorbs a sensible portion of barium salt.

K

quickly with iodine solution, using starch as an indicator. When employing a decinormal iodine solution (12·7 grms. I per litre), each cubic centimetre indicates 0·0089 Na_2S (=0·0031 Na_2O). A solution containing 3·256 grms. I per litre would indicate 0·001 grm. Na_2S per cubic centimetre. In the former case the number of cubic centimetres of decinormal solution divided by 10 can be deducted at once from the acid employed in test No. 1, whereby the sulphide is eliminated from the alkali test. Other sulphur compounds (except sulphate) need not be taken account of in fresh black-ash.

4. *Sodium Chloride.*—Neutralize 10 c.c. of the liquor as accurately as possible with nitric acid, preferably by adding exactly as many cubic centimetres of standard nitric acid (63 grms. NO_3 H per litre) as had been employed in test No. 1. Boil till all H_2S has been expelled, filter from any sulphur precipitated, add a little neutral potassium chromate, and titrate with silver solution (as described page 117). Each cubic centimetre of decinormal silver solution indicates 0·00585 grm. NaCl. A solution containing 2·906 grms. $AgNO_3$ per litre shows 0·001 grm. NaCl per cubic centimetre.

5. *Sodium Sulphate.*—Acidulate 10 c.c. with a very slight excess of HCl, boil, add barium chloride, filter, wash, and ignite the precipitated $BaSO_4$. Since the quantity is very small, it can be washed with hot water on the filter itself, which is then placed in the moist state in a platinum crucible and ignited. Each part of $BaSO_4$=0·6094 Na_2SO_4.

6. Prepare an average sample of all batches by pouring a certain quantity of the liquor belonging to each batch into a common vessel; *carbonate* this by passing CO_2 through its filter, evaporate the filtrate to dryness, and estimate in the residue Na_2CO_3, Na_2SO_4, and NaCl.

C.—TANK WASTE (VAT WASTE).

Take a large, really representative average sample, which should be kept protected from air, and of which 50 grms. should be weighed out *quickly* and in the *moist* state. Drying in contact with air would considerably change its composition. Moist tank waste may be assumed, without any great error, to contain 40 per cent. of water. Digest the above 50 grms. waste with 490 c.c. water of 40° C., which will yield 500 c.c. of liquid.

1. *Available Soda* (Na_2CO_3, or Na_2S).—Take 100 c.c. of the liquor, pass into it a current of well-washed carbon dioxide, heat the liquid to boiling, bring up the volume again to 100 c.c., pour through a dry filter, and titrate 50 c.c. of the clear portion with decinormal hydrochloric acid, of which each c.c. will indicate 0·0081 grm. Na_2O, or, in this case, 0·062 per cent. Na_2O of the moist waste.

2. *Total Soda* (*inclusive of Insoluble Sodium Salts*).—Heat 17·7 grms.* tank waste in a porcelain or iron dish with sulphuric acid of specific gravity 1·5, till all has been decomposed and converted into a stiff paste, evaporate to dryness, heat till all free sulphuric acid has been driven off, add hot water, scrape out the mass, and put it into a 250 c.c. cylinder. Neutralize any free acid left, and precipitate any magnesia present by adding some pure milk

* This amount is correct, not 18·6 grms., as a calculation would seem to show, because an allowance must be made for the bulk of the insoluble residue in the measuring vessels.

of lime (obtained from ordinary slacked lime by pouring off the first water, which may contain some alkali), fill up to the mark, allow to settle, take out 50 c.c. of the clear liquor, add 10 c.c. of saturated baryta water, pour the mixture through a dry filter, take 50 c.c. of the filtrate, precipitate all baryta by passing through the liquid CO_2 and boiling, filter, and titrate the filtrate with decinormal hydrochloric acid. Each cubic centimetre of this will indicate 0·1 per cent. of Na_2O in the waste, taking into account its bulk.

3. *Total and Oxidizable Sulphur.*—Boil 2 grms. of the waste with hydrochloric acid, filter, wash with dilute HCl, neutralize the filtrate almost completely by adding sodium carbonate, precipitate with barium chloride, filter, wash, and ignite the barium sulphate. From this is calculated the sulphur present as sulphate (*a*). Another sample of 2 grms. waste is oxidized by a strong bleaching powder solution and hydrochloric acid, or by a solution of bromine in strong hydrochloric acid. When a strong smell of chlorine is felt, all S is oxidized to sulphuric acid. Filter and estimate the SO_4H_2 in the filtrate. This indicates the total sulphur (*b*). The difference *b* − *a* is the oxidizable sulphur, *i.e.*, the theoretically recoverable maximum of sulphur in the waste.

D.—TANK LIQUOR (VAT LIQUOR)

Is tested while hot, or else it is kept at about 40° C., to prevent crystallization. Take out only small samples (2 to 5 c.c.) with an accurate pipette. This greatly furthers the work.

1. *Sodium Carbonate.*—Titrate 2 c.c. with standard hydrochloric acid. When employing methyl-orange as indicator, first add some cold water. From the cubic centimetres found deduct those found in test No. 2 and one-tenth of that in test No. 3.

2. *Sodium Hydrate* (estimated as on page 129).

3. *Sodium Sulphide* is estimated by decinormal iodine solution (as on page 129). The error caused by other sulphur compounds is hardly appreciable, and for practical purposes of no consequence. In any case this test must be made in order to rectify test No. 1.

4. *Sodium Sulphate* (as on page 130).

5. *Total Sulphur.*—Oxidize the liquor with bleaching powder and hydrochloric acid (as described C3, page 131), and precipitate by barium chloride.

6. *Sodium Chloride* (as page 130).

7. *Sodium Ferrocyanide.*—Acidulate 20 c.c. of liquor (or more) with HCl, and add *strong* bleaching-powder solution from a burette, constantly agitating. From time to time mix a drop of the mixture on a white slab with a drop of dilute ferric chloride solution, free from ferrous chloride. When no more Prussian blue is formed, but the mixture of both drops turns brown, all is oxidized, hence also all ferrocyanide is turned into ferricyanide. A drop of bleach solution in excess does no harm, but if too much excess has been used, or if too much liquor has been lost by taking out test drops, a fresh sample is taken out, which can this time be oxidized by running the requisite quantity of bleach liquor from the burette without losing much by making the drop-tests. This process gives quicker and more accurate results than adding an excess of bleach and driving out the chlorine by heating, in which case some ferricyanide may be decomposed. The oxidized liquor is

titrated with decinormal copper solution, containing 3·175 grms. Cu or 12·475 grms. crystallized cupric sulphate per litre, which precipitates yellow $Cu_3Fe_3Cy_{12}$. From time to time test a drop of the liquid by bringing it together on a porcelain slab with a drop of a *dilute* ferrous sulphate solution. So long as a blue colour is produced by the action of $FeSO_4$ on $Na_6Fe_2Cy_{12}$ more copper solution is added, till the test on the slab turns no more blue or grey, but reddish. Now no more $Na_6Fe_2Cy_{12}$ is present, and the $FeSO_4$ on the slab now reduces the yellow copper ferricyanide to red ferrocyanide. The first sensible reddening must be taken as the final reaction, although it vanishes after a short time. According to theory each cubic centimetre of the copper solution ought to indicate 0·01013 grm. Na_4FeCy_6; but recent experiments (*Chemische Industrie* 1882, p. 79) have shown this not to be the case. Too little copper solution is employed, and each cubic centimetre of this must therefore be put equal to 0·0123 grm. Na_4FeCy_6, or, still better, the copper solution must be standardized by pure potassium ferrocyanide.

8. *Silica, Alumina, and Ferric oxide (Parnell)*.—Supersaturate 100 c.c. of liquor with HCl, boil, add a large quantity of ammonium chloride and ammonia in excess, and boil till all smell of NH_3 has ceased. The precipitate settles easily, and can be well washed. On washing with hot water it turns intensely blue (by the formation of prussian blue?); on igniting it leaves SiO_2, Al_2O_3, and Fe_2O_3.

9. A large sample of the liquor is *carbonated* by passing CO_2 through it; it is then filtered, evaporated to dryness, and the residue tested for available alkali, Na_2SO_4 and NaCl.

E.—CARBONATED LIQUORS

Are tested in all respects like D. Bicarbonate is estimated by the following method, which is also applicable to testing the bicarbonate of commerce. Put 20 c.c. of liquor (or more if necessary) into a 100 c.c. flask, add 10 c.c. of seminormal ammonia (8·5 grms. NH_3 per litre, absolutely free from CO_2) and an excess of barium chloride; fill up to the mark with cold water, cork the flask well, allow to settle, take 50 c.c. of the clear liquid, and titrate with standard hydrochloric acid, of which x c.c. is used. The formula: $11(10-x)$ then indicates the milligrammes of CO_2 present in the liquor as bicarbonate. If the ammonia is not exactly seminormal, the figure 11 must be replaced by another corresponding to the milligrammes of CO_2 per cubic centimetre of the ammonia; and 10 must be replaced by the number of cubic centimetres of ammonia required for neutralizing 5 c.c. of normal HCl. In order to compare the CO_2 present as bicarbonate with the total CO_2, a fresh sample of the liquor is titrated with normal hydrochloric acid and methyl-orange at the ordinary temperature. The number of cubic centimetres used, multiplied by 22, indicates the milligrammes of CO_2 present as monocarbonate. The latter item added to the former yields the total CO_2.

The following formula admits of calculating the proportion of Na_2CO_3 and $NaHCO_3$ in a mixture containing both, if we know the amount of available $Na_2O=a$, and the total $CO_2=b$. There is present:

Na_2O in the state of $Na_2CO_3 = 2a - 1·409b$
Na_2O in the state of $NaHCO_3 = a$ less the above.

The total CO_2 present may also be estimated by the method of Lunge & Marchlewski (Zeitsch. f. angew. Chem., 1891, p. 229).

F.—TABLES.

1.—SPECIFIC GRAVITIES OF SOLUTIONS OF SODIUM CARBONATE AT 60° F=15°C.*

Twaddell.	Percentage by weight.		1 cubic foot of solution contains		
	Na$_2$O	Na$_2$CO$_3$	Na$_2$O	Na$_2$CO$_3$	48% ash.†
1	0·28	0·47	0·172	0·294	0·358
2	0·56	0·95	0·350	0·598	0·728
3	0·84	1·42	0·525	0·898	1·094
4	1·11	1·90	0·707	1·209	1·473
5	1·39	2·38	0·889	1·521	1·853
6	1·67	2·85	1·070	1·830	2·230
7	1·95	3·33	1·257	2·149	2·618
8	2·22	3·80	1·441	2·464	3·002
9	2·50	4·28	1·631	2·788	3·397
10	2·78	4·76	1·852	3·116	3·797
11	3·06	5·23	2·012	3·440	4·192
12	3·34	5·71	2·206	3·772	4·596
13	3·61	6·17	2·396	4·097	4·992
14	3·88	6·64	2·591	4·430	5·397
15	4·16	7·10	2·783	4·759	5·799
16	4·42	7·57	2·981	5·098	6·211
17	4·70	8·04	3·181	5·439	6·627
18	4·97	8·51	3·382	5·783	7·016
19	5·24	8·97	3·582	6·125	7·462
20	5·52	9·43	3·783	6·468	7·880
21	5·79	9·90	3·989	6·821	8·311
22	6·06	10·37	4·197	7·177	8·745
23	6·33	10·83	4·408	7·529	9·174
24	6·61	11·30	4·615	7·891	9·613
25	6·88	11·76	4·825	8·249	10·050
26	7·15	12·23	5·040	8·617	10·500
27	7·42	12·70	5·256	8·988	10·951
28	7·70	13·16	5·465	9·354	11·396
29	7·97	13·63	5·691	9·731	11·857
30	8·24	14·09	5·908	10·103	12·310

* OBSERVATION.—Special experiments have shown that the tables 1 and 2 indicate with sufficient accuracy, not merely the percentage of solutions of pure sodium carbonate, but also that of the dry residue in ordinary tank liquors.
† Equivalent to 31.

F.—TABLES.

2A.—SPECIFIC GRAVITIES OF CONCENTRATED SOLUTIONS OF SODIUM CARBONATE AT 86° F. (30° C.).

Twaddell.	Percentage by weight.		Lb. per cubic foot.		
	Na_2O	Na_2CO_3	Na_2O	Na_2CO_3	48°/₀ ash
28	7·97	13·62	5·662	9·681	11·80
29	8·21	14·04	5·86	10·02	12·12
30	8·46	14·47	6·06	10·37	12·64
31	8·71	14·89	6·27	10·72	13·06
32	8·96	15·32	6·48	11·08	13·50
33	9·21	15·74	6·69	11·43	13·98
34	9·46	16·18	6·91	11·81	14·39
35	9·71	16·60	7·11	12·16	14·82
36	9·96	17·04	7·33	12·58	15·27
37	10·21	17·46	7·54	12·90	15·72
38	10·46	17·89	7·76	13·27	16·17
39	10·71	18·32	7·98	13·65	16·63
40	10·97	18·75	8·21	14·08	17·10
41	11·22	19·18	8·42	14·40	17·55
42	11·47	19·61	8·65	14·79	18·03
43	11·72	20·04	8·88	15·18	18·50
44	11·97	20·47	9·11	15·57	18·97
45	12·23	20·90	9·34	15·96	19·45
46	12·48	21·33	9·56	16·35	19·92
47	12·73	21·77	9·80	16·76	20·42
48	12·98	22·20	10·08	17·16	20·91
49	13·24	22·63	10·27	17·57	21·41
50	13·49	23·07	10·52	17·98	21·91
51	13·74	23·50	10·76	18·39	22·41
52	14·00	23·93	11·00	18·80	22·91
53	14·24	24·35	11·25	19·20	23·40
54	14·49	24·77	11·47	19·61	23·90
55	14·73	25·19	11·72	20·03	24·41
56	14·98	25·61	11·95	20·44	24·91
57	15·22	26·03	12·20	20·86	25·42
58	15·47	26·45	12·45	21·28	25·93
59	15·72	26·87	12·69	21·69	26·48
60	15·96	27·29	12·94	22·12	26·95
61	16·20	27·71	13·18	22·54	27·47
62	16·45	28·13	13·44	22·97	27·99

2ʙ.—PERCENTAGE OF CONCENTRATED SOLUTIONS OF SODIUM CARBONATE, MEASURED AT 30° C.=86° F.*

Specific Gravity at 30°.	Degrees Twaddell.	100lb. contain lb.		1 litre contains Grms.	
		Na_2CO_3	Na_2CO_3, 10 aq.	Na_2CO_3	Na_2CO_3, 10 aq.
1·310	62	28·13	75·91	368·5	994·5
1·300	60	27·30	73·67	354·9	957·4
1·290	58	26·46	71·40	341·3	921·0
1·280	56	25·62	69·11	327·9	884·7
1·270	54	24·78	66·86	314·7	849·2
1·260	52	23·93	64·59	301·5	818·2
1·250	50	23·08	62·15	288·5	778·5
1·240	48	22·21	59·94	275·4	743·0
1·230	46	21·33	57·55	262·3	707·8
1·220	44	20·47	55·29	249·7	673·8
1·210	42	19·61	52·91	237·3	640·8
1·200	40	18·76	50·62	225·1	607·4
1·190	38	17·90	48·31	214·0	577·5
1·180	36	17·04	45·97	201·1	542·6
1·170	34	16·18	43·38	189·3	510·9
1·160	32	15·32	41·34	177·7	479·5
1·150	30	14·47	39·04	164·4	449·0
1·140	28	13·62	36·75	155·3	419·0

* This temperature has been exceptionally selected for tables 2ᴀ and 2ʙ, because the more concentrated liquors cannot exist as such at 15°C.

3.—INFLUENCE OF TEMPERATURE ON THE SPECIFIC GRAVITIES OF SOLUTIONS OF SODIUM CARBONATE.

0° C.	5°	10°	15°	20°	25°	30°	35°	40°	45°	50°
—	—	—	—	—	—	1·285	1·282	1·279	1·276	1·273
—	—	—	—	—	—	1·274	1·271	1·267	1·265	1·262
—	—	—	—	—	—	1·263	1·260	1·257	1·254	1·251
—	—	—	—	—	—	1·252	1·250	1·247	1·244	1·240
—	—	—	—	—	—	1·241	1·239	1·236	1·233	1·230
—	—	—	1·240	1·238	1·236	1·234	1·232	1·230	1·227	1·224
—	—	—	1·230	1·228	1·225	1·223	1·221	1·219	1·216	1·213
—	—	—	1·220	1·218	1·215	1·213	1·210	1·208	1·205	1·201
—	—	—	1·210	1·208	1·206	1·204	1·201	1·199	1·196	1·192
—	—	—	1·200	1·198	1·196	1·194	1·192	1·189	1·186	1·183
1·198	1·195	1·193	1·190	1·188	1·186	1·184	1·182	1·179	1·176	1·173
1·188	1·185	1·183	1·180	1·178	1·176	1·174	1·172	1·169	1·166	1·163
1·177	1·174	1·172	1·170	1·168	1·166	1·164	1·162	1·160	1·157	1·154
1·166	1·164	1·162	1·160	1·158	1·156	1·154	1·152	1·150	1·148	1·145
1·156	1·154	1·152	1·150	1·148	1·146	1·144	1·142	1·139	1·136	1·134
1·146	1·144	1·142	1·140	1·138	1·136	1·134	1·132	1·129	1·126	1·123
1·136	1·134	1·132	1·130	1·128	1·126	1·124	1·122	1·120	1·117	1·114
1·126	1·124	1·122	1·120	1·118	1·116	1·114	1·112	1·110	1·107	1·104
1·116	1·114	1·112	1·110	1·108	1·106	1·104	1·102	1·100	1·098	1·095
1·106	1·104	1·102	1·100	1·098	1·096	1·094	1·092	1·090	1·088	1·085
1·096	1·094	1·092	1·090	1·088	1·086	1·084	1·082	1·080	1·078	1·075
1·086	1·084	1·082	1·080	1·078	1·076	1·074	1·072	1·070	1·068	1·065
1·075	1·073	1·071	1·070	1·069	1·067	1·065	1·063	1·061	1·059	1·056
1·064	1·063	1·061	1·060	1·059	1·057	1·056	1·054	1·052	1·050	1·047
1·053	1·052	1·051	1·050	1·049	1·048	1·046	1·044	1·042	1·040	1·037
1·043	1·042	1·041	1·040	1·039	1·038	1·036	1·034	1·032	1·030	1·027
1·033	1·032	1·031	1·030	1·029	1·028	1·026	1·024	1·022	1·020	1·017
1·023	1·022	1·021	1·020	1·019	1·018	1·016	1·014	1·012	1·010	1·007
1·013	1·012	1·011	1·010	1·009	1·008	1·006	1·004	1·002	1·000	0·997

3.—INFLUENCE OF TEMPERATURE ON THE SPECIFIC GRAVITIES OF SOLUTIONS OF SODIUM CARBONATE.—*Continued.*

55°	60°	65°	70°	75°	80°	85°	90°	95°	100°
1·270	1·267	1·264	1·260	1·256	1·252	1·247	1·243	1·238	1·234
1·259	1·256	1·253	1·249	1·244	1·240	1·236	1·232	1·228	1·224
1·248	1·245	1·241	1·237	1·233	1·229	1·226	1·222	1·218	1·215
1·237	1·234	1·230	1·227	1·224	1·220	1·217	1·213	1·210	1·206
1·226	1·223	1·220	1·216	1·213	1·210	1·207	1·204	1·200	1·197
1·220	1·217	1·213	1·210	1·206	1·203	1·199	1·195	1·191	1·188
1·209	1·206	1·202	1·199	1·195	1·192	1·188	1·184	1·181	1·178
1·198	1·194	1·191	1·188	1·184	1·181	1·178	1·174	1·171	1·168
1·189	1·185	1·182	1·178	1·175	1·172	1·168	1·165	1·162	1·159
1·179	1·176	1·172	1·168	1·165	1·162	1·158	1·155	1·152	1·149
1·169	1·666	1·163	1·159	1·156	1·153	1·149	1·146	1·143	1·140
1·160	1·156	1·153	1·150	1·147	1·144	1·140	1·137	1·134	1·131
1·151	1·147	1·144	1·141	1·138	1·135	1·131	1·128	1·125	1·122
1·142	1·139	1·136	1·133	1·130	1·126	1·123	1·120	1·117	1·114
1·131	1·128	1·125	1·122	1·119	1·116	1·113	1·110	1·107	1·104
1·120	1·118	1·115	1·112	1·109	1·106	1·103	1·100	1·097	1·094
1·111	1·108	1·105	1·102	1·099	1·096	1·093	1·090	1·087	1·084
1·101	1·098	1·095	1·092	1·089	1·086	1·083	1·080	1·077	1·074
1·092	1·089	1·086	1·083	1·080	1·077	1·074	1·071	1·068	1·065
1·082	1·079	1·076	1·073	1·070	1·067	1·064	1·061	1·058	1·055
1·072	1·070	1·067	1·064	1·061	1·058	1·055	1·052	1·049	1·046
1·062	1·060	1·057	1·054	1·052	1·049	1·046	1·043	1·040	1·038
1·053	1·051	1·048	1·045	1·043	1·040	1·037	1·034	1·032	1·029
1·044	1·041	1·038	1·036	1·082	1·030	1·028	1·025	1·023	1·020
1·034	1·032	1·029	1·027	1·024	1·021	1·019	1·016	1·014	1·011
1·024	1·022	1·019	1·017	1·015	1·012	1·010	1·007	1·005	1·003
1·014	1·012	1·009	1·007	1·005	1·002	1·000	0·997	0·995	0·993
1·004	1·002	0·999	0·997	0·995	0·992	0·990	0·987	0·985	0·983
0·994	0·992	0·989	0·987	0·985	0·982	0·980	0·977	0·975	0·973

G.—ANALYSIS OF COMMERCIAL SODA-ASH.

When merely the *available alkali* (alkalimetrical degree) has to be ascertained, it is convenient to weigh out 15·5 grms., to dissolve in a 500 c.c. flask, and to take for each test 50 c.c. (in Germany, without filtering; in England, sometimes with, sometimes without). In this case each cubic centimetre of standard acid indicates 0·031 grm. Na_2O, or just 2 per cent. of available alkali (Na_2O). The standard acid is normal hydrochloric acid, containing 36·5 grms. HCl per litre, and standardized both with pure sodium carbonate and with silver nitrate. (Refer to Appendix.) The indicator is either litmus (in which case the liquor has to be boiled for some time) or more conveniently methyl-orange (which is used with cold liquors).

For a *complete* analysis of commercial soda-ash 50 grms. are dissolved in warm water.

1. *The Insoluble Residue* is filtered and washed, the filtrate and washings are diluted up to 1 litre, and the following tests are made with this liquor.

2. *Sodium Carbonate* is found by titrating 20 c.c. (equal to 1 grm. of soda-ash) with normal HCl, deducting the amount of No. 3. That of No. 4 is always too small to take notice of in this case.

3. *Sodium Hydrate* is estimated by barium chloride, according to page 129.

4. *Sodium Sulphide.*—100 c.c. (equal to 5 grms. of ash) are titrated with ammoniacal silver nitrate (refer to Appendix), containing 13·315 grms. Ag per litre, and indicating 0·005 grm. Na_2S per cubic centimetre. Heat the soda liquor to boiling, add ammonia, and run in the silver solution from a burette, divided in $\frac{1}{10}$ c.c., till no further black precipitate of Ag_2S is produced. In order to observe this more accurately the liquid is filtered towards the end of the operation, and the titration is continued if necessary. This filtration is several times repeated. Each cubic centimetre of silver solution indicates 0·1 per cent. of Na_2S in the alkali.

5. *Sodium Sulphite.*—Acidulate 100 c.c (equal to 5 grms. soda-ash) with acetic acid, add starch solution, and titrate with iodine till a blue colour appears. A decinormal iodine solution shows 0·0063 grm. Na_2SO_3 per cubic centimetre (in this case 0·126 per cent.). The solution mentioned on page 130 of 3·256 grms. iodine per litre shows 0·001615 grm. Na_2SO_3 (in this case 0·0323 per cent.). From this should be deducted the amount corresponding to test No. 4; 1 c.c. of the silver solution can be put equal to 1·3 c.c. of the decinormal or equal to 5·0 c.c of the weaker iodine solution.

6. *Sodium Sulphate.*—Acidulate 20 c.c. of the liquor (equal to 1 grm. soda-ash) with hydrochloric acid, precipitate with barium chloride, as on page 94, and weigh the $BaSO_4$, of which 1·000 part is equal to 0·6094 part Na_2SO_4.

7. *Sodium Chloride.*—Neutralize 20 c.c. (equal to 1 grm. soda-ash) exactly with nitric acid, preferably by adding exactly as many cubic centimetres normal nitric acid from a burette as had been used in test No. 1; then add neutral potassium chromate, and titrate with decinormal silver nitrate as described on page 117. Each cubic centimetre of this shows 0·00585 grm. NaCl.

8. *Iron.*—Neutralize 100 c.c. (equal to 5 grms. soda-ash) with sulphuric acid free from iron, reduce by zinc free from iron (p. 114), and titrate with 1-20th normal potassium permanganate, of which each cubic centimetre shows 0·0028 grm. Fe, or in this case 0·056 per cent. Fe.

9.—*Table for Comparing French, German, and English Commercial Alkalimetrical Degrees.*—The French or Descroizilles degrees mean the quantity of real sulphuric acid, SO_4H_2, neutralized by 100 parts of soda-ash. The German degrees express the available alkali in terms of sodium carbonate, Na_2CO_3. In England some works invoice in real per cent. of soda, Na_2O, as found in the first column of the following tables. The Newcastle test is based on the equivalent 32 for Na₂O, or 59·25 degrees for pure Na₂CO₃ and invoices fractions of degrees.

FRENCH, GERMAN, AND ENGLISH COMMERCIAL ALKALI-METRICAL DEGREES.

Real Soda Na₂O	German degrees Na₂CO₃	New-castle degrees.	French degrees.	Real Soda Na₂O	German degrees Na₂CO₃	New-castle degrees.	French degrees.
0·5	0·85	0·51	0·79	18	30·78	18·23	28·45
1	1·71	1·01	1·58	18·5	31·63	18·74	29·24
1·5	2·56	1·52	2·37	19	32·49	19·25	30·08
2	3·42	2·03	3·16	19·5	33·34	19·76	30·82
2·5	4·27	2·54	3·95	20	34·20	20·26	31·61
3	5·13	3·04	4·74	20·5	35·05	20·77	32·40
3·5	5·98	3·55	5·53	21	35·91	21·27	33·19
4	6·84	4·05	6·32	21·5	36·76	21·78	33·98
4·5	7·69	4·56	7·11	22	37·62	22·29	34·77
5	8·55	5·06	7·90	22·5	38·47	22·80	35·56
5·5	9·40	5·57	8·69	23	39·33	23·30	36·35
6	10·26	6·08	9·48	23·5	40·18	23·81	37·14
6·5	11·11	6·59	10·27	24	41·04	24·31	37·93
7	11·97	7·09	11·06	24·5	41·89	24·82	38·72
7·5	12·82	7·60	11·85	25	42·75	25·32	39·51
8	13·68	8·10	12·64	25·5	43·60	25·83	40·30
8·5	14·53	8·61	13·43	26	44·46	26·34	41·09
9	15·39	9·12	14·22	26·5	45·31	26·85	41·88
9·5	16·24	9·63	15·01	27	46·17	27·35	42·67
10	17·10	10·13	15·81	27·5	47·02	27·86	43·46
10·5	17·95	10·64	16·60	28	47·88	28·36	44·25
11	18·81	11·14	17·39	28·5	48·73	28·87	45·04
11·5	19·66	11·65	18·18	29	49·59	29·38	45·83
12	20·52	12·17	18·97	29·5	50·44	29·89	46·62
12·5	21·37	12·68	19·76	30	51·29	30·39	47·42
13	22·23	13·17	20·55	30·5	52·14	30·90	48·21
13·5	23·08	13·68	21·34	31	53·00	31·41	49·00
14	23·94	14·18	22·13	31·5	53·85	31·91	49·79
14·5	24·79	14·69	22·92	32	54·71	32·42	50·88
15	25·65	15·19	23·71	32·5	55·56	32·92	51·37
15·5	26·50	15·70	24·50	33	56·42	33·43	52·16
16	27·36	16·21	25·29	33·5	57·27	33·94	52·95
16·5	28·21	16·73	26·08	34	58·13	34·44	53·74
17	29·07	17·22	26·87	34·5	58·98	34·95	54·53
17·5	29·92	17·73	27·66	35	59·84	35·46	55·32

FRENCH, GERMAN, AND ENGLISH COMMERCIAL ALKALI-METRICAL DEGREES.—*Continued.*

Real Soda Na$_2$O	German degrees Na$_2$CO$_3$	New-castle degrees.	French degrees.	Real Soda Na$_2$O	German degrees Na$_2$CO$_3$	New-castle degrees.	French degrees.
35·5	60·69	35·96	56·11	53	90·61	53·70	83·77
36	61·55	36·47	56·90	53·5	91·47	54·20	84·56
36·5	62·40	36·98	57·69	54	92·32	54·71	85·35
37	63·26	37·48	58·48	54·5	93·18	55·22	86·14
37·5	64·11	37·98	59·27	55	94·03	55·72	86·93
38	64·97	38·50	60·06	55·5	94·89	56·23	87·72
38·5	65·82	39·00	60·85	56	95·74	56·74	88·52
39	66·68	39·51	61·64	56·5	96·60	57·24	89·31
39·5	67·53	40·02	62·43	57	97·45	57·75	90·10
40	68·39	40·52	63·22	57·5	98·31	58·26	90·89
40·5	69·24	41·03	64·01	58	99·16	58·76	91·68
41	70·10	41·54	64·81	58·5	100·02	59·27	92·47
41·5	70·95	42·04	65·60	59	100·87	59·77	93·26
42	71·81	42·55	66·39	59·5	101·73	60·28	94·05
42·5	72·66	43·06	67·18	60	102·58	60·79	94·84
43	73·52	43·57	67·97	60·5	103·44	61·30	95·63
43·5	74·37	44·07	68·76	61	104·30	61·80	96·42
44	75·23	44·58	69·55	61·5	105·15	62·31	97·21
44·5	76·08	45·08	70·34	62	106·01	62·82	98·00
45	76·94	45·69	71·13	62·5	106·86	63·32	98·79
45·5	77·80	46·10	71·92	63	107·72	63·83	99·58
46	78·66	46·60	72·71	63·5	108·57	64·33	100·37
46·5	79·51	47·11	73·50	64	109·43	64·84	101·16
47	80·37	47·62	74·29	64·5	110·28	65·35	101·95
47·5	81·22	48·12	75·08	65	111·14	65·85	102·74
48	82·07	48·63	75·87	65·5	111·99	66·36	103·53
48·5	82·93	49·14	76·66	66	112·85	66·87	104·32
49	83·78	49·64	77·45	66·5	113·70	67·37	105·11
49·5	84·64	50·15	78·24	67	114·56	67·88	105·90
50	85·48	50·66	79·03	67·5	115·41	68·39	106·69
50·5	86·34	51·16	79·82	68	116·27	68·89	107·48
51	87·19	51·67	80·61	68·5	117·12	69·40	108·27
51·5	88·05	52·18	81·40	69	117·98	69·91	109·06
52	88·90	52·68	82·19	69·5	118·83	70·41	109·85
52·5	89·76	53·19	82·98	70	119·69	70·92	110·64

FRENCH, GERMAN, AND ENGLISH COMMERCIAL ALKALI-METRICAL DEGREES.—*Continued.*

Real Soda Na₂O	German degrees Na₂CO₃	Newcastle degrees.	French degrees.	Real Soda Na₂O	German degrees Na₂CO₃	Newcastle degrees.	French degrees.
70·5	120·58	71·43	111·43	75·5	129·08	76·49	119·81
71	121·89	71·93	112·23	76	129·94	77·00	120·13
71·5	122·24	72·44	113·02	76·5	130·79	77·51	120·92
72	123·10	72·95	113·81	77	131·65	78·01	121·71
72·5	123·95	73·45	114·60	77·5	132·50	78·52	122·50
73	124·81	73·96	115·39				
73·5	125·66	74·47	116·18				
74	126·52	74·97	116·97				
74·5	127·37	75·48	117·76				
75	128·23	75·99	118·55				

H—CAUSTIC SODA.

1.—CAUSTIC LIQUOR.

(*a*) Test for *available alkali and sodium carbonate* (as described p. 138). An *exact* estimation of CO_2, which is rarely necessary in this case, could be made by expelling it with dilute sulphuric acid, and absorbing it in soda lime (p. 95).

(*b*) SPECIFIC GRAVITIES OF SOLUTIONS OF SODIUM HYDRATE
(60° F.—15° C.).

Twaddell.	Grms. per litre. Na₂O.	Lbs. per cubic foot.			Twaddell.	Grms. per litre. Na₂O.	Lbs. per cubic foot.		
		Na₂O.	48% ash.	60% caustic.			Na₂O.	48% ash.	60% caustic.
1	8·7	·23	·49	·39	11	41·6	2·59	5·41	4·82
2	7·5	·47	·98	·78	12	45·5	2·83	5·91	4·73
3	11·8	·70	1·47	1·17	13	49·4	3·08	6·41	5·13
4	15·1	·94	1·96	1·56	14	53·2	3·32	6·92	5·53
5	18·8	1·17	2·45	1·96	15	57·1	3·56	7·42	5·94
6	22·6	1·41	2·94	2·35	16	61·0	3·80	7·93	6·34
7	26·4	1·64	3·43	2·74	17	64·9	4·04	8·43	6·74
8	30·2	1·88	3·92	3·13	18	68·8	4·29	8·93	7·15
9	33·9	2·11	4·41	3·53	19	72·7	4·53	9·44	7·55
10	37·7	2·35	4·90	3·92	20	76·5	4·77	9·94	7·95

(b) SPECIFIC GRAVITIES OF SOLUTIONS OF SODIUM HYDRATE
(60° F.—15° C.).—Continued.

Twaddell.	Grms. per litre. Na₂O.	Lbs. per cubic foot.			Twaddell.	Grms. per litre. Na₂O.	Lbs. per cubic foot.		
		Na₂O.	48% ash.	60% caustic.			Na₂O.	48% ash.	60% caustic.
21	80·4	5·01	10·45	8·36	61	279·3	17·41	36·28	29·02
22	84·3	5·25	10·95	8·76	62	285·4	17·79	37·07	29·66
23	88·2	5·50	11·46	9·16	63	291·5	18·18	37·87	30·29
24	92·1	5·74	11·96	9·57	64	297·7	18·56	38·67	30·93
25	96·0	5·98	12·46	9·97	65	303·8	18·94	39·46	31·57
26	100·5	6·26	13·05	10·44	66	309·9	19·32	40·26	32·20
27	105·0	6·55	13·64	10·91	67	316·0	19·70	41·05	32·84
28	109·6	6·83	14·23	11·38	68	322·2	20·08	41·85	33·47
29	114·1	7·11	14·82	11·86	69	328·3	20·47	42·64	34·11
30	118·6	7·39	15·41	12·33	70	334·4	20·85	43·44	34·75
31	123·2	7·68	16·00	12·80	71	340·8	21·25	44·27	35·41
32	127·7	7·96	16·59	13·27	72	347·2	21·65	45·10	36·08
33	132·2	8·24	17·18	13·74	73	353·6	22·05	45·94	36·75
34	136·8	8·53	17·77	14·21	74	360·1	22·45	46·77	37·41
35	141·3	8·81	18·36	14·68	75	366·5	22·85	47·60	38·08
36	145·8	9·09	18·94	15·15	76	372·9	23·25	48·44	38·75
37	150·4	9·37	19·53	15·63	77	379·3	23·65	49·27	39·41
38	154·9	9·66	20·12	16·10	78	385·7	24·05	50·10	40·08
39	159·4	9·94	20·71	16·57	79	392·1	24·45	50·94	40·75
40	164·0	10·22	21·30	17·04	80	398·5	24·85	51·77	41·41
41	169·4	10·56	22·00	17·60	81	405·2	25·26	52·68	42·10
42	174·7	10·89	22·70	18·16	82	411·8	25·67	53·49	42·79
43	180·1	11·23	23·40	18·72	83	418·4	26·08	54·34	43·47
44	185·5	11·56	24·10	19·28	84	425·0	26·50	55·20	44·16
45	190·9	11·90	24·80	19·84	85	431·6	26·91	56·06	44·85
46	196·3	12·24	25·50	20·40	86	438·2	27·32	56·92	45·53
47	201·7	12·57	26·20	20·96	87	444·8	27·73	57·78	46·22
48	207·0	12·91	26·89	21·51	88	451·4	28·14	58·63	46·91
49	212·4	13·24	27·59	22·07	89	458·0	28·56	59·49	47·59
50	217·8	13·58	28·29	22·63	90	464·6	28·97	60·35	48·28
51	223·4	13·92	29·01	23·21	91	472·3	29·44	61·34	49·07
52	228·9	14·27	29·73	23·78	92	479·9	29·92	62·53	49·86
53	234·4	14·61	30·45	24·36	93	487·6	30·39	63·32	50·65
54	240·0	14·96	31·17	24·93	94	495·3	30·87	64·31	51·44
55	245·5	15·31	31·89	25·51	95	502·9	31·34	65·29	52·23
56	251·0	15·65	32·61	26·08	96	510·6	31·82	66·28	53·02
57	256·6	16·00	33·33	26·66	97	518·2	32·29	67·27	53·81
58	262·1	16·34	34·05	27·24	98	525·9	32·76	68·26	54·60
59	267·6	16·69	34·77	27·81	99	533·6	33·28	69·25	55·40
60	273·2	17·03	35·48	28·39	100	541·2	33·75	70·30	56·24

(c) INFLUENCE OF TEMPERATURE ON THE SPECIFIC GRAVITIES OF SOLUTIONS OF CAUSTIC SODA.

0° C.	5°	10°	15°	20°	25°	30°	35°	40°	45°	50°
1·367	1·364	1·362	1·360	1·357	1·355	1·353	1·350	1·348	1·345	1·342
1·357	1·354	1·352	1·350	1·347	1·345	1·343	1·340	1·337	1·335	1·332
1·347	1·344	1·342	1·340	1·338	1·335	1·333	1·330	1·327	1·325	1·322
1·338	1·335	1·332	1·330	1·328	1·325	1·323	1·320	1·317	1·315	1·312
1·328	1·325	1·322	1·320	1·318	1·315	1·313	1·310	1·307	1·305	1·302
1·318	1·315	1·313	1·310	1·308	1·305	1·303	1·300	1·297	1·294	1·292
1·308	1·305	1·303	1·300	1·297	1·294	1·292	1·289	1·287	1·284	1·282
1·298	1·295	1·293	1·290	1·287	1·284	1·282	1·279	1·277	1·274	1·272
1·288	1·285	1·283	1·280	1·277	1·274	1·272	1·269	1·267	1·264	1·262
1·278	1·275	1·273	1·270	1·267	1·265	1·262	1·260	1·258	1·255	1·252
1·268	1·265	1·263	1·260	1·257	1·255	1·252	1·250	1·248	1·245	1·242
1·257	1·255	1·252	1·250	1·247	1·245	1·242	1·240	1·238	1·235	1·233
1·247	1·245	1·242	1·240	1·237	1·235	1·232	1·230	1·228	1·225	1·223
1·237	1·235	1·232	1·230	1·227	1·224	1·222	1·220	1·218	1·215	1·212
1·227	1·225	1·222	1·220	1·217	1·214	1·212	1·210	1·208	1·205	1·202
1·217	1·215	1·212	1·210	1·207	1·204	1·203	1·200	1·198	1·196	1·192
1·207	1·205	1·202	1·200	1·197	1·195	1·193	1·190	1·188	1·186	1·184
1·197	1·195	1·192	1·190	1·187	1·185	1·183	1·180	1·178	1·176	1·174
1·187	1·185	1·182	1·180	1·177	1·175	1·173	1·170	1·168	1·166	1·164
1·176	1·174	1·172	1·170	1·167	1·165	1·163	1·161	1·158	1·156	1·154
1·166	1·164	1·162	1·160	1·157	1·155	1·153	1·151	1·148	1·146	1·144
1·156	1·154	1·152	1·150	1·148	1·146	1·144	1·142	1·140	1·137	1·135
1·146	1·144	1·142	1·140	1·138	1·136	1·134	1·132	1·130	1·127	1·125
1·136	1·134	1·132	1·130	1·128	1·126	1·124	1·122	1·120	1·118	1·116
1·126	1·124	1·122	1·120	1·118	1·116	1·114	1·112	1·110	1·108	1·106
1·115	1·113	1·112	1·110	1·108	1·106	1·104	1·102	1·100	1·099	1·097
1·105	1·103	1·102	1·100	1·098	1·096	1·095	1·093	1·092	1·090	1·087
1·094	1·093	1·091	1·090	1·088	1·087	1·086	1·084	1·082	1·080	1·078
1·084	1·083	1·081	1·080	1·078	1·●●●	1·076	1·074	1·072	1·070	1·068
1·074	1·073	1·071	1·070	1·068	1·067	1·066	1·064	1·062	1·060	1·058
1·064	1·063	1·061	1·060	1·058	1·057	1·056	1·054	1·052	1·050	1·048
1·054	1·053	1·051	1·050	1·048	1·047	1·046	1·044	1·042	1·040	1·038
1·044	1·043	1·041	1·040	1·038	1·037	1·036	1·034	1·032	1·030	1·028
1 034	1·033	1·031	1·030	1·028	1·027	1·026	1·024	1·022	1·020	1·018
1·024	1·023	1·021	1·020	1·018	1·017	1·016	1·014	1·012	1·010	1·008
1·014	1·013	1·011	1·010	1·008	1·007	1·006	1·004	1·002	1·000	0·998

2.—LIME MUD.

(a) *Sodium as Carbonate and Hydrate.*—Evaporate to dryness with addition of ammonium carbonate (in order to decompose the insoluble sodium compounds), repeat this, digest with hot water, filter, wash, and test the filtrate for alkali. The soda may have been originally present as NaOH or as Na_2CO_3. It is expressed in terms of Na_2O (0·031 grm. per cubic centimetre of normal acid).

(c) INFLUENCE OF TEMPERATURE ON THE SPECIFIC GRAVITIES OF SOLUTIONS OF CAUSTIC SODA. — *Continued.*

55°	60°	65°	70°	75°	80°	85°	90°	95°	100°
1·339	1·336	1·333	1·331	1·328	1·326	1·323	1·321	1·318	1·316
1·330	1·327	1·324	1·322	1·319	1·316	1·314	1·311	1·308	1·306
1·320	1·317	1·314	1·312	1·309	1·306	1·304	1·301	1·298	1·296
1·310	1·307	1·304	1·302	1·299	1·296	1·294	1·291	1·288	1·286
1·300	1·297	1·294	1·292	1·289	1·286	1·283	1·280	1·277	1·274
1·289	1·286	1·284	1·281	1·278	1·275	1·272	1·269	1·266	1·263
1·279	1·276	1·274	1·271	1·268	1·265	1·262	1·259	1·256	1·253
1·269	1·266	1·264	1·261	1·258	1·255	1·252	1·249	1·245	1·242
1·259	1·256	1·254	1·251	1·248	1·245	1·242	1·239	1·235	1·232
1·250	1·247	1·245	1·242	1·239	1·236	1·233	1·231	1·228	1·225
1·240	1·237	1·235	1·232	1·229	1·226	1·223	1·221	1·218	1·215
1·231	1·228	1·226	1·223	1·220	1·218	1·215	1·213	1·209	1·207
1·221	1·218	1·216	1·213	1·210	1·208	1·205	1·203	1·200	1·197
1·210	1·208	1·205	1·202	1·200	1·198	1·195	1·192	1·190	1·187
1·200	1·198	1·195	1·192	1·190	1·188	1·185	1·182	1·180	1·177
1·191	1·189	1·186	1·184	1·181	1·179	1·176	1·173	1·171	1·168
1·182	1·180	1·177	1·175	1·172	1·169	1·166	1·163	1·161	1·158
1·172	1·169	1·166	1·164	1·161	1·158	1·155	1·153	1·150	1·147
1·162	1·159	1·156	1·153	1·151	1·148	1·145	1·143	1·140	1·137
1·152	1·149	1·146	1·143	1·140	1·138	1·135	1·132	1·130	1·127
1·142	1·139	1·136	1·133	1·130	1·128	1·125	1·122	1·120	1·117
1·132	1·130	1·127	1·124	1·121	1·118	1·116	1·113	1·110	1·107
1·122	1·120	1·117	1·114	1·111	1·108	1·106	1·103	1·100	1·097
1·113	1·110	1·107	1·104	1·101	1·099	1·096	1·093	1·090	1·087
1·103	1·100	1·097	1·094	1·092	1·089	1·086	1·083	1·080	1·077
1·094	1·091	1·089	1·086	1·083	1·080	1·077	1·074	1·071	1·068
1·084	1·082	1·079	1·076	1·073	1·070	1·067	1·064	1·061	1·058
1·075	1·073	1·070	1·067	1·064	1·061	1·058	1·056	1·052	1·048
1·066	1·063	1·060	1·057	1·05■	1·051	1·048	1·046	1·043	1·040
1·056	1·053	1·050	1·047	1·0■■	1·042	1·039	1·036	1·033	1·030
1·046	1·043	1·040	1·037	1·034	1·032	1·029	1·026	1·023	1·020
1·036	1·033	1·030	1·027	1·024	1·021	1·019	1·016	1·013	1·010
1·026	1·023	1·020	1·017	1·014	1·011	1·009	1·006	1·003	1·000
1·016	1·013	1·010	1·007	1·004	1·001	0·999	0·996	0·993	0·990
1·006	1·003	1·000	0·997	0·994	0·991	0·989	0·986	0·983	0·980
0·996	0·993	0·990	0·987	0·984	0·981	0·979	0·976	0·973	0·970

(b) *Caustic Lime.*—Titrate as described (p. 125) with oxalic acid. This indicates NaOH as well, for which half of the amount found in test (a) may be assumed without any serious error.

(c) *Calcium Carbonate.* — Titrate with normal hydrochloric acid and methyl-orange, deduct from the cubic centimetres required those required in tests (a) and (b).

3.—FISHED SALTS.

Dissolve 50 grms. in 1 litre of water, and take 50 c.c. of liquor for each test.

(a) *Available Alkali* is tested for with normal hydrochloric acid.

(b) *Sodium Chloride.*—Neutralize with nitric acid, preferably running normal acid out of a burette, and proceed also in other respects as described (p. 117).

(c) *Sodium Sulphate.*—Add a slight excess of hydrochloric acid, precipitate with barium chloride, and weigh the $BaSO_4$ (p. 94).

(d) *Sodium Sulphite, Thiosulphate, etc.*—Add an excess of bleaching-powder solution, then hydrochloric acid, till the reaction is acid, and a smell of chlorine is produced (p. 131); precipitate with $BaCl_2$, weigh the $BaSO_4$, and deduct the amount found in test (c). The remainder is calculated as "Na_2SO_4 from oxidizable sulphur compounds."

4.—CAUSTIC BOTTOMS.

Dissolve 10 grms. in water, and filter. The washed residue is dried and ignited, and yields :—

(a) *Insoluble Matters.*—If necessary, the iron contained in these is estimated by dissolving in concentrated hydrochloric acid, reducing with zinc, adding manganous sulphate, and titrating with permanganate as on page 114.

(b) *Available Alkali* is estimated in the aqueous solutions by normal hydrochloric acid, using litmus or litmoid as indicator. (Methyl-orange is not available in this case, owing to the presence of alumina.)

(c) *Sodium Carbonate* is estimated as in commercial soda-ash (p. 138).

5.—COMMERCIAL CAUSTIC SODA.

The sample must be very carefully taken. (Refer to Appendix.) The single pieces must be freed from the modified outward crust by scraping it off before weighing. Dissolve 50 grms. of pure substance in 1 litre of water, and take single tests with a pipette.

(a) *Available Alkali* is tested in at least 20 c.c. (equal to 1 grm.) with normal HCl. If the caustic soda contains more than traces of alumina, methyl-orange cannot be used as an indicator, but litmus or litmoid should be employed. In the case of strong caustic this is unnecessary.

(b) *Sodium Carbonate* must be estimated by expelling the CO_2 with dilute sulphuric acid, and absorbing it with soda lime, as described (p. 95). The pumice saturated with cupric sulphate is left out here. Or employ Lunge & Marchlewski's gasvolumetric method (p. 96). The quantity of CO_2 being so small, any estimation by difference yields unsatisfactory results. Very approximate results can, however, be obtained by titrating first with phenolphthalein till the pink colour is discharged (when all Na_2CO_3 will have been changed into $NaHCO_3$), noting the amount of standard acid used, adding methyl-orange and more standard acid till the pink colour appears. The acid used in the second test × 2 indicates Na_2CO_3.

(c) *The Table for Comparing English, French, and German Degrees* is given on pages 139 to 141.

6.—SULPHUR RECOVERY (CHANCE PROCESS).*

1. *Estimation of Sulphur as Sulphides in Vat Waste.*—The apparatus consists of a small flask fitted with a stop-cock funnel and outlet tube connected with two Mohr's potash-bulbs, the first one being empty, the second one containing a strong solution of caustic potash. (In lieu of Mohr's bulbs a

---

* Partly from communications by Mr. H. W. Crowther, of Oldbury.

tube of the shape shown in fig. 6, p. 99, can be employed with great advantage.) It is preferable to connect the last potash bulb to an aspirator or Bunsen pump, to produce a slight vacuum. About 2 grms. of vat waste are put into the flask, and a sufficient quantity of water is added. Then hydrochloric acid, diluted with its volume of water, is run in from the funnel gradually. After the decomposition has ceased, the liquor is boiled, until the whole of the gases are displaced by steam, most of the steam condensing in the first empty potash bulbs. When enough steam has been produced to bring the first bulb of the second set, filled with potash solution, up to boiling heat, the tap of the funnel is opened, and the apparatus allowed to cool down. The potash solution is then transferred to a $\frac{1}{4}$ or $\frac{1}{2}$ litre flask, made up to the mark; an aliquot part is taken, diluted with a large quantity of previously boiled water (free from air), neutralized with acetic acid, and titrated with decinormal iodine, every c.c. of which indicates 0·0016 grms. S.

2. *Sulphur as Sulphide in Carbonated Mud.*—About 6 grms. are taken for analysis, and otherwise the test is conducted just like the preceding one.

3. *Sulphide-sulphur + Carbonic Acid in Vat Waste.*—This test (which is only exceptionally made) is carried out in a small flask, fitted with stopcock funnel, connected with a U-tube containing sodium sulphate to absorb any traces of HCl passing over, and a sufficient number of chloride-of-calcium tubes to thoroughly dry the gases. To the last of these are connected two weighed potash bulbs containing a strong solution of caustic potash, followed by weighed $CaCl_2$ tubes. The whole apparatus being connected, 2 grms. of vat waste are put into the flask, and some water is added. A stream of nitrogen is then passed through the apparatus to displace the air. [The nitrogen for this purpose is conveniently made by passing lime-kiln gases through a solution of caustic soda, then through a red-hot tube containing bright copper clippings to absorb any oxygen, and finally through solutions of caustic potash and barium hydrate.] Now the vat waste is decomposed by hydrochloric acid, and the contents of the flask are boiled. Afterwards a stream of nitrogen is passed through the apparatus for a considerable time to displace the H_2S and CO_2 in the flask and drying tubes. The potash bulbs and the last drying tubes are re-weighed, the increase showing the amount of $H_2S + CO_2$ in the vat waste employed. The potash solution is now transferred ▬ measuring flask, and the H_2S is estimated exactly as described in 1. Deducting the amount from the increase of weight of the absorbing apparatus, we find the amount of CO_2 present.

4. *Sulphur as Sulphide in Solutions of Calcium or Sodium Sulphydrates and Sulphides.*—10 cc. are diluted to 250, and of this liquid a convenient portion is taken out, strongly diluted with air-free water, acidulated with acetic acid and titrated with iodine, as in test 1. If thiosulphates are present, they are estimated as in 5, and deducted. If polysulphides are present, the sulphur which would be precipitated by an acid is not estimated by this method, but only that which would be liberated as H_2S by an acid.

5. *Soda, Lime, and Thiosulphate in Sulphur Liquors.*—In one sample of the liquor, say 5 c.c., estimate the total alkalinity, *i.e.* $Na_2O + CaO$, by standard hydrochloric acid and methyl-orange. Take another sample, say 50 c.c., pass pure CO_2 in till lead paper shows the absence of all sulphides, boil to decompose calcium bicarbonate, dilute with water to 500 c.c., allow the precipitate to settle, take 50 c.c. of the clear liquor and titrate again, the alkalinity this time being due to Na_2O only. CaO is found by the difference from the first titration.

Another sample of the carbonated liquor is titrated with decinormal iodine for thiosulphate. Each c.c. of iodine solution indicates 0·0064 S as thiosulphate.

6. *Lime-kiln Gases.*—CO_2 is estimated by an Orsat's apparatus, or a Honigmann's burette, or any other similar apparatus. When using an Orsat's apparatus, the test for oxygen can be made as on p. 86.

7. *Gas from Gas-holder.*

(*a*) *Hydrogen Sulphide + Carbon Dioxide* are estimated by an Orsat's apparatus or a Honigmann's burette, etc.

(*b*) *Hydrogen Sulphide Only.*—A wide-mouthed bottle of known capacity, holding about 500 c.c., is fitted with an indiarubber cork and two tubes, one nearly reaching to the bottom, the other ending just below the cork, both of them with stopcocks outside. Gas is passed through for some time, till it has entirely displaced the air in the bottle. Then 20 or 25 c.c. of standard potash solution is run in from a pipette, through one of the stopcocks, the bottle is well shaken, until the whole of the H_2S and CO_2 are absorbed, the contents of the bottle are poured into a measuring flask, the bottle is rinsed out completely, and the total liquid made up to the mark.

An aliquot portion is taken out, strongly diluted with previously boiled water, acidified with acetic acid, and the H_2S estimated by iodine. In this case a solution of iodine is employed containing 11·48 grms. I per litre, each c.c. of which indicates 1 c.c. of gaseous H_2S at 0° C., and 760 mm. pressure. For somewhat exact estimations, the temperature, pressure and vapour tension have to be taken into account; but it is unnecessary to observe the thermometer and barometer, and to make any complicated calculations, if a Lunge's gas-volumeter be present (p. 113). In this case the level-tube, C, of that instrument is placed so that the mercury stands at the same height in C as in the reduction tube B; the height of mercury in the latter is read off, which gives the volume occupied by 100 c.c. of dry air of 0° and 760 mm. under the atmospheric conditions of the moment; by this figure the number of c.c. of iodine solution, multiplied by 100, is divided, and thus the correction of the normal volume is effected.

8. *Exit Gases from the Claus Kilns.*—These contain SO_2 and H_2S. Both these gases, on being passed through iodine solution, produce 2HI for each atom of S; but whilst H_2S does not any further increase the acidity of the liquid, SO_2 produces its equivalent of H_2SO_4. Hence SO_2 and H_2S are measured together by the amount of iodine converted into HI, and SO_2 by the acidity present after the HI has been saturated with caustic soda. Since the current of gases carries away some iodine from the decinormal solution, the gases must be passed through caustic soda, or, even better, through sodium thiosulphate, to intercept this iodine. The manipulation is hence as follows: Aspirate one or more litres of the gases through 50 c.c. of decinormal iodine solution, contained in a bulb apparatus (fig. 6, p. 99), or other efficient absorbing tubes, followed by another apparatus containing 50 c.c. of decinormal thiosulphate soda solution. Empty the contents of both apparatus into a beaker. Now titrate with decinormal iodine and starch solution, till a blue colour appears. The number of c.c. of iodine solution used, if multiplied by 0·0016 grms., indicates the total sulphur present as SO_2 and H_2S. Now add a drop of thiosulphate to discharge the blue colour, then a drop of methyl-orange, and decinormal caustic soda from a burette, till the liquid has lost all pinkish shade. The number of c.c. of caustic soda used, less those of iodine used in the preceding test, multiplied by 0·0016, indicates the sulphur present as SO_2.

7.—NITRIC ACID MANUFACTURE.

A.—NITRATE OF SODA.

1. *Moisture.*—Heat 10 grms. cautiously to the fusing point, and allow to cool in a desiccator.

2. *Insoluble.*—Dissolve 10 grms. in water, filter, wash, and ignite. If there is a very appreciable quantity of organic substance present, first dry at 100° C. and weigh the filter with the precipitate before igniting it. The solution is used for the tests Nos. 4 to 6.

3. *Sodium Nitrate.*—From a very well mixed, finely-ground sample weigh in a narrow weighing tube about 0·35 grms. (which is facilitated by filling it to a mark*), cork the tube, and weigh. Pour the contents into the "nitrometer for saltpetre" containing 140 c.c. (described in the *Journal of the Society of Chemical Industry*, 1882, p. 15), taking care that the substance gets as much as possible upon the bottom of the top cup. The three-way cock must have been made to communicate neither above, nor below, nor sideways. Run in about 0·5 c.c. water, wait a minute till the nitre is nearly or quite dissolved, aspirate the solution into the measuring tube by cautiously opening the tap, the level tube being lowered, wash the cup with at most 0·5 c.c. water, and run in 15 c.c. concentrated pure sulphuric acid. Start the reaction as with the ordinary nitrometer (p. 112), and finish it by vigorous shaking. The level tube should be roughly put into position, in order to avoid any strong differences of pressure, and consequently possible leaking of the tap, and wait at least half an hour for cooling. Now adjust the level definitively, by allowing one division of mercury in the level tube for each 6½ divisions of acid in the measuring tube. Read off the volume of gas, but convince yourself whether it is actually under atmospheric pressure by pouring a little sulphuric acid into the cup and cautiously running it into the tube, as described on p. 112. Ascertain the temperature and the state of the barometer, and reduce the volume of gas by the tables 20 and 21 or 21ʙ to 0° and 760 mm. pressure. Thus x c.c. NO are obtained. Each cubic centimetre of NO is equal to 0·003805 grms. NaNO₃ (table, p. 112). The total divided by the weight employed equal a, and multiplied by 100 indicates the percentage, which is hence equal to

$$\frac{0.3805x}{a}$$

(N.B.—The nitrometer should be tested whether it really contains exactly 100 c.c. to the mark 100, by inverting it, filling in mercury to the mark 100, running it off, and weighing. It should weigh 1,360 grms. reduced to 0°, or 1,356 grms. at 15° C. If there is a difference, this must be allowed for in each reading.)

For the analysis of nitrate of soda, Lunge's *gasvolumeter* (described on p. 113) is even more to be preferred to the old nitrometer than for the analysis of nitrous vitriol. The decomposition of the nitre and evolution of NO are carried out in the vessel D, and the gas is then transferred for measuring into the tube A. In this case the gas-measuring tube A should hold 130 or 140 c.c., or, if a 50 c.c. tube is employed, only 0·15 grm. of sodium nitrate is employed for each test.

---

* The quantity of nitrate employed should be such that at the existing temperature and pressure the NO disengaged in the test is above 100 c.c., but not above 120 c.c.

4. *Sodium Sulphate* is estimated in the solution No. 2 by precipitation with $BaCl_2$ and weighing the $BaSO_4$. (Refer to p. 94.)

5. *Sodium Chloride* is titrated with silver nitrate. (Refer to p. 117.)

6. *Iodine* is proved by reducing the iodic acid with zinc, heating the solution with concentrated sulphuric acid, which liberates the iodine, diluting and agitating with carbon disulphide, which takes up the iodine, and is thereby coloured pink. The faintest traces of iodate are found by dissolving 5 grms. in 100 c.c. of boiled water, adding a little nitric acid, a few drops of a solution of potassium iodide in boiled water, and a drop of starch solution. In the presence of as little as 0·01 mgrm. I in 1 grm. of nitre, a blue colour will appear. A check test must, however, be made with the potassium iodide employed for this test, as this often contains some iodate.

B.—NITRE-CAKE.

1. *Free Acid* is titrated with standard alkali (p. 117). When larger quantities of ferric oxide or alumina are present, no indicator is employed, but normal alkali is added till the first flakes of a precipitate indicate the end of the reaction.

2. *Nitric Acid* should be estimated in the gasvolumeter, or in the nitrometer for acids (p. 111), its quantity being too small for the other nitrometer (p. 148), but the method employed is exactly the same as described in the last-mentioned place, viz., dissolving in the top cup in very little water, and decomposing with a great excess of sulphuric acid.

3. *Ferric Oxide and Alumina* (as pp. 117 and 118).

C.—NITRIC ACID.

SPECIFIC GRAVITY OF NITRIC ACID AT 15° C., COMPARED WITH WATER OF 4° C. (IN VACUO).

(Lunge & Rey.)

Twad-dell.	Percentage by weight.		Grammes per litre.	
	N_2O_5	HNO_3	N_2O_5	HNO_3
0	0·08	0·10	1	1
1	0·85	1·00	8	10
2	1·62	1·90	16	19
8	2·39	2·80	24	28
4	3·17	8·70	33	88
5	8·94	4·60	40	47
6	4·71	5·50	49	57
7	5·47	6·38	57	66
8	6·22	7·26	64	75
9	6·97	8·13	73	85
10	7·71	8·99	81	94
11	8·43	9·84	89	104
12	9·15	10·68	97	113
13	9·87	11·51	105	123
14	10·57	12·33	113	132
15	11·27	13·15	121	141
16	11·96	13·95	129	151
17	12·64	14·74	137	160
18	13·31	15·33	145	169
19	13·99	16·32	153	179
20	14·67	17·11	161	188
21	15·34	17·89	170	198
22	16·00	18·67	177	207
23	16·67	19·45	186	217
24	17·34	20·23	195	227
25	18·00	21·00	202	236
26	18·66	21·77	211	246
27	19·32	22·54	219	256
28	19·98	23·31	228	266
29	20·64	24·08	237	276
80	21·29	24·84	245	286
81	21·94	25·60	254	296
82	22·60	26·36	262	806
83	23·25	27·12	271	816
84	23·90	27·88	279	826

SPECIFIC GRAVITY OF NITRIC ACID AT 15° C., COMPARED WITH WATER OF 4° C. (IN VACUO).—*Continued.*

(Lunge & Rey.)

Twad-dell.	Percentage by weight.		Grammes per litre.	
	N_2O_5	HNO_3	N_2O_5	HNO_3
35	24·54	28·63	288	336
36	25·18	29·38	297	347
37	25·83	30·13	306	357
38	26·47	30·88	315	367
39	27·10	31·62	324	378
40	27·74	32·36	333	388
41	28·36	33·09	342	399
42	28·99	33·82	351	409
43	29·61	34·55	360	420
44	30·24	35·28	369	430
45	30·88	36·03	378	441
46	31·53	36·78	387	452
47	32·17	37·53	397	463
48	32·82	38·29	407	475
49	33·47	39·05	417	486
50	34·13	39·82	427	498
51	34·78	40·58	437	509
52	35·44	41·34	447	521
53	36·09	42·10	457	533
54	36·75	42·87	467	544
55	37·41	43·64	477	556
56	38·07	44·41	487	568
57	38·73	45·18	498	581
58	39·39	45·95	508	593
59	40·05	46·72	519	605
60	40·71	47·49	529	617
61	41·37	48·26	540	630
62	42·06	49·07	551	643
63	42·76	49·89	562	656
64	43·47	50·71	573	669
65	44·17	51·53	585	683
66	44·89	52·37	597	697
67	45·62	53·22	609	710
68	46·35	54·07	621	725
69	47·08	54·93	633	739

SPECIFIC GRAVITY OF NITRIC ACID AT 15° C., COMPARED WITH WATER OF 4° C. (IN VACUO).—*Continued.*

(Lunge & Rey.)

Twad-dell.	Percentage by weight.		Grammes per litre.	
	N_2O_5	HNO_3	N_2O_5	HNO_3
70	47·82	55·79	645	758
71	48·57	56·66	658	768
72	49·35	57·57	671	788
73	50·13	58·48	684	798
74	50·91	59·39	698	814
75	51·69	60·30	711	829
76	52·52	61·27	725	846
77	53·35	62·24	739	862
78	54·20	63·23	753	879
79	55·07	64·25	768	896
80	55·97	65·30	783	914
81	56·92	66·40	800	933
82	57·86	67·50	816	952
83	58·83	68·63	832	971
84	59·83	69·80	849	991
85	60·84	70·98	867	1011
86	61·86	72·17	885	1032
87	62·91	73·39	908	1058
88	64·01	74·68	921	1075
89	65·13	75·98	941	1098
90	66·24	77·28	961	1121
91	67·38	78·60	981	1144
92	68·56	79·98	1001	1168
93	69·79	81·42	1023	1193
94	71·06	82·90	1045	1219
95	72·39	84·45	1068	1246
96	73·76	86·05	1092	1274
97	75·18	87·70	1116	1302
98	76·80	89·60	1144	1335
99	78·52	91·60	1174	1369
100	80·65	94·09	1210	1411
101	82·63	96·39	1244	1451
102	84·09	98·10	1270	1481
103	84·92	99·07	1287	1501
104	85·44	99·67	1299	1515

2.—INFLUENCE OF TEMPERATURE ON THE SPECIFIC GRAVITY OF NITRIC ACID.

0° C.	5°	10°	15°	20°	25°	30°	35°	40°	45°	50°
1·424	1·414	1·407	1·400	1·392	1·385	1·378	1·371	1·363	1·356	1·349
1·413	1·404	1·397	1·390	1·382	1·375	1·367	1·361	1·354	1·347	1·340
1·402	1·394	1·387	1·380	1·372	1·365	1·357	1·351	1·344	1·339	1·332
1·391	1·383	1·377	1·370	1·363	1·356	1·349	1·342	1·335	1·330	1·323
1·380	1·373	1·367	1·360	1·353	1·346	1·340	1·333	1·326	1·320	1·314
1·369	1·362	1·356	1·350	1·343	1·337	1·330	1·323	1·317	1·312	1·305
1·359	1·352	1·346	1·340	1·333	1·327	1·320	1·314	1·308	1·303	1·297
1·348	1·342	1·336	1·330	1·324	1·318	1·311	1·305	1·299	1·294	1·288
1·338	1·332	1·326	1·320	1·314	1·308	1·302	1·296	1·290	1·285	1·280
1·327	1·321	1·316	1·310	1·304	1·299	1·293	1·287	1·281	1·276	1·271
1·317	1·311	1·306	1·300	1·294	1·289	1·283	1·278	1·273	1·268	1·263
1·307	1·301	1·296	1·290	1·284	1·279	1·273	1·268	1·263	1·258	1·253
1·297	1·291	1·286	1·280	1·274	1·269	1·263	1·258	1·253	1·248	1·243
1·287	1·281	1·276	1·270	1·265	1·259	1·254	1·248	1·243	1·238	1·234
1·277	1·271	1·266	1·260	1·255	1·249	1·244	1·238	1·233	1·228	1·224
1·266	1·260	1·255	1·250	1·245	1·240	1·235	1·229	1·224	1·219	1·215
1·256	1·250	1·245	1·240	1·235	1·230	1·225	1·220	1·215	1·210	1·205
1·245	1·240	1·235	1·230	1·225	1·220	1·215	1·210	1·206	1·201	1·196
1·235	1·230	1·225	1·220	1·215	1·210	1·205	1·200	1·196	1·191	1·186
1·224	1·219	1·214	1·210	1·205	1·200	1·196	1·191	1·187	1·182	1·177
1·213	1·208	1·204	1·200	1·195	1·190	1·186	1·181	1·177	1·172	1·167
1·202	1·198	1·194	1·190	1·185	1·181	1·177	1·172	1·168	1·163	1·158
1·192	1·188	1·184	1·180	1·177	1·171	1·167	1·163	1·158	1·154	1·150
1·182	1·178	1·174	1·170	1·166	1·162	1·158	1·154	1·149	1·145	1·141
1·172	1·168	1·164	1·160	1·156	1·152	1·148	1·144	1·140	1·136	1·132
1·161	1·158	1·154	1·150	1·146	1·142	1·139	1·135	1·130	1·127	1·123
1·151	1·147	1·144	1·140	1·136	1·132	1·129	1·125	1·121	1·118	1·114
1·139	1·136	1·133	1·130	1·126	1·123	1·119	1·116	1·112	1·109	1·105
1·129	1·126	1·123	1·120	1·116	1·113	1·110	1·106	1·103	1·100	1·096
1·118	1·115	1·112	1·110	1·107	1·104	1·101	1·097	1·094	1·091	1·087
1·108	1·190	1·102	1·100	1·097	1·094	1·091	1·088	1·085	1·082	1·079
1·098	1·095	1·092	1·090	1·087	1·084	1·081	1·078	1·075	1·073	1·070
1·088	1·085	1·082	1·080	1·077	1·074	1·071	1·068	1·065	1·063	1·060
1·077	1·075	1·072	1·070	1·067	1·064	1·061	1·058	1·056	1·054	1·051
1·067	1·064	1·062	1·060	1·057	1·055	1·052	1·050	1·048	1·045	1·043
1·057	1·054	1·052	1·050	1·047	1·045	1·043	1·040	1·038	1·035	1·033
1·047	1·044	1·042	1·040	1·037	1·035	1·033	1·030	1·028	1·025	1·023
1·037	1·034	1·032	1·030	1·027	1·025	1·023	1·020	1·018	1·015	1·013
1·027	1·024	1·022	1·020	1·017	1·015	1·013	1·010	1·008	1·005	1·003
1·017	1·014	1·012	1·010	1·007	1·005	1·003	1·000	0·998	0·995	0·993

2.—INFLUENCE OF TEMPERATURE ON THE SPECIFIC GRAVITY OF NITRIC ACID.—*Continued.*

55°	60°	65°	70°	75°	80°	85°	90°	95°	100°
1·342	1·335	1·329	1·323	1·316	1·310	1·303	1·296	1·290	1·283
1·333	1·327	1·320	1·314	1·308	1·302	1·294	1·288	1·282	1·276
1·325	1·319	1·312	1·305	1·300	1·293	1·286	1·280	1·274	1·267
1·316	1·310	1·304	1·298	1·292	1·286	1·279	1·274	1·267	1·260
1·308	1·302	1·296	1·290	1·284	1·278	1·272	1·266	1·260	1·254
1·300	1·294	1·288	1·282	1·276	1·270	1·265	1·259	1·253	1·247
1·291	1·286	1·280	1·274	1·268	1·263	1·257	1·252	1·246	1·240
1·282	1·278	1·272	1·266	1·261	1·255	1·250	1·245	1·240	1·234
1·274	1·269	1·264	1·258	1·253	1·248	1·243	1·238	1·233	1·228
1·266	1·261	1·256	1·251	1·246	1·240	1·235	1·230	1·225	1·220
1·258	1·253	1·248	1·243	1·238	1·232	1·227	1·222	1·217	1·212
1·248	1·244	1·239	1·234	1·229	1·223	1·218	1·213	1·208	1·203
1·238	1·234	1·229	1·224	1·219	1·214	1·209	1·204	1·199	1·194
1·229	1·225	1·220	1·215	1·210	1·205	1·199	1·195	1·190	1·185
1·219	1·215	1·210	1·205	1·200	1·195	1·190	1·185	1·180	1·175
1·210	1·206	1·201	1·196	1·191	1·186	1·181	1·176	1·171	1·167
1·200	1·196	1·191	1·186	1·181	1·177	1·172	1·167	1·162	1·158
1·191	1·187	1·182	1·177	1·172	1·168	1·163	1·158	1·153	1·149
1·182	1·177	1·172	1·167	1·163	1·158	1·153	1·148	1·144	1·139
1·173	1·168	1·163	1·160	1·154	1·149	1·144	1·140	1·135	1·130
1·163	1·158	1·154	1·150	1·145	1·140	1·136	1·131	1·126	1·122
1·154	1·150	1·146	1·141	1·136	1·132	1·128	1·123	1·119	1·115
1·145	1·141	1·137	1·133	1·128	1·124	1·120	1·116	1·112	1·107
1·137	1·132	1·128	1·124	1·120	1·116	1·113	1·108	1·105	1·100
1·128	1·124	1·120	1·116	1·112	1·108	1·105	1·101	1·097	1·094
1·119	1·115	1·112	1·108	1·104	1·100	1·097	1·095	1·090	1·086
1·110	1·107	1·103	1·100	1·096	1·093	1·090	1·086	1·082	1·079
1·102	1·099	1·094	1·091	1·088	1·084	1·081	1·078	1·075	1·071
1·093	1·090	1·086	1·083	1·080	1·076	1·073	1·070	1·067	1·064
1·084	1·081	1·078	1·075	1·072	1·068	1·065	1·063	1·060	1·056
1·076	1·073	1·070	1·067	1·064	1·061	1·058	1·055	1·052	1·049
1·067	1·064	1·061	1·058	1·055	1·052	1·050	1·048	1·045	1·042
1·058	1·055	1·052	1·050	1·047	1·044	1·042	1·040	1·038	1·036
1·049	1·046	1·044	1·042	1·039	1·037	1·034	1·031	1·029	1·027
1·040	1·038	1·036	1·034	1·031	1·029	1·026	1·023	1·021	1·018
1·030	1·028	1·026	1·024	1·021	1·019	1·015	1·014	1·012	1·009
1·020	1·018	1·016	1·014	1·011	1·009	1·007	1·004	1·002	1·000
1·010	1·008	1·006	1·004	1·001	0·999	0·997	0·994	0·993	0·990
1·001	0·999	0·997	0·995	0·992	0·990	0·988	0·985	0·983	0·981
0·991	0·989	0·987	0·985	0·982	0·980	0·978	0·975	0·973	0·971

3. *Chlorine.*—Saturate with sodium carbonate, free from chloride, till the reaction is neutral or faintly alkaline, and titrate with silver nitrate (according to page 117).

4. *Sulphuric Acid.*—Saturate almost completely with sodium carbonate and precipitate with barium chloride (as on page 94). If the acid on evaporating leaves any appreciable fixed residue, this usually consists of sodium sulphate.

5. *Nitrous Acid* or *Nitrogen Tetroxide* are estimated by running the acid from a burette into a measured volume of warm dilute potassium permanganate (according to page 110). If any of these lower oxides of nitrogen are present, the alkalimetrical estimation of nitric acid cannot be performed with methyl-orange, but some other indicator must be used.

6. *Fixed Residue,* consisting chiefly of sodium sulphate, with a little ferric oxide, etc., is estimated by evaporating to dryness in a place protected from dust, igniting and weighing.

7. *Iron.*—Precipitate with excess of ammonia, filter, weigh, and ignite the Fe_2O_3.

8. *Iodine* is proved by a short digestion with pure zinc, which reduces iodic acid and generates some nitrous acid ; the latter sets the iodine of the HJ free, and this can now be recognised by shaking up with carbon disulphide, which thereby assumes a pink colour.

N.B.—Tests Nos. 7 and 8 are only made with nitric acid sold as chemically pure.

D.—MIXTURES OF SULPHURIC AND NITRIC ACID.

Such mixtures are now sold for the manufacture of explosives, of colouring matters, etc. They are tested as follows :—

1. *Sulphuric Acid.*—Weigh off 2 or 3 grms. in a glass-cock pipette (fig. 9, p. 116). Run into a small porcelain dish, heat $\frac{1}{2}$ or 1 hour on the water bath, adding at last a few drops of water (to destroy any nitrososulphuric acid), until no smell of nitric acid is perceptible even on agitation. The expulsion of nitric acid is promoted by now and then cautiously blowing upon the liquid and agitating the capsule. Wash its contents into a beaker, and titrate with normal or semi-normal caustic-soda and methyl-orange. The titre indicates nothing but sulphuric acid.

2. *Nitric Acid.*—Weigh 2 or 3 grms. as before, run cautiously into some water, and titrate with litmus. The result, less the sulphuric and nitrous acid, indicates NO_3H.

3. *Nitrous Acid* is tested as on page 110.

4. As a check, *nitric* and *nitrous acid* are estimated together by the nitrometer.

8.—POTASH MANUFACTURE.
A.—POTASSIUM CHLORIDE.

1. *Moisture.*—Heat 10 grms. for some time to 150° C. and allow to cool in a desiccator.

2. *Potassium** (a) *In the absence of Potassium Sulphate* dissolve 10 grms. of the well-mixed sample in a half-litre flask, fill up to the mark and filter.

---

* Tests Nos. 2 and 3 are essentially as described by West and Zuckschwerdt, in Zeitschr. für Analyt. Chem., 1881, pages 185 and 357, and approved of by Professor Fresenius, and are recognised as binding for buyers and sellers at Stassfurt.

Put 20 c.c. of the filtrate (equal to 0·4 grms.) into a porcelain dish and add 7 c.c. of a platinum chloride solution, containing 10 grm. Pt. in 100 c.c. Evaporate on a water bath to a syrup, frequently agitating, so that most of the free HCl is driven off and the mass appears dry on cooling. When cool. pour 10 c.c. of 95 per cent. spirits of wine over it, triturate well and pour off the liquid through a filter, previously dried for an hour at 115°C. and weighed, pour on some more spirits of wine (rather less than before), triturate again, pour off the liquid and repeat this once more; now the alcohol should remain colourless and should not give any reaction for chlorine, otherwise the washing would have to be repeated. The double chloride of potassium and platinum, which is now pure, is washed on to the filter by means of a wash bottle containing alcohol. The filter is dried half an hour at 110–115° and weighed. The total quantity of alcohol employed should be about 50 c.c. Each part of K_2PtCl_6 is equal to 0·30521 KCl.

(b) *In the presence of Potassium Sulphate.*—Small quantities of this need not be noticed, but in mixtures containing much of this salt it must be converted into KCl by means of barium chloride. Dissolve 10 grms. in a half-litre flask in about 350 c.c. or 400 c.c. water and about 25 c.c. hydrochloric acid of 25° Twaddell, heat to boiling and add sufficient barium chloride to precipitate all the sulphate. The $BaCl_2$ solution employed should be almost saturated, and a litre of it should contain 50 c.c. aqueous hydrochloric acid. With a little practice it is easy to fix the point when nearly all the potassium sulphate is decomposed; a very slight quantity remaining has no influence on the result, but any excess of $BaCl_2$ would cause an error. If this way of proceeding should seem too uncertain, the sulphuric acid must be estimated in the usual way, and the calculated quantity of barium chloride added. Now fill the flask to the mark, shake up and allow to settle. An error is caused by the volume occupied by the barium sulphate, but the latter carries down a certain quantity of potassium chloride more than compensating that error, so that the result may be corrected accordingly (see below). The remainder of the analysis is carried out as in test No. 2a; special care must be taken to drive off all free HCl in evaporating, which is not quite easy when magnesia is present. The weight of K_2PtCl_6 found is corrected by calculating from the percentage of sulphate present, the c.c. of $BaSO_4$, viz.: 1g. $K_2SO_4 = 1·337g = 0·3$ c.c. $BaSO_4$; we call this quantity (a). In reality we have not had 500 ccm. of solution, but 500–a. But experience shows that a c.c. of $BaSO_4$ carry down as much KCl, as was contained in 2a c.c. solution; hence the result is too low, and must be multiplied by

$$\frac{500-a}{500-2a}$$

in order to indicate the real percentage. For instance, if the salt contains 70 per cent. K_2SO_4, 10 g. of it will furnish $7 \times 0·3 = 2·1$ c.c. $BaSO_4$, hence $a = 2·1$; consequently the weight of K_2PtCl_6 found has to be multiplied with

$$\frac{500-2·1}{500-4·2} = 1,0043.$$

If Na_2SO_4 occurs in any salt, it is, of course, equally necessary to calculate the $BaSO_4$ corresponding to it.

8. *Sodium Chloride* (of which sometimes a maximum percentage is stipulated) is estimated by a full analysis. Estimate KCl as above, then Ca (p. 117), Mg (p. 118), SO_3 (p. 94), insoluble matter and moisture. Calculate SO_3 as $CaSO_4$, or, if there is not sufficient Ca present, partly as $MgSO_4$

and K_2SO_4. If the SO_3 does not suffice for saturating all the Mg, calculate the excess of Mg as $MgCl_2$; the excess of Cl over that required to form KCl and $MgCl_2$ is calculated as NaCl.

4. *Magnesium* (as chloride or sulphate), if a guarantee has been given for a maximum not to be exceeded, is estimated as on p. 118, after precipitating the lime. It is generally calculated as $MgCl_2$.

B.—POTASSIUM SULPHATE.

Estimate :
1. KCl according to p. 117.
2. Free SO_4H_2 according p. 117.
3. Fe according to p. 114.
4. Insoluble, CaO, etc., just as in the case of sodium sulphate.

If a complete estimation of potassium is needed, employ the process, described sub A (*b*).

C.—LIMESTONE (Refer to p. 124).

D.—MIXING-COAL (Refer to p. 128).

E.—BLACK-ASH (Refer to p. 128).

F.—TANK-WASTE (Refer to p. 130).

G.—TANK-LIQUOR (Refer to p. 131).

H.—CARBONATED LIQUOR (Refer to p. 132).

I.—COMMERCIAL CARBONATE OF POTASH.

1. *Available Alkali* is titrated with normal hydrochloric acid, as on p. 138.

2. *Total Potassium* is estimated according to p. 156, A (*b*), so that all sulphate is converted into chloride. Of course, from the first more hydrochloric must be employed in order to decompose the carbonate.

3. *Chloride* is estimated by silver solution, p. 117.

4. *Sulphate* is estimated as $BaSO_4$, p. 94.

5. *Insoluble*, as on p. 138.

6. *Silicate.* Saturate the salt with hydrochloric acid, evaporate to dryness, moisten with HCl, evaporate again, dissolve in dilute HCl, filter, wash and strongly ignite the SiO_2. This test is only exceptionally made, and the potassium silicate is calculated together with the carbonate.

7. *Phosphate* is estimated by the magnesia process, and is treated like the silicate.

8. *Calculation of the Analyses.*—Calculate:

(*a*) K_2CO_3 from the difference between the total potassium and that corresponding to the Cl and SO_3 found.

(*b*) Na_2CO_3 from the difference between the total available alkali and the K_2CO_3 just calculated.

(*c*) KCl and

(*d*) K_2SO_4 as above.

(*e*) Water and

(*f*) Insoluble, if necessary also iron, by a special test.

9.—SPECIFIC GRAVITIES OF SOLUTIONS OF POTASSIUM CARBONATE AT 60° F. = 15° C. (Gerlach).

Twaddell.	Per cent. by weight. K_2CO_3	Kilogr. per cubic metre. K_2CO_3	lbs. per cubic foot. K_2CO_3	Twaddell.	Per cent. by weight. K_2CO_3	Kilogr. per cubic metre. K_2CO_3	lbs. per cubic foot. K_2CO_3
1	·54	5·4	0·34	38	19·74	234·9	14·65
2	1·08	10·9	0·68	39	20·22	241·7	15·07
8	1·62	16·4	1·02	40	20·70	248·4	15·49
4	2·16	22·0	1·37	41	21·17	255·2	15·91
5	2·70	27·7	1·73	42	21·65	262·0	16·33
6	8·24	33·4	2·08	43	22·12	268·8	16·76
7	8·78	39·1	2·43	44	22·60	275·7	17·19
8	4·32	44·9	2·80	45	23·07	282·6	17·62
9	4·86	50·8	8·17	46	23·55	289·6	18·05
10	5·40	56·7	8·53	47	24·02	296·7	18·50
11	5·94	62·7	8·90	48	24·50	303·8	18·94
12	6·48	68·7	4·28	49	24·97	310·9	19·38
18	7·02	74·8	4·66	50	25·45	318·1	19·88
14	7·56	80·9	5·04	51	25·89	825·0	20·26
15	8·10	87·1	5·43	52	26·34	831·9	20·70
16	8·64	98·3	5·82	58	26·78	838·3	21·12
17	9·18	99·6	6·21	54	27·23	845·3	21·56
18	9·72	105·9	6·60	55	27·68	852·8	22·00
19	10·26	108·4	6·51	56	28·12	859·9	22·44
20	10·80	118·8	7·41	57	28·57	867·1	22·89
21	11·31	125·0	7·79	58	29·02	874·3	28·34
22	11·82	131·2	8·18	59	29·46	881·5	28·79
28	12·33	187·5	8·57	60	29·91	888·8	24·24
24	12·84	143·8	8·97	61	30·34	895·9	24·68
25	13·35	150·2	9·37	62	30·77	403·1	25·13
26	18·86	156·6	9·76	68	81·21	410·8	25·58
27	14·37	163·1	10·17	64	31·64	417·6	26·04
28	14·88	169·6	10·57	65	82·08	425·0	26·50
29	15·39	176·2	10·99	66	82·51	432·4	26·96
80	15·90	182·8	11·40	67	82·94	489·8	27·42
81	16·38	189·2	11·80	68	83·38	447·8	27·89
82	16·86	195·6	12·20	69	83·81	454·8	28·36
88	17·34	202·0	12·59	70	84·25	462·4	28·88
84	17·82	208·5	18·00	71	84·67	469·9	29·80
85	18·30	215·0	18·40	72	85·10	477·4	29·77
86	18·78	221·6	18·82	78	85·52	484·9	80·23
87	19·26	228·2	14·28	74	85·95	492·5	80·71

9.—SPECIFIC GRAVITIES OF SOLUTIONS OF POTASSIUM CARBONATE AT 60° F. = 15° C. (Gerlach).—*Continued.*

Twaddell.	Per cent. by weight. K_2CO_3	Kilogr. per cubic metre. K_2CO_3	lbs. per cubic foot. K_2CO_3	Twaddell.	Per cent. by weight. K_2CO_3	Kilogr. per cubic metre. K_2CO_3	lbs. per cubic foot. K_2CO_3
75	36·37	500·1	31·18	95	44·60	657·8	41·01
76	36·80	507·8	31·66	96	45·00	666·0	41·52
77	37·22	515·6	32·15	97	45·40	674·2	42·03
78	37·65	523·3	32·63	98	45·80	682·4	42·55
79	38·07	531·7	33·11	99	46·20	690·7	43·06
80	38·50	539·0	33·60	100	46·60	699·0	43·58
81	38·91	546·7	34·09	101	46·98	707·1	44·09
82	39·32	554·4	34·57	102	47·37	715·3	44·61
83	39·73	562·2	35·05	103	47·75	723·5	45·11
84	40·14	570·0	35·54	104	48·14	731·7	45·62
85	40·55	577·8	36·02	105	48·52	740·0	46·14
86	40·96	585·7	36·51	106	48·91	748·3	46·66
87	41·37	593·6	37·01	107	49·29	756·7	47·18
88	41·78	601·6	37·51	108	49·68	765·1	47·70
89	42·19	609·6	38·01	109	50·06	773·5	48·22
90	42·60	617·7	38·51	110	50·45	782·0	48·76
91	43·00	625·6	39·01	111	50·83	790·5	49·29
92	43·40	633·6	39·51	112	51·22	799·0	49·82
93	43·80	641·6	40·01	113	51·61	807·7	50·36
94	44·20	649·7	40·51	114	52·00	816·4	50·90

10.—INFLUENCE OF TEMPERATURE ON THE SPECIFIC GRAVITIES OF SOLUTIONS OF POTASSIUM CARBONATE.

0° C.	5°	10°	15°	20°	25°	30°	35°	40°	45°	50°
1·589	1·586	1·583	1·580	1·577	1·574	1·571	1·568	1·566	1·563	1·559
1·577	1·575	1·573	1·570	1·568	1·565	1·563	1·560	1·557	1·554	1·551
1·567	1·565	1·563	1·560	1·559	1·555	1·553	1·550	1·548	1·545	1·543
1·557	1·554	1·552	1·550	1·548	1·516	1·544	1·541	1·539	1·536	1·533
1·547	1·544	1·542	1 510	1·538	1·536	1·534	1·531	1·528	1·526	1·523
1·536	1·534	1·532	1·530	1 528	1·526	1·524	1·521	1·518	1·515	1·512
1·526	1·524	1·522	1·520	1 518	1·516	1·514	1·511	1·508	1·505	1·502
1·516	1·514	1·512	1·510	1·508	1·506	1·503	1·500	1·498	1·495	1·492
1·506	1·504	1·502	1·500	1·498	1·496	1·493	1·490	1·488	1·485	1·482
1·496	1·494	1·492	1·490	1·488	1·486	1·484	1·481	1·478	1·475	1·472
1·486	1·484	1·492	1·480	1·478	1·476	1·474	1·471	1·468	1·465	1·462
1·476	1·474	1·472	1·470	1·468	1·466	1·464	1·461	1·458	1·455	1·452
1·466	1·464	1·462	1·460	1·458	1·456	1·454	1·451	1·448	1·445	1·442
1·456	1·454	1·452	1·450	1·448	1·446	1·444	1·441	1·438	1·435	1·432
1·446	1·444	1·442	1·440	1·438	1·436	1·434	1·431	1·428	1·425	1·422
1·436	1·434	1·432	1·430	1·428	1·426	1·423	1·420	1·418	1·414	1·411
1·426	1·424	1·422	1·420	1·418	1·416	1·413	1·410	1·408	1·404	1·401
1·416	1·414	1·412	1·410	1·408	1·406	1·404	1·401	1·398	1·395	1·392
1·406	1·404	1·402	1·400	1·399	1·396	1 394	1·391	1·388	1·385	1·382
1·396	1·394	1 392	1 390	1·388	1·386	1·384	1·381	1·378	1·376	1 373
1·386	1·384	1·382	1 380	1·378	1·376	1·374	1·371	1·368	1·366	1·363
1·376	1·374	1·372	1·370	1·368	1·366	1·364	1·361	1·358	1·356	1·353
1·366	1·364	1·362	1·360	1·358	1·356	1·354	1·351	1·348	1·346	1·343
1·356	1·354	1·352	1·350	1·348	1·346	1·344	1·341	1·338	1·336	1·333
1·346	1·344	1·342	1·340	1·338	1·336	1·334	1·331	1·328	1·326	1·323
1·336	1·334	1·332	1·330	1·328	1·326	1·324	1·321	1·318	1·316	1·313
1·326	1·324	1·322	1·320	1·318	1·316	1·314	1·311	1·308	1·306	1·303
1·316	1·314	1·312	1·310	1·308	1·306	1·303	1·300	1·298	1·295	1·292
1·306	1·304	1·302	1·300	1·298	1·296	1·293	1·290	1·288	1·285	1·282
1·296	1·294	1·292	1·290	1·288	1·286	1·283	1·280	1·278	1·275	1·273
1·286	1·284	1·282	1 280	1·278	1·276	1 273	1·270	1·268	1·265	1·263
1·276	1·274	1·272	1·270	1·269	1·265	1·263	1·260	1·257	1·255	1·252
1·266	1·264	1 262	1·260	1·258	1·255	1·253	1·250	1 247	1·245	1·242
1·256	1·254	1·252	1·250	1·248	1·246	1·243	1·240	1·238	1·235	1·232
1·246	1·244	1 242	1·240	1·238	1·236	1·233	1·230	1·228	1·225	1·222
1·236	1·234	1·232	1·230	1·229	1·226	1·224	1·222	1·219	1·217	1·214
1·226	1·224	1·222	1·220	1·218	1·216	1·214	1·212	1·209	1·207	1·204
1·216	1·214	1·212	1·210	1·208	1·206	1·204	1·202	1·199	1·197	1·194
1·206	1·204	1·202	1·200	1·198	1·196	1·194	1·192	1·189	1·187	1·184
1·196	1·194	1·192	1·190	1·188	1·186	1·184	1·182	1·179	1·177	1·174
1·186	1·184	1·182	1·180	1·178	1·176	1·174	1·172	1·170	1·167	1·164
1·175	1·173	1·171	1·170	1·168	1·166	1·164	1·162	1·160	1·157	1·155
1·165	1·163	1·161	1·160	1·158	1·156	1·154	1·152	1·150	1·147	1·145
1·155	1·153	1·151	1·150	1·148	1·146	1·144	1·142	1·140	1·137	1·135
1·144	1·143	1·141	1·140	1·138	1·136	1·134	1·132	1·130	1·127	1·125
1·133	1·132	1·131	1·130	1·128	1·126	1·124	1·122	1·120	1·117	1·114
1·123	1·122	1 121	1·120	1·118	1·116	1·114	1·112	1·110	1·107	1·104
1·113	1·112	1·111	1·110	1·108	1·106	1·104	1·102	1·100	1·097	1·094
1·103	1·102	1·101	1·100	1·098	1·096	1·094	1·092	1 090	1·087	1·084
1·093	1·092	1·091	1·090	1·089	1·087	1·086	1·083	1·081	1·079	1·077
1·083	1·082	1·081	1·080	1·079	1·077	1·076	1·073	1·071	1·069	1·067
1·073	1·072	1·071	1·070	1·069	1·067	1·066	1·064	1 062	1·000	1·058
1·063	1·062	1·061	1·060	1·059	1·057	1·056	1·054	1·052	1·050	1·048
1·053	1·052	1·051	1·050	1·049	1·047	1·046	1·044	1·042	1·040	1·038
1·043	1·042	1·041	1·040	1·039	1·037	1·036	1·034	1·032	1·030	1·028
1·033	1·032	1·031	1·030	1·028	1·027	1·025	1·024	1·022	1·020	1·018
1·023	1·022	1 021	1·020	1·018	1·017	1·015	1·014	1·012	1·010	1·008
1·013	1·012	1·011	1·010	1 008	1·007	1·005	1·004	1·002	1·000	0·998

10.—INFLUENCE OF TEMPERATURE ON THE SPECIFIC GRAVITIES OF SOLUTIONS OF POTASSIUM CARBONATE.—*Continued.*

55°	60°	65°	70°	75°	80°	85°	90°	95°	100°
1·559	1·553	1·550	1·546	1·542	1·538	1·534	1·530	1·526	1·521
1·548	1·545	1·541	1·537	1·533	1·530	1·526	1·522	1·518	1·513
1·530	1·536	1·532	1·528	1·525	1·522	1·517	1·513	1·509	1·505
1·530	1·527	1·524	1·521	1·518	1·513	1·500	1·504	1·501	1·498
1·520	1·517	1·514	1·511	1·508	1·504	1·500	1·497	1·494	1·490
1·509	1·507	1·504	1·500	1·497	1·494	1·491	1·488	1·485	1·481
1·499	1·497	1·494	1·490	1·497	1·484	1·481	1·478	1·475	1·471
1·489	1·487	1·484	1·480	1·477	1·474	1·471	1·468	1·465	1·461
1·479	1·476	1·474	1·470	1·467	1·464	1·461	1·458	1·455	1·451
1·400	1·466	1·464	1·460	1·457	1·454	1·450	1·447	1·444	1·441
1·459	1·456	1·454	1·450	1·447	1·444	1·440	1·437	1·434	1·431
1·440	1·446	1·444	1·440	1·437	1·434	1·431	1·428	1·424	1·421
1·439	1·436	1·434	1·430	1·427	1·424	1·421	1·418	1·414	1·411
1·420	1·426	1·423	1·420	1·417	1·414	1·410	1·408	1·405	1·402
1·419	1·416	1·413	1·410	1·407	1·404	1·400	1·398	1·396	1·392
1·409	1·406	1·404	1·401	1·398	1·395	1·391	1·388	1·385	1·382
1·399	1·396	1·394	1·391	1·388	1·385	1·391	1·378	1·375	1·372
1·390	1·387	1·384	1·380	1·377	1·374	1·371	1·368	1·365	1·362
1·390	1·377	1·374	1·370	1·367	1·364	1·361	1·358	1·355	1·352
1·370	1·367	1·364	1·361	1·358	1·355	1·351	1·348	1·345	1·342
1·360	1·357	1·354	1·351	1·348	1·345	1·341	1·338	1·335	1·332
1·350	1·347	1·344	1·341	1·338	1·335	1·332	1·329	1·326	1·323
1·340	1·337	1·334	1·331	1·328	1·325	1·322	1·319	1·316	1·313
1·330	1·327	1·324	1·321	1·318	1·315	1·312	1·309	1·306	1·303
1·320	1·317	1·314	1·311	1·308	1·305	1·302	1·299	1·296	1·293
1·310	1·307	1·304	1·301	1·298	1·295	1·292	1·289	1·286	1·284
1·300	1·297	1·294	1·291	1·288	1·285	1·282	1·279	1·276	1·274
1·290	1·287	1·284	1·281	1·278	1·276	1·273	1·270	1·267	1·264
1·280	1·277	1·274	1·271	1·268	1·266	1·263	1·260	1·257	1·254
1·270	1·267	1·264	1·261	1·259	1·256	1·253	1·250	1·247	1·244
1·260	1·257	1·254	1·251	1·248	1·246	1·243	1·240	1·237	1·234
1·250	1·247	1·244	1·242	1·239	1·236	1·234	1·231	1·228	1·225
1·240	1·237	1·234	1·232	1·229	1·226	1·224	1·221	1·218	1·215
1·230	1·227	1·224	1·221	1·218	1·216	1·213	1·210	1·208	1·205
1·220	1·217	1·214	1·211	1·208	1·206	1·203	1·200	1·198	1·195
1·212	1·209	1·205	1·202	1·199	1·196	1·194	1·192	1·188	1·186
1·202	1·199	1·196	1·193	1·190	1·187	1·184	1·182	1·178	1·176
1·192	1·189	1·186	1·183	1·180	1·178	1·175	1·173	1·169	1·167
1·182	1·179	1·176	1·173	1·171	1·168	1·165	1·162	1·159	1·157
1·172	1·169	1·166	1·164	1·161	1·159	1·156	1·152	1·149	1·146
1·162	1·159	1·156	1·154	1·151	1·148	1·145	1·142	1·139	1·136
1·152	1·150	1·147	1·144	1·141	1·138	1·135	1·132	1·129	1·126
1·142	1·140	1·137	1·134	1·131	1·128	1·125	1·122	1·119	1·116
1·132	1·130	1·128	1·125	1·122	1·118	1·115	1·112	1·109	1·106
1·122	1·120	1·118	1·115	1·112	1·108	1·105	1·102	1·099	1·096
1·112	1·110	1·108	1·105	1·102	1·098	1·095	1·092	1·090	1·086
1·102	1·100	1·098	1·095	1·092	1·088	1·085	1·082	1·078	1·076
1·092	1·090	1·087	1·084	1·082	1·070	1·075	1·072	1·069	1·067
1·082	1·080	1·077	1·074	1·072	1·060	1·065	1·062	1·059	1·057
1·074	1·071	1·068	1·065	1·003	1·060	1·057	1·054	1·050	1·048
1·066	1·062	1·059	1·056	1·054	1·051	1·048	1·045	1·041	1·038
1·056	1·053	1·050	1·047	1·045	1·042	1·039	1·036	1·032	1·029
1·046	1·044	1·041	1·038	1·036	1·033	1·030	1·026	1·023	1·020
1·036	1·033	1·031	1·028	1·025	1·022	1·019	1·016	1·013	1·010
1·026	1·023	1·021	1·018	1·015	1·012	1·009	1·006	1·003	1·000
1·016	1·014	1·012	1·000	1·006	1·002	0·999	0·996	0·993	0·990
1·007	1·004	1·002	0·999	0·996	0·993	0·990	0·987	0·984	0·981
0·996	0·994	0·992	0·980	0·996	0·983	0·990	0·977	0·974	0·971

M

9.—AMMONIA MANUFACTURE.

A.—GAS LIQUOR.

This liquor generally contains the ammonia principally in the state of carbonate and sulphide, which can be driven off by mere boiling, without employing lime or alkali, and which are indicated by alkalimetrical testing (*volatile ammonia*). There is, however, always a certain quantity of ammonia present in the state of salts not sensibly volatilizing by mere boiling, and not indicated by simple testing with standard acid. These are the chloride, sulphocyanide, sulphite, thiosulphate, sulphate, ferrocyanide (*fixed ammonia*). No other salts need be mentioned here.

For technical purposes, it is sufficient to make the following tests:—

1. *Volatile Ammonia.*—Dilute 20 ccm. of gas-liquor with 100 c.c. water, add 30 ccm. of normal hydrochloric acid, and boil till all CO_2 and H_2S is expelled. Retitrate with semi-normal alkali, employing the ordinary indicators. If the liquor is too much coloured to perceive the change of the indicator, dilute it with water or employ litmus paper. This process always admits of much greater accuracy than titrating the liquor directly with standard acid. Each c.c. of the latter corresponds to 0·017g. NH_3, or to 0·085 parts NH_3 by weight in 100 vols. of gas liquor; or to 0·4216 ounces of rectified oil of vitriol (at 93 per cent. SO_4H_2) per gallon of gas-liquor.

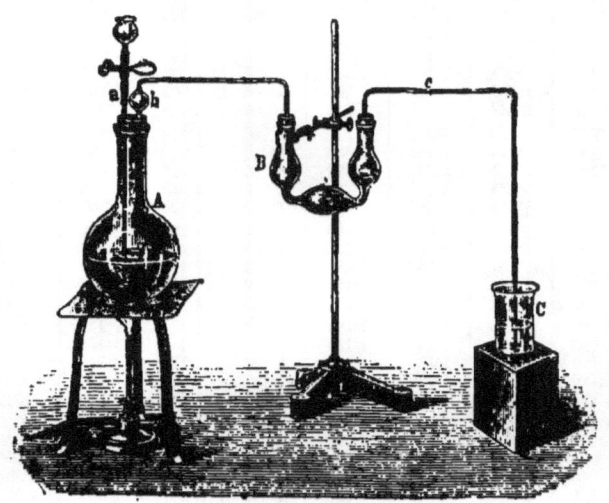

FIG. 11.

2. *Total Ammonia.*—Put 20 ccm. of gas-liquor, with about as much water, into the flask A, fig. 11, and charge the receivers B and C with 30 c.c. of normal hydrochloric acid previously diluted to twice its volume. The greater portion of this mixture should be contained in the U-tube B. Make

the connection and run an excess of milk of lime into A through the pinch-cock funnel a. Apply heat and keep up a gentle distillation for one or two hours, when all NH_3 will be driven off and absorbed in B and C. Unite the contents of these vessels and retitrate with semi-normal caustic soda. If a c.c. of this are used, $30-\dfrac{a}{2}$ indicates the c.c. of test acid, corresponding to the total ammonia, and calculated as in test No. 1.

3. *Total Sulphur.*—Add bromine water to 100 c.c. of liquid till the colour and smell of bromine are distinctly perceived, acidulate with pure HCl, boil till all bromine has been expelled, filter if necessary, neutralize the solution almost but not quite with pure sodium carbonate, and precipitate the SO_4H_2 formed with $BaCl_2$ proceeding as described p. 94.

Sometimes it may be desirable to deduct from the total sulphur that originally present in the gas-liquor as sulphate, which is estimated by boiling the unoxidized gas-liquor with HCl and proceeding as above.

4. *Sulphocyanide.*—Evaporate 50 ccm. of gas-liquor to dryness, heat the residue at 100° C. for 3 or 4 hours, digest it with strong alcohol, filter, wash on the filter with alcohol, evaporate all the alcoholic solutions to dryness, dissolve in water, filter from any residue, add a mixed solution of sul-phurous acid and cupric sulphate and heat gently, when cuprous sulpho-cyanide will be precipitated. Wash the precipitate into a flask, dissolve it in nitric acid, boil for some time, and precipitate the Cu as CuO by NaOH. The weight of $CuO \times 0.96 =$ the equivalent amount of NH_4 CNS (Dyson, S.C.I., 1883, p. 231). Or else proceed by titration, employing a solution of 6·2375 grms. $CuSO_4$, $5H_2O$ per litre, 1 c.c. of which is equivalent to 0·00145 grm. SCN = 0·00190 grm. (NH_4) SCN, which is added to a boiling solution, to which some sodium bisulphite has been added, till a drop of the mixture, brought into contact with a drop of a solution of potassium ferrocyanide in 20 parts of water, produces *immediately* a brown coloration (Barnes & Liddell, S.C.I., 1883, p. 122).

B.—SULPHATE OF AMMONIA.

1. *Estimation of Ammonia.*—The average sample, carefully drawn, is well ground up, passed completely through a sieve with 10 holes to the running inch, and a smaller sample is taken out of this. Weigh 17 grms. of the latter sample in a stoppered tube, dissolve and dilute it to 500 c.c. and place 50 c.c. of the solution without filtration into the apparatus fig. 11 (p. 162). The test is carried out exactly as in A No. 2. Each c.c. of the quantity $30-\dfrac{a}{2}$ is = 0·017g. NH_3 or = 1·0 per cent. The analysis of sulphate of ammonia is, however, best performed by the bromine method, in which the NH_3 is converted into elementary nitrogen. This method can be carried out in the "Azotometer," or in Lunge's gasvolumeter (p. 113), if the latter is provided with a "decomposing flask." The necessary "brominated soda" is prepared by dissolving 100 grms. 70 per cent. caustic soda in 250 grms. water, and cautiously adding 25 grms. bromine. The reagent must be kept in a dark, cool place, but even then does not keep more than a few days. The ammonium salt, preferably dissolved in water, is introduced into the

outer space of the decomposing flask F, fig. 12; 25 or 30 c.c. brominated soda is poured into the inner tube *a*. The cork *b*, having been already attached to the volumeter-tube by means of a short elastic tube, is pressed tightly down into the flask F, taking hold of this only by the neck; the pressure

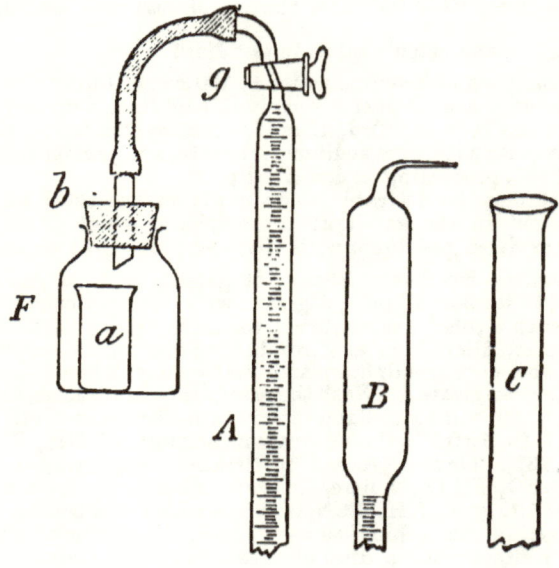

FIG. 12.

thus produced is relieved by momentarily pulling out the plug of the volumeter-tap *g*, having previously placed tubes B and C (fig. 7, p. 113) so that the mercury is exactly on the same level in both tubes. The mercury in tube A should reach right up to tap *g*, or else to some other point read off and taken as zero for the subsequent measurement. Now the flask F is tilted so that the contents of *a* run into the outer space; the flask is then shaken till no more gas is evolved. The mercury levels in A and C are made exactly to coincide, after waiting a quarter, or better, half an hour, in order to cool down the flask. ('This may be expedited by placing F, both before and after the operation, in a large vessel filled with water of the temperature of the room.) When the levels have been exactly adjusted, shut tap *g*, raise C, till the mercury in B stands at 100 c.c.; and now raise or lower C and B together, till the mercury level in A again exactly coincides with those in C and D. Now read off the number of c.c. of gas in A; each c.c.= 0·001285 grm. N=0·001561 grm. NH_3 (this includes the necessary correction for absorption or incomplete evolution of N). In order to save all calculations, dissolve 1·561 grm. sulphate of ammonia in 100 c.c. of water, and employ 10 c.c.=0·1561 grm. for each test; in this case each c.c. of gas contained in A=1 per cent. NH_3.

2. *Sulphocyanide.*—Refer to A No. 4.

C.—TABLES.

1.—SPECIFIC GRAVITIES OF LIQUOR AMMONIÆ, AT 15° C.

(Lunge & Wiernik.)

Specific Gravity at 15°.	Per cent. NH₃.	1 litre contains grms. NH₃.	Correction of the Specific Gravity for ± 1° C.	Specific Gravity at 15°.	Per cent. NH₃.	1 litre contains grms. NH₃.	Correction of the Specific Gravity for ± 1° C.
1·000	0·00	0·0	0·00018	0·940	15·63	146·9	0·00039
0·998	0·45	4·5	0·00018	0·938	16·22	152·1	0·00040
0·996	0·91	9·1	0·00019	0·936	16·82	157·4	0·00041
0·994	1·37	13·6	0·00019	0·934	17·42	162·7	0·00041
0·992	1·84	18·2	0·00020	0·932	18·03	168·1	0·00042
0·990	2·31	22·9	0·00020	0·930	18·64	173·4	0·00042
0·988	2·80	27·7	0·00021	0·928	19·25	178·6	0·00043
0·986	3·30	32·5	0·00021	0·926	19·87	184·2	0·00044
0·984	3·80	37·4	0·00022	0·924	20·49	189·3	0·00045
0·982	4·30	42·2	0·00022	0·922	21·12	194·7	0·00046
0·980	4·80	47·0	0·00023	0·920	21·75	200·1	0·00047
0·978	5·30	51·8	0·00023	0·918	22·39	205·6	0·00048
0·976	5·80	56·6	0·00024	0·916	23·03	210·9	0·00049
0·974	6·30	61·4	0·00024	0·914	23·68	216·3	0·00050
0·972	6·80	66·1	0·00025	0·912	24·33	221·9	0·00051
0·970	7·31	70·9	0·00025	0·910	24·99	227·4	0·00052
0·968	7·82	75·7	0·00026	0·908	25·65	232·9	0·00053
0·966	8·33	80·5	0·00026	0·906	26·31	238·3	0·00054
0·964	8·84	85·2	0·00027	0·904	26·98	243·9	0·00055
0·962	9·35	89·9	0·00028	0·902	27·65	249·4	0·00056
0·960	9·91	95·1	0·00029	0·900	28·33	255·0	0·00057
0·958	10·47	100·3	0·00030	0·898	29·01	260·5	0·00058
0·956	11·03	105·4	0·00031	0·896	29·69	266·0	0·00059
0·954	11·60	110·7	0·00032	0·894	30·37	271·5	0·00060
0·952	12·17	115·9	0·00033	0·892	31·05	277·0	0·00060
0·950	12·74	121·0	0·00034	0·890	31·75	282·6	0·00061
0·948	13·31	126·2	0·00035	0·888	32·50	288·6	0·00062
0·946	13·88	131·3	0·00036	0·886	33·25	294·6	0·00063
0·944	14·46	136·5	0·00037	0·884	34·10	301·4	0·00064
0·942	15·04	141·7	0·00038	0·882	34·95	308·3	0·00065

2.—SPECIFIC GRAVITIES OF SOLUTIONS OF COMMERCIAL AMMONIUM CARBONATE, AT 15° C.

(Lunge & Smith.)

Deg. Twaddell.	Deg. Baumé.	Spec. Grav'ty at 15°.	Per cent. Commercial Ammonium Carbonate.	Change of Spec. Gravity for ± 1° C.
1	0·6	1·005	1·66	0·0002
2	1·4	1·010	3·18	0·0002
3	2·1	1·015	4·60	0·0003
4	2·7	1·020	6·04	0·0003
5	3·4	1·025	7·49	0·0003
6	4·1	1·030	8·93	0·0004
7	4·7	1·035	10·35	0·0004
8	5·4	1·040	11·86	0·0004
9	6·0	1·045	13·36	0·0005
10	6·7	1·050	14·83	0·0005
11	7·4	1·055	16·16	0·0005
12	8·0	1·060	17·70	0·0005
13	8·7	1·065	19·18	0·0005
14	9·4	1·070	20·70	0·0005
15	10·0	1·075	22·25	0·0006
16	10·6	1·080	23·78	0·0006
17	11·2	1·085	25·31	0·0007
18	11·9	1·090	26·82	0·0007
19	12·4	1·095	28·33	0·0007
20	13·0	1·100	29·93	0·0007
21	13·6	1·105	31·77	0·0007
22	14·2	1·110	33·45	0·0007
23	14·9	1·115	35·08	0·0007
24	15·4	1·120	36·88	0·0007
25	16·0	1·125	38·71	0·0007
26	16·5	1·130	40·84	0·0007
27	17·1	1·135	42·20	0·0007
28	17·8	1·140	44·29	0·0007
29	17·9	1·1414	44·90	0·0007

APPENDIX.

A.—PREPARATION OF STANDARD SOLUTIONS.

INTRODUCTORY.

The analytical methods given in the foregoing pages are based upon the metric system of weights and measures. As there are still some laboratories using the English system, the following remarks, intended to facilitate the change of the prescriptions from the metric to the English system, may prove useful.

The unit of weight of the English system is the grain. All normal solutions are prepared so that 1000 grains by volume (100 decems) contain one equivalent of the reagent in grains, and consequently all normal solutions prepared on the English system are identical in concentration with those prepared on the metric system.

English burettes usually hold 1000 grains, and are divided into 100 parts of 10 grains each, called one decem. The decem corresponds to the cub. centimetre. As however this unit, the decem, is ten times the unit of weight, the following rules must be observed when any of the prescriptions are to be changed from the metric to the English system :—

Instead of Litre read 10,000 grains.

    ,,   Cub. centimetre read decem or 10 times the number of grains.

    ,,   Grams read 10 times the number of grains.

If, for instance, we are told to prepare a standard solution of permanganate by dissolving 15·820 grams of potassium permanganate in one litre of water, and that one cub. centimetre of such a solution indicates 0·028 grams of iron, we shall obtain a solution of equal strength by dissolving 158·20 grains in 10,000 grains of water, and one decem of this solution will indicate 0·28 grains of metallic iron. No errors can possibly occur if the reader will always substitute ten times as many grains for any number of grams, ten times as many grains, or an equal number of decems for any number of cubic centimetres, and 10,000 grains for every litre. Where we are directed to measure out by means of a pipette 50 cc., we take 500 grains instead, etc., but when speaking of the number of cubic centimetres on the burette we substitute exactly the same number of decems.

It will also be useful to remember that

grams per litre	= grains per 1000 grains.
,, ,,	= ounces per 1000 ounces.
,, ,,	= ounces per cub. foot (approximately).
grams per litre : 16	= lbs. per cub. foot.
grams per litre × 70	= grains per 70,000 grains.
,, ,, ,,	= grains per gallon.
0·4375 × grams per cub. metre	= grains per cubic foot.

kilograms per cub. metre	= lbs. per 1000 lbs.
$\dfrac{\text{kilograms per cub. metre}}{16}$	= lbs per 16 cub. feet.
	= lbs. per cub. foot.
16 × cub. metres per kilogram.	= cub. feet per lbs.
kilograms per square metre	= 0·205 lb. per square foot.
kils. per square metre × 4·89	= lbs. per square foot.

1.—NORMAL ACID AND ALKALI.

As foundation of Alkalimetry and Acidimetry we employ *chemically pure sodium carbonate.* This is tested for purity by dissolving 5 g. in water, which ought to yield a completely clear, colourless solution ; if, after super-saturating this solution with nitric acid, no opalescence is caused by barium chloride, or silver nitrate, the salt may be taken as sufficiently pure. Before using it, the sodium carbonate must be ignited in a platinum crucible at least for twenty minutes, so far that the bottom of the crucible becomes red hot, but that no fritting takes place ; the crucible is allowed to cool in the exsiccator, and out of it several portions of about 1 or 2 g. each are weighed directly one after another, to serve for standardizing the normal acid. The balance ought to turn at least with 0·5 milligram.

As normal acid, we prefer *hydrochloric acid,* which has the following advantages over sulphuric and oxalic acid, viz.:—1st, it is more generally applicable, *e.g.* also for alkaline earths; 2nd, its standard, first taken by pure sodium carbonate, can be most accurately checked by silver nitrate, far more accurately than that of sulphuric acid by barium chloride; 3rd, it does not change in course of time like oxalic acid.

Normal HCl is prepared as follows: Dilute pure hydrochloric acid to 1·020 spec. gravity (4° Tw.). Such an acid will be rather too strong. Fill a burette with this acid, and titrate with it one of the weighed samples of sodium carbonate spoken of above, the weight of which is w grams. Suppose that x ccm. of this acid had been consumed. As the acid is sure to be too strong, x will always be smaller than $\dfrac{w}{0·053}$, and we shall have to add to every x cub. cent. of the acid $\dfrac{w}{0·053}-x$. cub. cent. of water, and if the total quantity of acid of spec. gravity, 1·020 measures V cub. cent., the amount of water to be added thereto to render it correct will be n cub. centimetres, where $n = V\left(\dfrac{w}{0·053x}-1.\right)$

If accurate normal alkali is at hand, it may be employed by a completely analogous process for examining the provisional acid, reducing it to the normal strength.

In any case the mixed normal acid must be checked by titrating new samples of sodium carbonate, when x ought to $=\dfrac{w}{0·053}$. A further check is afforded by estimating the chlorine gravimetrically by silver nitrate; 10 ccm. (=0·365g HCl) ought to yield 1·435g Ag Cl.

The ordinary *indicator* in alkalimetry and acidimetry used to be tincture of litmus, which must be kept in open vessels, to avoid its being spoiled. When employing litmus, the liquid to be tested must be kept boiling for some time, in order to expel all CO_2; and normal acid must be added as long as on further boiling the colour changes back from red to purple, or blue. This prolonged boiling causes some alkali to dissolve from most descriptions of glass, which makes the testings inaccurate. A test with litmus rarely lasts less than half an hour, usually more. On the other hand, a test is finished in a few minutes, if litmus is replaced by a very dilute solution of methyl-orange (sulphobenzene-azo-dimethylaniline); but in this case the liquids must never be hot, but of the ordinary temperature, and none but mineral acids, but no oxalic acid may be employed. The cold solution of sodium carbonate is coloured just perceptibly yellow by adding a drop or two of the solution of methyl-orange, preferably by means of a pipette; if the colour is too intense, it will cause the transition into red on neutralization to be less sharp. CO_2 does not in the least act upon methyl-orange; only when all Na_2CO_3 has been decomposed, and a minimal excess of HCl is present, the yellow changes suddenly and sharply into pink. Hence the rule is to run in the normal acid quickly with constant agitation till the change of colour has taken place. The opposite change of colour from pink to faint yellow is just as sharp when titrating mineral acids with sodium hydrate or carbonate. The results are identical with those obtained by litmus, but they are obtained very much more quickly, and without heating the liquids. H_2S affects methyl-orange as little as CO_2, whence that indicator can be employed for directly titrating tank liquor and the like. In some cases methyl-orange fails to yield good results, from causes not yet ascertained, e.g. in chimney testing, but it can be employed in nearly all other cases. It is not applicable at all in the presence of nitrous acid.

Some laboratories prepare their standard acid twice as strong as the above, which naturally affects all the calculations given in this book. The object of this is to show the change of colour more clearly than with normal acid, but this is hardly necessary for methyl-orange.

The *normal alkali*, when intended to be used with litmus, should be as free as possible from carbonate, and should be constantly protected against absorption of CO_2 from the air, because otherwise the change of colour does not take place sufficiently rapidly, and markedly in cold liquors. A solution of sodium hydrate *entirely* free from carbonate is difficult to prepare and to preserve when in constant use. When employing methyl-orange as an indicator, an ordinary caustic soda solution may be employed without any special precautions. The caustic soda employed should not contain more than a very slight proportion of alumina; ordinary strong caustic nearly always fulfils this condition, or it may even be replaced by a solution of 53 g. pure sodium carbonate in 1 lit. water, which is employed cold, and which yields as accurate results as NaOH, no notice being taken of the CO_2 escaping with effervescence. The general use of this liquid is, however, inconvenient on account of the efflorescences on the burettes, bottle necks, etc. Weaker (e.g. fifth-normal, or even semi-normal) solutions do not show this drawback.

All standard liquors ought to be prepared and employed as nearly as possible at the same temperature, e.g. 15°C. If a correction be necessary, the table of the volumes of water at different temperatures (No. 22, p: 49) is sufficiently accurate for all practical purposes, for these dilute liquids as well. When they have stood for some time in bottles, a little water is evaporated and recondensed in the upper part of the bottles; the proper mixture must then be re-established by shaking up the contents.

Semi-normal ammonia serves for estimating the CO_2 of bicarbonates

(p. 132); but it can also be employed for general alkalimetrical purposes in lieu of sodium hydrate. Pure liquor ammoniæ of commerce, which does not produce any opalescence on adding barium chloride, is diluted to specific gravity 0·995; it is then tested with normal HCl, and diluted so far that it agrees with semi-normal acid, when it contains 8·500 g. NH₃ per litre. It keeps unchanged for some time in well-stoppered bottles, but must be frequently checked by titrating. *Decinormal ammonia* keeps almost constant in tightly stoppered bottles.

2.—POTASSIUM PERMANGANATE.

The ordinary solution is semi-normal, *i.e.*, it yields 0·004 g. oxygen per ccm. It serves, *e.g.*, for estimating nitrous acid in vitriol, for testing the nitrogen acids in the chamber exits, for testing manganese ore, for testing Weldon mud, etc.

Since iron only occurs in very slight quantity in the products of alkali manufacture, it is best estimated by means of a tenth- or twentieth-normal solution made from the semi-normal solution by dilution, and indicating 0·0056, resp. 0·0028 g. Fe per c.c.

The solution is made by dissolving pure crystallized potassium permanganate, and is then completely stable, if protected from dust and direct sunlight. Still, its titre must be checked in any case; all the more, as the article sold as "chemically pure" is usually not free from foreign salts. Of absolutely pure permanganate a quantity of 15·820 g. per litre would be required for a semi-normal solution. This quantity is dissolved for the first time; the check-test to be described now shows how much more salt must be added to bring the solution up to the standard, and this indicates the proper quantity for future preparations of test liquor from the same stock of solid permanganate.

The standardizing is effected by means of the finest, softest iron wire, so-called "flower wire," * which is preferable to oxalic acid, since the latter is not easily obtained with the theoretical percentage of water, whilst the uncertainty about the composition of the *finest* iron wire does not exceed 0·1 per cent. No sensible fault will be committed for all analytical purposes if the wire is assumed = 99·7 per cent. Fe. Before weighing, it is passed through emery paper, to remove any traces of rust. Weigh out 0·5617 g. wire (= 0·5600 g. Fe.; if the length is noticed, it is afterwards easy to hit the proper quantity almost at once); put it into a flask provided with an india-rubber valve (Fig. 10, p. 123), dissolve in dilute sulphuric acid by heating, allow to cool, and add permanganate solution from a burette till a faint but distinct pink colour has been produced, which lasts at least half a minute. The above quantity of iron ought to take exactly 20·00 c.c. permanganate. If this is not the case, a factor for correcting the difference is employed, or preferably the test liquor itself is corrected by adding the requisite quantity of solid permanganate. Suppose we have not used 20, but x ccm. of liquor, then we must in future employ $\dfrac{15·82 x}{20}$ grams of solid permanganate per litre, in order to produce an exactly semi-normal solution. Of course its titre must be checked again.

An excellent check upon the iron standard is the standardizing of potassium permanganate by decomposing it with hydrogen peroxide, and

---

* Not the steel pianoforte-wire, which contains more and irregular quantities of carbon. The objections made to its use by Blodgett Britton do not apply to flower-wire.

measuring the oxygen evolved in a gasvolumeter (pp. 113 and 164). Put 10 c.c. of the permanganate solution into the outer space of flask F (fig. 12); add 30 c.c. of dilute sulphuric acid (1:5 aq.); put 15 c.c. of hydrogen peroxide into the inner tube a; put the cork b in, relieve the pressure, and level the mercury as described p. 164. Then tilt F, shake a minute, allow 10 minutes to stand, shake up again, place tubes A and C so that the mercury is at the same level in both; shut tap g, raise C so that the mercury in B stands at 100; and, lastly, raise or lower B and C together, so that the mercury levels coincide with that in A. Each c.c. of gas found in A corresponds to 0·000715 grm. active oxygen in the permanganate employed, or 0·0000715 grm. O in each c.c. of the permanganate solution. The results agree very well with these of the iron test, and are more accurate than when standardizing with oxalic acid.

Permanganate is best employed in a burette with a lateral hollow glass-tap. Any change in its titre (from dust, etc.) is perceptible by a deposition of MnO_2 in the bottle. It is advisable to check the standard once every three months.

Permanganate can be used with perfect accuracy in the presence of free hydrochloric acid, if the liquids contain a considerable quantity of manganese salts; in other cases the same effect is produced by adding, say 1 grm. of manganese sulphate free from iron.

3.—IODINE SOLUTION.

Weigh exactly 12·7 g. of pure re-sublimed iodine (either bought as such or prepared by grinding up common iodine with 10 per cent. of potassium iodide and re-subliming) on a balance turning at least with 5 mg.; put it into a litre-flask already containing a concentrated solution of 15 to 18 g. KI, close the flask, agitate till the iodine is completely dissolved, and fill up to the mark. This deci-normal solution is checked by the arsenite solution (No. 4). Both solutions ought to be precisely equivalent, c.c. per c.c.

For estimating very slight quantities of sodium sulphide sometimes a special iodine solution is made, by dissolving 3·256 g. of pure iodine with 5 g. of potassium iodide in a litre, to indicate 0·001 g. Na_2S per c.c.

Solutions of iodine, especially the more dilute ones, keep a long time in well-stoppered bottles in a cool place, but they ought to be checked once a month by the arsenite solution.

Preparation of the Starch Solution.—Grind up 3 g. potato starch with a little water to a homogeneous paste; introduce this gradually into 300 g. of boiling water, contained in a porcelain dish, and continue the boiling till an almost clear liquid has been produced. Allow this to settle in a tall beaker, pour the clear portion through a filter, and saturate it with common salt. This solution, when kept in a cool place, is stable for some time; as soon as fungus vegetations are noticed in it, it is thrown away.

Very convenient is the soluble starch made by the process of Zulkowsky, by heating 100 parts of concentrated glycerine with 6 parts of starch to 190°C. for about an hour, pouring into water and precipitating the soluble starch with alcohol and filtering. This is kept in the state of a thick paste, not to be allowed to dry, and each time a small quantity is taken out by means of a glass rod.

4.—SODIUM ARSENITE SOLUTION.

This serves for standardizing the iodine solution, and as its volumetrical complement, especially in bleaching-powder testing. Employ commercial pure powdered arsenious acid; test its purity by subliming a little from a small capsule into a watch-glass, when there ought not to appear at first a yellow sublimate of As_2S_3 (which volatilizes more easily than As_2O_3); on heating more strongly it should leave no residue. Before using it the powder of As_2O_3 is kept for some time over sulphuric acid in a desiccator, and can then be weighed out without any special precautions, since it is not hygroscopical. For preparing a deci-normal solution, weigh out exactly 4·950 g. As_2O_3, boil it with 10 g. of pure sodium bicarbonate and 200 g. water till completely dissolved; add another 10 g. bicarbonate, and dilute on cooling to 1,000 c.c. This solution is altogether stable, and equivalent with 0·00355 g. Cl or 0·0127 g. I per c.c.

If really pure and dry arsenious acid has been employed, the above solution will be correct at once. But when preparing larger quantities of it, it ought to be checked by grinding up 0·5 g. iodine with 0·1 g. KI., heating this mixture in a small capsule on a sand-bath or upon asbestos-board till abundant vapours arise, covering with a dry watch-glass, allowing the major portion, but not the whole, of the iodine to sublime into the watch-glass, covering this with a second watch-glass which fits air-tight upon the former, and has been tared with it, and weighing. Slip the watch-glasses into a solution of 1 g. of potassium iodide (free from iodate), in 10 g. water, wait a little till the iodine is dissolved, dilute with 100 c.c. water, and titrate with arsenite. When the colour is only a light yellow, add a little starch-solution, and titrate exactly till the blue colour has just vanished. The c.c. of arsenite consumed, multiplied by 0·0127, ought to be exactly the weight of iodine employed.

5.—SILVER SOLUTION.

Weigh out exactly 17·00 g. of pure crystallized silver nitrate, preferably kept in a desiccator for a few hours, and dissolve in 1 litre. This yields a deci-normal solution, indicating per c.c. 0·00355 g. Cl., or 0·00365 g. HCl., or 0·00585 g. NaCl. By dissolving 2·906 g. $AgNO_3$ in 1 litre, a solution is obtained, indicating 0·001 g. NaCl. per c.c.

Ammoniacal silver solution, for Lestelle's estimation of alkaline sulphides, is obtained by dissolving 13·345 g. of pure silver in pure nitric acid, adding 250 c.c. liquor ammoniæ and diluting to 1 lit. Each c.c. of this indicates 0·005 g. Na_2S.

6.—COPPER SOLUTION,

for Hurter's ferrocyanide test, is obtained by dissolving 12·475 g. pure crystallized, not effloresced, cupric sulphate, in 1 lit. water. (Refer to p. 181.)

7.—OXALIC ACID SOLUTION,

for testing the "base" of Weldon mud, and caustic soda or lime in the presence of carbonate (pp. 123 and 124). Dissolve 63·0 g. pure, not effloresced, crystallized oxalic acid in 1 lit. water, and check the standard with normal alkali. This solution is not quite stable, especially when exposed to daylight; nor can it be employed for alkalimetry, when using methyl-orange as an indicator.

B.—RULES FOR SAMPLING.

1. *Ores and Minerals* (pyrites, manganese, coals, salt). (*a*). *Smalls, slack, salt or other substances not requiring to be crushed.*—Take a sample of about .1 lb. of each weighing tub, cart, or the like, by means of a scoop, so as to

obtain about the same quantity each time. Of railway trucks, which are tipped directly into the warehouse, take three samples, one from the middle and one from each end.* All these single samples are put in a cask and kept covered, to prevent the evaporation of moisture. When the large sample is taken, empty the contents of the cask on a level, clean, and hard place, spread it flat, heap it up in a cone at the centre by going regularly round with a spade; spread this heap again flat, and take a sample of about a quarter of the mass, by taking out with a spade two stripes crossing each other at right angles, and adding a little from the centre of each remaining quadrant. Treat this reduced sample exactly like the larger one, so that a third sample of about 5 lbs. is obtained. Mix this again thoroughly, and fill it into four (or more) wide-necked bottles of 4 ounces capacity, placed in a tight row on a sheet of paper, so that a portion of each handful gets into every one of the four bottles. When these are full, they are at once closed with tight-fitting corks; these are cut off straight above the bottle-necks and well covered with sealing wax, putting on the seals of both buyer and seller, or any other party concerned. The mixing and filling must be done as quickly as possible, in order to prevent the evaporation, or else the attraction of sensible quantities of moisture during the operation.

The above-mentioned sample bottles are handed over to the laboratory chemist, who has to pulverize their contents till they pass *completely* through a sieve with holes 1 mm. (= $^1/_{25}$in.) wide; nothing coarse must be left behind. From this, after thorough mixing, a smaller sample is taken and reduced to the degree of division necessary for analysis, by grinding in a steel or agate mortar, in the case of softer substances in a porcelain mortar. Manganese samples should not be treated in iron mortars. Moisture is estimated in an unground portion of the sample.

(b). *Ores in pieces requiring to be crushed.*—Large-sized samples must be taken if the lumps of the ore are very coarse. If the pieces are not above the size of an apple, and not too unequal, it is sufficient to take a sample from each tub, etc., as in (a), but with a shovel or scoop holding about 10 lbs. In the case of larger lumps, and of very unequal sizes, it is preferable to tip each tenth or twentieth tub or cart into a separate place, where the whole average sample is collected. At all events, the proportion between the large and small must be represented as accurately as possible in the average sample. This is now crushed down to the size of a walnut, either by hand or by machinery, leaving *no* larger lumps behind. The crushed material is thoroughly mixed by several times turning it over with a spade; it is then spread out in a flat heap and a smaller sample is taken, by lifting out two stripes crossing each other at right angles, adding something from the centre of each remaining quadrant. The reduced sample is crushed further, either in a large metal mortar, or preferably with a sledge-hammer on a flanged cast-iron plate of about 3 ft. square, bedded on a solid foundation; the latter process is much more convenient and cleanly than grinding in a mortar. The coarse portions are sifted out by a riddle of ⅛ in. holes and crushed again, till all has passed through. The product is reduced as in (a), by mixing, etc., to a quantity of 2 or 4 lbs., from which the sample-bottles are filled as prescribed above.

---

* At some factories very unsatisfactory results have been obtained with this mode of sampling; they prefer that described later on (in b), of taking a certain number of entire tubs, barrows, or carts as sample.

2. CHEMICALS.

Saltcake, soda ash, etc., if in bulk, are sampled as in No. 1 a. If packed in casks, each third, fifth, or tenth cask, according to the size of the parcel, is bored at one of its bottoms and sampled by means of an *auger* (fig. 13), which is inserted up to the centre of the cask, turning it round its axle all the while. The single cask samples are put into a large wide-mouthed bottle as drawn, till the sampling is over. Then empty the whole on to a large sheet of paper, mix thoroughly, crush any lumps with a spatula, and fill the 4-ounce bottles, previously prepared, exactly as described on No. 1 as for ores, observing the same rules for corking and sealing.

Bleaching powder, potashes, and any other substances which are liable to be quickly spoilt in contact with the air by attracting moisture, or from other reasons, are treated like the foregoing substances, but operating with the greatest possible speed, and keeping the large bottle for collecting the cask-samples well closed. The sampling is still more safely performed by taking away the upper end of the cask, removing the top layer to a depth of about two inches, taking a handful of stuff from the interior as far as it is possible to reach in, which should be nearly at the centre of the cask, and throwing it into the large bottles. In this case there is the least contact with air. Or else a sample-auger is employed, which is closed at its upper half, and is only turned round when its point has arrived in the centre of the cask; in this case the top layer does not get into the auger. Samples of bleaching-powder ought to be kept in a dark and cold place, and ought to be tested without any great delay.

Fig. 13.

Caustic Soda. Since the samples attract moisture and carbonic acid on their surface, even in well-closed bottles, the outer opaque crust must be removed by scraping before weighing out the tests (compare page 145). It should be borne in mind that the centre of the drum is of weaker strength than the remainder, because the foreign salts accumulate in the portion remaining liquid the longest. The average strength is best represented by the portions next to the bottom and sides of the drum, which solidify quickest.

Solid sulphuric anhydride cannot be sampled directly for analysis. An auger cannot be employed, as the mass is too firm and tough ; melting the mass in the drums themselves is out of the question, on account of the clouds of fumes. The following process is, therefore, employed : A large sample of the solid anhydride is mixed with so much exactly analysed "monohydrated" sulphuric acid that an acid of about 70 per cent. is formed, which is liquid at ordinary temperatures. This mixture is made in a stoppered bottle, and is gently heated to 30° or 40° C., the stopper being loosely put in, till the solution is complete, whereupon a small sample is taken out by means of Lunge & Rey's glass-tap pipette (p. 116).

C.—COMPARISON OF THE HYDROMETER DEGREES ACCORDING TO BAUMÉ AND TWADDELL, WITH THE SPECIFIC GRAVITIES.

B.	T.	Spec. Gravity.	B.	T.	Spec. Gravity.	B.	T.	Spec. Gravity.
0	0	1·000	15·4	24	1·120	29·3	51	1·255
0·7	1	1·005	16·0	25	1·125	29·7	52	1 260
1·0	1·4	1·007	16·5	26	1·130	30·0	52·6	1·263
1·4	2	1·010	17·0	26·8	1·134	30·2	53	1·265
2·0	2·8	1·014	17·1	27	1·135	30·6	54	1·270
2·1	3	1·015	17·7	28	1·140	31·0	54·8	1·274
2·7	4	1·020	18·0	28·4	1·142	31·1	55	1·275
3·0	4·4	1·022	18·3	29	1·145	31·5	56	1·280
3·4	5	1·025	18·8	30	1·150	32·0	57	1·285
4·0	5·8	1·029	19·0	30·4	1·152	32·4	58	1·290
4·1	6	1·030	19·3	31	1·155	32·8	59	1·295
4·7	7	1·035	19·8	32	1·160	33·0	59·4	1·297
5·0	7·4	1·037	20·0	32·4	1·162	33·3	60	1·300
5·4	8	1·040	20·3	33	1·165	33·7	61	1·305
6·0	9	1·045	20·9	34	1·170	34·0	61·6	1·308
6·7	10	1·050	21·0	34·2	1·171	34·2	62	1·810
7·0	10·2	1·052	21·4	35	1·175	34·6	63	1·815
7·4	11	1·055	22·0	36	1·180	35·0	64	1·820
8·0	12	1·060	22·5	37	1·185	35·4	65	1·825
8·7	13	1·065	23·0	38	1·190	35·8	66	1·830
9·0	13·4	1·067	23·5	39	1·195	36·0	66·4	1·332
9·4	14	1·070	24·0	40	1·200	36·2	67	1·335
10·0	15	1·075	24·5	41	1·205	36·6	68	1·340
10·6	16	1·080	25·0	42	1·210	37·0	69	1·345
11·0	16·6	1·083	25·5	43	1·215	37·4	70	1·850
11·2	17	1·085	26·0	44	1·220	37·8	71	1·355
11·9	18	1·090	26·4	45	1·225	38·0	71·4	1·857
12·0	18·2	1·091	26·9	46	1·230	38·2	72	1·360
12·4	19	1·095	27·0	46·2	1·231	38·6	73	1·365
13·0	20	1·100	27·4	47	1·235	39 0	74	1·370
13·6	21	1·105	27·9	48	1·240	39·4	75	1·375
14·0	21·6	1·108	28·0	48·2	1·241	39·8	76	1·380
14·2	22	1·110	28·4	49	1·245	40·0	76·6	1·383
14·9	23	1·115	28·8	50	1·250	40·1	77	1·385
15·0	23·2	1·116	29·0	50·4	1·252	40·5	78	1·390

N.B.—The Baumé degrees are calculated by the formula $d = \dfrac{144·3}{144·3 - n}$, water of 15° C. being put $= 0°$ and sulphuric acid of 1·842 at 15° C. $= 63°$; compare Lunge's Sulphuric Acid and Alkali, vol. i., p. 20. This is the Baumé's hydrometer, mostly used on the Continent of Europe; but other scales are in use there as well, and quite another scale for Baumé's hydrometer is used in America.

C.—COMPARISON OF THE HYDROMETER DEGREES ACCORD-
ING TO BAUMÉ AND TWADDELL, WITH THE SPECIFIC
GRAVITIES.—*Continued.*

B.	T.	Spec. Gravity.	B.	T.	Spec. Gravity.	B.	T.	Spec. Gravity.
40·8	79	1·395	50·9	109	1·545	59·5	140	1·700
41·0	79·4	1·397	51·0	109·2	1·546	59·7	141	1·705
41·2	80	1·400	51·2	110	1·550	60·0	142	1·710
41·6	81	1·405	51·5	111	1·555	60·2	143	1·715
42·0	82	1·410	51·8	112	1·560	60·4	144	1·720
42·3	83	1·415	52·0	112·6	1·563	60·6	145	1·725
42·7	84	1·420	52·1	113	1·565	60·9	146	1·730
43·0	84·8	1·424	52·4	114	1·570	61·0	146·4	1·732
43·1	85	1·425	52·7	115	1·575	61·1	147	1·735
43·4	86	1·430	53·0	116	1·580	61·4	148	1·740
43·8	87	1·435	53·3	117	1·585	61·6	149	1·745
44·0	87·6	1·438	53·6	118	1·590	61·8	150	1·750
44·1	88	1·440	53·9	119	1·595	62·0	150·6	1·753
44·4	89	1·445	54·0	119·4	1·597	62·1	151	1·755
44·8	90	1·450	54·1	120	1·600	62·3	152	1·760
45·0	90·6	1·453	54·4	121	1·605	62·5	153	1·765
45·1	91	1·455	54·7	122	1·610	62·8	154	1·770
45·4	92	1·460	55·0	123	1·615	63·0	155	1·775
45·8	93	1·465	55·2	124	1·620	63·2	156	1·780
46·0	93·6	1·468	55·5	125	1·625	63·5	157	1·785
46·1	94	1·470	55·8	126	1·630	63·7	158	1·790
46·4	95	1·475	56·0	127	1·635	64·0	159	1·795
46·8	96	1·480	56·3	128	1·640	64·2	160	1·800
47·0	96·6	1·483	56·6	129	1·645	64·4	161	1·805
47·1	97	1·485	56·9	130	1·650	64·6	162	1·810
47·4	98	1·490	57·0	130·4	1·652	64·8	163	1·815
47·8	99	1·495	57·1	131	1·655	65·0	164	1·820
48·0	99·6	1·498	57·4	132	1·660	65·2	165	1·825
48·1	100	1·500	57·7	133	1·665	65·5	166	1·830
48·4	101	1·505	57·9	134	1·670	65·7	167	1·835
48·7	102	1·510	58·0	134·2	1·671	65·9	168	1·840
49·0	103	1·515	58·2	135	1·675	66·0	168·4	1·842
49·4	104	1·520	58·4	136	1·680	66·1	169	1·845
49·7	105	1·525	58·7	137	1·685	66·3	170	1·850
50·0	106	1·530	58·9	138	1·690	66·5	171	1·855
50·3	107	1·535	59·0	138·2	1·691	66·7	172	1·860
50·6	108	1·540	59·2	139	1·695	67·0	173	1·865

D.—VALUE OF ALKALI PER TON.

Price per unit.	1%.	2%.	3%.	4%.	5%.
Pence.	£ s. d.	£ s. d.	£ s. d.	£ s. d.	£ s. d.
¾	0 1 3	0 2 6	0 3 9	0 5 0	0 6 3
$\frac{13}{16}$	0 1 4¼	0 2 8½	0 4 0¾	0 5 5	0 6 9¼
⅞	0 1 5½	0 2 11	0 4 4½	0 5 10	0 7 3½
$\frac{15}{16}$	0 1 6¾	0 3 1½	0 4 8¼	0 6 3	0 7 9¾
1	0 1 8	0 3 4	0 5 0	0 6 8	0 8 4
1$\frac{1}{16}$	0 1 9¼	0 3 6½	0 5 3¾	0 7 1	0 8 10¼
1⅛	0 1 10½	0 3 9	0 5 7½	0 7 6	0 9 4½
1$\frac{3}{16}$	0 1 11¾	0 3 11½	0 5 11¼	0 7 11	0 9 10¾
1¼	0 2 1	0 4 2	0 6 3	0 8 4	0 10 5
1$\frac{5}{16}$	0 2 2¼	0 4 4½	0 6 6¾	0 8 9	0 10 11¼
1⅜	0 2 3½	0 4 7	0 6 10½	0 9 2	0 11 5½
1$\frac{7}{16}$	0 2 4¾	0 4 9½	0 7 2¼	0 9 7	0 11 11¾
1½	0 2 6	0 5 0	0 7 6	0 10 0	0 12 6
1$\frac{9}{16}$	0 2 7¼	0 5 2½	0 7 9¾	0 10 5	0 13 0¼
1⅝	0 2 8½	0 5 5	0 8 1½	0 10 10	0 13 6½
1$\frac{11}{16}$	0 2 9¾	0 5 7½	0 8 5¼	0 11 3	0 14 0¾
1¾	0 2 11	0 5 10	0 8 9	0 11 8	0 14 7
1$\frac{13}{16}$	0 3 0¼	0 6 0½	0 9 0¾	0 12 1	0 15 1¼
1⅞	0 3 1½	0 6 3	0 9 4½	0 12 6	0 15 7½
1$\frac{15}{16}$	0 3 2¾	0 6 5½	0 9 8¼	0 12 11	0 16 1¾
2	0 3 4	0 6 8	0 10 0	0 13 4	0 16 8
2$\frac{1}{16}$	0 3 5¼	0 6 10½	0 10 3¾	0 13 9	0 17 2¼
2⅛	0 3 6½	0 7 1	0 10 7½	0 14 2	0 17 8½
2$\frac{3}{16}$	0 3 7¾	0 7 3½	0 10 11¼	0 14 7	0 18 2¾
2¼	0 3 9	0 7 6	0 11 3	0 15 0	0 18 9
2$\frac{5}{16}$	0 3 10¼	0 7 8½	0 11 6¾	0 15 5	0 19 3¼
2⅜	0 3 11½	0 7 11	0 11 10½	0 15 10	0 19 9½
2$\frac{7}{16}$	0 4 0¾	0 8 1½	0 12 2¼	0 16 3	1 0 3¾
2½	0 4 2	0 8 4	0 12 6	0 16 8	1 0 10

To find the value of intermediate strengths not given in the table, for instance—36% at 1$\frac{5}{16}$ per unit, find for 30%.........£3 5 7½
then for 6%......... 0 13 1½

The sum gives value per ton of 36%.........£3 18 9

D.—VALUE OF ALKALI PER TON.—*Continued.*

Price per unit.	6%.	7%.	8%.	9%.	10%.
Pence.	£ s. d.	£ s. d.	£ s. d.	£ s. d.	£ s. d.
$\frac{3}{4}$	0 7 6	0 8 9	0 10 0	0 11 3	0 12 6
$\frac{13}{16}$	0 8 1½	0 9 5¾	0 10 10	0 12 2¼	0 13 6½
$\frac{7}{8}$	0 8 9	0 10 2½	0 11 8	0 13 1½	0 14 7
$\frac{15}{16}$	0 9 4½	0 10 11¼	0 12 6	0 14 0¾	0 15 7½
1	0 10 0	0 11 8	0 13 4	0 15 0	0 16 8
$1\frac{1}{16}$	0 10 7½	0 12 4¾	0 14 2	0 15 11¼	0 17 8½
$1\frac{1}{8}$	0 11 3	0 13 1½	0 15 0	0 16 10½	0 18 9
$1\frac{3}{16}$	0 11 10½	0 13 10¼	0 15 10	0 17 9¾	0 19 9½
$1\frac{1}{4}$	0 12 6	0 14 7	0 16 8	0 18 9	1 0 10
$1\frac{5}{16}$	0 13 1½	0 15 3¾	0 17 6	0 19 8¼	1 1 10½
$1\frac{3}{8}$	0 13 9	0 16 0½	0 18 4	1 0 7½	1 2 11
$1\frac{7}{16}$	0 14 4½	0 16 9¼	0 19 2	1 1 6¾	1 3 11½
$1\frac{1}{2}$	0 15 0	0 17 6	1 0 0	1 2 6	1 5 0
$1\frac{9}{16}$	0 15 7½	0 18 2¾	1 0 10	1 3 5¼	1 6 0½
$1\frac{5}{8}$	0 16 3	·0 18 11½	1 1 8	1 4 4½	1 7 1
$1\frac{11}{16}$	0 16 10½	0 19 8¼	1 2 6	1 5 3¾	1 8 1½
$1\frac{3}{4}$	0 17 6	1 0 5	1 3 4	1 6 3	1 9 2
$1\frac{13}{16}$	0 18 1½	1 1 1¾	1 4 2	1 7 2¼	1 10 2½
$1\frac{7}{8}$	0 18 9	1 1 10½	1 5 0	1 8 1½	1 11 3
$1\frac{15}{16}$	0 19 4½	1 2 7¼	1 5 10	1 9 0¾	1 12 3½
2	1 0 0	1 3 4	1 6 8	1 10 0	1 13 4
$2\frac{1}{16}$	1 0 7½	1 4 0¾	1 7 6	1 10 11¼	1 14 4½
$2\frac{1}{8}$	1 1 3	1 4 9½	1 8 4	1 11 10½	1 15 5
$2\frac{3}{16}$	1 1 10½	1 5 6¼	1 9 2	1 12 9¾	1 16 5½
$2\frac{1}{4}$	1 2 6	1 6 3	1 10 0	1 13 9	1 17 6
$2\frac{5}{16}$	1 3 1½	1 6 11¾	1 10 10	1 14 8¼	1 18 6½
$2\frac{3}{8}$	1 3 9	1 7 8½	1 11 8	1 15 7½	1 19 7
$2\frac{7}{16}$	1 4 4½	1 8 5¼	1 12 6	1 16 6¾	2 0 7½
$2\frac{1}{2}$	1 5 0	1 9 2	1 13 4	1 17 6	2 1 8

To find the value of intermediate strengths not given in the table, for instance—36% at $1\frac{5}{16}$ per unit, find for 30%.........£3 5 7½
then for 6%......... 0 13 1½

The sum gives value per ton of 36%.........£3 18 9

D.—VALUE OF ALKALI PER TON.—*Continued.*

Price per unit.	20%.	30%.	40%.	48%.	50%.
Pence.	£ s. d.	£ s. d.	£ s. d.	£ s. d.	£ s. d.
$\frac{3}{4}$	1 5 0	1 17 6	2 10 0	3 0 0	3 2 6
$\frac{13}{16}$	1 7 1	2 0 7½	2 14 2	3 5 0	3 7 8½
$\frac{7}{8}$	1 9 2	2 3 9	2 18 4	3 10 0	3 12 11
$\frac{15}{16}$	1 11 3	2 6 10½	3 2 6	3 15 0	3 18 1½
1	1 13 4	2 10 0	3 6 8	4 0 0	4 3 4
$1\frac{1}{16}$	1 15 5	2 13 1½	3 10 10	4 5 0	4 8 6½
$1\frac{1}{8}$	1 17 6	2 16 3	3 15 0	4 10 0	4 13 9
$1\frac{3}{16}$	1 19 7	2 19 4½	3 19 2	4 15 0	4 18 11½
$1\frac{1}{4}$	2 1 8	3 2 6	4 3 4	5 0 0	5 4 2
$1\frac{5}{16}$	2 3 9	3 5 7½	4 7 6	5 5 0	5 9 4½
$1\frac{3}{8}$	2 5 10	3 8 9	4 11 8	5 10 0	5 14 7
$1\frac{7}{16}$	2 7 11	3 11 10½	4 15 10	5 15 0	5 19 9½
$1\frac{1}{2}$	2 10 0	3 15 0	5 0 0	6 0 0	6 5 0
$1\frac{9}{16}$	2 12 1	3 18 1½	5 4 2	6 5 0	6 10 2½
$1\frac{5}{8}$	2 14 2	4 1 3	5 8 4	6 10 0	6 15 5
$1\frac{11}{16}$	2 16 3	4 4 4½	5 12 6	6 15 0	7 0 7½
$1\frac{3}{4}$	2 18 4	4 7 6	5 16 8	7 0 0	7 5 10
$1\frac{13}{16}$	3 0 5	4 10 7½	6 0 10	7 5 0	7 11 0½
$1\frac{7}{8}$	3 2 6	4 13 9	6 5 0	7 10 0	7 16 3
$1\frac{15}{16}$	3 4 7	4 16 10½	6 9 2	7 15 0	8 1 5½
2	3 6 8	5 0 0	6 13 4	8 0 0	8 6 8
$2\frac{1}{16}$	3 8 9	5 3 1½	6 17 6	8 5 0	8 11 10½
$2\frac{1}{8}$	3 10 10	5 6 3	7 1 8	8 10 0	8 17 1
$2\frac{3}{16}$	3 12 11	5 9 4½	7 5 10	8 15 0	9 2 3½
$2\frac{1}{4}$	3 15 0	5 12 6	7 10 0	9 0 0	9 7 6
$2\frac{5}{16}$	3 17 1	5 15 7½	7 14 2	9 5 0	9 12 8½
$2\frac{3}{8}$	3 19 2	5 18 9	7 18 4	9 10 0	9 17 11
$2\frac{7}{16}$	4 1 3	6 1 10½	8 2 6	9 15 0	10 3 1½
$2\frac{1}{2}$	4 3 4	6 5 0	8 6 8	10 0 0	10 8 4

To find the value of intermediate strengths not given in the table, for instance—36% at $1\frac{5}{16}$ per unit, find for 30%.........£3 5 7½
then for 6%......... 0 13 1½

The sum gives value per ton of 36%.........£3 18 9

D.—VALUE OF ALKALI PER TON.—*Continued.*

Price per unit.	52%.			54%.			56%.			57%.			58%.		
Pence.	£	s.	d.	£	s.	d.	£	s.	d.	£	s.	d.	£	s.	d.
$\frac{3}{4}$	3	5	0	3	7	6	3	10	0	3	11	3	3	12	6
$\frac{13}{16}$	3	10	5	3	13	1½	3	15	10	3	17	2¼	3	18	6½
$\frac{7}{8}$	3	15	10	3	18	9	4	1	8	4	3	1½	4	4	7
$\frac{15}{16}$	4	1	3	4	4	4½	4	7	6	4	9	0¾	4	10	7½
1	4	6	8	4	10	0	4	13	4	4	15	0	4	16	8
$1\frac{1}{16}$	4	12	1	4	15	7½	4	19	2	5	0	11¼	5	2	8½
$1\frac{1}{8}$	4	17	6	5	1	3	5	5	0	5	6	10½	5	8	9
$1\frac{3}{16}$	5	2	11	5	6	10½	5	10	10	5	12	9¾	5	14	9½
$1\frac{1}{4}$	5	8	4	5	12	6	5	16	8	5	18	9	6	0	10
$1\frac{5}{16}$	5	13	9	5	18	1½	6	2	6	6	4	8¼	6	6	10½
$1\frac{3}{8}$	5	19	2	6	3	9	6	8	4	6	10	7½	6	12	11
$1\frac{7}{16}$	6	4	7	6	9	4½	6	14	2	6	16	6¾	6	18	11½
$1\frac{1}{2}$	6	10	0	6	15	0	7	0	0	7	2	6	7	5	0
$1\frac{9}{16}$	6	15	5	7	0	7½	7	5	10	7	8	5¼	7	11	0½
$1\frac{5}{8}$	7	0	10	7	6	3	7	11	8	7	14	4½	7	17	1
$1\frac{11}{16}$	7	6	3	7	11	10½	7	17	6	8	0	3¾	8	3	1½
$1\frac{3}{4}$	7	11	8	7	17	6	8	3	4	8	6	3	8	9	2
$1\frac{13}{16}$	7	17	1	8	3	1½	8	9	2	8	12	2¼	8	15	2½
$1\frac{7}{8}$	8	2	6	8	8	9	8	15	0	8	18	1½	9	1	3
$1\frac{15}{16}$	8	7	11	8	14	4½	9	0	10	9	4	0¾	9	7	3½
2	8	13	4	9	0	0	9	6	8	9	10	0	9	13	4
$2\frac{1}{16}$	8	18	9	9	5	7½	9	12	6	9	15	11¼	9	19	4½
$2\frac{1}{8}$	9	4	2	9	11	3	9	18	4	10	1	10½	10	5	5
$2\frac{3}{16}$	9	9	7	9	16	10½	10	4	2	10	7	9¾	10	11	5½
$2\frac{1}{4}$	9	15	0	10	2	6	10	10	0	10	13	9	10	17	6
$2\frac{5}{16}$	10	0	5	10	8	1½	10	15	10	10	19	8¼	11	3	6½
$2\frac{3}{8}$	10	5	10	10	13	9	11	1	8	11	5	7½	11	9	7
$2\frac{7}{16}$	10	11	3	10	19	4½	11	7	6	11	11	6¾	11	15	7½
$2\frac{1}{2}$	10	16	8	11	5	0	11	13	4	11	17	6	12	1	8

To find the value of intermediate strengths not given in the table, for instance—36% at $1\frac{5}{16}$ per unit, find for 30%.........£3 5 7½
then for 6%......... 0 13 1½

The sum gives value per ton of 36%.........£3 18 9

ADDENDUM TO PAGE 86.

Checking the working of fireplaces and firemen.—The estimation of CO_2 in the chimney gases, as described page 86, if combined with an observation of temperature, admits of checking both the efficiency of a special fireplace and the daily work of the firemen, according to a formula developed by Lunge in Zsch. f. angew. Chem., 1889, p. 240. A consecutive number, say from 10 to 15 testings for CO_2. are made by an Orsat apparatus in the flue leading from the fireplace to the chimney, and the mean volume percentage of CO_2 found is called n. At the same time a thermometer with very long stem, tightly inserted in the testing hole in such manner that its bulb is well within the flue, but that the scale can be read off outside, is observed at frequent intervals, and the mean temperature of the gases is called t', that of the air outside t. c is the specific heat of a cubic metre of CO_2, expressed in gram-calories; c' that of N or O (see below). The total volume of exit-gases, produced by the combustion of 1 kilog. of carbon burnt on the grate, is $= 1\cdot854 \left(\dfrac{100 - n}{n} \right)$ cubic metres, and the loss of heat in the exit-gases, expressed in gram-calories:

$$L = 1\cdot854\ (t' - t)\ c + 1\cdot854\ (t' - t) \left(\frac{100 - n}{n} \right) c';$$

the loss, expressed in per cent. of the heat theoretically given out by the carbon:

$$\frac{100\ L}{8080}.$$

The value of c' may be assumed for all temperatures $= 0\cdot31$; that of c varies with the temperature, and must be taken as follows:

If t' is below   150° C., $c = 0\cdot41$.
,, ,, ,, between 150–200° $= 0\cdot43$.
,, ,, ,,   ,,   200–250° $= 0\cdot44$.
,, ,, ,,   ,,   250–300° $= 0\cdot45$.
,, ,, ,,   ,,   300–350° $= 0\cdot46$.

ERRATUM.

Page 3. The atomic weight of Niobium is 94·2 (O=16) or 93·9 (H=1).

INDEX.